ABC Motion Pictures Presents
A JOHN FOREMAN PRODUCTION
A JOHN HUSTON FILM
Starring
JACK NICHOLSON   KATHLEEN TURNER

PRIZZI'S HONOR

Director of Photography ANDRZEJ BARTKOWIAK
Screenplay by RICHARD CONDON and JANET ROACH
From the novel by RICHARD CONDON
Music adapted by ALEX NORTH
Produced by JOHN FOREMAN
Directed by JOHN HUSTON

Berkley books by Richard Condon

AN INFINITY OF MIRRORS
PRIZZI'S HONOR

PRIZZI'S HONOR

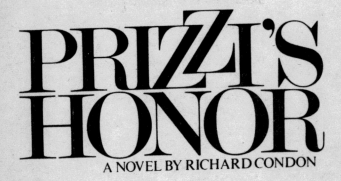

A NOVEL BY RICHARD CONDON

BERKLEY BOOKS, NEW YORK

For the Memory of
Benn Reyes

This Berkley book contains the complete
text of the original hardcover edition.
It has been completely reset in a typeface
designed for easy reading, and was printed
from new film.

PRIZZI'S HONOR

A Berkley Book / published by arrangement with
Coward, McCann & Geoghegan, Inc.

PRINTING HISTORY
Coward, McCann & Geoghegan edition / April 1982
Berkley edition / January 1983
Second printing / June 1985

ISBN: 0-425-08471-X

A BERKLEY BOOK ® TM 757,375
Berkley Books are published by The Berkley Publishing Group,
200 Madison Avenue, New York, New York 10016.
The name "BERKLEY" and the stylized "B" with design
are trademarks belonging to Berkley Publishing Corporation.
PRINTED IN THE UNITED STATES OF AMERICA

"But dreadful is the mysterious power of fate; there is no deliverance from it by wealth or by war, by fenced city, or dark, sea-beaten ships."

Chorus, *Antigone*

EDUARDO PRIZZI

Legitimate Enterprises and Political
Activities

Beniamino Sestero   Arrigo Gerrone

Lieutenants

CRIMINAL INCOME REINVESTMENT

Banking, Insurance, Interstate Trucking,
Electronics, Heavy Construction, Real Es-
tate Investment and Management (81
downtown and midtown buildings in 9
cities), Cable Television, Brokerage and
Underwriting, Personal Loan Companies,
Wineries, Food Manufacturing and Im-
porting; Fast Food Chain Franchising,
Theatrical and TV Motion Picture Pro-
duction, Phonograph Records, Video
Manufacturing, Hardcover and Paperback
Publishing, Magazine Publishing, 3 Law
Firms (NY, LA, Zurich), 11 Hospitals, 1
Flower Farm, 137 Hotels, 23 Laundries

GROSS ANNUAL BUSINESS
$1,770,000,000

Police, Judiciary, Legislative, Executive
Government at Federal, State, County,
Municipal and Ward Levels

THE PRIZZI FAMILY
(1918–   )

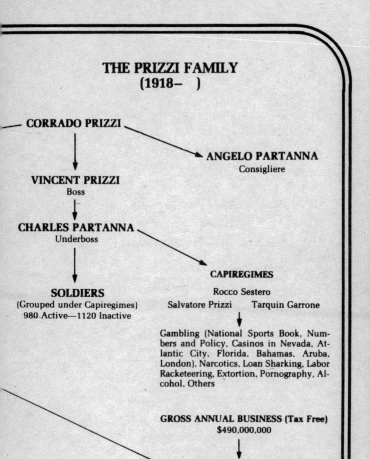

CORRADO PRIZZI

ANGELO PARTANNA
Consigliere

VINCENT PRIZZI
Boss

CHARLES PARTANNA
Underboss

SOLDIERS
(Grouped under Capiregimes)
980 Active—1120 Inactive

CAPIREGIMES

Rocco Sestero

Salvatore Prizzi   Tarquin Garrone

Gambling (National Sports Book, Numbers and Policy, Casinos in Nevada, Atlantic City, Florida, Bahamas, Aruba, London), Narcotics, Loan Sharking, Labor Racketeering, Extortion, Pornography, Alcohol, Others

GROSS ANNUAL BUSINESS (Tax Free)
$490,000,000

TO OVERSEAS BANKS
Switzerland, Panama, Bahamas, Nigeria

Chapter One

Corrado Prizzi's granddaughter was being married before the baroque altar of Santa Grazia di Traghetto, the lucky church of the Prizzi family. The bride shimmered in the exalting sounds of the choir and the chanting bishop. The groom, shorter but more intense than the bride, was her cousin, Patsy Garrone, a member of the inner Prizzi family.

The church was dressed with sensual shafts of light and the fur of holy music. Don Corrado Prizzi, eighty-four, sat on the aisle in the front pew, right side of the church. He was asleep, but even in repose his face was as subtly distorted and burnished as that of a giant crown of thorns starfish predator. Every few moments both small, sharp eyes, as merry as ice cubes, would open, make a reading, then close again.

Beside Don Corrado sat his eldest son, Vincent, father of the bride, a cubically heavy man. He clutched his kneecaps with both hands, frowning and humming, very softly, "The Stars and Stripes Forever." Beside Vincent was his brother, Eduardo, and his third "natural" wife, Baby. Eduardo called his wives Baby, not to sound colloquially American, as he had once explained to his mother, but because Cristoforo Colombo had named his first ship of discovery the Niña, which means Baby. "They are all little women," his mother had said. "How come you don't call them Pinta?" One thing was for sure, the family wisdom went, no one would ever call any of them Santa Maria. Eduardo wore the only elegance of the family: silver hair in high, teased waves, tailoring by Cifonelli (Roma), and money by Gucci.

Directly behind Don Corrado sat Angelo Partanna, his oldest friend and the family's counselor. He was a tall, scrawny, bald and relentlessly dapper man in his early seventies.

Behind the first two rows on the right side of the church, captured like pheromones in the thickening smell of hundreds of burning beeswax candles, in serried ranks, row upon row, were lesser Prizzis, one more Partanna, and many, many Sesteros and Garrones. Heavily larded among them were relatives from most of the principal families of the *fratellanza* in the United States. Sal Prizzi had married Virgie Licamarito, sister of Augie "Angles" Licamarito, Boss of the Detroit family. Two of the Garrone daughters had married the sons of Gennaro Fustino, head of the New Orleans family that controlled the entire southern rim of the United States. Don Corrado's niece, Caterina, was married to the son of Religio Carramazza, head of the Chicago family, and Don Corrado was second cousin to Sam Benefice, head of the New England family, and Carlo "Gastank" Viggone, Boss of the Cleveland combination.

Together, all sides of the *fratellanza* enterprises formed a loose conglomerate that was only able to operate as long as it could neutralize law enforcement on the one hand while sustaining cordial, continuing relations with its customer-victims on the other. The Prizzi family business depended entirely, in a way that no other business organization needed to, on strong relationships with the noncriminal sections of society. These relationships were kept in profitable repair by both sides. It would be a mistake to think of the Prizzi family as being "different" from "legitimate" society—continuing profits and mutual conveniences were established and encouraged by both sides. The Prizzis weren't "wrong-side" players making deals with strictly differentiated "right-side" players. Both sides had in fact evolved together in the long night of the money-tilted culture, helped each other, and were, combined, the most important part of the political and economic system of the society.

On the left side of the church, seated expressionlessly in the last half of the pews, were the working troops of the Prizzis and their *capiregimes*, an honor guard of about seven hundred men, a third of the available *soldati*. In front of them were the bag men from the chief inspector's squad, the borough squads, and the PC's squad of the New York Police Department, all in plain clothes. Alongside them sat the chief operating officer of one of the multinational conglomerates, the Papal Nuncio, the national union leaders, and the superstars of screen, opera, theater, TV, and the great world of sports. The groom's best man was the current light-heavyweight champion of the world. The bride's maid of honor was the reigning Miss America, who she had met that morning. In the first three pews, senators and congressmen sat side by side with high police officials, network anchorman, and the best and the brightest minds of the media, the district attorney's office, the attorney general's office, and the White House staff.

In the church choir lofts network TV cameras had been installed side by side with the Prizzis' own cassette taping units. Radio coverage was dense from this vantage point and the hum of their steady reportage joined the glorious song of the choir, the chanting of the bishop, the responses of the altar boys, and the clicking of plain, old-fashioned news cameras. A granddaughter of Corrado Prizzi was being married.

Charley Partanna sat in the eleventh row, right side, next to his cousin, movie executive Paulie Sestero. Charley was a large, lithe man of forty-two who resembled the late Phar Lap, with strong facial bones and a jutting chin, chrome eyes and brows like awnings. He had been a "made man" in the honored society since he was seventeen, the age at which his father had been made before him.

Charley Partanna was Angelo's son, Vincent's *sottocapo*, and the Prizzis' enforcer. When he was thirteen he had made his bones on the Gun Hill Road in the Bronx, where he had never been before that afternoon. His father had been unable to figure out any other way to ice Little Phil Terrone, the heaviest shit and boo dealer in the north Bronx, who always seemed to be at the center of a crowd of people. Charley was a kid in short pants. There were a lot of other kids, maybe thirty of them, milling around to get some of the silver money Terrone always threw around on them, and Charley just stepped out from behind a car and blew Terrone's head off. Then he dropped the gun and lost himself in the mob of other kids.

Charley was solid. Nothing shook him up. He made his plan then he walked through it deliberately, missing nothing. One time the police staked out an apartment. They had searchlights and bullhorns and snipers on roofs and in windows, the whole movie drill, to get at a hoodlum named Dimples Tancredi, who not only worked for the Prizzis but had killed two cops. Tancredi got a message out to the Prizzis saying that he was sorry but that he was going to have to make a deal to blow the entire Prizzi shit business on the East Coast to buy himself some time instead of being knocked off by the brooding cops. At least enough time so that his lawyer could get some things settled and the crazy cops cooled down. Don Corrado was stunned by Tancredi's intentions. He talked it over with Angelo Partanna and Pop said, "Why, my Charley will go in there and blast holes in that little prick." Charley was twenty. It was his fourth hit.

Eduardo Prizzi made a deal for a sit-down meet with the Brooklyn police brass and reassurances were passed around until everybody understood that all anybody wanted was for this fucking cop-killer to be dead while the Department got the media credit for it but wouldn't have to risk any more cops' lives.

Temporarily, the cops gave Charley a different name. In the newspapers the next day he became, without any pictures, First-Grade Detective George Fearons, complete with a police heavy rifle. He went up in the service elevator to the back door of the apartment Tancredi was trapped in and got him to move close enough to the door so that Tancredi could hear him explain the deal that the Prizzis wanted to make for him. That didn't get the door open, but it got Tancredi close enough so he could hear the proposition and Charley burned him through the door. Then he went down in the service elevator, handed in the riot gun, and told the cops how things were upstairs; four of them went up to the apartment, kicked down the front and back door for friendly TV crews, and blew eleven holes in Tancredi's dying body.

"There are even people here from Agrigento, Charley," Paulie said. He was a very short man when he was standing, but massively tall when he was sitting down. "See that turtle-faced guy over there? Four rows up? That's Pietro Spina. Now we are talking real old-country *fratellanza*."

"Never mind that," Charley said, "who is the great-looking head across the aisle, two rows up?"

They stared at the woman. "Great-looking?" Paulie said. She was okay. He would rate her about a 7.

"Jesus, Paulie, she's gorgeous!" Charley stared fixedly at the woman. She was handsome from some angles, but to Charley she was a classic, like the Truman win over Dewey. She was dark and she sat as reposefully as a swan.

"The name I don't know," Paulie said, "But she's gotta be a big friend of the family or else heavy media."

"If she's a friend of the family she's on the wrong side of the church."

The choir ran down for a few beats and Charley became aware of the sound of the taping cameras. Four camera set-ups! he marveled. Paulie had told him that the whole wedding was going to be made into a one-hour feature with music, titles, and special effects by Scott Miller; with Toni Muto, who had three records in the top fifty, singing "It Had to Be You" in the Sicilian dialect of her choice. The movie was going to be put on videocassettes and everybody at the wedding was going to get one so they could enjoy it in the years to come.

"Listen, Paulie," Charley said, "I want something."

"What?"

"As soon as the mass is over I want you to tell the head guy on the cameras to shoot stuff on that girl for me."

"Why not? You want it, you got it. Here," he took a card out of his side pocket and scribbled on it. "Give him this. He'll get whatever you say."

Amalia Sestero, in the row ahead of them, turned around and smiled. "Hey, Paulie," she said.

"Yeah?"

"Shut up and watch the wedding."

While the crowd was working its way out of the church, Charley moved fast and grabbed the head camera guy. He put a hundred-dollar bill in the man's hand, figuring it would work better than Paulie's card. "I am only trying to help the movie," he said. "See that girl over there? The beauty in the green-and-yellow dress?"

The man looked. "The beauty?"

"With the little white gloves! The one moving out into the aisle?"

"Oh, that one. Yeah."

"Shoot as much as you can get on her when we get over to the hotel, you understand? Save everything you get for me, you understand?" Charley had a harsh, metallic voice, metallic in the way heavy truck gears sound when they are covered with sand. It made a punishing sound even when he was singing Christmas carols. His voice, his size, and his ball-bearing eyes almost made up the cameraman's mind, but he was confused so he hesitated.

"Look, friend, I'd like to do it, but—"

"You want to eat this card?"

Charley put Paulie's card in the man's hand. The man nodded vigorously. "Certainly," he said. "My pleasure. She will flash up the footage."

"You ain't kidding," Charley said.

The decorators had turned the ballroom of the hotel into a replica of the old Palermo Gardens. Everybody from the old neighborhood who came into that room was kicked in the head by what they saw because what they thought they were seeing was their youth. It was such a terrific effect that three old ladies were laughing and crying at the same time.

"Hey, fahcrissake, look at *this*!" the head of the Bocca family yelled. "How about what these here people done here?"

Above the heads of the entering crowd the whole ceiling was festooned with crepe-paper ribbons: red, white, and blue from one side of the room to the central chandelier, and red, white, and green from the chandelier to the other side. Balloons jostled each other against the ceiling, bobbing with the rising warm air. Everybody felt good. What had been a solemn wedding turned into a party. People suddenly liked each other. Some people hugged. There was so much love in the room that Charley's heart filled with the foam of it, like a stein of beer pumped too fast.

Two long tables stretched down either side of the hall, holding up mountains of sandwiches. Dozens of steins of beer were being filled by Jewish waiters from the Prizzi chain of delicatessens around the city, which Ed Prizzi had put the family into because no matter where he was he couldn't seem to get a good (dry method) piece of corned beef. That had led the Prizzis into bakeries, which soon went national because nobody could get rye bread that had any crust, and before anyone knew it, the Palermo Maven delicatessens had gone national on a franchise basis, including the Jewish waiters.

A mass of Sicilian-speaking waiters were filling pitchers of elderberry wine from a large barrel. There were nine kinds of salad on the tables, mountains of *farfalline*, mounds of cold meat and piles of *salsiccia* and banks of pastries set among fourteen kinds of Sicilian candies and ice creams. Jesus, Charley marveled, even the orchestra was right—a piano, an accordion, a clarinet, and a bass playing a rock arrangement of *Giovanezza*. Above the stage, behind the band, were big eight-by-ten-foot sepia photographs of Arturo Toscanini, Pope Pius XII, Enrico Caruso, and Richard M. Nixon in heavy gilt frames.

A lot of the older men were dressed right, in tuxes, and the older women all wore the correct color for a wedding, black, but the young people and the civilians were schlocked out like *ziticones*. Charley wore a tuxedo. It was three o'clock on a summer afternoon but it was a Prizzi wedding and people should know how to pay respect.

One thing was right. Don Corrado's eighty-three-year-old sister sat at the door weeping happily in a black dress. As the guests came in they dropped either sealed envelopes or cash for the bride into the black drawstring bag she held between her feet. It looked like a sixty-dollar score. People in the environment liked to think of a thousand dollars as one dollar to confuse the tourists at Vegas, but the measurement became universal because so much money was lying around in heaps, pleading to be taken. Sixty dollars was sixty thousand dollars.

Charley had hustled a ride over from the church in a police car so he could be sure to get there first. He gave the sergeant who set it up a credit slip for six veal steaks packed in ice by the Prizzi meat company. When he got inside the ballroom he planted himself just inside the door and waited for her to come in.

She got there after about twenty minutes, probably she had stopped off in the john. He watched her drop her envelope, then he saw that she was with Maerose Prizzi, the bride's sister. He worked himself ahead of them in the crowd and positioned himself so that they couldn't get around him. What a face! She didn't look exactly Italian but she was beautiful. She had a mouth on her like a bunch of poppies and skin like he had never seen. He managed to stand as if he had been shoved in their way by the press of people near the door.

Maerose was a great woman even if she had screwed up. She was a very wop looker, all eyes and beautiful bones among the grabbing domes and dunes. She was almost as tall as Charley, with sad eyes and long fingers. She was a woman who had done everything right—except once.

"Hey, Charley!" she called out. "This is great. Meet my friend, Irene Walker. This is Charley Partanna."

She waited for him to speak. She was going to take her lead from him, which was very smart, he thought. How could a woman have such a face and (probably) such a body and also turn out to be this smart? He thought he could see her eyes change when she looked at him. To Charley she had something like the look which had come over Pizarro when he had first spotted the Peruvian gold. It was an expression of some kind of historic discovery.

Jesus, Charley thought, I never saw anything like this woman.

Maerose darted away into the crowd.

"How about a drink?" Charley said.

"Maybe a glass of wine to the bride and groom," she said. She had a voice like a jar of smoke! It just drifted out of her and, to Charley, it was visible. It had a color like Florentine gold, with a pink underpainting of the smoke out of a Roman candle on the Fourth of July. He was gonged by her eyes. Jesus! She had *healthy* eyes. They had fringes like on the lampshades his mother was always making when he was a kid. The white part was bright white and it pushed out the brownness of the rest like flowers coming off a pond. The brown was like maple syrup, then inside that, swimming around among tiny tangerine peels, were little goldfish, and they were changing his life. What would happen when he was able to break away from the eyes and look at the rest of her? He was dropped by this woman.

"Can I take you home? I mean—when you're ready."

She stopped a waiter who was carrying a tray loaded with glasses of champagne. Charley lifted two glasses off the tray. "I live in LA," she said.

"I meant to my home," Charley said.

Vincent Prizzi began to talk into the microphone on the stage. He was a cement-faced man with crinkly-gray hair, and he still had some of the old-country accent. He was so stolidly built that he seemed like the morganatic husband of Mother Earth, like the patron of rocks, television, and fallen cake. He introduced Don Corrado Prizzi to the guests. Charley stood at attention. He hadn't as much as seen Don Corrado for two years. A hush fell over the awe-whacked ballroom; not even the Jewish waiters made any noise in all the time it took the ancient, enfeebled body to shuffle across the platform to the microphone, an essence of violent death and corruption so vibrant that the assembly seemed to sigh with gratitude that this sine qua non was the prisoner of such withered flesh.

Of all the leaders of the *fratellanza,* Corrado Prizzi alone had steadily risen in strength and prestige, because he had never deviated from the code of omertà. In turn, it had preserved and protected him. He was the only one who attended both the Cleveland meeting in 1928 and the Apalachin meeting more than a quarter of a century later in 1957. Of all of those arrested at the Cleveland meeting in 1928, he was the only one whose photograph was no longer in the police files. For over sixty years his renown and power in the *fratellanza* had steadily increased while his power in the government of the United States had geometrically squared itself. He was the sole United States "friend" who had enjoyed a personal relationship with the late Don Calo Vizzini, who was so close as to be actually within the family of the present *Capo di tutti Capi* of Sicily, Don Pietro Spina, whose son had attended the wedding today.

Don Corrado tapped on his son's arm and motioned for him to bring his head down. Vincent bent over, nodding as he listened, then he turned back to the microphone.

"My father welcomes you to this great family occasion," he translated. "He says you are all going to have a good time. He offers his toast of love to the happiness of the bride and groom and wishes them many children."

Vincent lifted his glass. The eight hundred guests lifted their glasses. Everyone drank. The old man shuffled slowly off the stage and disappeared behind the piano into the curtain, one man clearing his way, another following him.

The music began again. It was "You, You're Driving Me Crazy," a great natural Peabody, the dance people were doing the last time Charley had ventured out on the floor with a woman. "Hey, how about a dance?" Charley said.

Maerose Prizzi grabbed Irene just as Charley was turning her toward the dance floor. "Phone call, Irene," she said.

"Phone call?" Charley said blankly, but Irene was moving away with Maerose and they got lost in the crowd. He stood where he was, wondering if she would come back, thinking he wouldn't be able to handle it if she didn't come back. Numbly, he began to make plans to keep his mind filled. As soon as the bride and groom got away, he would take Irene across the street to the cement park. They would sit on a bench and when they got tired of sitting they would walk around the block, then they would sit on the bench again and decide where they would go for dinner.

After twenty minutes of waiting he went looking for her. He couldn't find her. He saw Maerose dancing with Al Melvini and he moved around the dance floor in the direction in which they were dancing, waiting until the music stopped. He didn't want to cut in because Irene might come back and he didn't want her to think he was interested in any other woman. When Maerose came off the floor he stopped her. "Where's Irene?" he said.

"Irene?"

"You dragged her away to the telephone."

"Baby, how should I know?"

He was the last wedding guest to leave. He stood at the door, staring into people's faces, not having any idea of what he could say to her if she did come walking past with some guy. Well, he would talk to her. He had a right to talk to her and if the guy made any objections he would break all his fingers. But what if she didn't want to talk to him? What if she just gave him a wave and kept moving on or if he tried to stop her and she just froze him with a look?

When everybody had gone he gave the ladies' room pro five bucks to go in and make sure Irene wasn't sick in there or something. Nothing. He went to find the Head Cameraman.

"Did you get her?"

"Get what?"

Charley grabbed the man by his shirtfront and lifted him up on his toes. "You want to be dropped in a Dispos-All?" he asked the man plaintively.

"Listen, I remember now. I got the shots for you. Very good. You're gonna like it." Charley let go. "When do I see it?"

"We only shoot it, mister. I mean, we turn it in and it goes to the lab. You gotta take that up with the company."

"All right," Charley said. "I can do that."

He got into the beat-up black Chevy van in his tuxedo and drove out to the beach thinking that maybe it was just as well that she had disappeared because he would have had to drive her in this dumpy heap. But what the hell, he thought. He could have gone to the bell captain and rented a limousine. He could have left the Chevy and sent somebody in to get it tomorrow. When he got home to the four-room apartment that Maerose had decorated for him—without any books, though he hadn't noticed that omission in the nine years he had lived there—he took off his bow tie and sat on his small terrace overlooking the bay and thought the whole situation through. He had to find her. That was all. That was all there was to it. He wasn't going to spend the rest of life like some kid thinking about what his life would have been if she hadn't disappeared, he had to find her. It wasn't exactly kosher but he had to call Maerose and ask her. It could result in a whole series of pains in the ass but she was his only connection with Irene. He lifted the phone to his lap and dialed her number.

"Mae?"

"She isn't here. You want to leave a message?"

"Who is this?"

"This is the girl."

"You got a pencil?"

"Wait. I'll get a pencil."

She came back. "Okay."

"This is Charley Partanna. You want me to spell it?"

"No. I got it."

"So spell it."

She spelled it. "Good," he said. "You give me your name and I'm going to mail you ten bucks at that address."

"Ten *bucks*?"

"Yeah. What's the name?"

"Miss Peaches Altamont."

"All right, Peaches. Tell Miss Prizzi she has to call me no matter how late. She has the number."

"Yes, sir."

He hung up and called Paulie at his hotel. There was no answer. He went to a table and pulled open a drawer. He took out an envelope, put a ten-dollar bill into it, sealed it, then addressed it. He went out of the apartment to the mail chute across from the elevator and got a stamp out of his wallet. He put the stamp on the envelope and dropped it into the chute.

The elevator door opened and two men got out.

"Hey, Partanna," the big one said.

Charley felt a flash of panic, naked without a gun in the open hallway. The man flashed his shield. "Gallagher, Homicide," he said.

Charley relaxed. "What's up?"

"You don't want to talk about it out here."

"Sure. Come on in."

They went into the apartment.

"So?" Charley asked.

"Somebody hit Sal Netturbino this afternoon."

"Yeah?"

"At his hotel."

"Who did it?"

"Where were you between two and five today?"

"At the wedding, Corrado Prizzi's granddaugter's wedding."

"What did I tell you?" Gallagher said to the other cop. "They are all going to turn out to be at the wedding."

Chapter Two

One of Ed Prizzi's lawyers got Charley away from
the cops at ten o'clock that night. They had questioned him for over three hours but he had nothing to
tell them and anyway his mind was deep into how to
find Irene. Maerose had told him by the way she acted
that she knew Irene well, but suppose she didn't? If
she didn't then she was going to have to remember
who introduced her to Irene, and no matter how far
backward he had to go, he was going to come up with
a way to find Irene again. When he left police head-
quarters he went to a phone booth in a drugstore and
called Paulie at his hotel.

"I was just leaving for the airport," Paulie marveled. "It's a real freak thing. I am walking past the
phone to go out to the airport and it rings." Paulie
was a hysteric so he was in the movie business. He
always made everything out as if God had designed it
to happen only to him.

"Listen, Paulie," Charley said, "you remember the
pictures I wanted of that girl and you gave me your
card to hand to the guy?" Charley came over a telephone line like a talking brewery horse.

"Yeah?"

"The thing is how can I get it and put it on a
cassette?"

"You want it, we'll do it."

"Great. Thanks, Paulie."

"Is the girl an actress? You think we'd be interested in looking at her."

"You looked at her already. The girl in the church with the green-and-yellow dress."

"Oh, that one. Well, anyway. The thing is, you gotta look at the footage yourself, Charlie. Who else knows what you want?"

"When can I look at it?"

"Day after tomorrow. But at the studio. That's the only way."

"You got it. I'll fly out there the day after tomorrow. And I want to tell you something else, Paulie. I am glad you and me don't like the same kind of broads, because I don't like what you like, either."

"Charley!" Paulie said. "What did I say? I didn't say anything!" Charley hung up.

When he got back to the beach it was almost midnight. There was a message on the machine from Maerose. He called her. She sounded a little smashed so maybe she had gone to bed with pills.

"Charley, what is it with you?" she asked wearily. "You are something else, you know? I am pooped."

"Look, Mae, this is important or I wouldn't bother you. I got to know how I can get in touch with the girl, you know, Irene Walker."

"Charley, I only know her like an hour longer than you know her."

"Who introduced you?"

"Some people."

"Then, okay. Will you call those people who introduced you and run down where she lives?"

"I don't know, Charley."

"What do you mean you don't know?"

She sighed. "It's like cutting my own throat. It's pushing you further away."

"Who pushed who further away? Me? No, you. That's finished. That was almost ten years ago."

"Okay, okay. Ah shit. I had my shot but somebody bumped my arm."

"I'll appreciate it."

"I can't do it tonight, Charley."

"Okay. Tomorrow."

"I'll try."

"I can call you like noon tomorrow?"

"I'll call you. I don't know how I'm going to do on this."

After she had hung up she fell back on her bed, then turned over to stare at the wall. She had once had it made with Charley and her whole life, then they had that fight—some fight, she had made it a fight—and she went out of the joint with that guy and they wound up in Mexico City, drunk. She didn't know what to do so she stayed with the guy and they stayed drunk. Then one morning two of her father's people came in the door and beat the shit out of the guy while the fucking assistant manager just stood there. They made her get dressed and they never talked to her. They never said anything to her. They took her out of the hotel like a couple of cops and flew her back to New York. She sat in a room with her father and he stared at her until she wanted to yell at him. He looked at her like she was garbage. "You put shame on your family," he said. "You showed what you care about Prizzi honor. You were going to marry the son of your grandfather's oldest friend but you became a *passeggiatrice* instead. Thank God, your mother can never know what you did. She is safe from you with the angels. Listen to me! I am never going to talk to you again after this. Angelo Partanna says he forgives you, but Charley doesn't forgive you, you took his manhood from him. You can make believe you are a member of this family, make believe you are still my daughter, because that's the way your grandfather wants it, or you can get out—you are not in this family, you are not my daughter, and I am going to see to it that you stay an old maid for the rest of your life."

She didn't run into Charley for five months. He said, hello, how are you, just like nothing had happened. He wasn't even cold to her. She had lost him. She loved him and she had lost him and he never came near her again.

Chapter Three

Charley and his father had to spend most of the day with the chemist testing out batches of a shipment of *cinnari* that had just come in from Asia via Colombia. It was Grade A, Number 4 heroin and they stayed with the chemist while he cut it into wholesale lots and into dealer lots. In the midafternoon, while they were riding back through Long Island City, Charley remembered to tell his father he had been picked up for the Netturbino hit.

"Yeah. Ed told me," his father said. "But you couldn't be cleaner, right?"

"Who made the hit, Pop?"

"We did."

"*We* did? How come we did? I didn't know nothing about it."

"Well, that's the best way, ain't it?"

"Who hit him?"

"Outta town talent. It was a specialist kind of job."

"How come?"

"Vincent told me to set it up so we couldn't have nothing to do with it. There's going to be a rumble in the commission about it, but that has nothing to do with us. We was all at the wedding having our pictures taken, right? Don't get hot. It was good thinking."

"Jesus, it was great thinking," Charlie said.

He got back to the beach at 9:10 that night and

called Maerose as he sat out on the terrace. It was a louse of a night. Rain was pounding down and he had to stay in the far corner between the awning and the wall but he had always figured that anybody who had a terrace with such a view had to use it or let him go back and live in a tenement in west Brooklyn.

Maerose had Irene's number. "Let me tell you it was some job to get that, Charley," she said. "It would have been easier to get the number of the telephone booth on top of Mount Everest."

"I want to send you something really nice for this, Mae. What do you need? Tell me. Whatever."

She gave him the sad laugh. "Send me a Valentine," she said, "that's what I need."

It was 9:25. So it was 6:25 in California, a good time. Irene picked up on the third ring.

"This is Charley Partanna," he said. He held his breath.

"Charley Par*tan*na?"

"Yeah."

"This is ter*rif*ic! How did you get my number?"

"I asked somebody for it. You're not sore?"

"Sore? I am tickled. Where are you?"

"I'm in Brooklyn."

"Oh."

"But I have to be in LA tomorrow, but that won't take long. I thought—maybe we could have dinner tomorrow night."

There was a seven-beat pause. "All right," she said. "I think I can do that."

"Sensational. Okay. Then I'll pick you up. What's a good time for you?"

"Seven?"

"Great."

"But not here. Make it—well—how about the lobby of the Beverly Wilshire?"

"Sure. Okay. That's great. Sleep warm."

He pushed the disconnect button but he sat there

for a long time staring at the telephone. All his life he had just taken telephones for granted, like they were part of the furniture, for Christ's sake. What about when you needed a lawyer or a doctor? What about the thing it had just done for him, like it was nothing, like it was giving you the Gag of the Day or your horoscope, for Christ's sake? This telephone had changed his entire outlook on life. This telephone had delivered *Irene* to him. If he heard of any rotten kids ripping out a telephone booth like they did sometimes in the neighborhood, he was going to beat the shit out of them.

Just sitting in that hotel lobby under a shiny green balibuntal hat, which by itself could return millinery to a leading place in the arts, she had slowed down the lobby traffic, as Charley could see from across the lobby, to minus nine miles an hour. He studied everyone who was within sight of her in the room, pitying poor Paulie, and he imagined that he could see old men's eyes getting misty, room clerks and bystanders developing erections, and every woman who saw her realizing that she was doomed to hostile dreams that night. She had turned Charley's legs to water just by sitting there when he came into the lobby. He was holding on to the back of a chair as he stared at her; she looked up, lifted two fingers and fluttered them at him. He crossed the lobby and loomed over her saying, "I was scared I wasn't going to see you again."

"I called you," she said. "Maerose gave me your number. But you weren't in. I was going to call you again on Sunday morning." She was lying, but it was a nice kind of lie.

"No kidding?" That proved something to Charley, it proved that this wasn't going to be the one-sided thing he had been afraid it could be. "Let's go someplace," he said.

She stood up. She was just right, three inches

shorter than he was, but he hadn't remembered her this tall. "You got higher heels on?" he asked.

"Higher than what?"

"Higher than at the wedding."

"Oh! Yes. Yes, I do."

"I've got a studio car with a driver in the alley."

"Let's take my car. You drive."

He had never heard such a voice. Before he went home he was going to get Paulie to run some Garbo movies for him because Irene Walker had to sound like Garbo. He had read somewhere that some guy had paid fifteen hundred dollars for a dead rose that Garbo had kissed maybe twenty years before and he had thought that guy was a scimunito. But he understood now. He would pay fifteen hundred dollars for any rose that had even been in the same room with Irene Walker. Now he was in the same room with her and she liked him and soon she would kiss him and someday maybe they would auction him off and only God knew how much he would bring.

They walked out slowly past the elevators and the display cases and the restaurants to the wide, covered driveway. She said something to a car jockey and an amethyst-colored foreign car, a two-seater with the top down, was backed into place in front of them. Charley handed Irene into the car, gave the jockey some money and told him to send the studio car back, then he went around to the driver's side and got in.

"What kind of a car is this?"

"A Gozzy."

"A Gozzy?"

"It's a replica of a 1929 Mercedes. The Japanese make them in England for the Arab market. It's a great California car."

"It's a great anyplace car," Charley said as they drifted out of the courtyard. "Man, it must cost."

"Well," Irene said, "it wasn't free but, my God,

think what it will cost two years from now. What kind of food do you like?"

"Food?"

"You know, what kind of restaurant?"

"Outside? Outside is like a novelty to me."

"Aiee, do I have an outside restaurant for you."

They drove to the ocean, then up the Pacific Coast Highway, and Charley felt taller, better, greater, kinder, and smarter than he had ever felt in his life. He felt so good that he told her about the time in Lansing, Michigan, because that was the one thing he had experienced besides Irene Walker that always made him feel good.

"I am there on business and there is a blizzard. There was so much snow that almost all the people who worked in the motel couldn't get there. There was the assistant manager and the night auditor, that's all. The guests had to make their own beds and cook and keep the lobby clean and some of them were pretty lousy about it. I saw what a bind everybody was in and, anyway, I like housework and cooking. I live alone and you can't live like a peasant so I tell the manager I want to help out with the general situation. That guy gave me a smile I can still see, a really beautiful smile. I worked the switchboard, I worked in the kitchen, I tended bar—anyplace I could help out. Most of the guests were pretty good about the blizzard, like they lent each other newspapers and so on, but the other people, the beefers, just hung around the lobby and stared out at the snow going up higher and higher, and made trouble. On the third day, a freelance snowplow guy comes up to the door and he offers to clear out the whole parking lot and the road out to the main road and he wants four hundred dollars for this. The assistant manager naturally says he isn't authorized to spend that kind of money and anyway they have a contract snowplow guy. The people who live in the lobby make a big yell because he won't

make the deal. Two guys start to push him around so I
have to drag them into the lounge and bounce them
around a little. That quiets everybody down but they
sulk, and the other people, the good people, catch it
from them and they won't work anymore, they just sit
around the lobby and beef. I made all the beds. Then
I got behind the counter in the coffee shop and they
all ate. At four o'clock when it's already dark, the
contract snowplow comes to the front door and tells us
he has the snow cleared away and that we can get out
on the highway. The motel empties in like ten minutes
but only three of those bastards—pardon me—offer to
pay, which the assistant manager then tells them there
won't be any bills anyway. When everybody was gone,
the assistant manager, his name is Francis M.
Winikus, makes a speech to me about how I did the
right thing. I know I did the right thing but the speech
still made me feel very good. I call him up every
Christmas. It gives me a good feeling."

"I'm proud of you, Charley," Irene said. "You deserve to feel good."

He felt exalted. Talk about casting bread on water!
A couple of thousand miles and a couple of years later
and the bread comes down on me like a ton, Charley
thought. "Well, you got to pull your own weight," he
said.

They turned up into the hills and there was the
place, which Charley knew he would have to burn into
his mind because he knew he would never be able to
find it again—not that he doubted it existed, but he
felt himself being pulled forward so fast that there
could never again be any place he could go back to.

It must be a spic place, he thought, because the
waiter looked it and Irene asked him to bring something in what must have been Puerto Rican, which she
rattled off.

"What's he getting us?"

"You should see your face, Charley. It's got itself all set to resist something foreign."

"Yeah? Well, what is it?" He tried not to look worried or like a troublemaker.

"Fresh pineapple juice and rum from a blender."

"Say that name again."

"Jugo de piña con Bacardi."

"A Puerto Rican drink?"

"I suppose so. I've only had it in Cuba."

"That was Cuban you were telling the waiter? It sounds just like Puerto Rican."

They had another round. Delicious, Charley thought, and it tasted healthy. She got him to eat something called combo *nachos* and they were terrific. They laughed a lot, which make Charley feel tremendous because nobody else had ever thought he was funny. Very otherwise, in fact. After a while he got around to the nitty.

"You married?" he asked her.

"Not really."

"Even fake I want to know about."

"I was married once." She shrugged it off. "About four years ago. Then he left me and I don't know where he is. And I don't want to know."

"*He* left *you*?"

"Crazy, right? He just had a short attention span."

"What's that?"

"I suppose he got bored with me."

"Im*poss*ible!" Charley raised his voice and it almost shook the terrace furniture. People stopped eating. They looked around. Irene started to giggle, then she put her hand over his and looked right at him. "I was lucky it worked out that way," she said.

"I could find him."

"Let him stay lost."

"You might want to get married again someday."

"Could be. But until that time comes, I don't want to know about him."

"Marriage shouldn't be like that," Charley said. "I know it is a lot of times but that's not the way. I mean, my mother and my father had a marriage. It made me happy all the time she was alive. I get mad when I hear about the other kind and when it happens to you it tears up the whole road for me. I mean, I hate the guy for walking out on you, but I'm glad he walked out on you."

"I think the way you think about marriage. My mother and my father had a terrible marriage, but even then I could see how it could have been different. Anyway, I like your jacket, Charley."

"You like it? It's my cousin Paulie's tailor. He's in the movie business so I figured he should know. Not that I wear it much. New York, well they dress differently in New York. A jacket like this would stand out in New York. You don't want clothes for that. In fact, flash is bad. My father used to tell me that twice a week when I was a kid. He means all flashfront stuff but what he was saying to me is it's better to stand out because of what you are and how serious you are than to let clothes or cars or diamond rings do it for you. For men, that is," he added quickly.

"He's right, Charley."

"How come you aren't a wop and I meet you at Teresa Prizzi's wedding?"

"The bishop who married them wasn't a wop."

"He wasn't? Oh, yeah. He was a Polack."

"You think maybe I'm not a wop because my father was Polish?" She beamed on him.

"Walker is a Polish name?" He was astounded.

"It was Walcewicz. I was born Maida Walcewicz, but I shortened it."

"I figured maybe you went to college with Maerose."

"Something like that. How long will you be in LA?"

"Maybe till Tuesday."

"Do you have to get back?"

"Well, yeah. I'm in olive oil and cheese." He thought he caught a flicker of amusement in her eyes as he said that. He wondered, briefly, just how well she did know the family. "What business you in, you can afford a car like that?"

"Taxes."

"Taxes?"

"You know—death and taxes. I'm a tax consultant."

"Like what do you do when you consult?"

She gave him her tested-sentence answer. "Well, yesterday I had a client who had an interest in a bank and a financial account in a foreign country so I told him he had to file Treasury form nine-oh-two-two-one."

"Yeah?"

"I save them money. Like if a corporation pays ransom to a kidnapper for the return of a corporation officer, then that is deductible as a theft loss. It's technical, but that kind of thing."

"That is simply terrific, Irene. I really mean it."

He saw her for lunch and dinner for the next two days, Sunday and Monday. He kissed her on Sunday night. I am forty-two years old, he told himself, and this woman has got to be thirty-five and a kiss from her makes me drunk. He told her he loved her at lunch on Monday. "I gotta say it, Irene. I can't sleep, I can't eat. I love you. I am a grown man. Insurance companies will back me up that I am past middle age but nothing, nobody in my life, ever made me feel what I feel about you. I love you. That's it. That's everything. I love you."

She touched his lips with her fingertips, then pressed her fingers to her lips. "I think I am in love with you," she said.

"Not *in* love," he said fiercely. "In love is temporary, then you move on to the next in love. Everybody goes in and out of love. I know about this. I remember everything I ever read about it in the magazines. In love is just a lot of exohormones which is—wait a minute!—a hormonal secretion by an organism which affects the smelling of another person so as to alter it in a certain way. I never forgot that. I wrote it down till I had it pat. Or it is feedback which is—ready?—a reciprocal effect of one person or another person. That's what in love is. Who needs it?"

"Love," she said. "I mean—I love you, I think."

"That is not just good enough, that is unbelievable."

"It sounds like I hedged it. I just don't know how to say it because I never said it."

"Never?"

"I never loved anybody. All my life I had to protect myself, and you can't protect yourself anymore when you love somebody. I love you, Charley."

"I thought all the time about you saying that to me. Day and night. Now that I know how you see it, I have to say to you that everything is changed now. You don't need to protect yourself now. I protect you."

"We'll protect each other."

"You have to live in LA?"

"It's going to take me a little while to get out. My house, my business—I'm in pretty deep."

"Then I'll keep coming out here till we can get it all settled. I'll work in New York for a couple of days then I'll catch like a seven-o'clock plane out then I'll catch the Red-Eye back."

"That will be heaven."

"Can you sometimes get away to New York?"

"Sometimes."

"Listen—Irene—everything being even, would you marry me?"

"Everything being even? That's some mountain."

"Just suppose."

"Yes, I would marry you, Charley."

They made love Monday afternoon on his rented bed at the hotel. There was never anything like it. Not for anybody. Not in history, Charley thought.

Paulie ran the Irene footage for him at the studio. It was absolutely sensational stuff and, for once, Paulie didn't have any comments. They got it down to two minutes, forty-nine seconds, out of almost three minutes of stuff. One shot showed them standing together. It was a real John Gilbert-Greta Garbo deal that could have stood up against any love scene ever made, Charley thought. He couldn't get over the great way Irene looked at him. How come he didn't see it when it was happening? Well, maybe actually he did see it, but he didn't take in all of it. These were moments preserved on tape and Charley waited for Paulie to ask him if he could bring in all the movie directors on the lot so they could see how it happened when it was real. This guy was a sensational photographer, Charley thought. Christ, he makes me look tremendous! The color was brilliant. The necktie he had on was worth the eleven dollars he had given the booster for it. The sound was a lot of crowd noises but Paulie said they could put a filter on that and bring it down. There was one confusing shot in the batch on Irene, which Charley didn't have them include in the cassette. It was just a flash, almost. Maerose brought Irene to his father, then it was over.

Charley took the cassette back with him to New York. A studio car picked him up at the hotel on Tuesday morning. They were passing through Watts when the car's telephone rang. It was his father in New York.

"Hey, Cholly!" Pop said. "How they hangin'?"

"Terrific, Pop. You sound like you're in the next room."

"They got *rooms* in them Hollywood cars?" Pop said, and he broke himself up, yelling har-har-har into the phone for about half a mile. "Listen, Charley, we got a little problem here so come straight to the office when you get in."

Chapter Four

Charley went from La Guardia to the St. Gabbione Hotel Laundry where Vincent Prizzi ran his end of the family business. Pop was waiting for him.

"Before I forget," Charley said, "I got a gimmick maybe you or Ed can use." He told his father about the tax dodge on kidnap insurance that Irene had told him.

"That's a good wrinkle," Pop said, "where'd you get it?"

"Some tax expert. So—what's the problem?"

"Marty Gilroy is shorting payoffs again."

"What?"

"So break his legs."

"No, Pop. This proves it. Marty has to be stupid. If I talk to him that will make the second time and that ain't right. He don't give a shit. We only break his legs and the other bankers are going to think he is getting away on us."

"You want to hide him in the garbage?"

"I want to shove a *bruciatóre* in his mouth and keep it there until he signs a check for every dime he has. Then I want to take him out on the Island until his checks clear, then I want to break his legs and let him hitchhike home."

"Why is that different?"

32

"Because we will flash his certified checks to every banker and runner in Brooklyn and Queens and they will know Marty isn't getting away with only broken legs."

"That's very good. It'll keep Marty straight. I like Marty, he's a real hitter."

"Pop?"

"What?"

"Who was the girl you were talking to at the wedding?"

"What girl? Half was girls."

"A great looker in a green-and-yellow dress."

"A great *looker?*"

"Yeah—sure."

"Hey! I'm an old guy. I don't remember those kind of things like you do."

"Maybe if I showed you pictures?"

"Why not? But how come this is such a big deal?"

"She's a very special woman and I need to know all I can find out about her. Paulie has a movie shot of you and her."

"From where?"

"From Teresa's wedding. From after—at the hotel."

"Yeah? I'd like to see it."

"Can you come over to my place tonight? I'll cook you a meal. It's video, the picture. It takes a machine."

"I got a meet tonight."

"Well—as soon as you can."

"Sure, Charley."

"I'll go talk to Marty Gilroy."

Charley went to a phone and called Al Melvini, who was called "the Plumber" because he always threatened to flush people down toilets when he was on a job. Charley told him to be at The Corner in half an hour and to bring tools.

It was too early to call Irene in California. He went

out the back door of the laundry and got into his anonymous, black Chevy van and drove the four blocks to The Corner. He went into the luncheonette to see who was around. Phil Vittimizzare was eating a Danish while he played the pinball machine and two dealers were counting out decks of heroin at a table in the back.

"Hey, Cholly!" Mrs. Latucci yelled at him from behind the counter. "Come on. Have a cuppa coffee and give me a good horse for today."

Charley waved to her and stood next to Phil. "I'll be in the car," he said. "Take your time. We gotta wait till the Plumber gets here."

He started to go back to the Chevy van.

"Hey, Cholly!" Mrs. Latucci yelled. "First, give me a horse."

"Lady Carrot in the third at Pimlico," Charley said as he went out. The two dealers and Mrs. Latucci wrote the information down.

Charley got into the van and read a newspaper. There was still stuff about the Netturbino killing. Charley read the story as a piece of trade news. Netturbino had the lifetime habit of having a new hooker sent over to his hotel suite every afternoon at three o'clock, except Sundays, which he spent with three uncles who played *bocce* for a living in New Jersey. The police said whoever hit Netturbino had been welcomed by him, because he was alone and wearing only a bathrobe and a pajama top. Charley grinned. That was how to set up a tag, he thought.

Phil and Al got into the car. Charley drove.

"Manischewitz! what a beautiful day," Al Melvini said. "When the breeze is right and the sun is shining there ain't anyplace like Brooklyn. Where we going?"

"Marty Gilroy's," Charley said.

Marty Gilroy was a very large black man with a bushy moustache that joined his sideburns. He had the best disposition in Greater New York. "He is a regular Ronnie Reagan," Pop liked to say, because he admired a sweet nature. Marty was a Prizzi banker so there was no trouble getting into his inner office in the garage where he operated, but Charley knew that even the three of them would have a hard time with him so, smiling a greeting, he kept moving in and slammed Gilroy across his sideburns with a fistful of quarters while Gilroy was half-rising to greet him. When Marty hit the floor it was like a comet hitting a planet. Everything shook and seemed to keep shaking. Phil and Al lifted him back on his swivel chair and tied him to it, doubling up on the knots.

"Keep anybody out," Charley said. Phil left. Charley and Al waited for Gilroy to come around. It didn't take long.

"Where's your checkbook, Marty?" Charley asked.

"Top drawer," the black man groaned. "Charley, listen—"

Charley pushed the swivel chair back so he could open the drawer. He slid out a wide, three-tiered checkbook and a .38 caliber pistol. "Registered to you?" he asked. Marty shook his head. Charley put the gun in his side pocket and with the other hand took a leather notebook out of the opposite pocket. He read from its first page. "You got $208,439.21 in the A account, Marty. Make me out a check to cash for that."

"Listen, Charley—this a mistake. You trying to say I fucked the Prizzis around? Man, no way. Man, I am *set* with the Prizzis, what I need to do that for?"

"You shorted on payoffs again. You know it and we know it, and you know we know it. So make out the check. Untie the arm, Plumber. You right-handed, Marty?"

"Lefty," Gilroy moaned.

Charley moved behind Gilroy and pushed the barrel of the pistol into the base of his skull. Melvini untied the left arm. "Don't get wise," he said to Gilroy, "or I'll flush you right down the toilet."

Marty made out the check while Al held the checkbook steady.

"You got $86,392.17 in the B account," Charley read out from the small leather book. "Make it out Marty."

"Charley, that my kids' money. That the safety money."

"What the fuck is this, Marty? Make it out already!"

While Al retied Gilroy to a chair, Charley tore the signed checks out of the book. "Hey, Phil," he yelled. Vittimizzare put his head into the room. "Take these to Angelo Partanna," he said. "Okay, let's get Marty the fuck out of here."

It took three of them to manhandle Gilroy and the swivel chair into the back of the Chevy van. Four of Gilroy's runners watched them work, standing very still and wondering why *they* had to be witnesses. "Just keep your mouth shut and you're gonna be all right," Melvini said. "Start talking and you're gonna get stuffed down a toilet without a plunger."

Phil left to go back to the laundry with the checks. Charley and Al drove east on Long Island for about an hour and a half. They left Gilroy under his blanket on the swivel chair inside the van, which was inside a garage behind a frame house that was well into the fields behind Brentwood, while they went inside to keep cool, play cards, and wait for Pop's call. He called in two hours. "All certified," he said, and hung up.

Charley said, "Okay—now we take Marty over to the state park on the south shore. It'll be dark when we get there. Bring me a crowbar from the shed. Marty ain't gonna walk home."

When Charley got back to the beach that night, he

sat on the terrace and called Paulie in California. "Hey, Paulie," he said, "I told my father you got him in the movies and he's all set up. He wants to see it. You got a cassette yet?"

"Charley?"

"Yeah."

"Charley, don't get sore."

"Why should I get sore?"

"Your father called me this morning at my house and told me to burn the tapes on him and the girl."

"What?"

"That's what he told me to do, Charley. So that's what I hadda do. I mean—what else?"

"You did right, Paulie," Charley said, and hung up.

Charley had been a member of the honored society since he was seventeen. Ever since Charley had made his bones with Little Phil Terrone, when Charley had been thirteen, his father had pressed Corrado Prizzi for the boy's early initiation. Don Corrado had suspended all new membership for five years. Charley had been twelve when the last members had been made, and his father spoke so much about it at home that, gradually, the ritual acceptance into the *fratellanza* became a mystically important achievement for the boy.

Charley was twelve when his mother died. Had she been alive, Angelo Partanna would never have gotten away with giving Charley the Gun Hill Road contract when he was thirteen. But after that day, Charley became special to his father and, although the don concealed it better, to Corrado Prizzi. Charley lived and ate with his father, spoke like his father, thought like his father. Angelo Partanna knew only the environment, but he seemed to know what was happening in it from coast to coast: who had the most booze going for them, what the daily handle with layoff bookmakers was, which labor union was about to fall into which family's arms, who had killed whom and why. That was Angelo's job with the Prizzis, as *consigliere* he was supposed to know all those things. But he knew techniques as well and and he taught Charley how to garrote instantly, the right and the wrong way to throw a knife, and all of the methods of bribery that had been known to the most cunning of the friends of the friends for seven hundred years.

Charley was a big boy at fourteen, larger still at seventeen. He had left school and had been working for the family, learning the shit business, from the importing, to the cutting, to the distribution and price-fixing, to the financing of subdistributors and dealers, to the marketing that would widen the use of the product across the country. Although it was Vincent Prizzi who later got the credit for getting behind the unstable and more emotionally dangerous narcotic, cocaine, it was Charley's active marketing research into cocaine, through Paulie, among the population of the entertainment industry, which had him convincing the family in the early sixties that its time had come as *the* dope which could help to siphon off the prosperity of America's middle classes.

Charley was thirty when he put the Prizzis into the cocaine business with both feet, causing Don Corrado to believe even more in Charley's star. His business foresight obtained Charley's appointment as Vincent's underboss on the working side of the Prizzi family when Charley was thirty-two years old.

On the night of Charley's initiation into the friendship of the men of respect, the Prizzis had assembled forty "made" men at the St. Gabbione Laundry sorting room, in the basement. Charley had waited in an anteroom, amid the heady, strong, cleansing smells of soap and lye, with his fellow nominees: Dimples Tancredi, twenty-nine; his best friend, Gusto, twenty-three; Momo "The Cobra" Ginafonda, thirty-four, and two other guys who died from Asian flu within the following year.

Charley had taken it for granted that his father would be his sponsor, so that he and all the others, including the members, were astounded when Don Corrado himself came out of the meeting room and escorted Charley into the presence of the brotherhood to be sworn in.

Don Corrado was a robust fifty-nine years old when Charley was seventeen. He was, himself, fast becoming a national legend in the *fratellanza* and was already one of the nine richest men in the United States. Solemnly, he drove a dagger into the wooden table and, holding its hilt, said, "The first new member to enter the honored society within the Prizzi family for five years is the son of my oldest friend, Angelo Partanna, my *consigliere*. This son, who stands beside me now, is seventeen years of age, the same age his father was when he was sworn into membership before he left Agrigento, and the same age as I, myself, when I took the sacred oaths."

He placed a revolver at the base of the embedded knife. "Charley," he said in his piercing voice, "you are entering into the honored society of the brotherhood of men of the greatest courage and loyalty. You enter our companionship alive and you go out dead. You will live and die by the gun and the knife. Take my hand upon the knife."

Charley reached across the table, towering over the tiny Don Corrado, who said to him, thrillingly, "Does the *fratellanza* come before anything else in your life?"

"Yes," Charley said.

"Before family, before country, before God?"

"I swear it," Charley said.

"There are three laws of the brotherhood which must become a part of you. The first—you must obey your superiors, to death if necessary, without question, for it will be for the good of the brotherhood. Do you swear it?"

"I swear it," Charley said, his face shining.

"You must never betray any secret of our common cause nor seek any other comfort, be it from church or from a government, than the strength, protection, and comfort of this *fratellanza*. Do you swear it?"

"I swear it!" Charley said, his voice rising.

"Lastly, you must never violate the wife or children of another member."

"I swear it," Charley said humbly.

"Violation of these oaths will mean your instant death without trial or warning."

Angelo Partanna asked him to raise the first finger of his right hand. He pricked the finger with a straight pin and a tear of blood came forth. "This drop of blood symbolizes your birth into our family. We are one until death," Don Corrado said, reaching up on his tiptoes to embrace Charley.

"As we protect you, so must you protect Prizzi honor. Do you swear it?"

"I swear it before God," Charley said.

He kissed the don, then he kissed his father. The members applauded. The large room was alight with their admiration.

Chapter Five

His father's baffling order to Paulie made Charley
so restless that he had to scrub the kitchen floor to try
to calm down. He filled a pail with soapy water and
added his own formula of rubbing alcohol and straight
ammonia, because he had it from the Prizzi chemist
who cut the *cinnari* that it was stronger than house-
hold ammonia, and Charley insisted on a spotless
house. He had always been a Mr. Clean. His mother
had run the cleanest house in Brooklyn and nobody
needed anybody to tell him why clean, cleaner, cleanest was the only way, because that was the facts. He
rolled up his trousers, got down on his hands and
knees with the pail and a wire scrubbing brush, and
revenged himself upon the kitchen floor.

When he had finished, he washed all the windows
on the bay side of the apartment while the kitchen
floor dried. When he could get in there to begin to
make dinner he took the home-made *cuddiruni* pizza,
with the sardines, the cheese, the tomatoes, the garlic, the oregano, and a stuffed artichoke, out of the
freezer to let it warm up a little before he put it into
the microwave. All the hard cleaning work had made
him stop brooding about his father's order to Paulie.
He was hungry.

He took the *fungi 'Ncartati* out of the refrigerator

and looked at it lovingly: the best mushroom caps in the market, which he had grilled himself with breadcrumbs, minced anchovies, *pecorino*, garlic, lemon, and oil—and a little *prezzemolo*. Even Pop, a really heavy fork, preferred to eat at Charley's because the food came out like Momma's food.

He put the pizza into the microwave oven, took the cork out of a half-drunk bottle of red wine, set the kitchen table for one, propped up the *Daily News* against the wine bottle, and had himself another great dinner. How could restaurants stay in business, he marveled, when anybody who could read could cook?

He ate slowly. He chewed carefully. His mother had raised him critically on the point of chewing carefully and he knew, secretly, that he had the best bowels of anyone in the Prizzi family. He wondered if Irene chewed her food carefully. He tried to remember how she had eaten the food at the spic restaurant but he couldn't get it together. She had terrific skin and a fine, healthy deep chest. Her teeth were one of her best features, after her eyes. Her teeth were square and white and the gums were a good pink so, until he could actually check it out, there was no reason to worry. It stood to reason that she had to have been exercising those teeth all her life so, he reasoned, she had to have a great set of bowels.

But when dinner was over, while he was cleaning up, his mind went back to why Pop had called Paulie. He could see the shot of Pop and Irene in his mind very clearly. She was listening to Pop, concentrating on what he was telling her, and Pop wasn't making any wedding party conversation. They were standing alone and out of the way, in an alcove, and if Charley hadn't hit the photographer with the C-note and Paulie's card, nobody would have noticed them talking. How could Pop tell him he didn't remember talking to Irene when it was such an intense talk? Jesus, anyway, how could anybody say he couldn't remember Irene?

When he had put the silver away, Charley went back to the terrace and sat there with the telephone in his lap staring out at the bay, trying to figure out what he was going to do about Irene. He was in a different kind of business, after all. Women could certainly be expected to resist his business unless they were born into it like Maerose. If Irene had been connected with the family all her life she would understand that it was just another business that got the people what they wanted—but in this case, things the law said they couldn't have, because that kind of law got the politicians reelected. People had always gambled. People had always rushed in to grab sensations that they were told they couldn't have. People had reasons for not borrowing from banks. All that produced a lot of money and there were a lot of hoodlums who got ideas about stealing some of that money so the system had to have men like himself who put them down when they tried to make their grab. He had never wasted a legit guy in his life. He was like the chief security officer for the big business that got the people what they wanted and that was all. If Irene had grown up with that she would understand it, she would accept it the way Maerose did.

But she hadn't grown up with it, so what was he supposed to do—look for some other kind of work? Nobody in the family would understand what the hell he was trying to do if he did that. They would look right through him as if he wasn't there anymore and nobody would ever be able to trust him again. Anyway, what kind of business could he operate in? He had a future where he was. Vincent Prizzi was maybe sixty-five years old. His own father was seventy-four. Charley was next in line because he knew the operation backward and he had fear and respect going for him. All the other Prizzis on Vincent's side of the business were either dopes or kids. Most of the Prizzis were on the legit side of the business or they had left the family to be doctors or engineers or sports announcers. Don Corrado couldn't keep going forever, at eighty-four, but even if he did, when Vincent went, the don would put him, Charley Partanna, in charge of the whole thing. Was he supposed to turn his back on his life because he couldn't figure out any other way to marry a woman?

He sat quietly, sweating in the cool summer night, because he couldn't get a handle on what he was supposed to do. She was a married woman without a husband. Let him stay lost, she said. He began to think about that. They were going to need at least a couple of years together until she was educated at least a little bit to understand why he had to stay where he was. Sooner or later she would have to catch on that he was in the environment. She would put two and two together. The women would wise her up. She was an American. She knew that the country needed people like the Prizzi organization to get a little relief—why else would they lay on the glamour in the TV and in the books and in the movies, which always showed the people in the environment as being very glamorous people? Maerose would set Irene straight. After all, Irene didn't need to know *exactly* what he did. She would know that he was in the environment and that he counted in the Prizzi family. Very few people could prove what he did anyway. If he took his time about the whole business of wising up Irene they could be home free without her going into shock. She would gradually meet all the Prizzis, Sesteros, and Garrones and see what terrific people they were—warm, real, stand-up people.

But suppose the husband showed up before Irene was ready to have everything worked out for her? That could be bad. Also, it could even be bad if the husband stayed lost. He couldn't introduce a woman to the whole family unless it was seriously set that he was going to marry her. Don Corrado was a religious man. They couldn't get married if the husband stayed lost. A divorce was no good because the Prizzis, Sesteros, and Garrones didn't go for divorce. They were old-fashioned.

Irene needed to be made a widow. That was it. She had said herself that she had no use for the guy. She hadn't seen him for four years. If she was made a widow it couldn't hurt her. All he needed was the husband's name and a little basic information so his people could find him. But he had to be careful. Irene was smart. But maybe Maerose could get it out of her, then pass it along. He could have the husband set up wherever he was and have the job done on him. Nobody could connect him with it. Then he and Irene could get married at Santa Grazia's just like the rest of the family, and everybody would be proud to send them Christmas cards.

He was so elated that he called Irene.

"It's Charley."

"Aaaah."

"I'm a wreck."

"Can you get out here this weekend?"

"Jesus, I don't think so."

"Tell me."

"I love you."

"Truly?"

"It's real." He was helplessly in earnest. "Maybe it's not scientific but it's real."

"Scientific?"

"I read in a magazine that, according to a doctor, when two people try to make one stable couple that what they are doing is looking for what they thought they needed from their mothers."

"Charley!"

He wondered if he had made some terrible mistake.

"I can't even remember my mother."

"But that's the scientific part. Your head still knows what you think you needed from your mother whether you can remember your mother or not. That's what you need and it's a deep thing, an emotional thing, so when you think you see that in somebody that they can bring to you what you know you needed from your mother—that's what falling in love is. The magazine was very clear on that. A doctor wrote it."

"But, Charley, I can't suppose that what I wanted from my mother was that she be six foot two with a voice like a taxicab and an appetite for pasta like the entire Boy Scouts of Italy."

"No, not that. Not what you can see with your eyes. It's what you sense—like someone who will always protect you and take care of you, someone who will be kind to you and won't yell at you, someone who doesn't want *any*body else but you. It's possible, the theory."

"All I know is, whether I think I know it or know I know it, I have to know when I'm going to see you again."

"This weekend. Absolutely. I have to know that also. We have to be together this weekend."

He got to bed at eleven o'clock. He fell asleep thinking about how he had to get some hot airline blank-ticket stock from Ed Prizzi to set himself and Irene with plenty of back-and-forth transportation. At a quarter to twelve, the phone rang. It was Pop.

"Cholly?"

"Yeah, Pop."

"Vincent wants to see you."

"Tonight?"

"Tomorrow. Two o'clock."

"Okay."

"Not at the laundry. At Ben's."

Ben Sestero's house was where Corrado Prizzi lived.

"What the hell is this, Pop?"

"Whatever it is," Pop said, "it hit the fan tonight."

Chapter Six

Corrado Prizzi lived with his favorite child, Amalia Sestero, who took care of him as she took care of all of her children, her kitchen, her church, and her family's life. The house, as befitted a business executive who could expect rewards that matched his responsibilities, was in Brooklyn Heights with a magnificent view of lower Manhattan island, which could have been a foreign country to Don Corrado.

Neither the don nor his son Vincent owned anything. Houses, cars, furniture, jewelry, and equipment were all held in the names of various companies. As traditional men of respect they felt that it was more important to observe the rules of humility and austerity—and, perhaps to give the Internal Revenue Service no reason to assume that they could afford such luxuries, which would have required more than their meager incomes.

Amalia answered the door serenely, as if the armed doorkeeper were not there, and kissed Charley on both cheeks. "I got some *gelu i muluni* for you, Charley," she said softly in Sicilian, "for when after Poppa goes to bed."

She led the way to two sliding oak doors and knocked softly. A muffled voice inside told her to come in. She slid open the doors, Charley entered,

47

and she slid them closed again behind him. The room was paneled in dark wood. The furnishings were heavy and somber because it was a room for serious things—eating and meeting. The curtains had been closed. The wax fruit, in the basket at the center of the table, gleamed dully in the light falling from a central lamp, which had a red silk shade with peach-colored fringes, and only half-illuminated faces whose owners, as far as their business meetings were concerned, preferred shadows or darkness.

Vincent Prizzi and Pop sat at the bare dining room table. They were two elderly Italian-American businessmen in black suits, ties, white shirts and shined shoes. Their permanent expressions—pleasant, deferential, and courteous—had tightened into a grimness underscoring the respect paid to them throughout their communities. These included Brooklyn, Queens, Long Island, Miami, Vegas, Atlantic City, Phoenix and LA, the District of Columbia, London, Sicily, Turkey, Iran, Laos, Colombia, Mexico, and southern France, although neither of them had ever been beyond Brooklyn or Vegas.

Vincent Prizzi was built like a tractor. Everything about him was heavy: his speech, his jaw, and his justice. He was a man who took seriousness seriously. When he drank anything he always rushed it carefully around his mouth and through his teeth before swallowing it. He had once been his father's enforcer, when his father had been active in all operations on a day-to-day basis, just as Charley Partanna was Vincent's enforcer now. But he saw as little of Charley as he could because of the humiliation his daughter had inflicted upon Charley and himself almost ten years before. He knew it was wrong but he could not forgive Charley, either, for three reasons: first, for being the subject which had caused this stain upon Prizzi honor; second, for not getting married to some other woman so that the whole thing could be conveniently forgotten by all of them. How could he speak to his daughter or permit her to marry as long as the man she had wronged remained unmarried? Vincent's attitude to Charley was entirely proper, but formal and strained, because everyone who witnessed their relationship was aware that Vincent was incapable of actually feeling the degree of solicitude for Charley that he strained to project, overworking to convey that he wished with everything he felt that he could make up to Charley for what his daughter had done to him. At the same time, sharply aware that this was a weak position for a Boss to be seen in with one of his own people, he resented Charley for being the cause of his pain. And that was the third reason. Consequently, he dealt, not through Charley, his Underboss, but through Angelo Partanna, which only served to increase the powers of both Partannas throughout the family. But when he needed Charley, or when his father told him they needed Charley, he sent for him and suffered his presence.

Vincent's piercing eyes were frightening. They were as unremitting as laser beams, each glance a *keraunion*, that prehistoric artifact which was once believed to have fallen as thunderbolts. But Vincent's chilling gaze was caused by his nearsightedness and his vanity in refusing to wear eyeglasses. He moved about with difficulty—sometimes with a slight limp, sometimes with a more pronounced one. There were times when he could not walk at all. He sent one hundred dollars a week to the Little Sisters of the Grievous Wounds for them to pray in congress, asking St. Gerardo, patron saint of gout, to intercede for him.

Angelo Partanna was as much taller than Vincent (and ten years older) as Charley Partanna was taller than Angelo. Angelo's sweetness and amiable good cheer about murder and corruption were legendary in the environment. He was a man of brutal loyalty. Other men's pain, cupidity, and punishment were sim-

ple commodities to Angelo Partanna. He was dapper
in his way. After his wife, Charley's mother, died in
1950 he had emerged as a heavy ladies' man. He had
groomed white plates above the ears, below his vul-
ture-bald head, and his moustache was a white Puc-
cini-style. His skin was like dark, lumpy cocoa. His
nose was like a parrot's beak, a nose that had been
left behind centuries before in the DNA of some Arab
invader of western Sicily. Charley's resemblance to his
father was a matter of gesture and speech rather than
a physical similarity—horses do not look like parrots.
But they had the same ball-bearing eyes, opaque to
empathy. Both men, father and son, had been bred to
serve their feudal lords. Time had only *seemed* to
change for Sicilians.

The Partannas, father and son, were the prime
condottieri of the Prizzi family and guarded whatever
the Prizzis had, because what the Prizzis had, the Partannas, the Sesteros, and the Garrones—in that
order—shared.

"Siddown, Charley," Uncle Vincent said.

Charley pulled up a chair stolidly. He was accom-
plished at bearing Vincent's sufferance of him.

"I give that tip on the ransom insurance to Eduardo, Charley," Pop said. "He checked it out with the
insurance lawyers and they said it would work."

"Good," Charley said.

"Jesus, my gout is killing me," Vincent said.

Charley was listening with half his mind. He needed
to think about Irene and he couldn't help thinking
about Irene. The doctor in the magazine has got to be
right, he thought. How else could anybody account for
such a tremendous feeling grabbing two people
whether it was a convenient time or an inconvenient
time? It had to be that Irene and every other woman
he had loved had somehow signaled to him that she
could bring to him what he imagined, formlessly, he

had wanted from his mother. Not that his mother
hadn't given him those things, she hadn't deprived
him. She had been the most terrific woman in his life.
He wanted to be admired and his mother had admired
him, so all the more did he want to be admired by
women after she had gone. His mother had been busy
all day long, so maybe what he wanted as much as
getting her love and admiration was all of her time
whenever he wanted it. Things like that. Those signals
had come off Irene from the first moment they saw
each other. And he had fielded the same vibes from
Mardell Dupont, the crazy stripper in Jersey City
twenty years ago. He had gone out of his skull about
that girl and it lasted for fifteen months, until she
killed herself. The note said she had done it because
they had given her second billing but he always wondered, because it happened the day after he had been
indicted for the murder of Bummy Fein and Binky
what's-his-name. He thought it all out when it happened and he decided that Mardell had been born and
brought up a suicide, like all suicides. But she was
some woman—the beautiful way she spoke, like music, which his mother, for all her great points, never
did because she had been brought up in the old country. Mardell had loved him and had admired him and
she had been smarter than the whole Supreme Court.

Maerose, more than anyone else, Maerose proved
that the doctor in the magazine was right, because
Maerose was *all* the things his mother was as well as
what she wasn't. It was a powerful combination.
Maerose was a hot-blooded Sicilian woman who
needed to be run with all a man's strength, because
sometimes she thought she was her grandfather. But
she liked to drink and that was no good. She drank
too much one night when she was tired and she started
up a fight with him because he was dancing a lot with
Vera Bendichino, a Harvest Moon contest winner.
Then, to give it to him good, she left the party with

some guy nobody had ever seen before, also a juicer, and that was the end of Maerose's life with him. They found her drunk in Mexico. Her father sent her away someplace for five months and whatever they gave her made her vomit all over everything until she lost her taste for booze. She was on grass now.

Maerose was a tremendous woman in every way, but Charley knew that even if he had wanted her again (for a couple of years he wasn't sure whether he did or not) he couldn't have her, because the Prizzis were too ashamed of her for what she had done when she had been betrothed to him. But, in every way except the most important way, he loved her. She was brave just the way his mother had been brave, and she had a soft voice and an immense heart. The Prizzis had just left her lying there like a broken bottle for almost ten years and no one had seen her with a man, which didn't mean she never was with men, but there was so much sadness in her eyes that he thought the Prizzis had made her pay too much.

The four women of his life, including Momma, had a kind of amused classiness because they were proud of themselves, but they all carried some kind of pain with them, too, the way he did. With Irene he could lean way out and look all the way around at her pride and at her joy in being alive, but he could also see the pain. Maybe what the doctor in the magazine hadn't wanted to talk about was that people who fell instantly in love saw in each other some hope that the other would be able to lift the pain away, an impossible thing, but what the hell. That could be it. That could be why he and Irene loved each other.

The two sliding doors on the far side of the room were opened. Amalia came in, supporting the small, sere figure of Corrado Prizzi. They were followed by a deeply tanned man who wore sports clothes, which seemed comically garish beside the clothing of the others in the room. Amalia led the old man to the empty chair at the head of the table and gently helped to lower him into the seat. Nobody greeted the tanned man, who sat next to Charley Partanna, facing Vincent and Angelo. Amalia left the room. Don Corrado studied a yellow vase on a small sideboard beyond the far end of the long table.

"We all know Cyril Bluestone," Vincent said. "He is the president of our three hotels in Vegas and he is going to tell us what happened at the Casino Latino, the dirty bastards."

Bluestone said, "We only found out because the collectors had started in to ask where was the money, back East. Ten days after we pay out to an IOU signed by a roller with one-hundred-percent credit, if we don't get a check from them, the collectors go get it." He reached into his inside pocket. "I got fourteen IOUs here. The biggest one is for $60,000, the smallest one is for $43,000. All of them together come to $722,085. The trouble is that when the collectors go to get the money, the roller who signed the IOU either was dead from a bad cold or something before he signed the paper, or he was in Europe or someplace where he couldn't have signed the paper in Vegas. Every piece of paper is countersigned, that's the house rules, by Louis Palo and by a man in the cage, Marxie Heller. Every piece of paper. Okay, I check it out. For every date on every piece of paper, it was during the ten-day vacation which Jack Ramen, the casino manager, took for the first time in three years. When Ramen went on vacation, the shift boss, who was also the assistant casino manager, took over the job. He was Louis Palo. With the family. Very experienced casino man. But every piece of fake paper he takes to the cage, he takes to the number three guy in the cage, Marxie Heller, who had to be Louis' agent in the cage. They had ten days to operate. Ten days be-

fore Ramen came back to work. Ten days before the
collectors went out."

"Where are Louis and Heller?" Charley asked.

"Louis is dead," Vincent said. "Heller disappeared."

"Louis was laying across the front seat of his car in
the parking lot behind Presto Ciglione's bar past the
Strip," Bluestone said. "He hadda have set up a meet
out there because Louis was a very suspicious man."

"We all know Louis," Vincent said. "I know him
when he was a helper on an ice truck, forty years ago.
He came to my father, offered him his loyalty and
friendship, and asked my father to help him. He was a
suspicious man but he never forgot where his bread
came from. We taught him his trade. He wound up for
us in charge of the swing shift of our biggest casino in
Vegas, in charge of all the table games and holding
the deciding vote on keno and slot operations. He was
our second man in the whole joint because he knew
his stuff.

"He came up as a bust-out stickman. He was as
good as Con McCreary. He was a boxman and a floor-
man—and how many dealers are too dumb to move
up because they say they lose more money in tips than
they get in the extra salaries? Louis could deal, figure
operating expense, protect the bankroll, and work any
layout. He had great moves and a head for numbers,
but he could also control the rollers so they always
came back. But as good as he was at everything,
Louis' biggest strength was the way he understood
customer credit. He was like a machine, you know, a
computer . . ."

"I want to pernt out," Bluestone interrupted,
"while he was a shift boss, which is while Jack Ramen
was there, before Jack takes his vacation, and working
the floor, Louis could never have taken a shooter's
paper to the cage for him and got the money. Ramen,
the casino manager, could do that, but he wouldn't do

it. He made the shooters go to the cage themselves and identify themselves, so if Louis had tried it solo, even when he was acting casino manager, it would have looked fishy and somebody would have tipped me. But if Louis had his agent inside the cage, then he could hand in fake paper from high rollers whose credit could be looked up right in the file, and he and his agent would countersign that paper and put it with all the other paper that had come in, and the agent would pay out the money to Louis."

"I remember Marxie Heller now," Angelo said. "He wore a silver toupee on the job and he had dark brown bags under his eyes like his wife kept the coffee grounds in there, a big-assed, bossy guy with about thirty-two hundred dollars' worth of caps in his mouth."

"When I tell my father about Louis Palo," Vincent said, as if his father had stepped out of the room for a moment, "he sat for a while and remembered him. 'He wasn't a weak man,' my father said, 'except when flattery came into it. Louis couldn't resist flattery. He was worse, maybe, than the rest of us.' He liked clothes and his comfort. But, in all the years my father knew him, he was never a greedy man. I, myself, knew Louis was a brave man. He took Fufo Sapere, a maniac, in a bathhouse in Coney Island and he ran the crap game on Pier Nine like if he was handling schoolkids. So—my father thought—if a man is afraid of nothing, and if he isn't greedy for money, and he still isn't smart enough to figure out a gimmick as good as this one, then—well, my father asks himself—how did this happen? It must be a woman, my father decides. A woman could think for him and flatter him until he was helpless. Tell them about Marxie Heller, Cyril."

"Marxie Heller came to us four years ago from a man named Virgil Marowitz," Cyril Bluestone said. "Marowitz is a moneylender, not a loan shark, except that the law allows him to be a little bit of a loan shark. He has a chain of stores called Happy Finances in West Texas, New Mexico, and Arizona, and he has done very well with them."

"About seven years ago," Vincent interrupted, "Marowitz decides that he needs protection because he has the kind of a business which was too sweet to just let it lay there by some people. He knew Eduardo. He made a meet with Eduardo and he came to the meet with a lot of paper. He says cable television is the place to be and he wants to bring in the financing for us to establish this in the Southwest. Forty million dollars the cable layout cost—some of it his money, some of it through a credit line he got together. He and Eduardo worked out a deal and Eduardo told him we would manage it for sixty-five percent. Now you got to know this—Marowitz thinks that anybody in our bidniz is glamorous, like a movie actor or something. Marowitz like wants to be known on his gravestone as the man who knew more people in the environment than Jimmy Hoffa. It is like if all Charley ever wanted was to be known as the intimate friend of all the members of the National Council of Churches." He sighed. "Marowitz is a very weird fellow," he said, "and that brings us to Marxie Heller."

He sipped at a jelly glass of anisette. He nodded to Cyril Bluestone.

"Yeah," Bluestone said, "Marxie Heller. He used to be with the old Detroit outfit, all slobs. They ate opium like it was the breakfast of champions. He was good with figures. He got TB but, because he was steady, the boys set him with Abe in Phoenix and he moved there, but the lungs didn't get better so they laid him off. He must have met Marowitz and filled him with fairy tales about how he knew Capone and all lies like that, anyway Marowitz insisted on paying for Heller's cure. And when Heller came out of the sanatorium, Marowitz made a job for him in the finance companies. That was ten years ago. Four years ago, Marowitz sent me a strong recommendation to put Heller on at Vegas. He was a genius with figures, Marowitz said, and he hated to let him go but that Heller's wife couldn't stand Phoenix. We hired him. You know the rest."

"Where is the wife now?" Charley asked.

"In LA," Bluestone said. "I'll give you Heller's file with the wife's address and all the background."

"I think I should start with the wife," Charley said.

"After Marowitz," Vincent told him. "Tomorrow morning you fly out to Phoenix to see Marowitz. My father wants the money back and he wants you to lay it on Marowitz to take you to Heller."

"You think Marowitz was in on the scam?"

"How do I know, Charley? Louis couldn't have thought of it so who knows?"

Chapter Seven

Charley got to Phoenix at two P.M. It was hot. He rented a car, checked in at a downtown motel, and showered before he called Virgil Marowitz.

"Charley Part*anna*," Marowitz sang into the telephone. "What an honor! Are you in town? When can I see you?"

Charley hadn't been able to figure out any way to believe what Vincent had said about this man looking at people in the environment as celebrities, but it was all in Marowitz's voice so, against his own will, he tried to remember what Bogart did when he wanted to show that he was dangerous. He felt like four kinds of an idiot but he said, "We gotta have a little talk, Marowitz. I'm gonna pick you up in front of your office in twenty minutes. Be there." He hung up.

He put on a black short-sleeved sports shirt and black slacks and a pair of heavy shades. He got out the map of Phoenix the car rental company had given him and traced out the streets to the address of the Happy Finances office. He got into the car and drove there. There were four separate people in front of the building so Charley gave it a short blast with the horn and a short, roly-poly, grinning man came half-running, half-walking to the car. "Mr. Partanna?" he asked eagerly, with a voice that was pitched higher than an Abercrombie & Fitch dog whistle.

Charley nodded.

"I'm Virgil Marowitz." He opened the door and got into the car. "What a privilege and a pleasure, Mr. Partanna. May I call you Charley?" He clutched the sides of his head with both hands and keened. " I cannot get it through my head that I am riding through the streets of Phoenix with Charley 'the Enforcer' Partanna. My God!"

How does anybody talk to a freak like this? Charley thought. This was business! The Prizzis had been clouted for a gang of money! Bogart never did it in any of his picture shows the way Charley did it to Marowitz. "Listen to me, friend," he said. "I come here a couple of thousand miles to tell you that your man, Marxie Heller, stole $722,085 from my people."

"*Marxie*? I always thought his gang name was Moxie."

"Shaddap! You are going to make out a check for the seven-twenty-two then we are going to your bank to have it certified. All right? All right. I am going to ask you only once—where is Marxie Heller?"

"Mr. Partanna! I haven't seen or spoken to the man in more than four years. Where are we driving?"

"We drive till it gets dark," Charley said. "Then you get out and dig a hole with that shovel on the back seat, then I do the job on you and drop you in the hole and cover it up."

Marowitz turned around and looked at the back seat. There was a new shovel on it.

"Do I have any choice, Charley? *God*, this is exciting! I have dreamed about going along on an execution but I never ever imagined that I would be the gangland victim."

"Gangland?" Charley said.

"Do I have a real choice?"

"Two. Give me the money and Heller, and you can sleep in your own bed tonight."

"Well, then," Marowitz said, "no need to drive any

further. We can go straight to my bank and I'll make you out a counter check which they will certify."

"Okay." Charley said. "Where is Marxie Heller?"

"I purely don't know, Charley, so I cannot answer that question. But I could make a highly educated guess. But before I make that guess, I've got to tell you something. I just don't believe you'd kill me because of the complicated way the cable TV company is set up. The Prizzis own sixty-five percent of a forty-million-dollar investment in the cable only so long as I am well and strong enough to protect the revolving credit fund which pours in the operating money. I made the deal with the Prizzis because I thought I was beginning to need protection. If anything happens to me, that credit would just collapse. I designed it that way. Ed Prizzi knows that. Icing me, to put it in the *vivid* way you fellows say it, would be a hundred times more expensive for the Prizzis, in terms of their honor and their money, than the winkly little amount you say that Heller stole."

"Jesus, you are something else, Virgil," Charley said, exasperated, but admiring.

"Oh, I'll give you the certified check," Marowitz said. "Ed Prizzi will never let any of your people cash it, but I'll tell you what; if your uncle Vincent will give me the thrill of forcing me to appear in front of the Grand Council of organized crime, or even just the New York-Chicago families' Commission—either one of them the *final* court of American culture—for a ruling on whether or not I should pay the money because I recommended Marxie Heller for a job in Vegas four years ago, then I will *gladly* pay the fine if the council, in my presence, rules against me."

"Virgil—"

"Yes Charles?"

"Ah—shit!", Charley said, throwing a U with the car. "We'll go back to my motel and get out of this fucking heat while I call New York."

Vincent Prizzi told him to stay where he was, he would call him right back. He called back in seven minutes. "Somebody screwed up, Charley," he said. "Buy the man a drink."

Charley went to the quiet table in the corner of the air-conditioned bar. Virgil greeted him with a sunny smile.

"What a business!" Charley said. He called a waiter and ordered two *jugo de piñas con Bacardi*.

"How was everything back home?" Virgil asked.

"They gave you a lifetime pass," Charley said. The waiter brought the drinks.

"Say! This is an *extremely* refreshing drink," Virgil said. "I've *got* to get the recipe."

"Are you gay, Virgil?" Charley asked.

"Oh, a little." His face lit up. "Are you?"

"No."

"Oh, well. Don't worry about it."

"Where is Marxie Heller?"

"Such stick-to-it-iveness! Well, if I were one of the top executives of your organization, I would forget all about Phoenix, a four-year-old trail, and go back along the only trail which Marxie Heller ever followed consistently in all the time I knew him."

"What trail?"

"His wife."

"In LA?"

"Yoppee. Charley, this is a mag*nifi*cent drink. We must have another." He waved to the bartender. "Marxie said he had to get out of Phoenix because his wife couldn't stand it here. He said it was too dry for the asthma or something. I protested. Marxie was a very good figureman. He said he would greatly appreciate if I would smooth the way through my many *gangster* friends—pardon the expression—and get him work in Vegas. Naturally, I called Cyril Bluestone for him. He left and I never saw him again."

"You got any pictures of him, Virgil?"

"I have three or four very good snapshots. I keep a sort of Rogues' Gallery and I would absolutely *cream* with honor if you would consent to sit for me."

"My father is against any and all pictures," Charley said.

"I understand, Charley."

The bartender brought the new drinks to the table and Virgil asked him for a telephone. When it had been plugged in, he tapped out a number. "Hello, Killer?" he said into the phone. "This is me. Killer dear, I want you to go to Book Six of the gallery and study the index hard, go to the page holding the shots of Marxie Heller and bring them—now, please—to the front desk at The John H. Jackson Gusher Motel. I said, at the desk, dear. Please, Killer, do not make me angry." He hung up.

"He isn't really a killer," Virgil said to Charley, "I just call him that to give him a little side."

Chapter Eight

Marxie Heller's wife lived in an elegant fake-Georgian house in Westwood. Charley parked in the street about fifty yards beyond the house then walked back to make his way quietly up the driveway to the side door and let himself in. He closed the door quietly. Night was falling in blotters of darkness. He moved along a hall that led from the kitchen, looking for a room with a light, and there it was as he came around a sharp corner, gleaming out from under a door. Charley opened the door and found himself staring into the hooded, khaki-pouched eyes of Marxie Heller as he sat, dealing solitaire, at a large desk. Heller stared at him and blinked.

Charley didn't say anything.

"What do you want, my friend?" Heller asked.

"The Prizzis sent me."

Heller moved his right hand to open the drawer of the desk in front of him and Charley moved across the room and, both as a warning and as a precaution, broke Heller's wrist by lifting Heller's forearm with both his hands then crashing the wrist down violently upon the edge of the desk. Heller went under for a few seconds. Charley sat close to him and waited for his eyes to flicker again. He opened the drawer while he waited and took out a long knife. It had beautiful balance. It would be a great throwing knife. He slid it under his belt at the small of his back. Heller came around.

"Where is the Prizzi money, Marxie?" Charley asked.

"Who are you?"

"Charley Partanna."

"Oh, shit—Straight-Arrow Charley, the All-American Hood. Well, Charley, I am going to tell you I haven't got the money and you are going to say you don't believe me then everything is going to get rough for me, but that's the facts, I don't have the money."

"What's the difference, Marxie? What you did, things had to get rough for you anyway. Come on."

"Where?"

"Out to the car. Come on."

Heller got up. He stared at his ballooning wrist. "Jesus, this hurts," he said to no one at all.

"You won't need it," Charley said. Heller cradled the wrist in his good arm and shuffled out from behind the desk.

Charley said. "Up against the wall, feet apart, hands over the head." He found the gun in Marxie's bathrobe pocket. He unloaded the gun, put the bullets in his pocket and dropped the gun in the wastebasket. "Out," he said.

They went out the back door and Charley moved Heller into the two-car garage. He told Heller to swing the door open, they went inside. "The light, Marxie," Charley said, pulling down the garage door. Heller hit the switch. The light showed an Oldsmobile Cutlass and an empty space for another car.

"You had time to think," Charley said. "You want to tell me where the Prizzi money is?"

"If I knew, maybe I'd tell you, maybe I wouldn't, but I don't know."

Charley took a revolver, which had a sound suppressor fixed to its barrel, from a shoulder holster and shot Heller three times; once in the face, once in the chest, and once in the throat. He put the weapon away and opened the trunk of the Oldsmobile. He picked Heller up from where he had fallen beside the car and folded him into the trunk. He slammed the trunk lid shut, put out the light, opened the garage door and went back into the main house.

He sat in the darkened dining room just off the side door to the kitchen, which led from the driveway, and waited. He sat for thirty-five minutes before headlights came up the drive, pulling a car behind them. The side door opened and the woman came in, arms filled with shopping. She closed the door, crossed the kitchen and called out, "I'm home, dear."

Charley got up and moved into the kitchen doorway saying, "Marxie isn't here, Mrs. Heller."

She whirled around to face the voice.

She was Irene Walker.

Chapter Nine

She screamed. "Charley!"

He was speechless.

"What are you doing here?" she asked hysterically. "Why didn't you call? You always call. Ah, shit, Charley, you've ruined everything."

"Where's the money?"

"Money?"

"Where is it? Heller killed Louis Palo to get it, where is it?"

"Charley, I don't know what you are talking about. Did you ask Marxie? Where is Marxie?"

"He's dead."

"*Dead*?"

"All right, Irene. Where's the Prizzi money your husband stole from Vegas?"

She moved in a daze. "Maybe I know. He had a little bag. I'll show you." She left the kitchen and he followed her along a corridor out to a closet in the main front hall. She opened the door and shoved a satchel out with her foot. "It could be in there," she said. "That's the only place I know that it could be."

Charley lifted the satchel up to the top of a table. He snapped open the clasps and opened the bag. It was filled with money.

"I'm going to count this," he said. "Move over that way. I want you in front of me."

She moved.

He counted the money. He motioned for her to sit down. She sat down and he went on counting the money. "You're short," he said.

"*I'm* short?"

"I got three hundred sixty dollars here. Half!"

"Half?"

"Mrs. Heller, don't answer what I say with what I just said. Where's the rest of the fucking money?"

"Charley—I didn't even know it was there," Irene said. "So how could I know it was short? When Marxie came here three nights ago he had a big suitcase and that small bag. He just slung the small bag in that closet and he unpacked the suitcase."

"Then you knew he came to stay." Charley's voice was cold.

"Yes."

"Did you ask him about it?"

"Yes."

"And?"

"He said his lungs were bad again, that he had to go back to Phoenix but that he was so tired that I had to let him rest here for a few days."

"And you did."

"Yes."

"This is the worst night of my life," Charley said.

"I wanted him to stay, Charley. It was my chance to talk to him and get him to give me a divorce."

"You know what I remember?"

"What?"

"I remember you came in that kitchen door tonight and you yelled out, 'I'm home, dear.' Not just that you were home, or not just Marxie, but dear is how you called him."

"He *was* dear to me," she said slowly. "We had fourteen years together. I was a kid in Chicago and he was my friend. Not one time did he ever yell at me or hit me or take my money. I went to Detroit with him, then after he had to go to Phoenix, I went in and out to see him because he was my friend and he thought he was going to die. I loved him, not the way I love you, but I loved him like my father would never let me love him. Marxie was a funny, funny man. He had a terrific mind and he really cared about me."

"He ripped off the Prizzis for seven hundred twenty-two dollars!"

"Where is he?"

"I'll take him with me."

"For Christ's sake, Charley! He was my husband! He was good to me!"

"You're surprised? Seven hundred twenty-two dollars and you're surprised?" he said bitterly. "You still want to marry me?"

She stared at him sullenly.

"You want a little time to think about it?"

"I want you to have time to think about it," she said. "I mean what happened to Marxie isn't news to me. When he told me how he and Louis Palo took the money, I knew he was cooked. I knew they'd have to send you after him. He would be just as dead even if you had grown up to be a shoe salesman. So—what the hell—I'm not surprised, Charley. But you are. You're the one who is surprised. You sit in a stranger's house waiting for the stranger to come home and she turns out to be your woman. Your own woman. Shit, that is the real surprise, so, what I am saying is, you are the one who has to think about it."

"Think" was right. So she was Marxie Heller's wife. So she knew about the Prizzis, knew Marxie was stealing from them, knew what Charley's real business was. Had been *expecting* him to come after Marxie. When he hit that one, Charley decided to stop thinking for a while.

"Yeah. Okay. Marxie is in the Oldsmobile in your garage. I'll drive the Olds out to the LA airport and leave it in the parking lot. The cops will pick up on it. Is it your car?"

"No. And it has Nevada plates."

"Fine."

"Charley—do you believe me what I said about not seeing Marxie for four years?"

"Baby—he was just over the hill in Vegas. He moves in with you here because this is his house—the man had a fucking arsenal on him tonight, that was all—he brings a big suitcase in because he is running and you cook for him and lay down for him and when you come home of your own free will, you sing out to him 'I'm home, dear.' No. I don't believe anything you said." His voice rasped with bitterness. "Maybe if you were somebody else I would just blow you away. But it doesn't matter because there is nothing I can do to change how I feel about you even if I wanted that, but I can see your eyes, Irene. I believe them because that's what I want to see. I got to go back to New York and hand all this in, then Marxie Heller is finished for both of us. My people are going to ask about you and I am going to tell them lies. Then I'm going to come back out here, I think, and ask you again if you want to marry me."

"I want to marry you, Charley," she said.

Chapter Ten

He felt like somebody had handed him an armful of dead fish. Jesus, he thought, this has to be the original merry widow. I zip her husband while she's out tracking down specials in the supermarket, and she wants to marry me. What kind of a nothing woman is she?

What the fuck was he going to do about her? She had absolutely set the husband up because she had to know the Prizzis were coming for their $720. She was the bad guy. It had to be. She had to be the shit. With her mind, *and* with her body, she had to organize Louis Palo, that cunt-simple schmuck, and her own husband, to steal the money then to take the fall for her. There was only one thing he could do, what the Prizzis expected him to do; he was going to have to do the job on her and pack her in the trunk with the husband. But what about the rest of the money, the $360? If he zotzed her there wouldn't be anybody to tell him where to find the Prizzis' $360. He had to get whatever look had come on his face off it because she was beginning to look scared shitless.

"Listen, Irene," he said hoarsely, "I'm gonna tell you what you are gonna do. You are gonna stay awake tonight and think where that other three hundred sixty dollars is, you hear? I gotta lose Marxie and the car and get back to New York. I gotta do something and that's all I can decide to do right now."

70

"Okay, Charley," she said, "I will turn this whole house inside out until I find out where Marxie hid the money. When will you call me? When am I going to see you?" She felt like she was going to fold right there. She hoped she could stay standing. If she sat down that could look like some kind of guilt to him. His need to kill her was just beginning to fade out of his face.

"I don't know, Irene," he said. "I just don't know."

"You don't know if you'll see me again?" She had to hold him. She had to anchor him down on her side of the fucking swamp because if she let him drift away she knew he would come back and she would be dead.

"Shaddap!" he shouted. "The Prizzis are out three hundred sixty dollars and nothing happened to you."

"Marxie is dead," she said simply. "He was my friend. What is the loss to the Prizzis of some money which their insurance company is going to give back to them compared to what I have lost?"

"What are you, a professional liar?" he cried. "Five minutes ago you said you wanted to marry me, and you know, if you got a big loss on your hands, I am the one who fixed you up with it."

"Maybe there is something wrong with your emotions," she said, feeling safer because she had him talking and doubting what he thought he believed. "Marxie was dying. He had maybe a week, maybe ten days. I knew I was going to lose him. That is one legitimate set of emotions, okay? But you came in and gave it to him. When I left him, he was alive. When I walk in here, he is iced. What do you know—what do you care about a woman's emotions? Either way, he had to go, but nobody was set for your way, Charley."

"Aaaah, shit," he said. "Lissena me. Find the three hundred sixty. That's all. Find it and bring it to me."

He left the house by the kitchen door and drove the car and Marxie's body to the airport. He ditched the gun in an ashcan in Watts. He left the car in the air-

port parking lot for the rental people to find. He
caught the Red-Eye out of LA, disillusioned with the
most important thing in his life. Irene was a cold-eyed,
hard broad, that's what she was. Who needed a
woman like that? All that shit about being a tax consultant! It was disgusting! She was like some lowest
kind of hoodlum. He had almost broken his heart trying to figure out how he could explain to her about the
environment, while all the time she was setting up the
scam to beat the Prizzis out of the money. She had to
be laying Louis because there was no other way she
could get to Louis. Who else could have zotzed Louis
behind Presto Ciglione's? She stole the fucking money
and she did the job on Louis so she had to know that
the Prizzis would be sending somebody after her so
she figured it out that if she gave them Marxie and
half the $720 and came back with an armful of super-
market and that "I'm home, dear!" shit, anybody
would buy it that she was just a simple tax consultant
caught in some mystery web. The worst part of the
whole thing was that she had to know that the Prizzis
would send him after the money, and she had counted
on that as her insurance. And he had let her do it.

Shit! If he wasn't trapped on this fucking 747 somewhere over Arizona, he would grab somebody's car
and drive back to her fucking house and blow holes in
her, all over her.

He had himself a Seven-Up and a corned beef sandwich, automatically began to remember all of Irene's
good points. She was a tremendous woman, no two
ways about, he reminded himself. She drove a fifty-
two-thousand-dollar car, so she had to be a terrific tax
consultant. How many even men tax consultants made
enough to drive a fifty-two-thousand dollar car? She
could speak Puerto Rican like a native. She was crazy
about him. She had a terrific house and tremendous
clothes and she had probably gone to college with
Maerose Prizzi and that was all very nice, but the im-

portant thing, the unbelievable thing, was that she was crazy about him. He even had it on TV tape. As he measured Irene's pluses against her possible minuses, he began to calm down.

Could it be that Irene was two women, he wondered? That was possible. There had been a movie about that once and he could vaguely remember some magazine piece about it. The fact was, first and foremost, she was a wonderful girl. He knew what he knew and that was it. How could anybody fault a woman for marrying a man who had been good to her for most of her life? He told himself he should be grateful for that marriage because, at least, it had given Irene an understanding of the environment that she otherwise couldn't have had. She had probably figured that Marxie, a very sick man, needed her, so she married him. That was part of why she was a wonderful person. When he thought back on how close he had come to clipping her and stuffing her in the trunk with Marxie he felt terrible. But the surprise had been terrible. He had almost come apart when she turned around and he saw who she was. He had been ready, God knows he had been ready, but her goodness had come through and it had held him together. Her goodness, coming through like that, had let him know that he had to find time to think before he did anything that could have ruined their whole thing. Look how right that instinct had been. He had had time to cool off and look at the whole thing scientifically and he was going into Santa Grazia's tomorrow to light a couple of twenty-dollar candles in gratitude.

Above and beyond everything else, Irene had proved that she understood the environment. Even though he had done the job on her husband she had been willing to push that aside because she could see that the man had done a lousy thing to the Prizzis. He had stolen such a bundle of money from them that absolutely nobody, including the man's own wife, could look the other way. Next, it had to be that Heller had done the number on Louis. How could he have tortured himself with a fantasy that Irene had done the whole thing? There was no way Irene could have zotzed Louis. She understood the environment, yes. But that didn't automatically turn her into a hitter.

But—shit! If Heller had zipped Louis why was there only $360 in his satchel? If Heller had zipped Louis he would have the whole score. But because there was only $360, that didn't mean that Irene had to be the one who had iced Louis. The opposite was true. If the whole $720 had been in that house and if Heller had *really* been dying on his feet, *then*—maybe—somebody could say Irene had clipped Louis, as crazy as that had to sound.

When the plane landed in New York he didn't even bother to look at the time, he called Irene from the airport.

"Irene? Charley."

"Oh, *Char*ley!"

"You okay?"

"Are *you* okay?"

"I just wanted to let you know I landed. I'm here. At La Guardia."

"That is fabulous!"

"I'll call you later, hon," he said, and hung up.

He drove the Chevy van to the beach and fell asleep thinking that, after he got out of the meeting about the $360, he was going to get Pop out here, cook him a tremendous meal, then run the Irene Walker cassette for him so he could ask him some questions and get everything together in his head. They would get married after a while and she would move to New York, of course. He would ask Ed Prizzi to find her a classy office in Manhattan and throw her some tax business. Ed had so much going that they could double her take from what it had been in LA, no matter how much that was.

When he woke up, he felt great. He showered, singing the old-time tune "You Belong To Me." When he was shaved and dressed he checked out the food in the house, then went out to the stores to get everything his father doted on eating. He prepared most of the stuff for dinner then got into the van and drove to the St. Gabbione Hotel Laundry.

His father took him into Vincent's office. They shook hands and Vincent asked how everything went.

"Well, it went half right," Charley said. "Half the seven twenty-two I got back. Only half."

"Yeah?" Vincent said. "How do you figure that?"

"Louis and Heller—it figures—split the take in Vegas, then Heller goes to his wife's house in LA. Then Louis makes the meet out at Presto's and he's got his split on him and whoever's got the three hundred sixty, nailed him and lifted it."

"Louis is going to hang around Vegas for twenty-four hours? Then is he going out to some meet with half the split on him?"

"What else? That is how come the other three hundred and sixty dollars disappeared," Charley said calmly.

"Maybe."

"I talked to Heller in LA and he won't say anything. He says he don't know where the money is. So I pay him off. Then the wife comes home. I talk to her. No problem. She takes me to that money. I count it and there is only half there."

"You have to work her over?"

"She took me right to the satchel, no problems. She didn't even know there was money in the bag. She didn't know anything about him. She hadn't even seen him for four years."

"There is something fishy here," Vincent said, "and somebody's got our three hundred sixty dollars." He chewed his lip. "But you done great, Charley. There is going to be a couple of extra points in this for you."

As he walked with his father along the hall away from the meeting, Charley said, "You think Vincent was trying to tell me something, Pop? Like how he thinks it could even be me who copped the three sixty?"

"Aaa, that's Vincent's way. Don Corrado is gonna climb him about the money so he's got to look in every box."

"You think I should worry about it?"

"Well, not yet anyhow."

"Listen, Pop, why not come on over to my house for dinner tonight?"

"Sensational," Pop said.

"I got everything you like all ready and it's time I cooked up something really great for you."

"Sensational," Pop said.

"I want to show you the pictures of that woman I was telling you about. You know. The girl at the wedding? I got the video machine installed this afternoon."

"I always wanted to see one of those things work," his father said, "but it's got to be an early night."

The video recorder had been installed at three o'clock that afternoon. Charley told the man to have the machine copy something from Channel 13 because he didn't want to start it on junk, so the man had it copy "The Story of English Furniture" (Robert Adam) for about three minutes and Charley was sorry it had to be turned off, so the man said they could keep copying the same show while they looked at something else. They looked at a black-and-white 1937 movie for another couple of minutes and the man reminded Charley that everybody in the movie was almost fifty years older than they looked on the screen.

"If alive," Charley said. "TV movies are this country's biggest cemetery."

The machine worked! They had it play back about

two minutes more of "The Story of English Furniture" (Robert Adam), and when he knew he understood how to operate it, Charley tipped the man five and gave him the carton to take out with him. "Always tip just right," his father had taught him. "Never too much, never too little."

He slid the cassette marked IRENE WALKER into the machine. He pushed the PLAY button. He backed up rapidly to a chair, sat down, and she was in the room with him on the twenty-six-inch screen in gorgeous color. She was floating out of the car with Maerose in front of the hotel. Then she was dropping her envelope into the black silk bag at the door to Palermo Gardens, then he was holding her hand and they were smiling at each other in the boy-meets-girl scene of any movie. He pushed FREEZE FRAME on the remote control and gaped. It was the most beautiful thing he had ever seen. He started Irene moving again and when he got to the end of the two minutes and forty-nine seconds, he rewound the spool and started it running from the beginning again, exalted.

After three run-throughs he was filled with tremendous feeling. He had seen something vital; the way she kept touching him when they stood near each other. She wasn't just a toucher. She hadn't touched Maerose or Pop, only him. He was still exhilarated when Pop arrived for dinner. "Hey, Pop," he said manically, "you know what I got for you for your dinner tonight? I got *sisizzo ci 'U Cimulu*. Your favorite—right? What else, hah? I got some fresh shad, that's what else, which means for you some *alose in camicia* which I am going to feed you with a gang of *capotina*. How about that?"

"Listen, it's better than a McDonald's."

"You are The Man, Pop."

They had a subdued dinner because they concentrated on the food. Pop said, at least twice, that he swore to God he didn't know how Charley did it. "I'm telling you, Charley, I close my eyes and I think your mother cooked this." They never talked business while they were eating.

After the dinner he got his father in place in front of the television set with a jelly glass of anisette in one hand and a Pruelba cigar in the other.

"Now," Charley said, "I am going to show you the woman I asked you about." He started the tape and sat next to his father. They watched the pictures silently while Charley waited for Pop to tell him why he had told Paulie to get rid of Irene on that tape.

"That's some terrific invention," Pop said. "Whoever woulda thought you could get Pete Spina on with the cream of the police commissioner's squad?"

"Yeah—right. But what about the woman? How come you know her, Pop?"

"I didn't actually know *her*. I knew her father. Maybe I met her once, I think."

"Yeah? Her father?"

"He was a mechanic for Polack Joe Saltis' mob, the old Polack mob around the Stockyards in Pro'bition. They done hijacking and strong-arm stuff. They were never much of an outfit. Somebody did the job on the father after the war. Nobody missed him."

Charley was half-dismayed, half-elated. Well, Jesus, he thought, no wonder Irene understands the environment. She didn't need Marxie Heller for that. Her own father was a worker for a Chicago mob. She had lived in the middle of it, she grew up in it and she knew it and she was still a tremendous broad. He had just found out about her too fast, the way everything was happening too fast, that was why he felt a little sick. She knew the environment. She would understand completely.

"Hey!" he blurted out suddenly to his father. "How come you made Paulie kill that shot of her and you?"

"Well, what the hell, Charley," Angelo Partanna

said, "she was the outside talent we brought in to make the Netturbino hit."

The furniture of Charley's mind suddenly began to come loose, the pieces crashing into each other like unfastened objects aboard a ship at sea ploughing through a hurricane. The huge concert grand piano, at which he had sat with such dedication and absorption playing his ancient ballads to her, was careening across the decks of his mind, loosed and dangerous among the smaller objects that were hurtling through his consciousness, glancing off him or crushing and wounding him.

He had known many people in his business whose job was to kill other people and he had accepted them, some warmly, some with indifference. They were necessary. But they were men. Mostly, that she had taken men's work was what cut the gaping holes in Charley's hopes for the proper order of things. The people who did his kind of work were like all the other people who did things to win comforts and the acceptance of their peers and, like the other people, formed attitudes because of their work. They had to get the job done and, in his kind of work, it took a kind of detachment that, Charley knew, was something God had never meant women to have. He had known her for a few minutes and for an eternity, but even his eternity of valuing her had twisted the truth of her in his mind, until, against the meanings of his life, he had conjured with the bare information he had hoarded concerning her and had, himself, changed her into something she was not. She killed people by contract, for money. He felt deep pain. He was being crushed by the furniture of his mind inside the ship of his hope in a hurricane even while he knew she hadn't betrayed him. He had wanted so completely for her to understand the environment and now, with one sentence from his father, he knew where all her own invisible pain had come from, he was inside her, he had become her, but so much more than he had yearned to be, that it had tapped his joy and had left him empty again.

"What's the matter, Charley?" Pop asked.

"I don't feel so good, Pop," he said. "Maybe the food was off, or something."

"You like her."

Charley could not acknowledge that.

"You love her?" Pop's voice wasn't amazed. He was gentle. He was Pop, the consummate adviser, the wise man of all *consiglieri*.

"Pop, I can't talk about it now."

"You don't need to talk, I'll talk. She is a smart woman, the best. Look, Charley," he said quickly as his son turned away, "what do you know about her except what you feel about her?"

"What I know is all wrong."

"Whatta you mean—wrong? You think you can know everything about everybody? You know her a couple of days, a week maybe. Hey—what did you tell her *you* did for a living?"

"Olive oil and cheese. But she knew, Pop. She is what she is so she knew what I was and she didn't say anything. She went to the wedding to get the nod from you, then she went and did the job on Netturbino. She tells me she is a tax consultant."

"Charley, suppose it was the other way around? Suppose I told you, up front, that she took the contract on Netturbino and then you see her and she asked you what you do? You're gonna tell me that you woulda told her that you were the enforcer for the Prizzis?"

"No."

"We both know a dime-a-dozen bunch of guys who go around telling that they knocked off this guy and that guy and you *know* they are fulla shit. This woman is the McCoy. She figures you are gonna know about her sooner or later but she ain't gonna come out and tell you. Listen, Charley—anybody who has a hunnert thousand a customer bidniz like her can't take any chances with it, you know that."

"What a business for a woman!"

"You think she decided what business? Her father was a pig but she stuck with him until they found him under a pile of garbage in the city dump. She was a good daughter. Then she finds Marxie Heller and he was good to her. She went to Detroit with him and she saw him through the whole lung business, then he left her because he couldn't stand it to make a young woman like that try to settle down in Phoenix. So she goes to Chicago and gets a job with the wire, handling cash. They like her. They move her up. She was a courier and while she went back and forth across the ocean she studied the tax laws and she was good at it."

"So what's the use of being good at it if she's a piece man?"

"She's an American! She had a chance to win even more money so she grabbed it! She had a great front, her tax racket. She knew the environment. She had the connections. She knew there would always be special situations where a woman could handle it better than like Al Melvini or you. So she went out and did a great job. She's got it made, Charley."

"I don't know, Pop. This is a serious thing. We were going to get married."

"She would be a good wife, believe me. But Don Corrado and the family wouldn't understand that. Bring her to New York, sure. Live with her, sure. But you know the Prizzis. A woman, to them, belongs doing what she does."

"I gotta think, Pop."

"You remember what I said, you hear, Charley. You don't get crazy, you understand?"

Chapter Eleven

After Dom and Phil came with the car to take Pop home, Charley went out on the terrace and brooded. He was glad Pop's bodyguards had arrived just when they did because, for the first time in his life, he wanted to beat the shit out of Pop. He would have beat the shit out of Dom and Phil except for what it would have done to the furniture. He felt like going down to The Corner and seeing who was in the luncheonette and beating the shit out of them. What else could he do?

He suddenly felt sick and sprinted to the bathroom with his hand over his mouth, knocking over a coffee table and breaking a vase on the way. While he vomited he deplored having broken the vase. Where could he replace it? It had absolutely the color green that matched the stripe around the rug and the trees in the big painting. He would be three weeks trying to get the right vase, he thought, vomiting. Maybe somebody could bond this one together again so that the cracks wouldn't even show. Jesus, he certainly hoped so.

While he washed he knew that he hadn't gotten sick about what Irene did for a living, he was sick about the Prizzis' missing $360, which somebody had lifted off Louis Palo after they whacked him.

As he dried himself with sweet-smelling cologne he shook his head in disapproval. Louis Palo, the most suspicious man who ever ate a *cuddiruni* pizza, walking around with the $360 on him, had gone all the way out to a dump of a bar where the waitresses tricked in the parking lot, away out on the state highway, to a toilet like Presto Ciglione's, to meet somebody. Well, Louis would never have gone there, Charley knew, unless some doll he had wanted to win bad for a long time had handed him a line of shit and got him to go out there. Son-of-a-bitch!

He walked unsteadily out of the john and set the coffee table right. He picked up the pieces of pottery that had been a vase that Maerose had knocked herself out to find, wrapped them carefully in a sheet of newspaper, and put them into a drawer. He would have to tell Maerose what had happened and she would bawl the shit out of him. He really had it in for whoever had hit Louis.

He went out to the terrace to think. He sat down and looked across the bay and lighted a cigar. He tried blowing a smoke ring but the breeze took it away. Okay. It was impossible that Irene had hit Louis. But if Marxie Heller was dying in a couple of days he would be too weak to take on Louis. Anyway, the longest, strongest day of Marxie's life he couldn't take Louis. Louis was a rough customer and he was suspicious of everything. So who the fuck had iced Louis Palo? He got up and went back into the apartment. What was the sense of playing guessing games. He had to try for a little information. He went to the hall closet and rummaged inside it until he found a copy of the Las Vegas telephone book. He looked up the number of Presto Ciglione's bar and went back to the phone to dial the number.

"Put Presto on," he said. "Tell him it's New York." He waited.

"Presto? This is Charley Partanna."

"Well, hey! How about that? I mean, how are you?" Ciglione said.

"Listen," Charley said, "that night Louis caught cold, did he actually come into your place?"

"No. I was surprised. I mean, he never come in."

"All right. Okay. Keep it between you and me. Thanks."

Charley hung up. He went back to the terrace puffing on the big heater. That proved it. Louis hadn't gone out to the bar to meet somebody. He had gone to the parking lot to meet somebody.

No witnesses. Whoever had talked Louis all the way out there had then nailed him in his car in the parking lot, had stood in his car lights, had got in the car with him to do the job on him, and had lifted the $360. It *had* to be a woman.

Who was the woman Pop said was the best in the business? Who was the woman who was married to Louis' partner on the scam? Who was the woman who had given the Prizzis back $360, but who was holding out the other $360? Who was so gorgeous that Louis, totally suspicious Louis, would have grabbed his cock and forgotten his money? That's who.

Around and around and he came out always at the same place. Two guys are passing phony markers back and forth at the cage. They don't need anybody else in the scam with them. They are all the troops they need to rip off the $720 from the Prizzis. Louis didn't need to meet anybody in Vegas. He had scored. Marxie Heller left Vegas right away. Why did Louis wait? Louis waited for the only thing he had ever waited for—a broad. She had convinced him that she was going to leave Marxie and run away with him and the whole score and Louis was waiting in that car with his cock in his hand until she came out of the night and got in beside him and did the job on him. That was the only way. Irene had iced Louis and had racked up the whole $760. Then it figured that, maybe because

Marxie had been good to her but mostly because he was dying, she had divvied the money up into two piles so that when the Prizzis sent him to take her and Marxie she could do her impression of Lillian Gish and give him back half the money. He sat on the chair in the corner of the terrace, holding his stomach with both arms and rocking back and forth, gripping the cigar in his teeth, tears running down his face. Then he reached down for the telephone on the floor beside him, pulled it up into his lap and dialed.

"Maerose?" he said into the phone. "Charley. Charley *who?* Charley Partanna, fahcrissake! How many Charleys call you at this time of night?"

"Charley, what is this? It's a quarter to one in the morning! What do you want from me, another Polish broad?"

"Mae—Mae, listen—I broke the vase."

"What vase?"

"The special vase that matched the border on the rug. That vase you knocked yourself out trying to find."

"Charley, what are you, outta your head?"

"Are you alone?"

"Of course I'm alone, you klutz."

"I got to see you, Mae."

"About a vase?" But she heard the need in his voice. "You *got to* see me, Charley?"

"Yeah. Whatta you say?"

"Charley, what's the matter? What happened? You in trouble?"

Even Charley, even Charley at that nadir of his life, knew enough to answer, "Why should I be in trouble because I got to see you? I—I miss you. I need to talk to you. Okay?"

"After almost ten years, you suddenly miss me?"

"Can I drive in and see you?"

"Sure, Charley."

"Half an hour. Forty minutes tops."

He went to the mirror in the bathroom and combed his hair. He went to the bedroom and put a tie on. Then he took off the tie and his white shirt and put on the short-sleeve black sports shirt he had worn in Phoenix, smelling it carefully to be sure it was kosher, then dousing himself under the arms with cologne just to be sure.

Since her father had banned her from the Prizzi family, Maerose had lived in Manhattan in an apartment house on East Thirty-seventh Street off Park Avenue called the Matsonia. She had ten points in an interior decorating business on East Sixty-second Street and, in business, she used the name Mary Hoover. She was a good decorator and she handled the firm's male clients, the inside kind who could afford the prism paintings of James Richard Blake. Angelo Partanna, with an okay from Corrado Prizzi, was her go-between with the family. She was allowed to visit with them on Christmas and certain other holy days, like St. Gennaro's, and for birthdays, weddings, and funerals. At first, everyone talked to her except her grandfather, her father, Eduardo, the heads of the Sestero and Gennaro families and other men of the Prizzi family. Many of the women did not speak to her until Don Corrado mentioned that he wanted that changed, but by that time Maerose wouldn't speak to them. Charley, who was considered to be the cause of her exile, always said hello, if not much more. Angelo Partanna and Amalia Sestero were the only two people in the family who welcomed her. That had been going on for nine years and two months—"almost ten years" as the people said—but Maerose never missed a chance to cross the river to hold her head up among the Prizzis. Her fidelity brought Don Corrado's silent support in the third year, so that gradually many of the men including Eduardo, spoke to her with kindness when her father wasn't in the room, but her father would not change. Nor was it possible for her to get permission to visit her family—in a symbolic kind of way to enter Brooklyn—on any day other than the days that had been prescribed by her father.

Maerose Prizzi was a princess in exile, who longed for her home and her people while she lived about four miles away from them, and the objects of her longing were like planets to her sun—some farther away from her warmth, others closer—but the greatest part of her aching need to go back to Brooklyn was to live forever in bed with Charley Partanna.

She was strong. She had negotiated her visiting rights through Angelo Partanna when her father had been determined that she must be banished never to set foot there again. She used all of her intelligence and toughness and Prizzi determination to win back her rights to be with her family on Christmas, then holy days—because these were irresistible objects to her grandfather—then the weddings and funerals. She lost out on New Year's Day, the opening day at Shea Stadium, which was in Queens anyway, but at which the Prizzis held important concessions behind first and third base, and on Vincent Prizzi Day at the Palermo Gardens, at which the big Easter party was held. And all other days. When she saw that she had gotten as much as she could get, Maerose held to the bargain.

Angelo Partanna came to see her at the Matsonia every Friday at eleven A.M. to spend an hour with her and to bring her allowance from her grandfather, which was the five points he had given her in the restaurant supply racket. He brought all the family's news. Angelo's profession depended on his memory. She would always ask for Charley last, as she was walking with Angelo to the door, and Angleo would always say the same thing in different words, which went something like, "I think he longs for you, Maerose. But that was almost ten years ago—and, of course, there is the family." She would nod somberly, then Angelo would kiss her cheeks and go away for another week.

Maerose waited, certain of her father's forgiveness and of her place with Charley Partanna. Almost ten years and he had never married. If he saw women, he didn't bring them around the family presence. She understood as well as the men that honor was more important than love, and certainly more important than marriage and fatherhood. Honor was the face of a family and the heart and soul of a family. She did not know how she could restore the honor that had been taken away, but she waited for Charley.

In almost ten years, only once had she lost heart. Charley, who had never called her since she came back from Mexico City, all of a sudden called her to get a woman's telephone number from her. Christ, it had almost dropped her womb. And the woman was a contract hitter. She knew that only because Charley's father had asked her to go and get her at the hotel, take her to the wedding, and take her back from the church to the hotel so that Angelo could give her the office to take Netturbino—as it turned out. A real icewater dame. Jesus, it was like a knife, Charley calling to ask her that. Then Amalia told her about the woman's husband ripping off the Casino Latino with Louis Palo and how Charley had to ace the husband, all the time getting him closer and closer to the wife.

Maerose talked to Amalia Sestero every morning on the phone and she always asked what was happening with Charley and the Polack. Amalia would say that Charley was flying out there, then flying back, and how he walked around looking like he had been conked. So, when Charley called at that hour of the night to say he wanted to see her, Maerose knew that he figured he would get even with the Polack by cheating on the Polack with her. It was a start anyway. It was a lot better than the nothing she had gotten out of Charley for almost ten years, she thought.

She formed a simple-appearing but providentially devious policy for herself about Charley: she decided to hold to the policy with Charley that one thing could lead to another.

When Charley rang her doorbell at the Matsonia, Maerose was dressed in the spirit of the occasion. Her beautiful, blacker-than-black hair fell like Chinese silk below her shoulders and below her waist, framing her tremendous, aquiline, hawk-nose, Arab-wop face, setting off the oliveness dusted with that undercoating of pinkness that was the warm envelope of her body, and contrasted with the brilliant whiteness of her teeth as she smiled welcome upon the man she was convinced God meant her to have.

"Hey, Charley," she said. "What's with you?"

He took a deep breath. "We gotta—like—talk."

"You want to talk here or you want to come in and sit down and talk?"

"Sure," he said.

They sat beside each other on the large sofa.

The room was furnished like the interior of an important Chinese pagoda during the period of Napoleon II when the emperor had reigned over farmhouses stuffed with Middle American antiques. "Authentic, it ain't," Maerose had said to her partners, "but we're like custom tailors, you know? We've got to dress the set to get the maximum attention."

"Yes," said the senior partner, "But what if a client goes into shock after seeing this?"

"Listen, Gascoigne—the colors are right, that's what counts. Everybody sees shapes differently but the colors are forever."

"This is some beautiful set-up you got here," Charley said.

"Well—that's my thing."

"How come you got so many books?"

"I'm alone a lot."

"How come you didn't set me up with books at the beach?"

"You aren't alone a lot."

He had been trying to look only at her face. Not at her eyes, he couldn't look into her eyes, but he kept looking downward and he began to feel the talons scraping his scrotum because she didn't have anything on under that thing she was wearing, and it was thin enough so he was, almost, able to see her boobs. Jesus! What a pair of secondary sexual characteristics, as the doctor in one of the magazines had called them. He needed to adjust his clothing.

"I hear you're on boo," he said casually.

"I'm not *on* it. I smoke it, but I'm not on it. You want a stick?"

Charley couldn't decide what to say. Boo, cocaine, and shit were for squares. He and Pop had open contempt for any kind of user. Including juiceheads, ever since they had gone into the counterfeit whiskey-stamp business. Thinking about booze made him think of the spic place in California where Irene had got them the *judo de piñas con Bacardi*. To get his mind off that he said, "Sure. Why not?"

She opened the carved ivory box on the table and held it out to him. "I didn't know you were on this stuff," she said.

"I am not on it," he said flatly, taking a stick. "I don't even smoke it."

"What do you do—make brownies with it?" she asked, lighting up, inhaling deeply, and passing the joint to him. "What the hell do you want from me, anyhow, Charley?"

He drew on the grass, held it a long time, then said through the exhaling smoke, "I just wanted to talk to you."

"You drove all the way from Brooklyn at almost two in the morning just for that?"

He allowed his hand to rest on her knee, maybe more on her thigh. It was warm, nice, warm. "We wasted a lot of time," he said.

"Almost ten years? You call that a lot of time? How come you didn't wait till I was fifty?"

"Well," he said slowly, exhaling slowly, "you could be a fat wop broad by fifty."

"Yeah? By the time I'm fifty you'll look like the Plumber's father—if he had one. You want to do it, Charley? Is that what you want?"

"Hey! Come on! Take it easy. What the hell."

"Nobody took it slower and easier than you and me, Charley. Ten whole years. Answer the question—you want to do it?"

"Well, yeah."

"Okay, let's do it."

She stood up and began to get out of the three-ounce overcoat.

"With all the lights on?" he said.

She stood there in high-heeled mules, nothing else except for some heavy eye shadow, and she began to breath hard. "Yeah," she said, "right here. On the V'Soske rug. With the lights on."

"*Madonna mia*," Charley said.

An hour later they had made it on the rug, in her four-poster bed with the showbiz curtains, and with Charley seated on a little stool in her shower, because he was getting a little tired. He kept moaning into her ear about the velvetness of her skin, the deliciousness of her boobs, and the elasticity of her hips, until she told him to either talk dirty or shut up.

At seven o'clock she made him such a breakfast that he knew even he couldn't cook: *caciotti*, small, hot rolls filled with cheese, and a minced kidney, and some *sarde beccafico*, little sardines with a stuffing of bread crumbs, minced salami and pine nuts with a little lemon juice, a bottle of cold, white wine and a quart of black coffee.

Chewing, he looked up at her with dismay mixed with adoration. She had put a small apron on, but that was all. "I don't know what I'm going to do," he said.

"Yeah."

"What is 'yeah' supposed to mean?"

"Well, Charley, for Christ's sake, you say hello to me, when you think of it, for almost ten years—from the time I was nineteen years old—until you needed Irene Walker, then you use me like I was information at the telephone company and that was supposed to be it, right? Forever, right? Then you call me in a sweat at one in the morning and you gotta make it with me. So it figures you're in the worst trouble since I took off for Mexico City."

"Yeah? How do you know that?"

"What is my name—Jones? I am a Prizzi. I am Corrado Prizzi's granddaughter."

"Can I talk to you?"

"I don't know, Charley. I knew a couple of minutes ago but now I don't know."

"I was almost going to shoot myself last night."

"Ah, fahcrissake, Charley!"

He stared at her, nodding. His face was helpless. She had never seen that before.

She sat opposite him in the gadget-packed kitchen and they looked at each other as if they were both listening to all the digital clocks not tick. "Tell me about it, Charley."

"I can only tell *you*, Mae. It won't come out of me when I try to tell Pop and who else is there? I am doing this to you to make you feel bad so I'll feel better and that takes my manhood away from me. It dishonors me."

"Charley, how can I feel worse than I used to feel? That was the worst. That was how you feel now. I was going to kill myself, but what I had already done to

Prizzi honor would be nothing to my grandfather if I did that. But, what the hell, Charley, believe me—the calendar takes care of everything."

"I don't know what happened. I seen that woman in the church and inside my head it moved so that I was seeing everything different. It just happened. I seen her and I went. Then I caught up with her in California and we were together for a couple of days. Not like together—that was only once, that time—but we had time and I concentrated so I could remember and I thought I knew her."

Maerose took her lower lip between her teeth and held on.

"All right!" he said wildly. "Okay! So Louis Palo, who was so straight he could have been a Jesuit, gets himself inside the cage with a cashier name of Marxie Heller and they rip off your grandfather for seven hundred twenty-two dollars and some change. So your father sends me out to get back the money and to pay off the bad guys. Louis is already blown away. I handle Heller, then I wait in the house for his woman to come home—his *wife*, Maerose—and she turns out to be my woman!" He held his heavy hands up and out in supplication. "What was I gonna do? She gives me the bag with half the money and a big line of shit. I figured it all as soon as she turned around in that kitchen. Louis couldn't think of that dodge! Heller was dying from leaky lungs and he didn't care. *She* laid it all out. *She* went and grabbed Louis' cock and pulled him into the scam. *She* wasted Louis! *She* has the other half of the Prizzi's money. Oh, *shit!* Did I pack her in the trunk of Heller's car and move her out with him for the cops to scrape together at the airport? No. I come home and I tell your father she is clean. I tell your father that the guys who blew Louis away were the ones who walked with it."

"But, Charley—"

"To me that was nothing. I am straight all my life

and I lie to your father and that is still nothing! It's like because of how I pissed on my own honor that I find out—from Pop—that she is the piece man who took the Netturbino contract." He put his head into his hands and leaned on the table. "I love her. That is the rock which I can't move out of the way and which is too big to try to get around it. I love her."

"Well," Maerose said harshly, "what are you going to do?"

He produced a brass laugh. "I got to straighten it out," he said, "because I got to live with it."

She took a deep breath. "Then do it."

"How? What am I going to do? How am I going to do it?"

"Charley, even people in office jobs don't live so long, believe me. You do it. That's all, you just do it, and when you are dying—if you have time—you are going to know you did it. You'll get back your respect for yourself. You can't lose more respect for yourself if you get on a plane and go to California and face her."

He stared back at her, not believing that he had heard her solve his problems.

"Look, Charley," she said, as she walked into the living room to get the ivory box. "A woman like that thinks like that only in those situations. She was brought up with the idea that she had to make a score using what she had. So what did she have? A bent mind and a Saturday night special and she used them like notches in a tree to climb up toward the big scores. Well, look at her." Maerose passed him the lighted joint. "She made it. But, what the hell, Charley, because she's a thief and a hitter, that doesn't mean she isn't a good woman in all the other departments. You never needed to be a thief, but you are the enforcer for the family and that never kept you from doing right. You see what I mean? What the hell, if she was some fashion designer like, or just a rich broad, and you got it together with her, it couldn't last for thirty days. You and this woman see everything with the same kind of eyes. You are lucky you found out in time, you know that, Charley?"

He began to sob with relief. She stared down at his bowed head, smiling with Sicilian triumph, and she left the room.

Chapter Twelve

Six days before Teresa Prizzi was married in New York, Irene Walker, naked, slid out of bed beside Louis Palo, wishing that he would wash his hair. She was a handsome, if not overly handsome, woman but she had something more important than looks winning for her. She had calm, she had the stillness that soothed violent men.

Irene slipped into a blue silk dressing gown that had cost her $825 retail. She got into a pair of imported French mules that had cost her $150 retail.

"Where you going?" Louis asked with a muffled voice.

"Coffee!" she sang.

"What time is it?"

She glanced at the Patek-Philippe light clock on the mantel ($3,500, retail). "Coming up to a quarter to eight," she said. Louis grunted and turned over like a stock car at a county fair, driving the pillow into the headboard of the bed.

Irene put the coffee on, then took a shower, scrubbing her hair. She was dressed in a Dior suit ($695, retail) when the coffee was ready. Irene bought everything at retail because that was the legitimate way. "Buy from a fence and who do you take it back to when it turns out lousy," she said to Marxie Heller.

"What kind of a rat race is it for people who don't even have a fence but they've got to buy wholesale to keep their self-respect? People with money. You think there is any class in buying wholesale? Class is retail."

She carried the two china cups and saucers, the spoons, cream and sugar on a tray to the table at Louis' bedside. "Okay, lover," she said.

He threw back the bedclothes and sat up looking as if his eyelids had been stitched to his chin. He reached out. She guided his hand to the cup. He lifted the cup to his mouth. "Hey!" he said, his eyes popping open. "Where's the coffee?"

"In the kitchen. The pot wouldn't fit on the tray."

"You certainly have a different point of view, Irene," he said admiringly. "A lot of people wouldn't hand me an empty cup."

"It got you awake, right?"

"Yeah. Just like coffee."

She came back with the coffeepot and filled his cup. "We are ready to go, Louis. Tonight is the first night."

"Those are beautiful markers you got together."

"It cost a lot of money."

"They are perfect."

"Jack Ramen leaves when you get there today. Ten days for the action. Two markers to Marxie tonight, three tomorrow night, one Tuesday, and so on. Fourteen markers. That gets us $722,085. How about that?"

Louis grinned. "Inflation dollars," he said.

"Oh, sure. Sixty percent to you because you have the toughest stand, and twenty percent each to Marxie and me. We fly out to Rio and live happily ever after."

"It depends, the ever after."

"Depends on what?" Her clear brown eyes were bright with curiosity.

"Charley Partanna."

"How come?"

"You know about Charley?"

"I know he handles the rough stuff for the Prizzis."

"You better believe it."

"He's just another enforcer for another big organization."

"Charley is something else. He don't just do what they tell him to do, he don't look around and if he can't find it, forget it; Charely takes Prizzi money very serious. It is like their honor with him when they tell him somebody ripped them off and he's got to make a lesson for everybody. Charley never stops. He worries. He nags the people. He waits and he keeps working. What I'm telling you, Irene, is that we shouldn't figure we are home free because we make it to Rio."

"I don't understand. Marxie told me about Charley. He says Charley is practically a square."

"Very funny—a Sicilian square. But I know what you mean and that is what makes Charley so dangerous. He really believes he is in charge of Prizzi honor. He hurts when anybody rips them off or doesn't pay respect to them. That's the whole thing I am talking about. You remember Joey Labriola and Willy Daspisa?"

"The guys who turned about four years ago?"

"Yeah."

"What about them?"

"Where do you think they are now?"

"Somewhere. Plastic surgery. New Social Security cards with new names. They are probably in the paint business in Winsted, Connecticut."

"Charley found them."

"How?" She was impressed.

"It took him almost three years, and a change at the top in administrations. He kept leaning on Ed Prizzi to squeeze the facts out of the government, to make them tell where Joey and Willie were. They cost the Prizzis about six hundred dollars and Charley couldn't stand it. How much money didn't matter. They done it to the Prizzis, that's all Charley knew. His father raised him right. Let somebody dishonor you and they got to be paid back, is what he taught Charley, and he's right. The Prizzis wouldn't have any business if anybody thought he could take whatever they had."

"Jesus, I can't believe it. Charley broke into the witness protection program?"

"Yeah. He did it. Look. They were big in the papers. They made the government's case then they dropped outta sight. Six Prizzi soldiers went into the joint. That alone costs the Prizzis eighty dollars a year for their families. You say, how can he find two guys with new faces and new prints and new paper in a country this big? In a world this big? Charley never sees it that way. It is a direct line for Charley, between him and whoever crosses the Prizzis. He makes them call a Commission meeting. He was on the phone every day to all over, reminding every *capo* and all the hustlers all over that it was their duty to look for Joey and Willy. But people are people. They got other things on their mind. After a while they fob him off, then he really leans on Ed Prizzi. Ed gets hot about it after a while. He tells Charley to lay off. Charley won't lay off. Charley keeps after him. Ed calls a meeting. Don Corrado Prizzi is at the head of the table. Vincent is there. Angelo Partanna is there, and the three *capiregime*. Charley makes them such a speech that nobody could tell him to lay off. He wants Joey and Willie because of Prizzi *honor*. They got to pay, that's all. Don Corrado tells Ed to go ahead. It takes them eight months and some very big federal politicians. They get the run-down on Joey and Willy straight from the government."

"Jesus!"

"You know what Charley did? He finds them in a furniture business in Yakima, Washington. The funny thing is they done what they done because they are queer for each other. Yeah. That's the facts. Jesus. Sicilians. Anyway, Charley rents a house in Yakima and he has the agent put out that he needs furniture, which the agent gets a commission on. He sees a lot of furniture guys but they don't have what he wants. So the agent sends Joey over. The doctors done a good job on his face. Not a new face, you know what I mean, but you don't make him right away. Joey don't know me, so Charley has me be the front. I go over to their warehouse and I look. Willy is there, the second time. Gold bracelets, shirt open to the knees, long yellow hair. Jesus. I say what I need is an expert eye for them to tell me what is the right size of stuff, like whether it will fit nice at my place. So we make a date for some drinks, then we gonna go out to the house, me and Joey and Willy. Well, Willy is very, very gay by this time, maybe because he is the interior decorator partner; Joey is the one with the prices. So we go out to the house, I got them fulla wine and pasta, and the house is like outside town. They are sitting down when Charley comes in, and Joey vomits all over. Willy faints. We take them down to the cellar and this is where the real Charley comes through. He don't yell at them and tell them a lotta shit, he *explains* the situation to them like it is important thing that they have everything straight. He tells them, calm and quiet, what they were when they come to the Prizzis— young punks working that shitty three-card monte layout, always running. He tells them, year by year, how they did pretty good and how, when coke got very big, the Prizzis put them into good slots in that business. Joey is crying now. Willy is saying, 'What are you gonna do, Charley? The government is gonna blow you up, you lay a glove on us,' and all stuff like that. Charley is like their father. He only wants them to understand they did wrong by their own people. They still don't get it that they are dead. They think he wants something else, I don't know what. What do you want from us? they ask him. I want you to make some phone calls, Charley says, and I want you to say you are sorry you done what you done. That's all? they want to know. He nods his head. 'Who do we call?' they say, and Charley gives them the names and the private telephone numbers of four *capi di mafiosi* around the country. He picks up the phone and dials the first number. He speaks in Sicilian. 'Don Abramo,' he says into the phone, 'this is Charley Partanna.' He listens. They exchange greetings. 'I am sitting here,' he says, 'with Joe Labriola and Willy Daspisa, the boys we talked about a couple of years ago. They want to talk to you. Just a minute.'

"He hands the phone to Joey. Joey says, 'What do I say?'

"'Tell him you did wrong to the Prizzis and that you deserve to cook in hell for that,' Charley said.

"Joey took the phone. 'Don Abramo?' he says in a shaky voice, 'this is Joey Labriola. I say to you that I have put a shame on the Prizzis. I deserve to burn in hell for this.' He looked up at Charley. Charley pointed his cigar at Willy. Willy took the phone and he said exactly what Joey had said. Four calls. At the end of each call Joey and Willy are looking better.

"'Now we will call Don Corrado,' Charley said, dialing.

"'Amalia?' he said in Sicilian, 'this is Charley calling Don Corrado.' He waited. '*Padrino*,' he said, 'I have Joey Labriola and Willy Daspisa.' He listened. Joey stood up to take the phone. 'Yes, *padrino*. Yes.' Charley hung up.

"'He forgives you,' Charley said.

"Joey and Willy embrace each other. They are so relieved they are crying.

"'But he wants your thumbs,' Charley said.

"They whirled around. 'What?' Willy said, and Joey couldn't say anything.

"'Did you expect that all this would cost you nothing?'

"'You can't do that to us!' Willy screamed.

"Charley shot them both in the stomach. When they fell down he took a hatchet out of a drawer. He knelt down beside each man and, spreading each man's arm across the floor, chopped off his right and left thumbs. It brought them back. Their eyes rolled in their heads, then they focused on Charley. He stared down at them. He is a hard man, but he was soft with triumph that night, I can tell you. He said, "The Brooklyn cops will get your thumbs. Our man will see that the official sheet with your print gets to the papers. You will be famous again! Famous!' and he shot them through the kneecaps. They made a lot of noise, I can tell you. Charley says, like Joey and Willy are listening to him, 'We'll hang around till you guys quiet down.' After about twenty minutes—who could stand that kind of noise?—he shot them in the head and we left."

Irene stared at Louis. "We aren't going to stay in Rio, Louis," she said, "we are going from there to South Africa where the sun always shines, where nobody can find us because there isn't hardly anybody there."

Not that she had ever intended to go anywhere with Louis after they made the score.

She drove to her office in the amethyst Gozzy ($53,000, retail, with plates) thinking about Charley Partanna who, if she ever thought of him, she would have imagined to be another hoodlum like her father. She was grateful to Louis for telling her about Charley Partanna. She thought about a mob as a mob no matter what the family name was. Anybody who used his head could have robbed Polack Joe Saltis blind. She decided she needed to take some kind of course on Sicilians. They were too dumb to protect their money, then they went crazy for revenge as soon as somebody took it. Maybe her work was too specialized, so that she never got to see the big picture. There had to be more to it than just money with the Sicilians. They were all macho flash and they were so fucking *dumb*. She couldn't get past that shit about their honor, when they lived by turning on each other for any rotten edge or one fucking dime. Their religion was betraying their families and their friends, they were the lowest kind of shit on earth, and if she kept thinking like that she could get herself killed.

She had never looked at every job just like every other job. That's why she was the best. So—she was going to start all over again and begin to study each hoodlum as different from every other hoodlum, not just as Polack hoodlums, or Jewish or Sicilian hoodlums, but as dangerous animals capable of doing her grievous harm. They had to have at least two minds: the group mind that made them need to be a part of a family, and a separate individual mind that let them survive inside the grinding, double-crossing mass of their families, betraying their own people for money again and again, fifty thousand times. She was sure that it was the *macho* disease that made the Sicilians so fucking dumb. The family lived only for power— and money, because it meant more power—but it was the use of subtle power subtly manipulated to move great mountains (as with Charley Partanna's problem, which ultimately needed to be solved by an attorney general of the United States moving in his expensive ways his wonders to perform) that had made them what they were. Money, beyond a point that they had left behind long before, was only grease for the chariot. All those who followed behind the chariot gained money but, in appropriate measures, they were following the chariot because of the prodigious power on the chariot. It could do anything, because it had all the shit and coke, sixty-seven national sports to take five hundred million chump bets every day on, broads, loan sharks, labor unions, cops and politicians and judges, and a couple of hundred "legitimate" industries. It could go anywhere because all the people wanted them, and the people elected the politicians. She shivered deliciously with the thought of sharing all that at the top. She was a woman but as she saw it, looking back over the years that had taken her from a Chicago slum to the driver's seat of a Gozzy, that was an advantage.

She saw that she would have to know Charley Partanna. He had things that she did not have. She had things that, perhaps, he did not have. He was steadfast. Well, Marxie was steadfast in a shaky kind of way. Marxie did as he was told and he was glad to have her there to guide him. Charley Partanna was loyal, and although she did not know whether he loved the people to whom he paid loyalty, he loved loyalty as a separate thing, by itself, because he had been trained that way. Marxie was more dependent than loyal, because he was a half-a-lung man running a seventy-woman stable. Marxie needed women to help him get through life. He had been caught with his opportunism (and his cock) showing many times. He was more loyal to switching loyalties. Charley Partanna was strong. Well, no one could say Marxie Heller was strong.

She didn't know anything about Charley Partanna except what she had heard, and that was never good enough. When she had the time, which would probably be never, she would have to get to know Charley Partanna. In the meantime there was hardly anything more important than spending as much time as she could thinking about how she was going to protect herself from him when everything hit the fan at Vegas after the morning of the eleventh day.

She slid the key into the lock of a door marked WALKER & WALKER, TAX CONSULTANTS, in gold leaf on simulated mahogany, with smaller letters in the lower righthand corner that said By Appointment Only, and locked the office door behind her when she went in. She went through the mail, almost all of it from the Treasury Department, Internal Revenue Service, but with four letters from clients. She dictated the responses to the letters into a machine after consulting files and tax references, twice telephoning lawyers, then she put the dictation sleeves into a large manila envelope that was addressed to a stenographic service, telephoned the service to send a messenger to get them, then checked the telephone answering machine attached to a telephone on the far left side of her long desk.

It was an eccentrically, if sumptuously, furnished office. There was no anteroom because there was no staff. The room was approximately thirty feet by thirty feet, on the corner of the twenty-third floor of a new building, with four windows that overlooked Beverly Hills. The desk dominating the room had been a military map table; an oak top, four feet wide, eight feet long, upheld by oak horses. At each end of the desk a telephone sat, connected to a telephone answering machine. There was steel engraving of Pilsudski. There was a romantic painting of Chopin at a piano. There was a framed photograph of Marxie with a lot of Teamster brass and Richard Nixon. A wheeled filing cabinet was concealed in portable window boxes packed with plants, the sides of the boxes concealing the filing cabinets underneath. The large side table had once been a casino craps layout. All the walls of the room on the windowless sides were lined with tax law reference books and schedules. Through connections here and there, Irene did a net tax consulting business that averaged out at about sixty thousand dollars a year; the lesser part of her income, but her solid front.

She played back the single message on one of the far-separated telephone answering machines through the blower. It was a rough New York Italian voice. It said, "Room eight-oh-five, Peak Hotel, Brooklyn, Thursday, July twenty-third. Somebody'll pick you up and take you to the meet. Bring tools."

The twenty-third was six days away. The twenty-third would be the seventh day of the Vegas scam.

She called a tax-burdened client and told him they could have lunch.

When Irene answered the knock on the door of Room 805, at the Peak Hotel, a beautiful Italo-Arabic-looking woman was standing there. "Hello," the woman said, "are you Irene Walker?" Irene nodded. "I'm Maerose Prizzi. I'll take you to the wedding."

When they got to Santa Grazia's, Maerose told her to find a seat on the left side of the church. "I'll pick you up as soon as the mass is over," she said. Irene collected her repose like a pussycat and sat serenely watching the wedding, wondering whether she would be home this time tomorrow, deciding that things must be moving right along at Vegas because no news was good news and Marxie had never failed to call her whenever things were going wrong.

After the mass she found Maerose at her elbow and they were assigned a limousine to themselves to take them to the reception. In the car, Maerose gave her a sealed envelope. "You drop this in the silk bag at the door on the way in," she said.

Once they were inside the door into the reception room, which had been decorated as if for a Polish wedding, Maerose spotted somebody and called him over. This must be the contact. Then Maerose introduced him and she knew it was the contact. It was Charley Partanna, the legendary Charley Partanna. She gave him her full attention. Maerose darted away into the crowd. Charley looked at her like she was some kind of new species so she figured he had never worked with a woman on a hit. They all got used to it.

She let him do the talking. "How about a drink?" he said.

"Maybe a glass of wine to the bride and groom." Jesus, he was a big man. He was like a high rectangle of meat and hair. He had a nice smile and that threw her off. It didn't go with his business. His voice came up from his belly like in buckets of mud, she thought, but it was a listening voice, it responded to what it was talking to. Nice clothes. Most men she knew wore expensive clothes but not many wore nice clothes. It was an Italian and Polish necessity to wear a tuxedo to an afternoon wedding, but Charley's jacket was quiet and black and it had natural shoulders, on him like an ox yoke, and the whole effect—no bright green ruffed shirt, no magenta bowtie, no wine-red lapels, and no yellow commerbund—made him seem to her more like a real man than a headwaiter at an acid-dropping party.

Someone began to talk into a sound system from the stage and it took her a few moments to register that it was Vincent Prizzi, but there was no mistaking who came out next, the grand old man, Corrado Prizzi, the oldest and most powerful surviving chief executive in the entire national Combination.

They made the speeches short. Charley asked her to dance. It was a great tune from when she had been a little kid, "You, You're Driving Me Crazy." She answered Charley with her big brown eyes but as they turned to go onto the dance floor, Maerose Prizzi told her she had a telephone call so she knew, all of a sudden, that Charley had meant something entirely different by the way he had been looking at her. He wasn't the contact. She followed Maerose through the crowd, thinking, Charley Partanna has gone fruit about me, and she measured how she felt about that. It was good, because she liked him. It was very good because, since they were deep into the Vegas action, which Charley Partanna was going to figure as being a shot at Prizzis' honor, and since he would be the bloodhound they would send out to tear them to ribbons, she needed Charley Partanna on her side. If she was reading him right, this was her lucky day.

Maerose led her to an alcove off a side room, off the ballroom, and didn't introduce her to the tall, thin, old man who was standing there. She left them alone. It was Angelo Partanna. He showed her his expensive false teeth in a brilliant and courtly smile, then he threw the smile away, and there was nothing to look at in the face except those ballbearing eyes.

"It's a contract on Sal Netturbino," he said. "Waldorf, twenty-one hundred, at three o'clock—one hour and ten minutes—he is expecting a woman he never saw. She won't get there. He'll think you are her."

"A hooker?" Irene asked.

"Yeah."

"I can do a hooker," Irene said.

"When you go out, after you clip him, go to the downstairs bar. Ask for Johnny. He's a bartender. Tell him you think there might be a message for Mrs. Bronstein. He'll give you the envelope and he'll let us know everything is copacetic." He smiled and nodded so she left.

She got a cab to the Waldorf. She went straight to the twenty-first floor and Netturbino's suite was right near the elevator. She rang the bell and decided to be a demure hooker type. He opened the door ready for action. His bathrobe was open and he had no pajama bottoms on. His dong wasn't flapping. It was like an extra arm. "Hey! Right on time!" he said with the kind of desperate concentration that comes to men with a hard-on.

"I'm Rhoda Bronstein," she said, whacking her cheekbones with her eyelashes. "I'm sorry but I have to use your john."

Charley said. "I live alone. I keep a
ouse so I figure wherever I'm living,
se. Is that the restaurant? Up there?"

Charley began to ask her if she was mar-
whole protection for the Vegas job fell
s had to go anyway, because he actually
she would go away with him to Rio or
l Louis was going to be the Prizzis' first
they found out, because he was in the
Marxie was dying. He didn't give a shit
ed and he was only going through the
is job so he could leave her a stake. She
take Louis and give Marxie to Charley
l to give Charley a little extra reason for
arxie so he would do everything more
let Charley pull the whole story of her
of her. None of it was true except that
kie were married.

en eighteen years old, hustling her ass in
el lobbies and bars, and getting fifty per-
en away from her by The Outfit, when
kie. He wasn't a pimp. He collected from
from the pimps. He was plodding and
bout it but he was a jagged man inside.
he had been a child and her father had
r mother, about four times a week, Irene
understood that she had some kind of
hat calmed men who were jagged inside.
her signals. He was a watery, tentative
ife but whenever, all through their time
had needed him to move, he had moved.
of maybe seventy hookers he was collect-
t, with what was to prove to be unerring
ndability (if absolutely no other kind), he
have a drink in the fall of 1963 at the
se. After a while he asked her to move in
hen, in the spring of 1964, he told her he

"Be my guest!" he said expansively. "But don't take all day about it."

She went into the john, closed the door, screwed the noise-killer to the piece and went back into the living room and killed Sal Netturbino. *Then* she peed.

had a job as a bookkeeper with The Outfit in Detroit and he asked her to marry him. She had been knocked flat on her ass by the idea, but just the same, she liked Marxie. He needed her and Christ knew she needed him. She didn't have the indifference that successful hustlers have. She wasn't a born suicide and she wasn't a slob. She was attracted to numbers and Marxie knew all about numbers, so she cried all over him and said okay. They moved to Detroit. The Purple Gang had gradually converted from a Jewish mob to a Sicilian family. Marxie was a carryover from the old days, a part of the sentimental notion that Jews understood numbers better than the Sicilians. It slowly became clear to both of them that Marxie had a lot of things wrong with him: his lungs were shot, his heart was weak, he was a bleeder. After ten years in that climate, he couldn't stand up to it anymore. By that time she was a courier delivering the Nevada skim for certain people and carrying it to Miami for the first split, then to New York for the second split, then to Chicago for the final split between Chicago and Cleveland. They moved her up then to the overseas routes, carrying the cash to Zurich, Geneva, Panama, Nigeria, and the Caribbean; long flights with lots of time to crack the tax books.

Marxie could be a drag, in fact a real pain in the ass, but the record certainly showed that he had been a good luck charm for her. It had been Marxie who had gotten her into her real work, at the top of the heap. There was a jeweller in New York who The Outfit used to move out hot stones in bulk, and he was switching the good stones for shitty ones, so there were a lot of complaints. He ran a diamond store on Forty-seventh between Sixth and Fifth, and the place was always filled with women looking for bargains they thought they could talk some guy into buying for them. Joe Licamarito, Marxie's boss, was furious that this momser thought he could get away with such a ripoff, and he wanted to have one of the New York families send a team into the store and give it to the jeweller. Marxie happened to be a good friend of Joe's. "Lemme tell you, Joe," he said, "the best thing for this job is a woman. She'll hit him and get closed in the crowd so fast nobody'll have anything to talk about."

"A woman?" Joe says, "Where do I find a woman for a job like that?"

"I got her," Marxie says.

Marxie brought it up while they were doing the dishes that night. "You stand at the counter. You pick the stone you want to buy," Marxie said. "The jeweller bends over to open the case while you open your handbag as if you are getting the money. You blow him away, drop the gun in the crowd, mix with the other women, then rush out on the street yelling when they rush out on the street yelling."

"What does it pay, Marxie?" Irene asked.

"Twenty-five thousand."

"No kidding?"

"That's nothing, Irene. Once it gets around the Combination that there is a classy woman contract hitter, you're going to see that price go up to triple."

Irene took the job, and everything developed just the way Marxie had said it would except that, with the inflation, she got herself one hundred thousand dollars for the Netturbino job, and there were always three, sometime four of them a year.

Marxie wanted to be her agent for lining up the work, for fifty percent, but she gave him such a look, no words, that he said, very quick, "No, that wouldn't work. I'd be involved. I'd be the corroboratory." She told him he could give her telephone number to Joe Licamarito in Detroit. After that she invented her system. She romanced a beautiful kid who was a student genius in the electronics lab at UCLA. The kid worked out the relay from the telephone in Kansas

City, an empty room in Kansas City, to the telephone answering machine in Beverly Hills. Then she bought a second number in Columbia, South Carolina, which also went directly to the answering machine in Beverly Hills. The relay was untraceable. Like Wow! for her business.

So she told Charley that she had been married once, for a couple of weeks, about four years ago. She told him she was a Polack, something she hadn't admitted since she was eighteen years old. She told him she was in the tax consulting business, which was the truth. She handled a small piece of the tax work for the Syndicate in Southern California. Then, all of a sudden, something happened that she certainly should have foreseen but didn't. She went to bed with Charley Partanna and she was ready to swear to God that there had never been anything like it. Not for anybody. Not in history, she thought.

She was in love with Charley Partanna. She *loved* Charley Partanna, or however else his demanding rules said they had to feel it.

Chapter Fourteen

She did the number on Louis Palo in his car in the parking lot. She was wearing hot pants and a bandanna so that Louis could see plainly that she had no gun on her as she got out of the Avis and ran across the lot, as happy as a bride, to run away with him. Marxie had fixed the gun under the dashboard of Louis' car, on the passenger side. While she kissed Louis she pulled the gun away from the magnets and shot him through the head. She lowered him across the front seat as she got out of the car. Then she got into the back seat so she could lean over and go through his pockets. The money was in the trunk of the car, with his suitcase. It was packed into a satchel.

She carried the satchel to the Avis and drove to Reno. On the road, early in the morning, she changed into a pretty dress. She flew from Reno to LA, picked up the Gozzy and drove to her house. When she got there, Marxie was in bed. He was in bad shape. He had hemorrhaged twice.

"I can't get moving, Irene," he said.

"Rest, Marxie. Don't talk."

"They're going to come looking for their money. We should be on our way to Hong Kong right now, but I just ain't got it in me, Irene." He coughed badly into a handkerchief. "They got this house in the file."

"Marxie, please! I'll think of something." She had thought of something fourteen days ago and Marxie was dying anyhow.

"Tell them I come in here and held a gun on you," he said. "Tell them you don't know anything about any money."

She went to the small room where she looked at television, and counted out the money into two equal piles. She put one of the stacks back into the satchel, because that was Marxie's cut, and stashed the satchel in the closet in the front hall. Her half would go into the vault at the bank. If anything happened to Marxie, like any minute, she figured she would have a right to the whole score.

The next day Marxie insisted on sitting up. They got him into a dressing gown with a pistol in one pocket and she sat him behind the desk in the television room with a pack of cards. That day, and the next, he played solitaire while he was dying. They were short on food so Irene went shopping. It was time. They had to get here soon, she thought. She could feel another presence when she came back from the supermarket, as she came into the kitchen, so she went into her performance as the happy wife.

"I'm home, dear," she sang. Then she heard Charley's voice behind her and, thank God, everything was ready for him. As she whirled to face him she was thinking of Marxie. She knew the hard, hard life was over for Marxie.

Everything worked. She took him to the money. She kept herself in a kind of shock. She *experienced* her own innocence. Then Charley admitted to her what he suspected and told her what he wasn't going to do about it. He wasn't going to kill her. He loved her. She had never meant anything so feelingly in her life when she said, "I want to marry you, Charley."

They would have to get it back to where it was or take it far beyond where it was. He was miserably unhappy with himself, but that was his own fault. He couldn't prove anything. She had given them back half the money voluntarily. They had nothing to connect her with Louis. Only Marxie, but Marxie had been her husband, and they knew better than anyone what wives had to go through in that business because of husbands and, besides, Marxie was dead. If she lived out her innocence for Charley, it would get better day by day. He would be all right. They were both going to be all right, and in the meantime she was $360 ahead.

She had to keep the money, certainly, but she had to hold on to Charley most of all. Jesus, she thought, how could anybody knock somebody by calling him a Boy Scout? The fantastic thing about Charley was that he *was* a Boy Scout. Charley paid his dues to his life. Charley believed. She had to get him back to find out how much she had hurt him by being the cause of making him turn on what he believed in. She had to make him believe that she understood the things he believed in—loyalty, the Prizzis' honor, the deep necessity of responding to the trust he was held in, which told him to do the work no matter what the effort or the cost.

Because there weren't too many guys in the business who were in their thing, people who could do their kind of work, she had prospered. She knew it wasn't only because she was a specialist, or because she was a woman. Even for the rough work, clipping crappy little hoodlums, not taking out top people, the business only had about a twelve percent yield of workers: butchers, stranglers, and quality workers. The Prizzis could put 2,100 people on the street but they had maybe 150 workers, no more, and of the 150, probably 100 were just a bunch of shtarkers who could pull at one end of a rope that was looped around some poor fucker's neck, while some other lump pulled at the other end.

Charley was a legend as a worker. Charley had taken contracts in broad daylight, out in the open with dozens of witnesses, and had walked away when the job was done because he had everything going for him that a top worker was supposed to have *plus* he had going that he knew that he was right when he blew that guy away. It had a lot to do with power, sure. But Charley didn't throw his power around. It had nothing to do with money. No piece man with any family ever got paid by his family for making a hit. Most of them were animals. What kept Charley from being an animal, she knew, was that Charley had *emotion*. Charley knew he was serving a purpose, not a buck. The purpose was to do every job like an artist, so that class shone out so much the bosses were forced to pay more points for a hit so they could be absolutely sure.

It was different for her, she figured. She wasn't locked into any family, she was a straight, commercial freelance who couldn't expect any protection from anybody if she didn't do the job right, which was why they paid her the big money. She didn't have to believe in anything but her head and her nerves, but now that Charley had come into her life, she could feel how cold it was out there. It was one thing to work alone, but she had never been able to live alone, and her luck—good and bad—had brought her Marxie. She knew she would have to die alone but, what the hell, so did everybody else. The thing was, if she could only get Charley back, she might not be as safe as she was right now, but she could live inside him and learn to think like him, and when she did and she was able to believe the way Charley believed then, what the hell, maybe they could take a chance on having some kids, maybe they could throw away all the shit that most of her life was made of and she could live, because she believed.

She considered her chances like a chemin de fer player against a bank. First, she had to get Charley to listen to her. She had to tell him what she did mainly

for a living. It would shake him up, but he saw that
kind of work from the inside. He knew the mechanics,
the economics, the reasons. She felt it was eighty-
twenty in favor. She had to convince him that they
saw things the same way and that was why they loved
each other.

On the bad side she saw the Vegas scam, which
broke down into different pieces. One, she had to
convince Charley that she had nothing to do with it.
How could they trace anything to her? On the other
hand, Louis was dead and Marxie was dead and only
half of the money had turned up. They couldn't ever
show that she had any connection with Louis, but
Marxie was hanging around her neck like a fish. He
was the only connection they had and they had often
moved on much less information than that.

She had made one mistake, probably because she
was working on her own and not polishing her reputa-
tion for the future. Maybe the mistake was good.
Maybe any mistake on any hit was so out of character
for her that they would automatically rule her out. But
she didn't really think so. She had left Louis in Nevada after she shot him. The Commission, which was
the arbitration council made up of the five families
from New York plus Chicago, had set down a rule
that nobody could do a job on anybody in Nevada
unless they took the body to another state and
dumped it. Somebody in the Commission could decide
to make a noise with that, just to crowd the Prizzis,
and the Prizzis would have to straighten it out the only
way they could straighten it out, by clipping whoever
they decided had wasted Louis.

So—she loved Charley more than she had ever
loved anything, but if she was ever going to give
Charley kids she needed Charley to stand off the
Prizzis if they began to move in on her as the only
connection to dead Louis *and* the money.

She reminded herself that they weren't going to be

seeing her as Marxie Heller's little widow, a work-
horse housewife who just happened to be washing the
rugs the day the Prizzis found half the money in
Marxie's house. Very soon, Angelo Partanna was
going to bring it up that she was such a part of the
environment that they had just paid her one hundred
dollars to blow Sal Netturbino away. They couldn't
pin any scams on her but they would know she wasn't
legit, and they could take it from there.

She really *needed* Charley Partanna.

Chapter Fifteen

It was a beautiful Sunday morning. Manhattan Island, across the river, looked clean and serene, as if it really existed only upon airline calendars. Vincent Prizzi picked up his father at 6:45 to attend the working man's mass, in a black Lincoln sedan driven by Phil Vittimizzare with Zingo Poppaloush, a Greek guy, riding beside him. They were both workers. Poppaloush's family had been Greek when it migrated to Sicily 673 years ago. It would be hard to take him for a Greek, but he was proud of the little edge it gave him. Behind the Lincoln, two and a half car lengths back, came a new Toyota some parishioner had given to Don Corrado, which was registered in the name of the Hurry Up Sandwich Company of Rockrimmon, Connecticut. Cucumbers Cetrioli drove it, separated from Willie Lessato by a sawed-off shotgun.

Father and son were dressed for church in black suits with white shirts and black ties. Don Corrado wore a sporty white cloth fedora.

"You know what I heard on the late news last night?" Vincent said.

"What did you hear?"

"They took a poll and sixty-seven percent of the American people think that what they all call the Mafia is the most efficiently run business organization in the whole country."

"That is a genuine compliment. That comes from the heart."

"All I can say is, there must be a lot of dopey American businessmen."

"What do they care? There aren't involved. They go to work at nine and they quit at five. All they get is a salary, so what do you expect?"

The small religious procession halted in front of the Church of Santa Grazia di Traghetto. Vincent got out on the open street side, slammed the door and hurried around the back of the car to open the car door for his father. He and Zingo helped the old man out of the car then, as was correct, established for many years, two Little Sisters of the Precious Blood appeared as if by God's will, and stood silently before the don, scowling piously. He nodded to Vincent. Vincent gave each nun a fifty-dollar bill, thus establishing Don Corrado as a casual, as well as an institutionally charitable man, but reserving for his son the prayers of the Little Sisters for the relief of gout.

Cetrioli and Willie stood at the back of the church throughout the mass. Phil and Zingo sat in the reserved pew directly behind Don Corrado and Vincent. Don Corrado slept through the mass and Vincent, even as he went to communion, hummed once-popular musical comedy selections silently inside his head to keep himself from thinking about whether he was ever going to get his daughter off his back.

When the mass was over, Cetrioli and Willie came down the aisle and stood as a screen between the Prizzis and the congregation while the church emptied. When it was empty, Father Malgaragno came hurrying out of the vestry to walk with Don Corrado to his car, Vincent leading, Cetrioli and Willie behind, then the don and his confessor, then Phil and Zingo.

"Did the bishop enjoy the wheel of *parmigiano stravecchio* which I sent him?"

"Don Carrado! He eats it with red wine, with white

wine, and when he is alone I think he eats it with champagne."

"It is very good with champagne. How is the young people's baseball team going?"

"We could win the league championship this year. We have two fine pitchers and three heavy hitters."

"The church should have its own Boy Scout troop. There is nothing equal in the world to what a boy brings to scouting and what he gets out of it."

"That is an excellent suggestion, Don Corrado. It has been on my mind for some time."

"Do you want me to mention it to the diocese?"

"It would help, Don Corrado. It could make the difference."

"I will talk to them tomorrow morning."

The old man held up his arms to kiss his priest before getting into the Lincoln. The two cars drove to Sheepshead Bay, where they boarded a seventy-eight-foot power launch (Don Corrado forbade the word yacht), which was owned by the Tarrawonga Golf & Country Club of Hillsboro, North Dakota. Don Corrado had some difficulty getting aboard, but his will prevailed. The launch moved slowly out, past Sunday fishermen, outboards, and sailing boats, and cast anchor in the middle of the bay. The crew went below. The captain remained on the bridge. The four soldiers played cards in the bow, while Don Corrado and his son sat under a striped awning in fishing chairs at the stern of the vessel.

Vincent unwrapped two roasted pepperoni sandwiches to break his fast. Before he bit into the first one, he poured his father a jigger of olive oil, which the old man lifted in toast to his son before he drank it down. While Vincent demolished the pepperoni heroes his father spoke to him quietly.

"You have been my strong, sure son," he said in the Agrigento dialect. "You were a lion."

Vincent chewed and nodded with gratitude, wondering about the past tense.

"You have never sought reward for yourself but you have earned a vaster reward than your family can ever give to you."

Biting into the sandwich, Vincent held up an admonishing hand, an action forced upon both of them by his modesty.

"You must be recognized before the world," his father said. "You must be acknowledged. The world must see your father's pride in his son. You have won the distinction of peace."

Vincent realized that something was happening. His father was glowing with intentions. He took a much smaller, warier bite of the sandwhich, chewing it more like a chipmunk than like a lion. "What's goin' on, Poppa?" he asked.

Don Corrado gazed at him with doting fondness. "You got that gout, you got that blood pressure, you got those kidneys, and you got to carry the cross of a daughter's shame all because of the pride you have in your family," he said. "You gave all of us everything you've got and still you give us more. Well, let me tell you this, Vincent. The left hand knows what the right hand did and it is now going to try to give back a little."

Vincent became concerned. When his father got like this there was no way to head him off. He had his mind fixed on something and he was going to get it and there was nothing that could change that. "Poppa, listen," he said, in a flash of panicked realization that if his father was easing him out then Charley Partanna would be Boss, and Vincent didn't want anything good for Charley Partanna.

"You listen," his father said. "You worked for us, you gave, and now we are going to show what gratitude can be. I have talked to the Commission and to some of the key people on the Grand Council. I have laid it on them what I want and they have gladly given me the right to offer you *the* job as the moderator in Vegas. You are going to supervise our three hotels there, but—most of all—you are going to be the

Principe Azzurro and the *parlière* of the national sports book in this country. How about that, heh, Vincent? You are going to live in a $935,000 house right on the golf course with a big swimming pool and a lot of those chairs they lay down on, and you can take any four soldiers in the family you want with you." He got to his feet and tottered toward his son with his arms outstretched. "You have made me happy, son," he said, "because you have earned this."

Intense relief went to every tired cell of Vincent's body. God had removed him from his daughter's shame. God had seen to it that he would be far away from all the hassles of New York and also protected from Maerose. He would have peace. He would be cutting the national sports book for two percent, the most profitable financial institution in the world. He could get Angelo to come out sometimes when he needed to keep up on what was going on at the laundry, and maybe Poppa would let him organize western Canada from there. But, holy Jesus, the corded and sensual wonder of the relief was that he wouldn't have to pretend to suffer about Maerose anymore. He was free.

"That is a terrific opportunity for me, Poppa. I ain't been feeling so hot. I think if I stayed in Brooklyn, I might slow down. I need the kind of light they got out there. I think I can really build the sports book. Who is gonna take over, Poppa? Charley?"

"One thing at a time," his father said. "This is your day. We don't think about anything or anybody until we get you settled in Vegas. I am going to give a banquet for you. Something nobody is going to forget for a long time."

Vincent embraced his father. "The whole thing is, Poppa," he said huskily, "that all my life, I can never get done thanking you. You made everything for us, two thousand people, you made everything for us. I don't know what any of us would be if you hadn't thought of it first, even Ed—Angelo Partanna and Charley—all the people, all of us."

When he stepped back his eyes were filled with tears.

"I owed it to all of you," his father said, "because you have all loved honor."

Cetrioli's honking laughter drifted back to them from the bow of the ship. Seagulls dove for garbage in the thick water. Seventy-one thousand eight hundred and forty-three toilets flushed simultaneously into the bay.

Chapter Sixteen

Charley caught a ten A.M. flight out of La Guardia for LA that Saturday morning. He kissed Maerose goodbye an hour before, then he kissed her again because he couldn't get used to her—the soft hardness and the hard softness and the delicious taste; then the goodbye feeling got so tremendous that he laid her on the rug just inside the front door and she came like a lunch whistle and cried.

He had to ask Irene a couple of questions, and he knew she would have the answers, and whatever the answers were going to be, they were going to be good enough for him. He had lived alone all his life, fahcrissake, because he always put the job first. Well, he was putting the job, and the Prizzis, and their honor, second—sixteen lengths back. Something had gone out of whack inside him when he had lied to Vincent. He *knew* Irene had scammed the Prizzis. He knew it had to be Irene who had zotzed Louis Palo. He knew it had to be Irene who had set the whole thing up. He had lied to the Prizzis. He hadn't clipped the woman and stuffed her in the trunk of the car with Marxie. There only had to be once when you got down to nitty like that, he told himself. He had changed. He didn't seem to give a shit about what he

owed to the Prizzis. He couldn't understand that. All
he wanted now was that scamming woman. Maybe he
was growing up. He was forty-two years old and
Marxie Heller had called him Straight-Arrow Charley,
the All-American Hood, like that was what a lot of
people were calling him behind his back. Well, fuck
that. He had done everything to deliver for the Prizzis
and what the fuck was he—some kind of a cock-
amamie junior executive who hadn't even seen Don
Corrado for like two years. He had maybe eight hundred, nine hundred dollars in Switzerland to show for
all that straight-arrow shit. Vincent must have fifteen
million.

Irene *counted* with him. He didn't want to do anything if he didn't have Irene. Irene was the whole
thing. That was it. So he would ask her a couple of
questions and take whatever she handed back to him.
Holy *shit*! What a business!

As soon as he got inside the airport building he
went to a telephone.

"Irene? Charley."

"Oh, Charley, thank God."

"We need to sit down."

"Where are you?"

"At the LA airport. Look, I'll meet you at that restaurant. The spic place, outside?"

"When?"

"I'll check in at the hotel and so on, then how about
one o'clock?"

"I'll pick you up at the hotel."

"No! I mean, I just want it to be out in the sun
when I see you. How do I get there?"

"Charley, it's not easy to find."

"Okay. I'll take a cab." He hung up.

When he got there he asked for the manager and
the same spic waiter as before told him it was the
manager's day off. Charley gave him fifty dollars. "I'm

going to sit at that table," he said, pointing at a table at the far end of the terrace that overlooked the ocean. "I don't want anybody to sit near me, keep a fence of three empty tables between me and anybody else."

The man grinned and shrugged. Charley sat down. Irene got there at ten minutes to one. She looked tremendous. She moved unhurriedly across the terrace wearing a smile and he didn't care what else. They both did a funny thing, they extended their hands to be shaken.

As soon as she sat down the waiter came back and she talked in Puerto Rican, or whatever.

"You order the pineapple?" he said.

"Yes."

"I been all shook up," he said.

She sighed, puffing out her cheeks and blowing it out hard.

"Irene, let me tell you something. I know about you. I know you clipped Netturbino and I'm just as sure that you scammed us with Louis and your husband at Vegas."

She lifted her head and the force of her serenity was narcotic. He could feel calm settling over him, which only happened when he was with her. Instinctively, he knew that the doctor in the magazine article had been wrong. This feeling had nothing to do with what he needed from his mother, it was entirely what he needed from this woman.

"I did the work on Netturbino, Charley," she said. "But I had nothing to do with what Marxie and his partner did."

"Nothing? Yeah? How come?"

"That's not the business I'm in, and if I was into scamming, I wouldn't have handled it that way."

"You know something? Vincent Prizzi doesn't even think Louis would have handled it that way, and he never thought Louis was very bright. Also, he says that if there was only the two guys in it, they would be doing it the way Louis called it because there was no way your husband was going to run Louis."

"Whatever they did, Charley, I had nothing to do with it."

"You think Louis Palo would sit in his car at night out behind a place like Presto Ciglione's? You think he would have pushed it right up to the night before Jack Ramen was due to get back to the casino? You think he would have taken an easy split on that kind of money with your husband, just like Marxie was some made man or something? If he *did* sit in that car waiting for somebody, the only one he woulda let get near him was your husband because maybe your husband was bringing more money—but what money? They had scored the money. Louis would have zipped your husband and he would have been on his way to Reno or San Francisco by the time he was hit in that parking lot."

"I don't know what they did," she said with effortless calm.

"The gun was under the dashboard. Louis was so suspicious that he checked his engine for a bomb every time before he started the car, even if he was going out for an ice cream cone. That's how he was built. But he would have let you walk up to the car and get in."

She let him see the pain in her eyes, but she kept looking at him, then, slowly, as if she were taking an oath on the head of a child, she shook her head slowly, three times, then murmured in a voice so low that he could only read her lips, "No."

"I have to ask you, Irene. I can't live with myself unless we talk about this."

"I understand you," she said. "I haven't slept much because I saw how much of your life is tied to the Prizzis' honor. Some insurance company will pay for the scammed money, but you are the one who feels violated by what Louis and Marxie did. You say to yourself that the Prizzis trust you, and only you, to get the money back, and whether you get it back or not, you have to deal with whoever betrayed the Prizzis.''

"Jesus," Charley said, "seven hundred and twenty-two dollars is a lot of money."

"They got half back."

"Three hundred and sixty is *still* a lot of money!"

"You can't stop *every*body from shaking the money tree! People scam the people with the money."

"Yeah," Charley said hoarsely, "something like that. But I didn't tell them what happened to the money. I covered for you. I lied, and to me—and to the Prizzis—that is the same as if I was in on it."

"You didn't cover for me, Charley. No matter how you've got that stuck inside your head, you didn't cover for me because I had nothing to do with it." She wasn't vehement. She didn't go wild with impatience and frustration. She was calm. She was true all the way, but Charley was wound up.

"I walked away with my father after the sit-down with Vincent Prizzi and, like I was crazy or guilty or something, I asked him if he thought Vincent thought *I* had copped the other half of that money. I'll never forget the look that came into my father's eyes." He lifted his hands helplessly.

"Are we going to get married?" she asked quietly.

He stared at her. "Jesus, what a question!" he said. All the hardness left his face. The doubts were gone. "You mean that?" he said. "After everything I been dumping on you?"

"Oh, Charley!"

"All right! That's it! That settles everything. The Prizzis have to believe me because I believe you."

Gratitude to God, to Charley, to her mother, who had taught her the wastefulness of arrogance, and to Marxie, who had taught her how to lie, poured into her, exalting her. She thought that this might be the only important minute of her life. Her eyes filled with tears and she smiled.

Charley blew his nose loudly.

"Look, Irene. My father knows how I feel about you—so maybe he thinks the same way I thought. But he's a wise man. He didn't try to stop Nature. He said, bring her to New York, live with her, but since the family knows she is a worker—you can't marry her. After all, you know what I mean. They can't have a hit woman hanging around with the women in the family."

"Come on, Charley! The women in the family have to hang around with the men in it, and they do worse things than clean, fast hits every day."

"Certainly. Sure. Of course. But you can see how Pop was just staying ahead of them. He says to me, I can't marry you. But my father was with only one woman all his life until my mother died. One woman. I don't have to draw any maps for my father."

"Are you sure, Charley? It won't get you in deeper with yourself?"

"It's none of the Prizzis' business," Charley said. "You are going to have Maerose as your family friend anyway and when you have her it's like you got an army. Come on, we're going to Mexico. We'll buy clothes there. We're going to get married."

It didn't work out exactly that way. Irene was sure she wasn't going to get married for the first *real* time in her life in a bunch of pick-up clothes from some beachside boutique, so they went back to her house and before there was even any thought about packing clothes, they were in the bed where Irene had made it with Louis Palo and where she used to make it with Marxie and it was so tremendous that they kept putting the packing off, until it was a quarter to seven.

Irene cooked a dinner that was part Polish, part Sicilian, and part Mexican. "I never ate food this good," her fiance said and, what with the strains of the day, the Olympic sex with Maerose the day before, the travel, his anguish over Irene, the post-Olympic sex with Irene, then the four-pound meal with the bottle of French wine (Petrus '70) that Irene had produced, Charley fell like an obelisk into bed.

When she was sure he was sleeping, Irene went to the TV room where Marxie had liked to play solitaire and called her telephone answering machines at the Beverly Hills office. It was half past ten. The South Carolina machine had recorded a male, reasonably cultivated voice, which was pitched on the high side. The voice said, "Would it be possible to have a meeting in Dallas on the ninth of August? This would be a full-fee job." Irene smiled in the low-key lighting; full-fee was one hundred dollars. "Let's make it for lunch at one o'clock in the coffee shop of the Hilton Inn on Central, at Mockingbird. Look for me at the sixth table near the window on the left side as you come in. We'll supply the tools."

She checked the calendar. The ninth would be six days from tomorrow. A short honeymoon was better than no honeymoon. She erased the tape and snapped out the light.

They were up and out at seven the next morning. "Charley," she said before they got out of bed, "there is a lot of red tape if people aren't Mexican nationals who want to get married. It could take like three weeks to set up."

"Yeah?" Charley said.

"I had to check it out once, two years ago, for a friend of mine."

"Yeah?"

"Tijuana's the place. Then we get a plane out for Acapulco."

"Let's go."

While they were dressing, Irene told him they had six days, that she had a business meeting in Dallas on the ninth.

"What kind of business?"

"Work."

"How much do they pay you for one of those?"

"One hundred dollars for this one. It depends. Mob people—but still tricky hits—run about seventy-five dollars."

"How many do you get a year?"

"Three or four."

"Yeah? That many?"

"That's not many when you consider the population of this country."

They finished packing and Irene called for a taxi.

"Okay," Charley said, "how long you going to be in Dallas?"

"I don't know. Maybe three days. They do the groundwork."

"No more living on two coasts, okay, Irene?"

"We'll be married. Everything changes. You're my husband. I've got to build on that. We have to live together."

He rushed across the room and held her face in his hands tenderly. He kissed her face softly, on the eyes, on the soft cheeks, on the softer mouth. "I can't believe it," he said.

They were married in Tijuana, using two professional witnesses and a justice of the peace (Joseph Tierney Masters, JP, "Your Blue Heaven"). "Jesus," Charley said, "it should be by a priest. There is something wrong here."

"It could be even more legal this way," Irene said. "Anyway, when we get to Brooklyn you can get something up with your own priest. A little bit of this kind of excitement goes a long way. It is terrific to feel so legitimate. I agree we ought to get married a couple of more times."

They flew to Acapulco. After they were settled in at the hotel, Charley called his father at his home number in New York.

"Pop? Charley."

"Hey, I ain't seen you around."

"I'm in Mexico."

"Yeah? How's the weather?"

"It's hot or it rains."

"Whatta you doing in Mexico?"

"I got married, Pop."

"The contractor?"

"Yeah."

"Keep it to yourself, Charley."

"I just wanted to tell you."

"Give Dwye Williams a call."

"Anything special?"

"No. He'll see that they comp you at the hotel and the restaurants."

"Ah! What's his number? And maybe he's got some fresh airline ticket stock. We could use it."

"When you coming back?"

"The ninth."

"The contractor coming with you?"

"Later. She has to get everything together."

"If we need you, I'll call Dwye. And, hey, Charley."

"Yeah, Pop?"

"Congratulations."

"Thanks, Pop."

"We'll hope for the best."

Charley went down to join Irene at the swimming pool. The gold lamé bikini she had on made her so stacked that he got a hard-on.

"Hey, Charley," she said, grinning widely. "Who you got in there with you?"

"Pay no attention to it," Charley said. "maybe it'll go away. You know Dwye Williams?"

"No. Should I?"

"He runs the thing for us in Mexico."

"Oh, *that* Dwye Williams. Jesus, he used to be a big man."

"My father wants me to call him."

"You going to see him?"

"Probably."

"Do it right away, then we'll have all the rest of the time for us."

"Sure. You want to come?"

"No. It would make me too sad."

Dwye Williams had been the mayor of Philadelphia once. He was so well set politically that even after he had given the keys of the city to the mob, even after he had the citizens of the city whimpering on their knees and groping in the darkness because he had stolen them so blind, in order to get him out of the way (for his own safety and the safety of his party from certain public investigation), he had been appointed ambassador to Mexico, where he served out his full term, perpetually drunk in a wise-owl sort of way.

When a new administration swept him out, Dwye Williams went into private law practice in Mexico City; well, not a law practice exactly, he was more a consultant. He didn't go home because that had been one of the conditions of getting him out; he could never go home.

The business of exporting cocaine, shit, and boo from Mexico to the States was developing big, and the Mexican *coyotes* were trying to tear away pieces of it so Dwye, with his official connections, made various high officers of the Mexican government full partners, and the river of dope became an ocean of dope as it oozed and moved across the thousand-mile-long frontier, into the nostrils and veins of Americans.

Charley called Dwye from the lobby of the hotel. Dwye insisted on sending a car for him, asked for the name of his hotel, saying he would handle it, saying the car would be there in ten minutes.

Charley waited in the air-conditioning in a chair

near the front door. He felt queasy about Mexico because it made him think of the Plumber and Little Philly Zanzara jerking Maerose around and beating up that guy while they made her watch because her father told them to do it that way. The Plumber was very embarrassed and had apologized to Mae at least once a year every year after that. Charley wasn't exactly sorry that he and Maerose had somehow lost each other, but sometimes, especially since the only night they had ever been together, even including the endless time they had been engaged and he had walked around on his toes with frozen balls, he felt a sweet longing to be with her, just to have her around, not to fuck her or anything, just to have her around because she was his friend. They were in different parts of his mind and his life, Irene and Maerose. There was no place they could ever join: oil and water. He was the happiest man in the world because he had Irene, but he owed Maerose for straightening him out, because he wouldn't have Irene if Maerose hadn't made him sane again. Jesus! He was never going to see her again and it made him sad.

The doorman came over to tell him that the car was there.

The car took them to the airport. "What the hell is this?" Charley said.

"Mr. Williams is waiting for you at his office in Mexico City," the impeccably blank-faced, Swedish-looking driver said.

"He's out of his fucking mind!" Charley said. "I thought he was around the corner. That's five hundred miles away. Back to the hotel. Don't fuck me around."

"Yes, sir."

They drove for two miles in silence.

"I am—and the car is—at your service. Mr. Williams wanted me to be sure to tell you that after you refused to fly to Mexico City."

"That's very nice," Charley answered. "Leave me the car. We don't need you."

"Mr. Williams wants to be sure that you are comped wherever you want to go, sir."

"That's different. Okay. Be out front about half-past-seven tonight."

They agreed that it was the greatest honeymoon anyone had ever had. "That sounds dopey," Irene said, "but I would bet my next fee at thirteen to five that the combined people of New York, Brooklyn, Detroit, Chicago, and LA, one on one, never got laid fifty-one times in five days and watched three people pulled out to sea by the undertow to drown right under their window."

"The pasta wasn't bad, either," Charley said weakly.

They were packing to leave a day early because Pop had called to tell Charley he had to come back to New York. "Something come up, Charley," he said. "The grand jury is going to indict you and Don Corrado wants to get that out of the way before he calls this meet."

"What meet?"

"A top family, both sides, meet."

"*Both* sides?"

"Yeah."

"About the Vegas scam?"

"I don't think so. I mean—what would both sides know about the Vegas scam—right?"

"Yeah."

They had a short goodbye at the airport. Irene cried. Charley blew his nose. He was flying through to Kennedy. Irene was headed for Dallas.

Chapter Seventeen

Irene checked in at the Plaza of the Americas and watched a movie on TV. She went to bed at eleven after having dinner in the room. She slept as late as she could the next morning, until 8:30, then she stretched the time by bathing, washing her hair, sewing on a small tear in her nightgown from when Charley had rolled over on her, and having a slow breakfast, sending things back and complaining that the waiter had forgotten the hot milk. At a quarter to one she got into a taxi for the twelve-minute ride to the Hilton Inn at Mockingbird and Central. She counted six tables along the window at the left and sat down opposite a fat man who was wearing a green suit, a bright pink shirt, and a green tie. He said, in that almost cultivated kind of high voice, "Hello, there. We haven't talked since you were in Columbia, South Carolina."

"Yes?" Irene said. "What number?"

He told her the number of the phone at the left end of her desk.

They ordered omelets for lunch, hers cheese, his strawberry. "What's the layout?" Irene said, and after that the whole thing played itself out in two days.

The contract was on some local lawyer who was tight with the mob until he held out on them. An independent oil operator, the fat man's client, had sued the lawyer for breach of contract, negligence, fraud, and misrepresentation. The oilie had hired the lawyer to bring an antitrust action against two oil companies for conspiring to fix oil prices. A federal jury returned a 27.2-million-dollar verdict, and the attorney was awarded 2.7 million in fees, but the appeal yielded a settlement for ten million dollars under which the oil companies agreed to pay 1.5 million immediately, and the rest over a five-year period. The lawyer didn't bother to tell his client about the settlement and refused to give an accounting of the money. Also, he didn't mention it to the boys. The oil man had sued and the lawyer was tying everything up with court postponements until it looked like three years before the oil man could get at the money. So he wanted the lawyer dead. The boys okayed it.

The lawyer lived at one of the big downtown hotels, so the fat man wanted Irene to go into his rooms dressed as a chambermaid and substitute for his high blood pressure pills identical cyanide pills the same size and shape, mixing them in with the prescribed ones.

Irene said that Texas juries understood using guns to clip people, because that was the American way, making it easier for the judge to let somebody like that off, but were very strict about poisoning and almost always returned against. She asked the fat man if the client had anything against shooting the lawyer. There were no objections so Irene called the lawyer, told him a story involving a hundred-million-dollar estate that she had inherited by will and out of which "some model" was trying to cheat her, and the lawyer invited her to his office at 9:15 the next morning.

She wore widow's weeds with a heavy black veil when a secretary took her in and closed the door. It was a big room with lots of heavy curtains and leather to kill the sound. Irene shot him, holding the gun un-

der the desk, pointed through the deskwell. It hardly
made any sound. Then she walked around the desk
close up and let him have it twice through the head.
She left the body there and went out to the secretary's
office. "He asked me to tell you to give him at least
fifteen minutes while he goes over the papers on my
case." The secretary gave her a sappy nod and a smile
and Irene asked if she would show her out to the elevator. It was an hour and five minutes before the secretary went in to check something with her boss, after
holding eight phone calls, and by that time Irene was
on her way to LA to pack up for the move to New
York, to close the house, and to leave the full fee in
her safe deposit box at the Beverly Hills bank.

Chapter Eighteen

On the afternoon of the day he talked to his son in Acapulco, Angelo Partanna made his regular Thursday call at Amalia Sestero's house in Brooklyn Heights to have a glass of elderberry wine and to pick up whatever casual instructions Don Corrado had accumulated during the week. Amalia knew how to make sensational Sicilian sweets, so it was the visit he enjoyed most in all the week.

He was sitting in the kitchen of the large house, wiping his smooth brown bald head, sipping wine, and nibbling on *cubaita*, the instructions from Don Corrado in his pocket, when Amalia asked him how Charley was.

"Between you and me, and don't let it go any further at least for the time being," Angelo said, "Charley just got married. He's in Mexico."

"*Married*? Charley? My God."

"He's forty-two years old."

"Who did he marry, for God's sake?"

"A California girl."

"He can certainly keep a secret. What's her name?"

"Irene Walker."

"That's no Sicilian name."

"She's American. She's a tax consultant. Very nice. Very smart."

"That is some terrific news."

"Well, let's see how it goes. A mixed marriage."

"And she's not in the environment."

"Yeah. That's what I meant."

Ten minutes after Angelo left, Amalia couldn't hold in news like that any longer. If there was one person in the world who was entitled to know, it was Maerose Prizzi. She called Maerose at her office. "Mae, I got some news."

"Yeah?"

"Charley Partanna just got married."

Maerose didn't answer. She put the phone down on the desk and walked away from it to look out the window. After a while she could hear it squawking so she went back, sat down, and picked it up. "Is she a woman named Irene Walker?"

"How did you know that?"

"I heard he was seeing her."

"Well," Amalia said, "I don't know how you look at it, but the way I look at it, it's the end of an era. You know what I mean, Mae?"

"What?"

"I think if you write a letter to Poppa now and you tell him the news and you say you think the time has come to let you come home, that he will tell Vincent that he's got to do it."

"Thanks, Amalia."

"I'll be right there with him when the letter comes. I'll encourage him."

"Jesus, I'd like to come back just to have it on my father."

"That isn't the only reason and you know it."

Maerose answered grimly that she was now in a kind of war.

"Write the letter now, Mae," Amalia said.

Maerose got on the telephone and canceled the two remaining appointments of the afternoon. It was raining heavily so she called the switchboard. "Check me out on all calls for the rest of the day, Edwina," she told the receptionist, "I've got a lot of planning to do in here." She locked the door of her office and sat down with a large yellow pad. Her grandfather was suspicious of typewriters.

Dear Grandfather (she wrote in Sicilian):
   I am twenty-nine years old and I have had to live away from my family since I was nineteen. Charley Partanna, whom I wronged, is now going to get married to a woman from California. He is happy. He has forgotten all about me.
   I am asking you to talk to my father and to tell him that I have suffered enough because of what I did almost ten years ago. I am asking you to ask my father to forgive me. Your loving grand-daughter,

                                        Maerose

   Angelo Partanna moved very carefully. He had confided the news to Amalia Sestero because she would tell Corrado Prizzi. Corrado would think about it for a while then he would call Vincent. Angelo had to be sure Vincent knew about it before Corrado told him, so that Vincent would be ready when his father gave him the news.
   He walked down the hall and put his head in at the doorway to Vincent's office. "How about an early dinner tonight?"
   "Sure. Where you want to go?"
   Vincent always said that but they always wound up at Tucci's.
   "How about Tucci?" he suggested.
   "Great. You want to pick me up at six o'clock?"

   They talked baseball in the car on the way to Tucci's. Angelo didn't know a baseball from a *cocómero* but he had learned the patter after years of talking to Vincent, so he could fake the responses. As soon as they got to Tucci's things got serious. They studied the menu, which they stared at five nights a week.

Tucci's had a bar in front, six tables, and a jukebox. Tucci's wife and daughter-in-law took turns working in the kitchen. Vincent's driver, who was also his bodyguard, had his dinner up front at the bar.

Tucci was a Neapolitan.

"I think I'm going to have that fisherman's soup *di Pozzuoli*," Vincent said adventurously. It was on the card twice a week, and whenever it was on the card, he ordered it.

"Good. Me, too."

"Hey, look! He's got *peperoni imbottiti*! Whatta you say?"

"Lovely, lovely."

They had a bottle of the Tears of Christ, grown in the lava at the foot of Vesuvius. It was Vincent's happy moment of the day, but it never lasted very long, so Angelo went to work for his son.

"Vincent? Whatta you know? Charley got married."

Vincent wasn't able to take that in. He stopped his wine glass in midair and put it down on the table. "Charley got *married*?" His small eyes went opaque. He stopped looking at Angelo. His mouth contorted into a tight ugly scar, until he realized what he could be showing to Angelo. He brought his napkin up to his face; then he forced himself to drink the wine.

Angelo nodded gently. He knew what was happening inside his friend's always predictable mind. For almost ten years, Vincent had pretended to feel shame and sorrow over what his daughter had done to Charley, but as the years went on, more and more he had blamed Charley for Maerose's unhappiness and his own misery over the way things had turned out.

How could his daughter be expected to marry and come home to her family when the man she had shamed kept the shame alive by staying single? Even if she never got married again, and he knew in his heart she must never marry after what she had done, Charley's public mourning over what had been done to him still stood in the way of Maerose's ever being allowed to come home. For almost ten years he had had to go out to a lot of goddamn restaurants like Tucci's and get heartburn because Charley had made his daughter keep living in New York when she should have been keeping house for him and cooking his meals for him.

Charley had to be the cause of the girl's running away to Mexico in the first place. He had probably wanted her to do shameful acts, and she couldn't stand that—she had run away. If she had been engaged to anyone except Charley, almost ten years ago, she would be married by now and he could be living with them, eating the only kind of food that could sit on his stomach, not this Neapolitan garbage of Tucci's. Charley Partanna had forced his daughter to shame her father in front of the family. Charley Partanna had caused him more pain than anyone else in his life. Charley Partanna didn't deserve to have a wife—a housekeeper, a cook, a companion—after what he had caused Maerose to do to himself, to herself, and to her father. He controlled his anger as well as he could because Angelo Partanna was his father's oldest friend.

"Who did he marry?" His voice shook. His eyes would not look at Angelo. Vincent knew Charley couldn't be marrying inside the family because he would have known about it long ago. What did he do—marry into one of the other four families? That could be good and that could be bad.

"He married a California woman," Angelo said.

"She's not in the environment, I understand. She's a tax consultant."

"Not in the environment? Jesus, Angelo, what are the women going to talk to her about? Jesus, we'll all have to shut up every time she comes into a room."

"Well, they're married," Angelo said. "They're in Mexico on their honeymoon right now."

It was a calculated risk. Angelo was the only one who knew who had made the Netturbino hit, because that was the way the system was designed. That was what insulation was. No witnesses. No corroboration. Because of the traditional system of insulation Vincent had no need to know who had made the Netturbino hit. If Vincent had wanted to know, he would have asked him, but he never asked him. That was one trouble area. Then there was the other trouble area; that Charley's wife had, just over three days ago, been the wife of Marxie Heller, who had ripped off the family for $722. Both trouble areas were dynamite. He didn't see how Charley was going to survive it if Vincent found out about either one. The first was a violation of the Prizzi, Sestero, and Garrone women, bringing in a contract hitter as one of the family's wives. Nobody would hold still for that. The second was even more serious than honor; it involved almost three-quarters of a million dollars stolen from the family, of which only $360 had been returned. In fact, Angelo thought, all things considered, it would be impossible for Charley to be in a worse situation than he had gotten himself into. Maybe, and even so it was too big a maybe, if Charley had happened to meet and marry this woman like three years after the scam, then nobody could say he was connected with it. But he had zipped the woman's husband, then he had married the woman four days later, and since it was a matter of record that the woman was a worker, a worker who had the $360 that she gave back to Charley, it figured that she had clipped Louis Palo, and Vincent, feeling about Charley the way Vincent felt about Charley, if he ever was able to put the two things together, could make a deadly case against Charley about the whole $722, and the wife.

Angelo had thought it all through. He was a professional thinker about things criminal. He was the only one who knew Charley's wife had done the Netturbino work. He was the only one who could make the connection that Charley's wife was Marxie Heller's widow. He was Charley's father before he was the Prizzis' *consigliere*, so he had to take the chance of being the one to tell Vincent that Charley had gotten married because from now on, if anyone brought it up, Vincent would say he knew all about it and didn't want to talk about it.

The next afternoon at five o'clock, Maerose Prizzi rang the doorbell of the Sestero residence on Brooklyn Heights. She had had her hairdresser come to her apartment at one o'clock and the beautician came at three. She knew how her grandfather liked to see her so she had them transform her into a young virgin, shining with beauty and goodness. Ugo Bustarella was on the door and he was delighted to see her.

"Jesus, it's got to be four years, right? Jesus, you look marvelous," he said.

"Ugo! You got so *fat*! Florrie must be feeding you six times a day."

He grinned. "Florrie three times, Mrs. Sestero three times. Come on. I'll take you down to Mrs. Sestero. She's inna kitchen."

He stood the riot gun in the corner behind the front door and led the way happily to the stairwell. "Hey, I can find the kitchen," Maerose said. "I only been here like two hundred times. Tell Florrie hello for me." She went down the stairs to the kitchen.

Amalia was waiting for her. She sent the girl on an

errand upstairs, then she said to Maerose, "He got your letter and it made him very happy. He has told Vincent to come over here tonight. He's going to make Vincent bring you home."

Maerose stood very tall and straight. She took in a deep breath and held it. She exhaled slowly then she said, "I am going to make my father pay. I am going to give him the next ten years the way he gave me the last ten years."

"There is no joy in revenge," Amalia said. "Revenge is something Sicilians talk about, but when they get it, it turns to nothing in their mouth."

"I am Corrado Prizzi's granddaughter. When my father told me I was no longer his daughter, he stopped being my father to me, too. When he threw me out and kept me out for ten years, calling me a streetwalker, telling me he would see that I stayed an old maid for the rest of my life, looking at me like I was a piece of shit on the few times every year that my grandfather made him let me come back, he was spitting on my honor. It isn't revenge. I do it for honor."

Corrado Prizzi wept as he welcomed his granddaughter back into the family. He was such an old, old man, she thought, so frail and helpless, then she remembered who he really was. "It will be settled tonight," he said. "Your father will come to see me tonight."

"I wrote to you, not only to be restored to the family, grandfather," she said. "I want to be allowed to take my place in my father's house. He is a lonely man. I want to cook for him and to keep his house for him. I want to be allowed to make up to my father for all the pain I have caused him."

When she left her grandfather, Maerose Prizzi hurried to Santa Grazia di Traghetto. She lighted three candles, one for her father, one for Charley, one for herself, and put a twenty-dollar bill into the reposi-

"Why not?"

"She's a decorator in New York. She decorated this whole place." His face lighted up. "Say—she could get stuff for you, for this place, wholesale."

Irene froze for a second. "I never buy wholesale or boosted stuff," she said. "What do you care, Charley? Anyway, I have nine whole rooms of stuff in California. Beautiful stuff. The best. You're going to be crazy about it. You're going to love it when I'm done."

"So? What's for dinner?"

"I am trying something new. It's a very special meat and wine stew, very French, you know, farmhouse French."

"No pasta?"

"With this dish, which is called *la daube de boeuf Provençale*, you get little *farfallini*, which is absolutely okay for this recipe."

"Believe me—it is okay for any recipe."

The telephone rang. It was Pop.

"Heh, Charley!" he said. "So Ed Prizzi took care of everything. That's nice. Listen, ten o'clock tonight at Ben Sestero's. They can't wait anymore with this."

"Sure, Pop. When are you going to come over and meet the bride?"

"I met the bride, remember? Anyway, she's not sentimental. Depending on how things work out at the sit-down tonight, figure me dinner on Sunday."

"Great." They hung up at the same time.

"They have set a big meet tonight at ten," he told Irene. "The same one Pop talked about when he called me in Mexico."

"Big sit-downs bring big money," Irene said, stirring a pot slowly.

"If everything is even, Pop is coming over here for dinner on Sunday.'

Irene put a lid on the pot. "Okay. Sensational. Then tonight we are going out for dinner and this stew is going to sit for two days until it is the most tremendous stew ever smuggled out of France when I give it to your father on Sunday."

"You sit down and have a glass of wine," Charley said. "Let me cook the dinner, which, you are going to have to admit, is going to be better than eating out."

"How? What are you going to make?"

"I am going to make you something terrific."

"What?"

"I am going to make you *pasta con le Sarde* from Palermo, which it is some great pasta shells, like *maruzzi*, about a pound, baked with sardines, secret amounts of chopped anchovy, fennel, raisins and pine nuts, in oil, and seasoned with saffron. Then, after I get you drunk on that, I am going to make love to you all night."

"Well, at least until half past nine when you leave for the meeting."

"Ah, the hell with the food," he said, grabbing her, "we can eat anytime but I couldn't eat anyways tonight, looking at you."

He arrived for the meeting on Brooklyn Heights five minutes early. The guard, a new Agrigento boy named Sam Falcone, opened the door. Amalia Sestero greeted him, kissing him on both cheeks. "They are all in there," she said. "I'll bring Poppa down now." She took Charley to the sliding doors, opened them, and he went into the room. She closed them behind him.

Don Corrado's chair was empty at the head of the table. Vincent was seated to the right of it, Ed Prizzi to the left of it, the protocol being set by the order of their birth, not by how much money they brought in, which bugged Ed. Angelo sat at Vincent's right and there was an empty chair for Charley at his right facing Ben Sestero and Harry Garrone, seated at Ed's left. A stranger sat at the foot of the table. He was a somber man with a nose like a rope, a large stomach and two gold watch chains draped across his gray flannel vest. As Charley went around the table at that end nobody introduced him so Charley ignored him.

Almost as soon as Charley's seat touched the chair, the sliding door opened and Amalia brought Don Corrado into the room and settled him in his chair, which faced all the others. Everyone stood. The don motioned Amalia out of the room with his left hand and, as she left, he said, in Sicilian, that he was happy to see that Charley was cleared of the charges that had been brought. Charley thanked him.

"The gentleman at the far end of the table is Alvin Gomsky," Don Corrado said, in English, with his indistinct sandpiper voice, "and he is treasurer of our bank. I have asked Mr. Gomsky here so that you could hear from his own mouth what is happening."

He looked sweetly at Gomsky for his statement. Mr. Gomsky had only been able to understand every other word because of Don Corrado's rich accent but Ed had told him what he was there for.

"The president of the bank is stealing from the bank," Mr. Gomsky said, "and, if he is allowed to keep up his scheme of bad foreign exchange deals, it will all be over for the bank within nine months or maybe fourteen months."

"Thank you, Mr. Gomsky."

"We will look at the books tomorrow morning," Ed said.

"We will talk about that," Don Corrado said. "Thank you, Mr. Gomsky. See Mr. Gomsky to the door, Arrigo," he said to his youngest son-in-law.

"Eduardo will tell you about it," Don Corrado said in Sicilian when Gomsky had left the room. Eduardo began to speak with full salesman's voice, collecting the minds of the others, which had been scattered by the outrageous enormity of the news. Don Corrado closed his eyes, perhaps the better to concentrate.

"The bank was always like a cousin to me," Ed Prizzi began, speaking in the Agrigento dialect. "The bank made everything happen, and not only with the money it generated. The man who bought seventy-five percent of the bank from us is a Neapolitan named Rosario Filargi. He calls himself Robert Finlay and anyone named Filargi who would call himself Finlay would also have to be stupid enough to think that we wouldn't protect the remaining twenty-five percent of the bank which we own. The treasurer of the bank, Mr. Gomsky, whom you met tonight, has told us— you heard him—that Filargi is bleeding the bank to death with crooked foreign money deals and that, if we don't protect the bank, that it will be dead in a year."

"How about a fink like that?" Angelo said. "We should cut his balls off, the fucking fink."

"You got enough for us to do that, Eddie?" Vincent asked his brother.

"Poppa worked out a plan," Eduardo said. "You got to hear the whole story."

"Okay,"Vincent said.

"So where did Filargi's money come from, to buy the eighteenth-biggest bank in the United States? Well—there is a bunch of robbers in Italy at the very top of the government, just like here, from big business, big money. We are like little stickup men robbing gas stations in the Depression, compared to these people. We are what one slot machine is, compared to everything in Vegas compared to these people."

He filled the jelly glass in front of him halfway with anisette, then passed the bottle across to Vincent. Vincent wet the bottom of his glass because of his gout and passed the bottle to Angelo. Ed Prizzi didn't speak again until the bottle returned to his end of the table.

"These men had to have a way to get their money out of Italy, into Switzerland, so they wouldn't have to pay taxes, so Filargi opened two banks across the border from Como, in Chiasso, and Filargi's people would pick up the bales of cash from these people and take them to Filargi's Swiss banks. He did so well for them that he was able to convince them that they shouldn't keep all their eggs in one Swiss basket, and he got the money from them to buy seventy-five percent of our bank. But Filargi's name should be changed again, to *spingularu*, because he can never steal enough. Now he is stealing from their seventy-five percent and from our twenty-five percent, but he dishonors us more than he dishonors them, because we feel it more."

"The loss of the money or the honor?" Arrigo Garrone asked.

Charley looked at him with such brutal questioning that Garrone became pale.

"Harry was trying to emphasize that we feel the loss of both more than anything else," Ed Prizzi said smoothly. Angelo patted Charley's leg under the table.

"Still, it is my father's honor and my father's money which has been put in peril here, so I will tell you my father's plan for dealing with Filargi. Some men suffer when you take life away from them, because life is sweetest to them. To Filargi, my father has decided, money is sweetest, so that is what we are going to take away. We will leave him his life without money, and without any way to get money."

Don Corrado opened his tiny eyes. He looked into the face of every man at the table, nodding. "That is how Filargi must pay," he said. "I was able to figure it out because Charley gave me the key which showed me the way to justice for Rosario Filargi."

"*I* gave the key?" Charley said blankly.

"You brought me the key that kidnap insurance

premiums are deductible from the income tax. Eduardo will explain."

Don Corrado closed his eyes. Everyone looked at Ed Prizzi.

Chapter Twenty

"Very recently," Eduardo said, "Mr. Gomsky has persuaded his fellow directors of the bank to take out two million, five hundred thousand dollars worth of kidnap insurance to cover all bank officers. The amount of the coverage represents twelve percent of what our twenty-five percent interest in the bank is worth. Naturally, we will have to share up to twenty-five percent of the costs of the high premium rate for the policy, but, as Charley has established for us, that cost will be tax-deductible, and the ransom mo___ the bank will have to pay will also be deductible, in the event that one of the officers of the kidnaped—if Filargi were to be taken, for e the kidnapers themselves would get two m hundred thousand net as ransom and the company would have to pay."

"Thank you, Eduardo," Don Corrado s you, Beniamino. Thank you, Arrigo. now. Please—on the way out—please t come for me."

The three men left the room.

"I think I am getting an ulcer," "What kind of a thing is that at my

"Don't drink milk," Angelo said. acids flow. It makes the ulcers wors

"Who drinks milk?" Vincent said as Amalia came into the room for Don Corrado, leading him out of the room. She closed the sliding doors quietly.

"My father has a terrific plan here," Vincent said to the Partannas. "We are going to put a two million five price tag on him after we take him, then we are going to leave a trail for the Feds so that they can prove that Filargi organized the whole thing to have himself kidnaped so he could cheat the insurance company out of that kind of money. Jesus, talk about felonies! They will give him ten consecutive life sentences for stealing that much money from such a company with the clout that an insurance company has."

"Tremendous!" Angelo said, kissing his fingertips and throwing the kiss into the air. "Now you are learning how a real 'narugnutu should be handled, Charley."

"That ain't all my father has figured out for Filargi," Vincent said. "When Filargi is picked up for engineering his own kidnapping, our people in Italy and Switzerland are going to put the pressure on the *papaveri* who were his partners in buying the seventy-five percent of the bank from us, by telling them how much Filargi was stealing from them on the crooked foreign exchange deals, and they are going to squeeze their government to bring Filargi to trial in Rome, so that if he ever gets out of the joint in this country, he going to face at least twenty-five years' time in some king Italian prison. In the meantime, as soon as y pick him up here, our people will organize the k's stockholders to take him for every dime he has he world and what they can't get at, the Italian *ocannonati* will take away from him. Believe me, the next fifty years he's in the joint here or in he's going to have plenty of time to figure out nderstand that he had to be out of his mind he decided to piss on the honor of the Prizzis."

s a beautiful piece of work, is absolutely all any-an say," Charley said humbly.

"Well," Angelo said, "when you figure that we are going to be able to buy at least fifty percent of the bank back from the Italians after it hits the fan, it certainly is a beautiful piece of work."

"There is going to be points in this for you, Charley," Vincent said, somberly, because he was talking about giving out the family's money.

Charley began to protest politely but Vincent held up his hand. "My father wants it that way. Fair is fair. You come up with the gimmick that is going to cook this guy. You are going to get five percent of this job. Five points on two million five is a nice score."

"Hey, Charley!" Angelo said. "A hundred twenty-five dollars! How about that?"

"What can I say?" Charley said, "it is very generous."

"Well, you are a married man now," Vincent said blankly. "You can use the money."

There was a thoughtful silence. Angelo coughed lightly. Charley thought, shit! Here comes the knife about Maerose again.

"Well, anyways," Vincent said, "you gettin' married finally lets Maerose off the hook."

"God bless her," Angelo said. "Now back to the Filargi job."

"It's a job I should be doing myself," Vincent said, "as my father's son I should be the one who sets Filargi up, but I got this fucking gout and now, I think, this fucking ulcer, and my father don't think the Little Sisters' prayers to St. Gerardo will work in time."

"When you get gout like that, you really got gout," Angelo said.

"How do you want me to handle it?" Charley asked deferentially.

"You're in charge. You pick your own people. We don't want to know. You run the show. We got the working side of the operation all worked out. You take Filargi on a Monday afternoon at his hotel, because Tuesday is a good news day and for the rest of the week. He goes home for lunch, fahcrissake, the head of the eighteenth-biggest bank in the country and he goes back to his hotel and fries himself an egg in the middle of the summertime."

"When?"

"Soon. We'll give you plenty of notice. My father has to work out how the payoff is going to be picked up."

"We got a layout of Filargi's floor at the hotel, Charley," Angelo said. "You take that home and study it. Everything is marked with circled numbers for the moves you got to make and it's got the positions marked with arrows beside it. Once you got it absolutely clear in your head, I'll come over to your place and we'll go over it."

Chapter Twenty-one

Charley and Irene had spread the floor plan out across the kitchen table and the back of one chair and he was going over it with her carefully. "If you spot anything soft, speak up. All right. This is the forty-first floor of Filargi's hotel. There are only three apartments to a floor up that high. Okay, that is Filargi's apartment facing the elevator." He touched the plan where the circled number one appeared. "Every day, when Filargi is ready to go back to the office, his bodyguard goes out that door first and rings for the elevator. When the elevator comes he puts it on Hold, then he goes back and raps on Filargi's door."

"Filargi always waits for the rap?" Irene asked.

"Yeah. That's their SOP. On Monday, when the bodyguard goes to the elevator button, my second man will come out of the apartment on the south side, across the hall from Filargi's place but beside the elevators, so when the bodyguard puts the car on Hold, my man will pin him down inside the elevator. As soon as the bodyguard is handled, I come out of the north-side apartment, straight across the hall beside the elevators, and I rap on Filargi's door. He comes out. I take him to the elevator where my second man is with the bodyguard, push the button for the garage basement, and push the No Stop button. Al Melvini

163

will be waiting at the bottom. We walk Filargi to the car Zanzara has waiting there and we take Filargi out to the Island."

"What happens to the bodyguard?"

"My second man takes him up to the roof on a No Stop trip and does the job on him."

"Pretty clumsy," Irene said.

"Pretty *clumsy*?"

"Charley, fahcrissake, if the bodyguard sees a man outside that door, he isn't even going to call the elevator. If the second man comes out while he's waiting for the elevator to come up, the bodyguard is going to drag out his piece and maybe whack him. It's a licensed piece. He's a licensed man, which the insurance company is going to say Filargi has to have with him wherever he goes. The insurance company tells him, don't take chances."

"You think we should drop the guy right there and bring Filargi out?"

"Well, I certainly don't think you should take him all the way to the basement, then bring him all the way up to the roof before you clip him. But the clumsiest part is with the second man. You've got to have a woman to do that stand."

They were in the middle of a heavy discussion when the doorbell rang and Pop arrived. He listened to Irene's argument and shrugged. "She's right, Charley," he said. "A woman should do that stand."

"Look," Irene said, "listen to me. A woman should take a fake baby out of the south apartment after the bodyguard pushes the button for the elevator, smile at him nicely, fuss with the fake baby, then, when he puts the elevator on Hold, let *him* rap on the door for Filargi and get him all the way out in the hall. When they are both out there, she throws the baby at the bodyguard who, naturally, tries to catch it, and while he is doing that she covers him with her piece. *Then* you come out of the north apartment, Charley, while the woman takes the bodyguard back into Filargi's apartment, and does the job on him in there. By that time you are going to have Filargi in the elevator car and you'll be on your way down to the basement."

"That's good," Pop said.

"Fahcrissake," Charley said, "where are we going to find a woman for a stand like that?"

"Where?" Irene said. "Me."

"You? Listen—wait a minute—I didn't get married so my wife could keep working."

"Charley, lissena me. Irene is right," Pop interrupted. "No matter how you look at it, we will be taking chances any other way. Even Don Corrado is going to agree with me when I tell him why a woman has to do the stand."

"You fellas work it out," Irene said, "I have a terrific meal in danger in here so, please, go out on the terrace and look at the view."

She shooed them out of the kitchen.

The two men went out to the terrace. Charley closed the glass door carefully, then he turned to his father with desperate impatience. "Pop, what the hell is the matter with you? You got to turn her off this thing! Fahcrissake, Pop!"

"Charley, she's right and you know it. That is a woman's stand there by the elevator. A woman has to do the stand, and throwing the fake baby—that is terrific."

"Pop, lissena me. Sooner or later the Prizzis are going to find out that Irene and me are married. If they *then* find out that I used my own *wife* on this job, man, that is really going to shake them up. It would get *out*, Pop. Every family in New York would fall down laughing that the Prizzis now use their *wives* on jobs. Pop, fahcrissake! You know how the Prizzis are about honor! They could have me clipped for this. At the very least they would clip my wife."

"Charley, siddown a minute. Lemme talk, all right?" Charley sat down and Pop pulled a chair close to him and sat down, looking into Charley's eyes. "In the first place, who is going to know? The bodyguard? Irene will clip the bodyguard. Filargi won't even know she's in the action, he'll be so scared. Now second— and it should be first—there is no more important job than this job. This job Don Corrado sees as his monument. You ever hear of a soldier or a *caporegime* getting five percent of a two million five price tag for a job? Any job? A hundred twenty-five dollars? You bet your ass you didn't. It's got to go right, the job. This is the *bank* Don Corrado is protecting here. The bank he put together when he first came to this country, the bank that brought me to this country, the bank that made the whole business possible, and he figures he doesn't have much time left and that it is right that he should complete a circle with his life and end by getting his bank back for ten cents on the dollar, and then let Eduardo build it all the way back up again. Charley, lissena me. This ain't no two million five ransom deal. What is that? Its nothing. It's just to ruin Filargi. The real money in this thing is that we see that Filargi's trial smears the bank enough so that them Italians don't want to have anything to do with it and they are glad to sell it back to our dummies for ten cents on the dollar. This is like a sixty-, seventy-million-dollar deal for the Prizzis, Charley. Nobody is ever going to know your wife was on this job— fahcrissake—she never leaves the forty-first floor until you have Filargi on the Queensboro Bridge already! But even if it was *possible* for the other families to know that your wife did a number for you on this job, what the hell, people forget, so maybe it wouldn't be so great for the Prizzi honor but what is a little honor compared to seventy million dollars—right?"

"Well, yeah, when you put it that way, Pop. But Irene's got to be paid for doing the stand."

"Of course. She's a *specialist*. When I clear it with Don Corrado that there is no other way except we use a woman here, he will not only agree—because it makes so much sense—but he is going to know that a specialist, a woman, a woman who comes up with the idea of throwing the fake baby at the guy, has to get the top dollar."

"How much, Pop?"

"One hundred dollars."

"I think more. I swear to God, Pop, that stand is worth one hundred fifty."

"I won't say yes, I won't say no, because it isn't up to me. Lemme get back to you tomorrow night."

Irene tapped on the glass door to the terrace and motioned them into the room, her lips moving. Pop opened the door. "My God, have I got a meal for you!" Irene said.

Chapter Twenty-two

Vincent sat with his father in the Sestero house on Brooklyn Heights. He listened with growing emotion as Don Corrado spoke. They were alone. It was hot in the room because the don liked to keep a fire going all year around.

"Your daughter has suffered. Ah, I know! You have suffered too, but compassion says we must make ourselves look to the end of suffering. Jesus teaches us that. The Holy Mother is the personification of that. A natural period has come to an end. After almost ten years of wandering in the wilderness outside her family, your daughter—my granddaughter—has asked for forgiveness because the man she had wronged has symbolically ended the ritual punishment of all of us by marrying another woman. Maerose is released. You are released. I am released. Honor is protected. So I have asked you to come here to beg you on my knees to forgive your daughter and permit her to come home. Look—here is her letter. Read the letter, Vincent. See how the child loves you, perhaps because of the punishment which you inflicted upon her because she had sinned against honor and knew she must be punished. She wants to take care of you. You need that, Vincent. You have lived too long in loneliness. Open your arms. Say to me that I may send her to your open arms. Let us love each other. Each of our days are numbered."

Tears were pouring down his withered cheeks when he finished. Vincent was sobbing. They enjoyed a long moment of purging, happy emotion, then Vincent said, "Send her to me, Poppa. We will make up those years to each other. She is my daughter again."

Maerose was in Presto Ciglione's office, upstairs over the bar, in the big bar, dance hall, and old-fashioned gambling hall out beyond the western end of the Strip in Vegas while her father and grandfather were exploring the mysteries of compassion in Brooklyn. She carefully laid out three headshots of Irene on the desk in front of Ciglione, a classical early-talkies type of hoodlum, who spoke flawless Sienese Italian.

Next to the three photographs Maerose counted out ten one-hundred-dollar bills.

"You know who I am—right?" she said.

"Yes, miss."

"You understand that this thousand dollars is for you—right?"

"Yes, miss."

"Did you ever see this woman?"

"She was here twice. Alone. She had one drink, maybe looked around, and left."

"When?"

"A couple of weeks ago, maybe three weeks."

"Around the time Louis Palo was hit?"

"Yes, miss."

"Presto, lissena me. I'll go downstairs for ten, fifteen minutes. You bring your people up here one by one. Ask your people if they ever saw this woman on the night Louis Palo caught it."

"Sure, miss."

Maerose left the office and went down to sit at a table at the far end of the bar, away from the staircase. She ordered a Shirley Temple.

"A what?"

"You heard me. You want me to have Mr. Ciglione explain it?"

"It's all right. I'll look it up."

"Not too sweet," Maerose said.

Twenty minutes later the bartender came to the table and said, "Mr. Ciglione wants to see you now, miss."

Maerose put a ten-dollar bill on the table. "That's for you," she said and walked to the stairs.

Mr. Ciglione was waiting for her with a pretty young woman in a waitress uniform.

"Tell the lady about the night that fellow was shot," he told her.

"Well, if you're sure it's okay."

He nodded gravely.

"I was using a Toyota Celica as a trick room out in the parking lot with a truckdriver john and, as I lifted my head up, I seen this woman in hot pants run into the headlights of a car which was the car the guy was in who they hit. My trick is all knocked out because he had a lot to drink and he had just come so he don't pay any attention. In like three minutes, the woman gets out of the front seat and gets in the back seat, then like three minutes later she gets out of the car and goes to the trunk and takes out a satchel, then she goes back to the car she came from. I *think* it was the car she came from, and she drives away. I forgot all about it until Mr. Ciglione asked me just now."

"Did you look at the pictures carefully?" Maerose said.

"That's her. That's the same broad."

"Thanks." Maerose nodded to Mr. Ciglione. He took a roll of bills out of his pocket, peeled off two fifties and gave them to the girl. "Buy yourself a cigar, honey," he said.

"All right," Don Corrado said. "That's settled. I'll

tell my granddaughter she can go home. Now we have to settle the bank business so that Charley can go ahead. Please tell Eduardo to come in now."

When Ed Prizzi had settled into a chair, Don Corrado passed out Mexican cigars and began to talk.

"We're going to make the bank pay the ransom for Filargi overseas, Eduardo, so you got to have your people set it up."

"Overseas?"

"Number one, it is outside the jurisdiction of the kidnaping—the local police can't do nothing and Interpol is just a telegraph office anyhow which tells the local police what is happening but, of course, out in front, Gomsky at the bank, who will be in charge of the payoff, will tell the cops that the bank is going to pay the money over to the kidnapers in the States— like in Central Park or something—so that while they wait around here, we can collect the money there."

"Where overseas, Poppa."

"I was thinking Panama, Lagos in Nigeria, like maybe Aruba, one in Hong Kong, and maybe one in São Paulo. You pick two banks in each place. Gomsky sets it up with one bank to pay out five hundred dollars to a courier who signs Filargi's name to the receipt in a code number, you know, Filargi, not Finlay, his new name. Then, when we blow it off, the police investigation will show that Filargi's couriers then take the five hundred to the second bank in the same town and have them transfer it to a numbered account in Lichtenstein which I want you to have opened by our bank in Zurich. Even if—and it's going to be impossible, believe me—they can establish criminal motives, except against Filargi, they are still not going to be able to trace that money to anybody except Filargi and after a couple of years the Lichtenstein bank will ask the Swiss bank to invest the money in U.S. securities and, when we are ready, we cash them in plus the appreciation."

"That is very good, Poppa," Eduardo said.

"That is *tremendous*," Vincent said. "That is a sensational wrinkle. The problem part of any snatch, irregardless, is always the payoff. They are always nailed when they reach for the ransom money. We could turn this into a very, very nice business in this country with a wrinkle like that."

"No, Vincent," Don Corrado said sadly. "Stick to the harmless rackets which bring people a lot of pleasure and which they want. Start snatching big shots and the media starts screaming, they get the people all agitated, the politicians see right away that they can't protect us because the people don't want them to protect us on a thing like that, and we've got ourselves a lot of heartaches. Besides, the payoff, the way it is set up for Filargi, could be one of those things that only works once."

"You're right, Poppa," Vincent said contritely.

Angelo Partanna sat with his old friend in the overheated study on Brooklyn Heights at six o'clock that evening, explaining in exhaustive detail why Charley had decided that a woman had to do the second man's stand on the forty-first floor of Filargi's hotel. When he came to the part where the woman tossed the fake baby at the bodyguard, Don Corrado nodded his appreciation of the fine point. "That is really professional," he said. "And much better than my way."

"Then it is okay?"

Don Corrado nodded.

"It *is* a woman," Angelo said. "And that *is* a specialist."

"Give her whatever she wants, my friend," Don Corrado said, "this is my monument."

Chapter Twenty-three

The Prizzis had rented the north side apartment on the forty-first floor of Filargi's hotel in devious ways eight days before the Monday on which Filargi was to be taken. Angelo Partanna sent matinee theater tickets and a luncheon invitation for two at one of the city's heaviest restaurants as the grand prize of a community contest that the woman tenant of the south apartment couldn't remember entering, but which she was delighted to have won. Irene checked into the south apartment at 1:25 P.M. of the day they were going to take Filargi. Charley took his place in the north apartment at 1:37. Filargi's bodyguard would come out of the east apartment, Filargi's, at between two and six minutes after two o'clock.

Irene moved as coolly as always. She inflated the rubber doll and wrapped it in the swaddling that she carried under her coat. When the whole package was weighted and put together in its Baby Bunting sack, all that was needed was sound effects to convince anyone that it was a baby. She grinned as she put the package together, thinking of the look on the bodyguard's face when she tossed the baby at him. She took her place in the south apartment. Charley waited behind his north door.

On schedule, at three minutes after two, the

bodyguard came out of the east apartment. He was a wiry-looking, medium-sized man with a blue-black underbeard and a loud red, purple, and white necktie. He pressed the elevator bell. Within ninety seconds the elevator door opened and the bodyguard stepped into it to push the Hold button. He left the open car and crossed the hallway to the door of Filargi's apartment and knocked. The door opened immediately. Filargi, a man of about sixty-three, short, plump, and nervous-looking, wearing a bow tie and a Panama hat, appeared immediately. As soon as the spring locker of the door closed behind him, Irene opened the door and, carrying the baby, stepped out into the hall. Both the bodyguard and Filargi half-turned to look at her. Irene was about three feet from the bodyguard, her purse open behind the baby so she could grab her piece, when she said, "Catch!" and tossed the baby at the bodyguard.

The bodyguard sidestepped the baby and let it fall to the floor. He went for his gun. Irene pulled her piece out of the purse. Charley came out of the north apartment, gun in hand. The second elevator door opened directly beside Irene and the bodyguard as they pulled the guns. A woman in her middle fifties started to come out of the elevator car just as Irene shot the bodyguard. The woman said distinctly, staring at Irene, "I must have the wrong floor." Irene shot her in the face.

The doors of the second elevator began to close. Irene leaped forward to stop them. Charley sprinted in behind Filargi and jammed the piece to his back and slammed him up against the mail chute between the two elevators while Irene went in, punched the Hold button, then dragged the woman's body, which had been knocked backward by the force of the bullet, out of the car by the feet, the dress riding up to the hips to show the tops of pantyhose and dead-white belly skin. When the body was out Irene released the

Hold button and pressed G to send the elevator back to the lobby.

"No bloodstains," she said to Charley.

"Jesus," he said, "I thought that elevator was going to take her down to the street."

Charley manhandled Filargi, grabbing him by the upper arm and pushing him toward the bodies. "Come on!" he said. "We gotta move this shit out of here." Filargi, pale with shock, watched Charley take the bodyguard under his arms and drag him across the threshold of the south apartment, telling Filargi to bring in the woman.

"I can't," Filargi said. "I don't have the strength."

"Take one arm," Irene said. "I'll take the other." Together they dragged the woman's body into the south apartment. Its shoulder caught in the side of the mail chute. Irene had to jerk the arm to drag the body free.

"I had to hit her, Charley," Irene said, "she was looking right at me."

"It's okay," Charley said. "You had to do it."

They left the south apartment, closing the spring lock on the door, the unlucky woman sprawling obscenely over the legs of Filargi's bodyguard, and pushed Filargi into the holding elevator. Charley pressed the Basement and Express buttons and the car fell from the forty-first floor.

"He let the baby hit the floor," Irene said. "Suppose it had been a real baby? It could be dead, the son-of-a-bitch."

"What are you *doing?*" Filargi said. "What are you going to do with me?"

"Lissena me," Charley said. "You are going with us. When we get down to the garage you are going to lay down on the floor in the back of the car. That's all you got to know."

"You are *kid*napping me?" Filargi said. "Are you crazy?"

"All right. Here we are," Charley said. The doors opened and Al Melvini was standing there, chewing gum. "What did you do," he asked, "take a coffee break?"

They walked Filargi rapidly along the short entrance to the garage, through revolving doors, and out into the open back door of a Buick sedan. "Get in front, Irene," Charley said. He and the Plumber pushed Filargi into the back seat, got in and shut the doors. Filargi lay on his back on the floor. The plumber saturated a handkerchief with chloroform and strong, sweet, sick-making fumes filled the car. He pressed the handkerchief over Filargi's face. Filargi struggled weakly, then Melvini covered him with a blanket. "Okay, Dom," he said and the car moved sedately to the exit of the garage. Dom Bagolone was driver and second helper. Like the Plumber he was a made man. They drove east across town to the Queensboro bridge. No one spoke until they were in Long Island City, then Charley said, "What did you lay in for dinner?"

"I thought the chicken cacciatore," Melvini said.

"This is Irene."

"Pleased to meet you," the Plumber said.

"Likewise," said the driver.

They settled Filargi in the cellar room of the house in Brentwood. Charley called his father at eleven o'clock that night.

"On schedule," he said.

"You better come in," Pop said.

"When?"

"Ten tomorrow. At the office." Pop hung up.

"They want me and Irene in New York," Charley told the Plumber. He included Irene because, according to the original plan before the dumb broad pushed the wrong button, she wasn't supposed to be there anyway.

"What'll we do for a car?" the Plumber asked.

"Whatta you need a car for? You going someplace?"

"You coming back?"

"I'll be back tonight."

"That's great. Then we'll have a car. I feel naked without a car."

"Charley, bring a case of canned tomatoes," Dom said. "When we stocked up the house we forgot the tomatoes."

Charley made a careful note. "Somebody must have lost their mind," he said. "Don't try to cook anything until I get back," Charley said. "We don't want Filargi to have any complaints." That got a laugh.

They left Brentwood at three A.M. for the drive into the city. Charley took Irene to their apartment at the beach. They took a shower together, then they made love. Afterwards, lying motionless, intertwined naked upon the sheet in the air-conditioned room, Irene said, "I can't get it through my head that that son-of-a-bitch sidestepped the baby. Suppose it was a real baby? It could have been crippled for the rest of its life."

"What the hell, Irene. You don't think he thought that was a *real* baby?"

"What the hell else could he think?"

"Anyway, he wasn't paid to bodyguard no baby," Charley said.

At ten o'clock Charley was in his father's office at the St. Gabione Hotel Laundry.

"We got a little trouble, Charley," Angelo Partanna said. "That woman you hit at Filargi's was a police captain's wife."

"Oh, boy!" Charley said. "That does it. How do you like a dumb broad who pushes the wrong floor?"

"They don't know we took Filargi yet. The woman

with the theater tickets came home and she finds the two people piled on top of each other. The baby out in the hall—you know, the doll—helps the media to confuse everybody as usual so it looks like tomorrow before anybody notices that Filargi is missing."

"That guy never caught the baby. Irene threw it and he just sidestepped it."

"Very professional," Angelo said.

"When do you lay the first ransom note on the bank?"

"Well! We figured three days after the papers know Filargi is gone. Now this throws the whole thing off, because tomorrow is Wednesday, when they figure it out that Filargi is gone, then we come into the weekend, and the bank is closed. So I suppose we'll mail the first letter on Friday and they'll get it next Monday."

"I think we should have one more guy at Brentwood. That would give them three eight-hour shifts out of every twelve."

"Fuck that," Angelo said. "They're just sitting on their ass. Let them work it out. They're getting a nice piece of money so how can I justify one more guy at that kind of money? Anyway, you're going to drive out there every other day. That'll give them a little time off."

"Well," Charley said, "we're going to catch a lot of heat from that dumb broad being a police captain's wife."

Chapter Twenty-four

Maerose telephoned to Amalia to ask, in humble spirit, for an audience with Don Corrado, so that she might thank him for the meaning he had returned to her life by convincing her father that she should be allowed to come home. Amalia, her good friend, called back within the hour to say that her grandfather would see her at five o'clock that afternoon.

Maerose arrived, dressed in black, and knelt before Don Corrado's chair to kiss his hand. He flushed at the old-fashioned flavor of the obeisance, clucked over her and bade her sit in a chair beside him and hold his hand.

The ladies near Corrado Prizzi understood that he liked to hold females' hands, not for amorous reasons, no longer at any rate, but because of the tactile sensuality of the hand's plumpness or softness or definition—and because he believed he could flow into their bodies and minds through their hands as he had once felt the power of the *Capo di tutti Capi* of all Sicily flow into him when he was a boy.

He held Maerose's hand and, with his tiny, icy, augur-eyes, bored into her consciousness. Beyond the wide window, Manhattan lay out at his feet like a field of stone asparagus, and beyond that stretched America in a sheet of endless pavement. "Amalia has told me," he said with his ruffled voice, "that you wish to thank me for bringing you home, but I am the head of our family—who else should have gone to your father and pleaded for the only place for you in the world where you belong? You are blood of my blood, flesh of my flesh, and as long as I am able, I will think of your well-being."

"Thank you, Grandfather," Maerose said, his match in the bravura aspects, "you have drawn me back from Purgatory. I am a part of you and the family again. Only that could fulfill me."

"I wish you had been a son. You have the sensitivity and you have the strength to endure. Would you like a cookie?"

"It is I who must offer a gift to you, Grandfather."

"I love gifts. I think I have always enjoyed gifts."

She opened her purse and took out an envelope. She opened the envelope and removed three photographs. She gave them to the don.

"Ah! Who is this handsome lady?"

"That is Charley Partanna's wife, Grandfather."

"His *wife*? When? Why wasn't I told of it? Weddings, births, and funerals are the most important things a family can share."

"It was sudden, Grandfather. In California."

"Well, well."

"Grandfather, this is my gift to you. Not only the pictures but what they mean. Do you remember that Louis Palo was killed?"

"Yes."

"He was shot in a car in the parking lot of Presto Ciglione's place outside of Las Vegas."

"I remember."

"I took the pictures to Ciglione, a respectful man. I lay them down under his eyes and I asked him to show them to the people who worked for him—who were there the night Louis caught it. There was a girl who had been out in one of the cars in the parking lot and she said she saw the woman in these pictures get out of a car and walk to the car where Louis was hit. Then after a few minutes there was like a pop and she got out of Louis' car and opened the trunk and took out a satchel then went to her own car and drove away."

"The woman who married Charley?"

"Yes, Grandfather."

"That is serious talk, Granddaughter."

"She stole seven hundred and twenty-two thousand dollars from you. She gave half of it back to save herself. She still has your three hundred and sixty thousand dollars."

"What do you want me to do?"

"She did the job on Louis, she stole the family's money. She dishonored us. So she must pay, isn't that right?"

"But what would that do to Charley?"

"Charley married her. He married her right after she gave back half the money. I'm not saying that he knew anything about what she had done, but he knew she was involved somewhere because her husband was Louis' helper on the whole scam. Charley has to put her in the ground. That is what his penance has to be. Doing the job on her."

"Now you are his priest. You examine the sin and you prescribe the penance." He gazed at her with admiration. "You are like me," he said, with the affection that can come from any mirror. "We forgive nothing."

She lowered her eyes.

"I must think about it," the don said. "I must ask some questions. It is my duty as the head of the family to prevent injustice."

Chapter Twenty-five

When Maerose moved back into her father's house after almost ten years of exile, she took great care to be sure she looked like a ruined spinster. She pulled her hair back into a tight bun at the back of her head. She wore no makeup, but powdered her face carefully, then worked in a few lines under her eyes with a black eyebrow pencil. She wore a black shawl and black dress and she pretended that she could not look him in the eye.

Vincent stared at her, remembering the vital, beautiful young woman he had forced out of his life. In the years she had been gone he had thought about her constantly, and he had seen her living in the same kind of tenement flat his family had lived in when he had been a boy, facing an airshaft and the sound of the rats dragging off the neighbor's baby, but he had never thought of that changing her physically. He began to weep as he looked at her. He held open his arms as tears poured down his face, and took her to himself, the top of his head just below her chin while her hardened eyes glinted with pleasure. She wondered how long she would have to stay in this dump before she could get the job done. She had kept the apartment at the Matsonia in New York; had negotiated a leave of absence from the interior decorating firm. She hoped that she would have ruined her father, destroyed Irene, and recaptured Charley in three months' time—maybe two, maybe four.

During the next week, she worked silently and ceaselessly as a penitent in her father's house and he wasn't able to tell her that she must stop this, because that was what he thought women were for, and because on his best day Vincent wasn't a communicator.

He saw his daughter rise with the sun, scrub floors, wash sheets, cook meals, make beds, and polish furniture (after she had applied the Charles Addams makeup grimly every morning), and since he believed that the beautiful girl who had once been the light of his life was a broken woman, and since it was impossible, under Sicilian rules, to blame himself for what had happened to his daughter, and since, at the instant he had forgiven his daughter, all possiblity of blame had been removed from her—Vincent therefore blamed Charley. Shit, Charley had behaved as if he had been forced into the betrothal with her. Now that Vincent had to look at the results of that betrothal, to look day after day on this woman who had been so vital and beautiful and who had been turned into a crone whom he would never be able to get off his hands, Vincent was able to hate Charley openly: secretly to the world, openly to himself, the Sicilian way.

More than only taking his beautiful daughter from him and giving him this indifferent slattern in return, there had been a defilement of Prizzi honor. He was Vincent Prizzi. There was nothing that a Prizzi could value and cherish and protect more than honor and Charley had walked up to it, unzipped his fly, and pissed all over Vincent's only irreplaceable possession. So long as Charley remained alive, that was how long Vincent would choke on his shame.

He began to scheme. Since the day Charley had come back from doing the job on Marxie Heller, Vin-

cent had been convinced that something was fishy.
Somebody had killed Louis Palo to get all the money.
Half to Marxie Heller. All right. Half to Louis. All
right. Whose half had Charley brought back and
where was the other half? Charley must have copped
the money. Every day Vincent convinced himself further that Charley must have copped the missing half of
the money. What kind of Boss was that? When Vincent went to Vegas, Charley would be Boss—a Boss
who started out by clipping his own family for $360!

Since Maerose had come home, Vincent had not
gone out at night. He sat with his daughter in the living room that had not been changed in the twenty-one
years since his wife had died and, because she hardly
said anything, he began to talk more and more against
Charley and, by her silence, his daughter encouraged
him in his hatred.

He began at the beginning and covered, again and
again, all of the ground that had become the swamp of
his honor.

Did Maerose think Charley had ever cared for her?
She did not answer nor did he expect an answer. Had
Charley ever tried to see her since she had come back
from Mexico almost ten years ago? She did not answer. He said he was sure that Charley had never tried
to see her because he had no use for her. He had accepted the honor of marrying into the Prizzi family but
he had no use for her. Maerose protested the first few
times her father told her this. Each night he brought
all of it up again she allowed him to see her agitation
more and more, a little bit at a time. On the fifth
night, after he had spent the day brooding over how
he could prove that Charley had ripped his family off
for $360, he charged into his daughter like the ex-
hausted bull that he was, bellowing out his shame that
because of one foolish mistake by a nineteen-year-old
girl, Charley Partanna had manufactured the excuse to
turn his back on the daughter of Vincent Prizzi, the

granddaughter of Corrado Prizzi, because he had no use for her.

"He had use for me, Poppa," Maerose said. "He came to my place in New York the night before he left to marry the woman in California and he forced himself on me and did it to me."

"Did it to you?" Vincent said in confusion, unable to sort out semantically what he was convinced he had heard.

"He fucked me, Poppa," Maerose said. "Three times. Maybe four. I can't remember."

Vincent slapped her heavily across the face, knocking her sideways, off the chair. "You wash out your filthy mouth, you hear? Who are you talking to here? You are speaking to your father."

She got back on the chair, holding her face. "Well, that was it, anyway."

"The dirty bastard!" Vincent yelled. "He did that to you? Charley Partanna? Are you sure?"

"Am I sure? Poppa, you should see the size of him, you should—"

"*Stop*! How can you say such things to your father? Where is your honor?"

"Charley Partanna destroyed my honor, Poppa. Are you kidding? I have no honor anymore."

Vincent rushed out of the room. He left the house. He walked the streets. He schemed.

The next night they sat again in the moldering living room. Maerose knitted. Vincent glowered. After twenty minutes he said, "Do you know that Charley has betrayed us in another way? He robbed us for three hundred and sixty dollars."

"Poppa, listen. Not Charley. The wife ripped you off. The wife was the brains behind the whole thing, then she killed Louis Palo to get the money. This is one thing which Charley had nothing to do with."

"Whatta you talking about? Sure, all right, the wife was in on it, but so was Charley. They needed the husband, Heller, because he was inside the cage at Vegas, but as soon as they had the money, Charley clipped the husband. Fahcrissake, he married the woman before the husband was cold. Charley killed the husband so he could get the wife."

"No."

"Whatta you mean no? Stop saying No!"

"Lissena me. Poppa. You know the cassette? The one Paulie had made of Teresa's wedding? I had them make prints from that cassette of the wife."

"Prints?"

"You know—pictures. They were good shots. I took them to Presto Ciglione's in Vegas . . ."

When she had finished speaking, Vincent stared at her. "I'm going to talk to Don Corrado tomorrow." But he said nothing about agreeing that Charley Partanna should be free and clear.

Chapter Twenty-six

Vincent telephoned the house on Brooklyn Heights the next morning just before noon. He was told by Amalia that his father was having a very good day and could see him at five o'clock. Vincent went out the back way at the laundry. He didn't tell Angelo Partanna, or anyone else, where he was going. It was a matter between himself and his father.

They sat in two Morris chairs in the enormous side room that had been converted into an apartment for the don. It was a living room and bedroom all in one. The colors were different shades of blue; soothing, restful, and calming. The room had been designed, furnished, and decorated by Maerose Prizzi but, because of the enforced alienation between her grandfather and herself at the time, had been executed by her colleagues.

The Morris chairs were something else, wholly apart from the other furniture of the room. The Morris chairs had been in use ever since Vincent could remember, from when his mother had been alive and his father had been a young man.

"What do you want to do, Vincent?" his father asked.

"Well, I am saying that Charley has to be hit. He married the woman who ripped us off as soon as they

187

got the whole deal together. Charley set the whole thing up. Charley has to pay."

Don Corrado pursed his lips and made a steeple with his fingers. "Lissena me, Vincent. Nobody gets taken out until we get our three hundred sixty back. Even then—and I am going to talk now about ethics. Hitting both of them or either one of them would create an ethically impossible situation. Charley is our own best soldier, our enforcer, your *sottocapo*, a tremendous, reliable man. His father is my own *consigliere*. These are very important considerations. What I am saying to you is that if the money is returned, then unless we want to have to kill Angelo Partanna and a lot of the Partannas' friends, then this is something which deserves clemency. Even if we only do the job on the wife we don't only have the Partannas on our back. You *know* what a case the Partannas could make with the Commission, and what a stain it would be upon our name throughout the *fratellanza* if we were to harm the wife of anyone in the brotherhood. She is Charley's wife. We can't take a chance with a thing like that. We have to think about clearing a thing like that with the Commission."

"Whatta we gunna do?" Vincent demanded. "Are we gunna just let them get away with this?"

"First, Filargi must be arrested and charged. That is the big one, Vincent," Don Corrado said. "Then I will ask Charley's wife to give back the money, but I am not going to talk about it with Charley."

Chapter Twenty-seven

What had made Vincent sensitive to life was the emergence of his brother Ed as the dominating force within the Prizzi family. Corrado, the father, was the natural force of the family and Vincent had never questioned that. But he considered that Ed had gained his power by means unfair to his brother; Ed had insisted upon being educated.

Vincent, always a mature, strong boy with much brutality, had left school at twelve to work with his father. When he took the oath as a made man, at twenty, with Angelo Partanna as his sponsor, he imprinted it upon his mind. Vincent was able to feel each point of the oath of fealty to the *fratellanza* subjectively, as if it were an oath to protect himself. Reciprocal aid to all members of the society in any case of need whatsoever. Absolute obedience to superiors. An offense against one is an offense against all and must be avenged at any cost. Never reveal the names or secrets of the society or look to government processes for justice. Vincent was obdurate about obeying those rules because he was a Prizzi, at the top, and they had been made to protect him.

But Ed had never had any interest in being made. Ed had graduated from high school high in his class. Vincent mocked him when Ed asked for his father's permission to go to college. He was shocked and ashamed when Ed entered law school. In Vincent's view, his brother had copped out and Vincent stood behind the old Sicilian proverb, "The less things change, the more they remain the same." Ed was trying to change everything. What the fuck good was an education in the rackets? When his boyhood pals, Ben Sestero and Harry Garrone, went away to study whatever it was they said they were studying, Vincent even had moments of worry, wondering how the family was going to carry on.

He was encouraged when Charley Partanna had the good sense to quit high school after two years but bitterly resentful when Charley went back to night school to finish after he had been made.

Vincent was a schooled resenter by the time Ed came back and took over the family's business side. Poppa made no objections. Poppa said Ed and Ben and Harry were going to triple the business, maybe more. Vincent had never grasped what Poppa had been building on the legit side all through the years, but when Ed came back, a lawyer, Vincent began to see and to resent deeply that *his* operation, the *real* business of the family which had financed all the rest of it with the tax-free capital, had become the dog that was wagged by Eduardo's tail.

The realization of Ed's dominance came over him so suddenly that it was like a shot on the head with a hammer. Ed was legit. He knew how to go anywhere. Ed was in and out of Washington, Camp David, the friend of presidents. He took senators and congressmen and cabinet secretaries on hunting trips or boat rides in the Caribbean or to his place in Palm Springs, where Vincent refused to go. But never to Vegas. Ed was too pure for Vegas.

Ed never even married. He stayed "engaged" to different women and the three he had around him the longest were called his "natural" wives. This was a friend of the cardinal! Of Billy Graham! Of Rabbi Kahane! Ed got away with anything. He never seemed to work. He was always on the telephone or in an airplane. He ran a tremendous business, but that was the least part of why Ed's shadow had kept Vincent in perpetual night. Ed was one of the people who ran the *country*, fahcrissake. He had so much clout that when any other family in the entire *fratellanza*, or the Jewish combinations, or the blacks who had come up so fast, had to get something done at the federal level, they went to Ed. Ed knew everybody's price, so Ed was The Man.

What was Vincent? He ran the troops—period. He was muscle. The newspapers called him a hoodlum. They called Ed a leading industrialist. His own daughter had been unable to respect him, so she had shamed him in front of the entire environment in the United States by acting like a nothing whore and costing herself her whole future as the wife of the man who was sure to take her father's place in the family someday. Now Charley Partanna—son of the man who Vincent and his father and even Ed trusted most in the world—had shown him that he had no respect for him. Charley had betrayed his family but it had been directed against Vincent. He had wanted to dishonor Vincent and he had left that honor in the gutter by the time he was through. Because of that and because of what he had done to Vincent's daughter, Vincent had become obsessed with the idea that Charley had to be hit.

He called Casco Vagone, the *consigliere* to the Bocca family in downtown New York.

"Hey, Casco! Vincent. How they hanging?"

"Hey, Vincent!"

"I gotta be in New York today and there's some business we got to go over."

"Where you want to make it?"

"How about we'll eat?"

"You got it. The Pavone Azzurro. One o'clock."

Casco was an old buddy. They had been made the same year, 1935. Casco was maybe six years older than Vincent. They cut up old touches throughout the lunch, remembering details of people and jobs that they were sure they had forgotten. When they were drinking the coffee Vincent said that four of his boys had cased a fur warehouse in the Bocca family's country and he wanted permission to whack it.

"Well, like you say—that is our country, Vincent. So we would have to have the usual arrangement."

"Of course. Certainly. I will personally be responsible."

They worked out the details for the distribution of the proceeds of the robbery, then Vincent said, "I want a telephone number from you. I want to get in touch with the best freelance hitter around."

"Angelo Partanna has them numbers."

"I know," Vincent said.

"Well, if you want the best, it costs."

"How much?"

"About seventy-five dollars."

"I need the number, Casco."

"You got it. It's a Kansas City number. Also, the worker is a woman."

Vagone wrote on the inside of a folder of paper matches. "It's a woman, but she is the best."

Vincent went to a telephone booth in the Roosevelt Hotel in midtown and called the Kansas City number. The automatic relay switched the call to the machine in Beverly Hills. The machine said: "This is an answering machine. Please leave your message at the sound of the tone." It was a woman's voice. The tone sounded and Vincent said, "Meet me at—uh—the little park, Paley Park, on Fifty-third offa Fifth in New York. Full price. I will have a copy of—uh—*Popular Mechanics* beside me on the bench so you'll know it's me. Nine-twenty A.M. Tuesday the first of September." He hung up.

Vincent was in place in Paley Park at 9:05 to be sure he could get a bench. All the benches were empty. Irene came in at 9:15. She hesitated for a fraction of a moment when she saw who the client was, then she registered that Vincent had never seen her so he couldn't recognize her as Charley's wife.

She walked directly up to the bench and sat down. "Whoever heard of a really popular mechanic?" she asked pleasantly.

"You the contractor?" Vincent said.

"Yes."

"Okay. How much?"

"It depends. Some are simple, some are tricky. Who do you want whacked?"

"A Brooklyn fellow by the name of Charley Partanna. You know him?"

Irene looked at him sardonically, raising her eyebrows. "That could be a very tricky hit," she said. She didn't take the time to think about Charley. This was business. First, a price, then she could think.

"How much?"

"Charley Partanna has a lot of experience," Irene said. "And he is dangerous. It would be fifty-fifty that he would do me before I could do him."

"How much?"

"I couldn't take the chance for less than one hundred."

"That's ridiculous, lady. I mean, that is a really mixed-up number."

"If you can buy it for less, so buy it for less."

"They told me seventy-five."

"You told me Charley Partanna."

"Ah, shit!" Vincent said. "I'll go to ninety."

"Remember, I'm out in the cold. Nobody can get me out but me. That's why it's gotta be one hundred."

"All right."

"How soon?"

"Right away."

"I need time to lay it out. I need to watch him. I

have to know the best place to take him—listen, maybe I won't take him at all. If it doesn't look right to me, I won't take him."

"When you going to know?"

"Tell me where I can call you. I'll call you by two weeks."

"Look, that don't work with me. You took the call. You come to New York because you know what your work is. Maybe is nothing." He took an envelope from the inside pocket of his shapeless dark jacket and tossed it on her lap. "That's fifty dollars. The first payment. What are we here, a bunch of schoolboys with the maybe? You're supposed to be the best in your business."

Irene took up the envelope and opened its loose flap. She looked at fifty thousand-dollar bills. They were well-used bills. She took out and rubbed them together.

"When is the next payment?" she asked.

"When you make the hit. All right. Two weeks if you want. He is in and out of town right now anyway." Vincent brought out a postcard. On its address side someone had written Charley's address at the beach and under it the address of the St. Gabbione Hotel Laundry. She turned the card over. There, in four colors, was the scene of the beach at Coney Island, where you couldn't even see the sand there were so many goddamn people. "The top one is where he lives. The bottom one is where he works. You can routine the hit with that."

Irene put the envelope in her purse, telling herself she would figure it out later. "On the next payment," she told him, "give me half in hundred-dollar bills."

"Fahcrissake, I'll need a suitcase."

"Whatever." Fifty dollars was fifty dollars, she told herself. At the back of her mind she thought that maybe, before the time came to make the hit, she could do the job on this peasant and everything would be solid because she would still be fifty dollars ahead.

She let herself hear Charley's voice. She watched him while he was eating and felt him all around her when he was making love to her. Fifty dollars couldn't give anybody memories like that.

Irene had lunch alone at Schrafft's and thought the whole proposition through. On the plus side was the high fee. Also she was going to make a big score from yesterday's Filargi grab. Already she had made more this year than the President of the United States admitted he made. On the minus side was the fact that it wouldn't be worth that much or almost any amount of money to do the job on Charley, because he was irreplaceable. She would like it to work out that she would be offered one-hundred dollars to bury Vincent Prizzi, but there was no way that she could clip Charley. So, fuck it, she would mail the deposit back and be out the hundred. Maybe, since Vincent had it in his mind to have Charley whacked, maybe she should hit Vincent. But there was always the chance that somebody else would get the idea to hit Vincent and, if they did, there was always the chance that she would be offered the work and maybe get the hundred back.

She ate chicken salad and pondered upon love. How could somebody be worth more than a hundred dollars, she thought. What could she buy with Charley? He was a luxury. She had gone the luxury route from day one as soon as she was able to, and she *bought* the luxuries, she hadn't given up a big bundle just for the privilege of being able to buy them. She paid for the luxury of Charley with her body every night. It was terrific, there had never been anything like it, she supposed that was part of what love was, but that was her ticket of admission. She paid when she cooked. She paid by having left California to live in Brooklyn, she paid by not having her Gozzy, so Charley as a luxury was all paid for. The hundred dollars was separate. Jesus! She thought of her mother lying in the corner of that stinking stockyards tenement in Chicago after her father had punched dents in her and she wondered what the fuck love could be if her mother could put up with an animal like that year after year and if she could give up a hundred dollars because love had punched some dents in her, too.

Chapter Twenty-eight

On the day after Irene's meeting with Vincent in Manhattan, Maerose called her at the beach and said that Corrado Prizzi would like to see her at five o'clock that afternoon. It was two o'clock, Irene was vacuuming, and she wanted to wash the awnings because Charley had complained that morning that they hadn't been washed all month, but Irene knew what had to be done so she asked how to get to the meeting. Maerose said she would drive out to get her. Irene said that would be too impossible a trip so Maerose said she should take a taxi to the Peak Hotel in the Heights and that they could meet in the lobby at a quarter to five.

At four o'clock she called Charley and told him where she was going. "What the hell is that all about?" Charley said. "I don't get it."

"He probably just wants to welcome me into the family," Irene said.

She got into the taxi almost cold with the fear that Vincent Prizzi would be at his father's house. She had only seen Vincent twice before in her life, once up on the stage at Teresa Prizzi's wedding party and once at Paley Park, but that was a lot of times in one bunch considering the length of her life, and there had to be trouble for her if he saw her again while she was standing next to someone who could explain who she was.

Maerose was there when she got to the hotel; beautiful and blithe. She was the friendliest girl Irene had ever met. They walked up the hill to the Sestero house, chatting about Charley. When they got to the door Maerose said that was as far as she had been invited to go, but that she would wait at the hotel to drive Irene home. Irene thanked her and explained that she was going to phone Charley when her visit to Don Corrado was over, that they were going into New York for dinner.

The armed guard at the front door passed her to Amalia who took her upstairs to the don's sitting room. The old man was delighted to see her. He asked Amalia to put a chair close to him so that he could hold her hand as he talked to her. When she had finished tucking Don Corrado in, Amalia left them.

"You are a fine-looking woman," Don Corrado said. "What a surprise you gave us with this sudden wedding to Charley."

"The time just seemed right," Irene answered gaily. "We sort of swept each other away."

He patted her hand. "I understand," he said. "I was young once. But the marriage has troubled me."

"Why is that?"

"You know what hard facts can do to faith, dear child." He spoke English slowly, well, and with care. His accent was strong but he said everything well. "The people at Presto Ciglione's place in Nevada have looked at pictures of you and have told us that you killed Louis Palo." He held her hand tightly, looking directly into her face. He smiled at her.

She could not speak. Like someone who is drowning, scenes and events of her life crowded into her mind. She clutched the old man's hand tightly with terror, staring at him.

"Under ordinary circumstances," he said gently, "I would have had to turn you over to Vincent's people, because such things have to be punished and those who steal must pay."

She could not control the trembling of her arms and body. She could not take her eyes off his cold, tiny eyes. "However, now you are the wife of my godson, who is the son of my oldest friend, so—in the calm quiet of this room I have searched my compassion for some way to show clemency to you."

"What can I do? Just tell me what I can do," Irene said.

"You have the other half of the money which Charley brought back to us," he said flatly.

Against all of her sensibility Irene nodded her head.

"Was Charley in this with you?" he asked.

"No! He believed me when I told him that it was Marxie's split. He doesn't even know that I was in it with Marxie and Louis. He doesn't have any idea that I did the number on Louis and took all of the money from him, that Marxie never saw any of it. He thinks I just took him to where Marxie kept the money. He told me he suspected me—on the day he asked me to marry him he told me—that he felt that I was somehow a part of the whole scam, but then he decided that I wasn't, that I couldn't have been, otherwise he couldn't have married me." She knew she was talking for Charley's life because by now her own had been all settled one way or the other. She felt the sweat running under her arms and between her thighs.

"Charley is a good man. Charley has honor," Don Corrado said. He sighed. "Well, then my child, you may have five days to get the three hundred sixty dollars and to put it in my hand together with the fifty percent penalty for what you have done to us. Will five days be enough time for you?" he asked considerately.

"Yes. Oh, yes!" She wanted to scream the answer
with relief.

"Five days. Five hundred forty dollars."

She met Charley at six o'clock at the Peak Hotel
and they drove into Manhattan for dinner.

"Charley, for a change, let's not eat Italian
tonight."

"Sure. But where is a good Polish restaurant?"

"I have to go to LA in the morning."

"How come?"

"I have to settle the office lease and there are things
I want to ship back to the beach for us. I'll be back
Friday night."

"I'll be all day tomorrow out on the Island with Filargi anyway."

"How is he?"

"He hurts. What did Don Corrado want?"

"You know—welcome to the family and like that."

"That's terrific. I can't believe it. That is a very serious honor, being welcomed into a family in the
fratellanza by the head of the whole family. I mean,
particularly for a non-Sicilian woman."

"The Prizzis really are an arm and a leg outfit,
aren't they?"

"What do you mean?"

"Well, like the route they laid out for Filargi."

He was surprised. "Baby, that's the business we're
in. The Prizzis are the most successful outfit in the
country because they hit hard. People remember when
they get through doing business with the Prizzis."

"Jesus, I keep thinking about that woman getting
off at the wrong floor. Man, she really lucked out."

"Irene, come on. She was a witness."

"What luck! She pushes the wrong button in an elevator and she's dead."

"Where are we going for dinner?"

"I'm not so hungry."

"You want to take in an early movie? Then we could eat after the movie and you'd be hungry."

"Yeah. A movie."

"One of the houses on Third Avenue," Irene said. "But even later I don't think I'm going to be hungry."

Charley drove her to the airport at 8:30 the next morning. Before they left he filled in the stolen ticket stock that he had picked up from Ed Prizzi's office for a round-trip, first-class flight. They just had time to buy some newspapers before the flight was called and then she was gone.

After takeoff Irene opened the first paper. She turned to an article on page two:

STILL NO LEADS IN KILLING OF POLICE CAPTAIN'S WIFE

There was a picture of a woman's body laid out neatly on a police stretcher. There was a boxed picture of a police officer inset beside it.

"Police say they still have no leads in the murder of Victoria Calhane, wife of Police Captain Martin B. Calhane, director of the Organized Crime Unit, NYPD. Mrs. Calhane was found dead in a luxury suite on the forty-first floor of the Hotel Vanguard in New York Monday night by the tenant of the murder apartment. Mrs. Calhane's body had been dumped upon the body of Eugene Gormley, forty-six, a private investigator and professional bodyguard.

"In the hotel corridor outside the murder apartment the police found an inflated rubber doll encased in a baby's swaddling garments but no explanation of this has been offered by the police.

"Mrs. Eliot Shenker, tenant in the murder flat, said, 'It was terrible. They were both shot in the face.' Mrs.

Shenker had returned from a matinee performance of a Broadway play when she discovered the bodies.

"Captain Calhane went immediately to the scene of the crime. He said his wife had gone to the hotel to attend a charity auction at the hotel's roof garden on the forty-third floor."

Irene put the paper down. The silly bitch was going to the forty-third floor so why did she press for the forty-first floor? Holy shit! She leaned back and closed her eyes. Not only had she hit a cop's wife, but it had to be a cop who worked over hoodlums. It was really going to hit the fan this time. She picked up the paper again, because something was wrong with the story but she didn't know what. Then it hit her. There was nothing in there about Filargi. A big banker had been snatched and nobody knew anything about it yet—after nearly three days!

She felt like changing planes in LA and going straight on to Hong Kong.

When Charley got to the office there was a message to call Amalia Sestero.

"Heh, Amalia!"

"He wants you to come for lunch with him today, Charley."

"Sure. Great." Charley had the feeling it wouldn't be great. After years he was suddenly seeing too much of Don Corrado. Each time he saw him things got rougher than before.

"He likes a late lunch. Two o'clock—okay?"

"Sure. Great. Fine, Amalia."

Irene took a taxi from the LA airport to the Beverly Wilshire Hotel. She walked from the hotel to her office, where she checked the answering machine for calls, but there was nothing. She went to the window and let the light in. It was a sparkling sunny day and she asked herself how anyone could live in Brooklyn, a double dump, if they had a gorgeous house like hers in sunshine and cleanliness like this? Someday, she told herself, she was going to find out what the hell love was, and when she did, she was going to shove it up the guy who invented it. She had never been in such trouble. The biggest hood in the country was after her money. The New York Police Department was looking for her like she was the bubonic plague. There wouldn't be any easy answers if they got her, no Prizzi lawyer would be able to get her out of this one, and all because of some horseshit called love. She had thrown away a sweet, uncomplicated business, a gorgeous house in the most perfect climate in the world because of this love shit. She wished she had Marxie back. He was a deadbeat and useless but she had been safe with him for seventeen years. They had made out all right and now she had to dig out $540 of her own money, and throw away a sweet $100 contract, and practically hand it over to one of the richest men in the country—for what? Because he said so and because he would have her clipped if she didn't. The law wanted to clip her and the bad guys wanted to clip her. Jesus, $640!

She got a briefcase out of the closet. It had cost her almost a thousand dollars, retail, and it was a beautiful thing to touch. She left the office with it and went to the bank on Wilshire Boulevard.

They gave her a private cubicle in the vault room and brought in her boxes. This was her entire lifetime of work here. This was her blood mixed with a couple of gallons of her cold sweat. She didn't think she could stand it. She thought of the condition of the underwear of the men she had scored when she had been hustling in Chicago, before Marxie came along. She thought of the pimples on their thighs and the coarse hair on their backs, and their breath, and she made herself sick. She thought of trying to keep warm for the first fourteen winters of her life while her father snored like chains caught in moving machinery and while her mother whimpered, then drank, then whimpered and drank some more. She was supposed to hand $540 over to that old man! More than half a million dollars! People who paid taxes had to work for eighteen years at $127 a year in order to accumulate $540 in one piece. She put her face in her hands and wept bitterly. Why the fuck had she ever met Charley? If she had just gone along the way it was meant to be, she and Marxie could be in Singapore by now, or somewhere on the South Island of New Zealand where the pickings were all sheep, and that didn't interest the mob. She and Marxie could be in a clinic in Switzerland right now, getting over an operation on their faces and on their prints. They could have new paper and go anywhere, but she had to run into Charley and all the love shit.

She knew she should empty all the boxes on that table and run right now for the airport and fly over the Pole to Zurich and make her connections. Ten days from now she could have a new face and new prints and new paper. She would have her money and she would be safe.

But no Charley. Even for $540 she didn't think she could hack it without Charley.

Charley drove to Brentwood after he left the office. The Plumber was on duty, reading some tit magazine, and the place was a mess.

"What are you guys, animals?" Charley said indignantly as he went from the kitchen, piled with dishes and garbage, to the living room, which had plates of half-eaten sandwiches and sour beer glasses on almost every surface. "What do you want? A knock on the head? This is not only childish it is unhygienic."

"Charley, whatsa matter with you?"

"All right! where's the vacuum cleaner? Where's the scrub pail?"

"How do I know?"

Charley picked Melvini up by the front of his collar and knocked him over the back of a sofa. "You are going to get this place *clean*, you hear. Where the fuck is Dom? Get him down here." He kicked Melvini. "And don't give me any crap about how you'll stuff me down the fucking toilet because that's where you and Dom are going if this place isn't cleaned up in one hour."

Dom appeared at the stair landing. "Heh, what the fuck is going on?" he said. "I'm tryna sleep here."

"The Soap Fairy wants you," the Plumber said.

"Get down here, you slob," Charley roared. Dom hurried down the stairs. "All right. You, clean up all this shit laying around in here," he pushed the Plumber's shoulder, "then work that vacuum cleaner wherever you can find carpets or curtains. You, you little prick, get in there and wash those dishes. And when you finish that you are going to scrub the floor. You hear me? Move!"

The two men scurried to work. Charley went down the cellar stairs to the room where they kept Filargi. He used two different keys to open two padlocks. Filargi was writing a letter.

"How's it?" Charley asked.

"The men are pleasant. The food is good," Filargi said.

"You look all right."

"I am well enough. I can't stop thinking about that woman as she got out of the elevator, but maybe that will go away. I have nightmares about that awful woman coming to get me. I can't get her face out of my mind. She didn't change a flicker of an expression when she shot that defenseless woman in her face."

"That woman who got clipped was a goddamn dummy," Charley said. "She pressed the wrong button."

"What's going to happen to me?"

"It looks very good for you, Mr. Filargi. Next Mon-

day the bank gets the ransom routine. You know
about the bank being insured for the money. They
make the payoff and we turn you loose. That's the
whole bit."

"When?"

"Maybe two-three weeks."

"You are really going to let me go?"

Charley nodded gravely, thinking of what Don Corrado had in store for this poor son-of-a-bitch.

"You don't care that I can identify you and the
woman and those two men upstairs?"

"Mr. Filargi—look. You were standing there when
we did the job on your bodyguard and on that lady.
We are going to let you go free. But if you get into
that shit of telling the police you can identify us, then
you'll be dead. No matter where you are, you'll be
dead. So it's not such a hard choice. Anything you
want me to bring you from New York?"

"Well—I have this short list of books. And, if you
can do it, I'd like to have a television set down here."

"Certainly. Why not?"

Charley went in to find Pop to talk about Don Corrado sending for him but Pop was at a breakfast meeting with two basketball coaches. Charley got into the
panel truck and drove to The Corner. Nobody was
there. Mrs. Latucci was all smiles. "Coffee onna
house," she said. "You know what the Lady Carrot
paid? Twelve to one. I had ten bucks going three
ways. Jesus, it was terrific. Whatta you got for today,
Charley?"

"Today is nowhere," Charley said. "There isn't a
race in the country I would bet."

"How you betting the pennant?"

"It's too early. Two more weeks. I'll give you the
word in two weeks."

Phil Vittimizzare came in, ordered a Danish, and
went to the pinball machine. "Heh, Charley," he said.

"What happened to the Plumber? I don't see him around."

"Beats me," Charley said.

"He missed mass Sunday," Vittimizzare said primly. "Father Doniger asked me about him."

"He'll show up," Charley said. "You know the Plumber."

He left the luncheonette and drove to a downtown Brooklyn movie place. He had two hours to kill and a war movie was playing. He sat in the loges and after about twenty minutes some creep came over and sat beside him. Then the guy put his hand on Charley's thigh so Charley turned his arm over across his kneecap and broke it. He changed seats to the other side of the theater. What the fuck kind of a world do we live in, he thought, if you got to be molested by degenerates right in a Brooklyn theater?

He drove the Chevy to Brooklyn Heights, parked it illegally around the corner from the Sestero house, and rang Corrado Prizzi's doorbell.

Don Corrado was known as the heaviest fork in the history of the *fratellanza* on the Eastern seaboard. He had a small glass of olive oil for breakfast and another small glass of it for dinner. He ate only one meal a day, but to see the amount of food he was able to pack so effortlessly into that tiny frame, containing a stomach about the size of a doll's derby and intestines no longer than a skipping rope, was like watching a great illusionist work. He never had more than one guest at lunch, and never more than one lunch guest in a month. Because he couldn't bear to share even a small part of the food from his table.

He greeted Charley in an abrupt and preoccupied way, because his mind was entirely on the meal to come, then led him to the trough.

They began with a glass of Sicilian wine, Mamertino, which was semisweet, very strong, golden-white wine with a powerful aroma.

"Charley—tell me how it happened that you had to hit a cop's wife on that job?"

"*Padrino!* you never saw anything like it. The broad pushed the wrong elevator button. The door opens the minute the second man shoots the bodyguard. The woman is standing right there. She makes all of us. She had to go."

"I knew it had to be something like that. But it's making a real storm, Ed says. The entire department is gone crazy because you hit that woman."

"How come? Why?"

"Charley, you didn't hear me! That was not only a cop's wife you did that number on, that was the wife of the captain who runs the organized crime squad, and when they finally figure out that Filargi was grabbed they are going to make it into a mob operation and God know how much heat they'll generate."

The soup arrived. It was called *Le Virtù* and it contained pork sausages, meat balls, greens, vegetables, and pasta. Even though Charley had been warned about Don Corrado's lunches since childhood, he mistook the giant's soup, the hero's soup, for the main course and came back for seconds. The don put away four bowls of it, just as if it were cement going into a mixer. After that he poured each of them a glass of red wine, Corvo di Casteldaccia, dry and delicate, while Amalia served them the spiral pasta from Abruzzi, *ricci di Donna*, over which she had poured a stew made of roasted crabs with tomatoes, garlic, and pieces of toast; pungently aromatic. Charley looked up at her sharply as she came to serve him, after having served the don, and she lowered her eyes, nodded slightly, and gave him just a spoonful of each of the dishes on her tray. Don Corrado didn't notice the omission. He ate two large portions before he spoke again. "Amalia, dear one," he said, "I have a feeling for pasta today. We could be in for an early winter. Could we possible have another pasta? Is there any way you could do that?"

"I made some *panzerotti*, Poppa."

"Do I remember that? What's that?"

"You love it. It's fried *cappiddi d' Angilu* surrounding *cannaruozzoli* stuffed with *mozzarella*, ham and eggs and tomatoes, onions, and anchovy."

"It smells so good!" the little old man sang, clapping his hands. "It is from Bari, the birthplace of Urban the Sixth."

Suddenly Charley was released by the wonderful aromas, all of the beautiful food, and by the don's consumed and consuming appreciation of every bite of it. He felt safe. He was no longer afraid of this hungry little old man whose name or presence had been as terrifying as garlic to a werewolf for all of Charley's life. These were the sights and sounds of his mother's kitchen, the haven of havens. This was the tremendous food of his childhood and all of his life. His second wind as a great *golóso*, as a gargantuan *ghiottone*, returned to him in one piece as if the Holy Ghost had been seated on his shoulder with a napkin tucked around where his chin might have been. Charley signaled to Amalia with his eager eyes, piled high the *panzerotti* upon his plate, and dug in. Don Corrado nodded gleefully, chewing with great zest.

Charley had a vision of himself at Don Corrado's advanced age, enjoying such food on and on until, at last, his bowels failed; he would be the envy of every Italian-American to whom his legend would be told. Food was like money or power. You took it into yourself and you defied the other guy to get any of it. All it took was one meal with Don Corrado to get that through his head.

He saw clearly, in a sudden vision, that because of the kind of work he did in the business he was in, he might not last as long as Don Corrado. In fact there was a statistical chance that he might not last out the year.

As he ate he pondered his mortality. He decided that when he delivered the Filargi contract to Don

Corrado, as required, as the don graciously handed
him his share of the payoff money, while the old man
was in high spirits because of the seventy million dollars he was now going to make by getting back the
bank at ten cents on the dollar, he would shut himself
out from the muscle work, with all of the odds it offered against his length-of-life span, and ask the don
for the family's national sports book out of Vegas,
Miami, Atlantic City, Dallas, New York, and LA,
turn in the fifty million a year net to the Prizzis and
take his steady end of five million a year and let the
other guy knock himself out.

Irene would be proud of him for thinking of taking
over such a dodge. There would have to be a certain
amount of rough stuff before they got established,
sure. No one was going to just hand it to him, but
every family had its basic sports book, which made the
American mania for sports possible, and that was
going to be Charley Partanna, backed up by a wife
who had a real head for figures. The oncoming food,
which had drugged him, awoke him again. The next
course arrived.

After the *panzerotti* they had boiled fresh tuna and
a tart called *pitta ripiena*, which was made of layers of
ricotta cheese, layers of fried pork, layers of cacio-
cavallo cheese, layers of sausage, and layers of hard-
boiled egg. Charley silently ignored the tart.

"And now," Don Corrado said, breathing easily as
he poured from a bottle of Eloro wine, "the main dish
which I took care to inquire about this morning, dear
Charley, because you were to be my luncheon guest, a
supreme dish from our own Agrigento, *coniglio in
agro e dolce*, cooked the way the great *gabellotti*, the
Spinas, my darling wife's own family, cooked rabbit,
in a sweet-sour sauce—different from any *argo e dolce*
found anywhere else in all of Italy—in a sauce having
pieces of eggplant, celery, olives, capers, almonds,
honey and lemon. It will exalt you."

They finished off with various little cakes, tarts and sweets such as *'Nipitiddata* and *'Nfasciatelle* and *'Scursunera*, an ice flavored with the essence of jasmine.

"We must discuss our business," Don Corrado said to Charley, "or else we would have a proper dessert— unless you would care for some of Amalia's famous *cassata*—in both styles."

"No, thank you, *Padrino*. All of these sweets and cakes are dessert enough for me."

"Then I shall try your *cassata* cake, Amalia, chilled but not frozen, stuffed as only you can do it, with ricotta and candied fruits and chocolate. And we will both have, of course, a glass of the Malvasia."

After lunch the two men settled down in the Morris chairs in Don Corrado's sitting room and looked out at the hackles that rose from the neck of the city in lower Manhattan. They drank coffee and smoked large *maduro* Mexican cigars. Don Corrado said, "Never once in your life, Charley, have you been less than my favorite of all the family."

"You were my sponsor when I was made, *Padrino*. I have tried to live up to that honor," Charley answered in his flawed Sicilian.

"How well I remember. You swore absolute obedience and you have lived by that oath."

"You made that possible, *Padrino*."

"Charley, let me tell you that you made possible so much of our family's success. You are the best worker we ever had—and that includes both Vincent and your father. You never failed on a contract and you always got the last dollar."

"I wanted to repay you for the faith you had in me."

"I have even greater faith. More faith in you than ever. And so has my son, Eduardo."

Obliquely that struck Charley as an odd note. Why not Vincent? He was Vincent's Underboss, so why should Don Corrado speak of Ed's faith in him? Ed Prizzi had always stayed strictly away from him. They had spoken to each other indirectly at rare meetings, but the only other contact Charley had ever had with him had been through a bank of criminal lawyers.

"Charley," Don Corrado said, leaning forward to touch Charley's knee lightly to emphasize their intimacy, "Vincent is a sick man. The blood pressure is very high—dangerously high, his doctor tells me—the pain of his gout distracts his mind, but worst of all are his kidneys. This is confidential, you must remember that, but Vincent's kidneys are shot."

"Well," Charley shrugged, "modern medicine—"

"We are going to move Vincent out to Vegas. The three hotels can use one central adviser who has the authority Vincent would bring the job. We got to firm up a fixed odds line on the sports for the whole country without shaking up the Justice Department too much. The casino action is nothing compared to the sports book."

"I know," Charley said. Jesus, he thought, why do I always think of everything a year too late?

"You wonder why I'm telling you all this, Charley?" the don asked, smiling.

"Yeah."

"Because you are going to take over Vincent's job here."

Charley blinked.

"That's right," the don said, popping a blue-black grape into his mouth. "You are going to run everything. You are going to be Boss."

"Me?" Charley said.

"You and me and your father will work out a deal on how many points you're going to get. Less until we get Vincent all the way out on deals he set up, but still you got to do yourself forty dollars a week and have the biggest organization in the business—twenty-one hundred people out on the street for you. What do you say, Charley?"

Charley let himself go for a few seconds so that at least he could enjoy the *idea* of all that money and power being all his, but he knew it didn't happen that way. Vincent was the don's oldest son. It was a Prizzi business. The Prizzis would decide together if Vincent was to do the impossible and give up what he had to go out killing time in Vegas because of a couple of dumb kidneys. Then if such a miracle were passed and they all agreed that it was the best thing to do, Vincent would call Charley in and lay it out for him. And after he laid it out he would tell Charley how many points he was going to have to kick back to get the job. Charley wouldn't get all the points until Vincent was dead, then, when the time came for him to hand over, he would set up the next guy.

"I am speechless, *Padrino*," Charley said to the don. "This is an honor and a privilege beyond my dreams. How can I show my gratitude? How can I thank you?"

Don Corrado's little eyes brimmed with tears. He took a brilliantly white handkerchief out and dabbed his tiny, sunken eyes. "This is an even greater day for me than it is for you, Charley," he said with a trembling voice. "To be allowed to witness the son of my oldest and dearest friend in the world assume the duties of my own son fills me with joy and emotion."

"When will this begin, *Padrino*?" Charley had cold foreboding. Irene's scam in Vegas filled his mind. It was impossible that Don Corrado would ever forgive or forget the loss of any amount of money through betrayal and theft and this was a great big bundle of money.

"For the time being, it must be our secret. You must not even tell your father."

He was being set up! It had to be! A jolting stab of certainty that he was being set up socked itself into Charley. The change-over involved a three-hundred-and-sixty-million-dollar business. Don Corrado would not make a move involving any matter of policy, either small or as large as this, without talking it all over, testing every angle with his *consigliere*, who was Angelo Partanna, but he had just said Pop wasn't supposed to know.

"I understand, *Padrino*."

"Vincent will be ready to move out when the Filargi thing is all settled. Not long. About three weeks before we can collect the payoff and you can let Filargi go so that he can go to the police and suddenly find himself in prison. On the day Filargi is arraigned for trial, Vincent will move out of the laundry and you will move in."

Chapter Twenty-nine

Angelo Partanna had a call from Lieutenant Hanly, bagman for the chief inspector's office, who wanted a quick meet.

"Certainly, Davey," Angelo said. "Wherever you say."

They made a date at the usual place, Chez Hans, an Irish restaurant near Prospect Park, for the next day. When Angelo got there, with Charley as his listener, Hanly had brought along a police captain named Kiely from the PC's squad. Kiely had the rank but Hanly ran the meeting.

Everyone was effusively cordial. Highballs arrived and the Partannas let them rest on the table in front of them. They all ordered corned beef and cabbage, the only food item that Hans ever seemed to sell. Hanly and Kiely did most of the talking. It was mostly about sports and national politics.

After Angelo passed around Mexican cigars Hanly got down to the basics.

"I don't know if you guys kept up with it," Hanly said, "but it was hard to miss—the murder of Captain Calhane's wife."

"I seen that," Angelo said. "Like you say, it would be hard to miss it. It was a terrible thing. We sent flowers to the funeral and—well, what can you say?"

"Well, it shook us up, Angelo. Believe me. We see it the same way you would see it—it's a family loss, the whole Department feels it. Everybody—I mean cops on the beat and the bosses. And we gotta do something about it, respect has got to be paid, Angelo."

"We are with you, Davey. Anything. If you know anything we can do, if we can put the word out to every family to find whoever done this, or anything else, we want to do it."

"Well we are asking all the families for that kind of help, of course. And we will appreciate it because we know that you know how we feel about this. But that isn't the whole thing. I am here to tell you and the Prizzis the same thing we are telling every family in this town. All contracts are off until we get the killer of Vicky Calhane."

"How do you mean that, Davey?"

"We have to come down hard on you, Angelo. A week from now half the horse rooms in Brooklyn, for example, will be out of business and the people will be held on high bail."

"We are gonna break you guys on the narcotics," Kiely said. "This time when we go in and take it, you won't be getting any of if back. Every racket you run is gonna get it." His eyes were vindictive. He smiled unprofessionally when he said, "Business is gonna get very bad for you guys." Kiely had strong traces of a North-of-Ireland accent. Hanly was a redhead with a bullet-dented jaw. Both men had calm eyes from years and years of the good life.

"Davey," Angelo said softly, "I been doing business with the guy who has your job in the Chief's office since I was a young fella in the twenties. Over the years I worked with the PC's squad, too, and the divisions, and the borough guys. We only had one rule, an easy rule, and mostly we have done business that way."

"I know," Hanly said, "but circumstances alter cases. What can we do?"

"If you take our money," Angelo told him, "you let us alone. Every one of our people working on the street has a contract with your people, insurance, we pay for them to work, your people give them their license to work. The all-borough squads protect that."

"Look at it our way, Angelo. It's got to be a point of honor with us and you guys, of all people, have to see that."

Angelo sighed. "Okay. How much time do we have? Can you give us three days?"

"Listen, Angelo, you can have *no* days. We're being pushed for results, now. We toss the first banks today, then the broads tomorrow, the bookies Saturday, and so on."

"The public ain't gonna like this, Davey. Shut down all the gambling and narcotics and loan-sharking and broads and you are going to have a much worse crisis than the baseball strike."

"Take away the coke from the very important people is like holding out hamburger on a working man," Charley said. "They are going to panic then lean on you."

"How long can it last?" Hanly said, "right, Charley?"

Charley shrugged. "With you guys working on it and every family in the combination working on it, you ought to have your man inside a week."

"That's it." Hanly said. "That is exactly it. I give it a week."

"But if it takes more than a week, Davey, I just want to say that you guys are gonna hurt a lot sooner than we hurt. The ice has got to stop for you, today. It's human nature to get to depend on that kind of money coming in over the past eighty, ninety years."

Kiely leaned across the table. His voice was hard

and cold. "Sure, we'll hurt, Angelo. But we'll have
the dirty rat who hit Vicky Calhane."

As they rode back across Prospect Park in Charley's
van on the way to the laundry, they chewed on their
cigars and thought about what had happened. Charley
said, "How long do you think they can stand it without the pad?"

"Listen, I'd hate to count how many weeks they
kept the lid on and lived on cops' pay when Arnold
Rothstein was hit and they had to get his files before
the reformers got them. This is worse, I think. They
have their own kind of *omertà*, the cops. They are no
different than us except they all wear the same suit.
When that dumb broad who pushed the wrong floor
went down, it was like every one of their wives had
leaned on the bullet. It is their honor, Charley. You
got to watch your step when you are fucking around
with somebody's honor."

'Well, it's very close to home for me," Charley said.
"This kind of pressure is very dangerous."

"We have our own honor, Charley, never forget
that. We protect our women. If necessary, you can hit
the Plumber and Dom because outside you and me,
nobody else knows who did the job on the woman."

"The Plumber and Dom think I hit her," Charley
said. "But Filargi knows who. And, correct me if I am
wrong, but nobody is gonna ice Filargi when seventy
million bucks is involved."

"Listen," Angelo said, "—we are talking about
Corrado Prizzi's honor. Nobody is gonna get near
Irene."

Chapter Thirty

The day after his talk with Don Corrado, Charley was still hollow with fear. Don Corrado had written him off, but he needed him to run Filargi until the time came to turn him loose. Charley thanked God that He had made him a worker, not just a rackets guy. If they were setting him up, then maybe they were setting themselves up, because like two days before he set Filargi loose, Charley, maybe with a little help from Irene, would wipe out Don Corrado and Vincent and Ed Prizzi.

It was 3:40. Irene's plane would get in from the Coast at 6:20. He decided to go straight to the airport and wait for her to get in. As he drove along the Belt Parkway he thought of going to the beach and picking up the blank airline ticket stock, then taking off from JFK to Zurich to assembly his money, then going on to New Zealand, but he knew he and Irene would have to have more muscle than just running. He thought vaguely about turning but he didn't have much confidence in the government's Witness Protection Program either. Ed Prizzi had been an enormous factor in organizing big campaign money for the new president and he'd be set up as soon as he walked into it.

He drove slowly to kill time. He parked the car at

La Guardia and went to a newsstand. He bought a
paper and went into the coffee shop.

BANK PRESIDENT KIDNAPED

DIRECT LINK TO CALHANE KILLING

the front page said. A hotel chambermaid had found
Filargi's bed not slept in for two nights and the bank
had called on the morning of the second day to ask the
hotel to check Filargi's apartment to see if he was all
right. By that time they had traced the dead
bodyguard's papers to a one-man office in Long Island
City, and his records showed that he had been guard-
ing Filargi. That was Wednesday. The cops had tried
to keep a lid on the story, but by Friday Gomsky had
seen to it that somebody spilled it to the papers. The
combination of a police captain's wife and a bank
president would keep it on the front page for the rest
of the week and Charley knew that no ransom instructions would be sent to the bank until the really heavy
pressure had died down and the media was ready to
give it another tremendous shot.

There had to be five more days before the bank got
the ransom demand. Maybe more than that because a
bank and an insurance company, not people, were involved in making the move. It would take about three
weeks before they could agree with the cops on how
to make the payment. There would be one set of letters to the insurance company telling them to pay off
in Central Park, where there would be two cops behind every tree, while the real letter would go to
Gomsky at the bank, telling him to set up the payoff
in Lagos, Hong Kong, Aruba, Panama, and São
Paulo. So maybe it would be a full month before he'd
be told to let Filargi go.

Charley nursed a beer and read the sports page until
6:10, then he drifted out to find a call board to locate
Irene's gate number and went to stand near it to wait.

The flight was early. Irene came out of the gate yelling and waving. They grabbed each other and held on. She said, "You look lousy, Charley. What's the matter?"

"Better we'll talk about it in the car." He took her small case. She tried to hold on to it, but he took it. What have you got in there?" he said. "The family jewels?" She grinned weakly.

They drove in the battered black Chevy van out toward the parkway entrance. Irene said, "What's the matter, Charley?"

"You ready?"

"Yeah."

"Don Corrado called me over for lunch with him yesterday. That Amalia is some sensational cook. So after lunch he says to me how sick Vincent is and how they are going to move him out to Vegas to take care of the action at the three hotels and that I am going to take over Vincent's job and Vincent's points."

"Charley! That is te*rrif*ic!"

"Yeah?"

"Why not?"

"They are setting me up."

"Why should they set you up?"

"Well I don't know. But it has to have something to do with the three hundred sixty dollars. And Louis Palo. No matter what else, it's got to be that Don Corrado knows all about that."

"He knows. I couldn't figure a way to tell you, but he knows."

"Who told you that?"

"He did. The day we had dinner in town—the day before I flew out to LA. When I told you he had me over there to welcome me into the family."

"Holy *shit*, Irene. Then that is why he is setting me up. He knows. He has you cold and you're my wife so we both got to get it."

"Oh, Charley!" Irene began to cry softly.

"Baby, I love you. You understand that? Love is for keeps with me. I won't let *any*thing hurt you. You're my woman."

"Jesus, God, Charley, how I love you."

"Listen, we have time. The don said the whole thing is on ice until the cops get Filargi," Charley said earnestly. "He wants me to keep the Filargi thing together, then they move. We've got three weeks, a month, to get ready. Then you and me are going to take them before they can take us."

Irene took a deep breath and exhaled slowly. "Charley," she said, "you know how my jobs are lined up?"

"No."

"The customers call a number in Kansas City or South Carolina, then that call is relayed to my answering machine in LA."

"Telephones can do that?"

"Yeah. So—I got a call a couple of days ago and it says: full fee, meet me in Paley Park on Fifty-third in New York."

"A *park?* On Fifty-third?"

"Yeah. Who do you think the customer is?"

"Who?"

"Vincent Prizzi."

"Whaaaat?"

"Yeah."

"What the hell? If Vincent wants somebody clipped, *I* do it!"

"Not this time. That would be suicide. He put out the contract on you."

"Vincent? On *me?*"

"Well, he did."

"Wait a minute. Vincent gives you a commission on me? He is buying my wife to clip *me?*"

"Charley, fahcrissake! He don't know I am your wife. He called the KC number! He tells me it's worth a seventy-five. I tell him you would be a very tricky hit. In the end we get it up to a hundred."

"That's crazy. The Plumber would have to do it for nothing. Any one of my boys, for nothing."

"Baby! Don't be offended! He wanted a specialist. Don't ask me why."

"I'll tell you why," Charley said. "He don't want the family to know that he has put out a contract on me. The don is setting me up, but when they think they are going to take me, he isn't going to spend any one hundred dollars to have the number done. That's what he has workers for, to blow people away for nothing. But, and this is the nitty, if Vincent is paying out one hundred dollars for a specialist to take me out then, number one, he's got to be crazy—I mean out of his head about something he thinks I done to him—and, number two, he's gotta be using his own money; not that he doesn't have it, but spending one hundred dollars has to hurt him more than the fucking hit would hurt me."

"One thing is for sure," Irene said dryly, "we are in bad with your family. Now what do we do? You know what Louis Palo told me? He said that even if we went to Rio, or any place, that you would find us, because that's the way you are built. Do the Prizzis have anybody else like you? Do they have another guy who wouldn't give up on us?"

"What do they need? They have Don Corrado to remember. They are Sicilians. Don Corrado tells five other guys to remember and he makes them swear that if he dies, the other guys remember. They are all over this fucking world. We go in a restaurant in Uganda and a spade tells some clerk at the Italian legation who passes it to Palermo and they move it to the don in New York and the word goes out—this much money for our thumbs. Maybe two thousand people in Africa are out after our thumbs unless he says he wants them to ship him my whole head. If we are going to run then we have to have face jobs. We have to have new prints and papers. We have to be entirely new and still think every minute that they're watching us."

"Then what are we going to do?"

He swung the car into a side street and stopped it next to a curb. "We are going to use Filargi to get us out, somehow. Don Corrado won't let anything touch us as long as we have Filargi."

"You mean we can negotiate this thing?"

"The Prizzis need me. How much I don't know, but there is such a bundle here that we need them."

"You don't know, Charley. You never asked me how much that old fuck decided to charge me for scamming him."

"Whatta you mean?"

"He gave me a choice of being hit or tearing five hundred forty dollars out of my safe deposit box. I have it right here and I'm supposed to hand it to him. Jesus, I looked at my money in one of my boxes at the bank and I almost busted out crying. How I worked to get that money, pounding into their heads—Marxie and Louis—what they had to do and how they had to do it and getting a fight on it every way because I was a woman and therefore they knew better."

"But how come five hundred forty?" Charley asked.

"Prizzi wants his three hundred sixty plus a fifty percent penalty—five hundred forty dollars of my blood, all gone because of a bunch of Sicilians who have been up to their ass in pathological crime for seven centuries and who have to cheat, corrupt, scam, and murder anybody who stands between them and a buck. It's a peasant mentality, Charley, and I can't stand that."

"Irene, listen—fuck the Prizzis."

"Charley!" She was genuinely shocked to have heard that from him.

"I have you and you have me. The Prizzis can't always win."

"But what are we going to do now?"

"There is only one thing we can do," Charley said. "We gotta talk to my father."

Chapter Thirty-one

Angelo Partanna's bland face broke its lifetime pattern and showed them anger, which climbed toward an explosion point as its fuse burned shorter and shorter. When Charley finished with his report on Don Corrado's setting him up and Vincent's putting out a contract on him, Angelo stood up abruptly, walked out to the terrace, shut the door, and stayed there for almost ten minutes staring out across the bay. When he came back he was his old self. "There is nothing to get hot about," he said. "It's just business, except with Vincent."

"Well, what the hell is it with Vincent?" Charley asked.

"Ever since his daughter came home she's been making his life miserable. It starts up his gout and the blood pressure and he blames you for not marrying her in the first place, ten years ago."

"Marrying who?" Irene said.

"Maerose," Charley told her.

"*Maerose?*"

"That's the way our minds work, whatta you going to do?" Angelo said to Charley. "But the sweetest part is that is that Vincent tries to put the contract with the guy's own wife to do the job on him. That is something."

"What are we going to do?" Irene asked.

"You had it coming. There is no way out of that," Angelo said to Irene. "Whacking Louis Palo was bad enough. He was a made man in our family so if he rated getting clipped, we had to do it. But robbing the Prizzis of three hundred and sixty dollars," he held up both hands, "nobody can hold still for that, Irene."

"Pop, Irene and me have been over that, we know all that, so what are we supposed to do now?"

"The absolutely first thing is that she's got to give back the three sixty. And if the don wants a fifty percent premium she's got to pay that, too. That is for openers."

"All right. I already got that straight in my head," Irene said, "then what?"

"First hand over the money. We ain't going anywhere until Don Corrado has that money. He can't believe anything unless you give back that money. We won't have any way to argue unless you do what you said and give him back his money. You and Charley are going to be taking big chances in the next couple of days and the only way you are going to come through is if you keep these deals separate and give him back his money so that he can see that you are serious when you lay out the deal that is going to keep you alive."

"What deal?" Charley said.

"You have to take away the only thing Don Corrado wants. Filargi, the golden Filargi he needs to get back his bank for ten cents on the dollar and win sixty million, maybe seventy million dollars. You have to snatch Filargi again, this time from the Prizzis. You understand me?"

Charley nodded. "I was thinking of something like that," he said. Angelo looked at Irene. She nodded sadly and turned away from him. She walked to the hall closet, took a small overnight bag from it and brought it out to stand it at Angelo Partanna's feet.

"There's the five hundred and forty," she said. "Give it to him for a little while, but before we give him Filargi, I want that money back."

"This is the story on Filargi," Angelo said, sitting down in the nearest chair. "Almost a year ago Don Corrado and Ed Prizzi had a meet with Filargi and they laid out for him Ed's scheme to milk the bank with the crooked foreign currency deals. They told Filargi they would even take only a fifty-fifty split on everything he could steal from the bank. He refused them. He called them bad names and he told them if they ever came near him again that he would see that they were put in prison. He told them he was going to write down the whole conversation just in case they decided to send some people after him and that it would go to the DA's office if he was hit. Now, anybody else except Corrado Prizzi would have let it go at that and moved along to some other scam, but Corrado buys himself an inside man at the bank—that fellow Gomsky—and talks him into going through with the ripoff for only twenty-five percent, a nice saving. Corrado tells me that this way not only is the pot that much sweeter, but that he can set up Filargi to get much worse than just getting buried—he will be ruined as a witness against the Prizzis. You got to hand it to him. There is nobody like him in this business."

"Jesus, I'm quitting," Irene said.

"What do we do with Filargi?" Charley said.

"First you get him. How many people they got out there holding him down?"

"Two, but they're my people. They do what I tell them."

"You think the don trusts anybody?" Angelo asked him amiably. "Where have you been? We use our suspicions instead of our brains in this business. Vincent told every man on that job that he is responsible for getting Filargi into court. They are all paid extra for watching each other."

"Then—too bad," Charley said. "They got to go, then."

"What do we do with Filargi when we have him someplace else?" Irene asked Pop.

"You negotiate. You send the letter to the don saying that you got Filargi and that you want to talk but only through an acceptable third party. Corrado will ask me who the third party should be and I will tell him that I am the best man for the job because you aren't going to trust anybody else."

"Then we have to trust you," Irene said.

"Yeah," Angelo said, smiling broadly at her. "That's right. But it's easier than running for the rest of your life then getting iced anyway, right?"

She stared at him. Then she grinned. "Yeah, right," she said.

"Filargi is worth sixty-seventy million to the Prizzis plus total control of what is maybe about the eighteenth-biggest bank in the United States, because they have to win if they get Filargi, and the biggest win is planting him in the joint here and in Italy for the rest of his life while they buy back the bank from the Italians at ten cents on the dollar. What are you next to seventy million dollars? Nothing."

"Yeah," Irene said, "but they're Sicilians so—present company excepted—they are basically dopes who think with their balls. They are, man for man, the biggest dummies I have ever gotten rich off so what if they turn us down?"

"How can they turn you down?" Angelo said blandly, spreading his open-palmed hands out in front of him. "If they turn you down, Filargi goes in to testify against them. You and Charley will turn and go into the government's Witness Protection Program and testify against them. The don, Eddie, Vincent and all the rest will be in the slammer for complicity to defraud, for murder, for—ah, shit! you name it—and not only will they never survive the prison terms they get but it will be the end of the Prizzi family." He walked to the window and stared out at the bay. "I think maybe I can make the cops lean even heavier on the street people. That ought to take the Prizzis' minds off thinking how they can blow you two away."

"How?" Charley asked.

"It could turn out to be a good thing that Irene zipped the broad who pressed the wrong floor."

Chapter Thirty-two

After he had straightened out some basketball betting patterns for the following week, and made the arrangements for the delivery of edges on the national professional tennis circuit, Angelo called Davey Hanly at the chief inspector's office. He said he was Chester Feinstein calling and Hanly said he would call him right back. It took Hanly twenty minutes to get to a pay phone on Broome Street that should have had a tap on it for the past thirty years, but didn't.

"Angelo? This is the call-back."

"Hey, great. Look—lemme pick you up in front of the usual place at twelve o'clock, okay?"

"I'll be there," Hanly said and hung up.

They drove slowly around Prospect Park in Angelo's six-year-old Ford. Angelo said, "I got a lead on the Calhane hit. It ain't concrete. But this much I know, if you guys can double your pressure on every joint operating in the five boroughs, I think it's possible that somebody might give you the hitter."

"Jesus, I don't know, Ange. We're limping along on like half pay now. Shutting down half the action is costing us hundreds of thousands of dollars a week."

"It was just an idea, Davey. Some people are sick and tired of being hassled and I think they could talk to certain other people. The Prizzis are only interested in one thing—getting the Department what it wants, the hitter, and getting back to business as usual for both sides."

"Lemme talk it over with my people. You got to be operating on information and you never had bad information. My people can go on the shorts if that will turn up the prick who shot that fine woman."

"It could speed things up for all of us, Davey."

Four days later, the police arrests clogged up every precinct house in the city, including Staten Island. The police redoubled their raids on handbooks and gambling houses. The hookers were driven off the streets and herded out of joints that had been protected by the pad for thirty years. What Dewey did to the prostitution business in the thirties, the NYPD was doing in spades to every moneymaker that the cousins had. The squads lifted sixteen million dollars in street price worth of narcotics. They came down so hard on bookmaking, on the street and on the phones, that nobody could figure the losses. The war affected seventeen separate national sports, which had created millionaire jockeys and tennis players, tens of thousands of golf courses, hockey rinks, and stadia, and a billion-dollar dependence on all of their stars by an army of barking media men and advertisers. Race tracks, ball parks, jai alai frontons, basketball courts, dashes, jumps, passes, throws, toboggan runs, yacht races, space shots, thoroughbred horses, shuffling fighters, and doped greyhounds generated sales of billions of dollars' worth of television sets, hundred of millions of gallons of beer. Each week, in bets alone, cost the citizens more than any foreign war. When the New York police shut all of this down it cost the media, the equipment manufacturers, and the air-conditioning industry—plus the team owners, and the thousands of players of the hundreds of industrialized games—the attention and patronage of the New York trading area, because if the games could not be bet upon they didn't exist for the people. But most of all it cost the direct recipients of all of that betting cash—the New York Police Department and the Mafia families and Syndicate affiliates.

Chapter Thirty-three

All police leaves were canceled. Rich hoodlums were arrested on sight and held for twenty-four hours before being booked, then arrested again as fast as the lawyers could get them out. The heat was heaviest on the Prizzis. The police had quickly made the connection between Filargi and the family's bank, which had been sold to Filargi's group, and Hanly tipped Angelo off, saying that every Prizzi phone had been bugged. All telephone contact with the house in Brentwood was broken. If such calls had to be made, they would be placed by either Vincent or Angelo from different public telephone booths.

Vincent was arrested twice; and his three *capi* and about two hundred of his button men, as if they were moving through a revolving turnstile.

"What is this?" he asked a sergeant named Keifetz from the borough squad. "This is the third time I been here in two days on the same thing."

"Who did the job on Mrs. Calhane, Vincent?" Keifetz asked him.

"Who's that?"

"The woman who was wasted when Finlay got snatched."

"How do I know? Everybody asks me! I don't know nothing!"

"Vincent, let me tell you something which is strictly inside, you dig? Your family owns twenty-five percent of Finlay's bank. That's the connection. Nobody else has any direct connection. Your people took Finlay and on the way out they murdered Mrs. Calhane."

"Keifetz, lissena me. What do I know about kidnaping? Am I crazy? I got a business. What do I need cowboy stuff for?"

The police weren't only tossing people in Brooklyn. They were just as grim about it in New York and the Bronx. Every time they broke up a mob score or bounced soldiers and workers around, they planted that the Prizzis had once sold their bank to Robert Finlay.

After eight days of being hassled the Bocca family called a meeting of the five New York families at a rented meeting room on the third floor of a straight bank on Fifty-first Street. The bosses attended with their *consiglieri*. The meeting was opened by Quarico Bocca, who controlled, among other things, about sixty-eight percent of the prostitution in the country.

"They ain't kidding around," he said. "They are costing us all money and they are going to keep leaning on us until we give them whoever hit that cop's wife. All I know is one thing here. The cops keep telling my people that the guy who was snatched the day the broad got it also did big business with the Prizzi family which everybody knows about anyway, including the Prizzis. Now I want to make this a short meeting. I want to put it to a vote that Vincent Prizzi and his *consigliere* take a break and talk it over then come back in the meeting and tell us what they're going to do about it. All right? Raise your hand if you are in favor." He sat down.

"Hold the hands. We don't need no hands yet," Vincent said, getting to his feet. "Angelo and me are going home now, we ain't going outside to have a meeting. Who do you think you are talking to? I am

Vincent Prizzi. When most of you people had holes in the ass of your pants or you was sticking up gas stations we was the biggest family in this country and now that some of you have learned how to run broads and roll drunks we can still buy and sell you. We lose more when the cops are in an uproar than any of you. We don't like it. But you ain't going to tell us how we run our business whatever it is and I ain't saying that what you are talking about is a part of it. We'll decide what can be done. If something can be done then we'll do it. Anybody here doesn't like it, you come and get us. We ain't taking any shit from any outsiders about family business. If you want a war, we'll get one for you. Otherwise do the best you can. Don't tell Prizzis how to run their business, and I mean most of all a scummy little pimp like you, Signore Fatalone," he said directly to Bocca.

He stood up. Angelo Partanna rose with him. They moved out of the meeting room, slowly and quietly, while the eight men around the table looked at their cigars.

They rode back to Brooklyn in Angelo's little Dodge. "You would think they would figure it out," Vincent said as they rode through the Midtown Tunnel. "Who has more to fall back on, us or the cops? We own the pad. They get their main juice from it. So they go ahead and bounce the guys around on the street for a couple of weeks. How much more? You think they're gonna go back living on their salaries after eighty-five years on the pad? Every dime they cost us, it costs them thirty cents. Sure, their heart bleeds for the dumb broad who pushed the wrong floor. They got to do that. It's a family thing. But all the time they are thinking of the business thing. They bounce us around, we don't pay them. They don't get paid, they hurt. Everybody understands they got to forget so we can get back to business. What I'm saying is, Angelo, is that Bocca lost his head in that meeting.

He wants to be a hero with cops he runs? He wants to insult Prizzi honor so it gets back to all the cops on his pad? You noticed nobody else wanted to push us around today, only Bocca. Well, whatta you think, Angelo?"

"Bocca has done so much time that he gets a little hysterical," Angelo said. "He is like a person who has a lot of accidents, they finally figure out that he don't know it, but he wants to have accidents. That is how Bocca is about spending time in a federal joint. His own people are beginning to figure him out and they don't like it."

"Why does anybody want to spend time in the joint? Hey! Look out for that crazy son-of-a-bitch! A woman. Jesus, every time there is a crazy driver it's a woman. Anyhow, why should Bocca want to be sent to the joint?"

"He has terrible luck with women. He treats them like they was some kind of beast," Angelo said. "He throws chairs at them when company is there. He makes them sleep on the floor sometimes. He breaks their dishes. No woman is going to take that kind of a life. So they make it impossible for him. His wife, his girls he has stashed around. They dump on him all the time. One of these days one of them is going to wire up his car. That's what his own people think."

"Maybe we should do it for them," Vincent said.

"Believe me, Vincent. He's going to suffer more the way he is."

"Who was the second man on the Filargi stand?" Vincent said.

"Only Charley knows. You said Charley should run it with his own people. Why, Vincent?"

"Why? What the meeting was about today is why."

"Vincent, we've got to move very carefully here. Kidnaping is a federal offense, which is the same as first degree. They burn people for it. The FBI has taken over. If we go fucking around with making cops

happy by turning in the second man on that stand,
then we are implicated as accessories before and after
and what is just a thing with New York cops becomes
a whole federal kick in the head."

"Yeah."

"Charley knows. Charley was on the job. The
Plumber maybe knows if the second man went out
with them. And Dom. But if anything goes wrong it's
only them guys who get it. *We* got no connection with
it. If the cops get the second man from us, they are
going to sweat it out of him who the other people
were. The other people—except Charley—might also
start to talk. They could pull us all into it so, from the
heart, Vincent, I am saying to you that the only thing
we can do is to forget any cooperation on whoever
shot that police captain's wife."

"I see what you mean."

They drove in silence through Queens and into
Brooklyn. "I was thinking about what my father
would do," Vincent said. "You know how he is about
family honor, well, that is how he sees what the police
are going through. The wife of one of their people got
it. They made a big reaction and now they can't back
down. We got to deliver. What I am saying is that Ed
can talk to them. He can show them why nobody can
turn in whoever shot that dumb broad because that
would tie them in with the Filargi thing and the whole
federal thing. Ed can say that we will deliver the *body*
of whoever made the hit, in any shape, manner, or
form that they say and with a complete signed confession shoved down his throat on delivery. When we
give back Filargi, he would make the ID. The television would take it from there. The papers would take
it from there. They would cooperate on the angle of
how the cops shot it out with this prick who hit the
broad who pushed the wrong floor and how they got a
confession then how he escapes and they have to gun
him down. Department citations, everything. They get

what they got to have and everybody goes back to business the way it is supposed to be."

"That could work. That is neat and tidy," Angelo said.

"I'll check it through with my father then we got to bring Charley in to give us the second man."

Angelo reached Charley at Brentwood that night.

"Charley, lissena me. You got to take the man by noon tomorrow at the latest. Come in tonight and get Irene and we'll set up the routine."

Angelo hung up.

Chapter Thirty-four

Eight hundred and twenty-six engraved invitations for the banquet at Palermo Gardens honoring Vincent Prizzi went out at the end of July for mid-September, causing high excitement and a lot of speculation in the family. The Palermo Gardens had always looked great inside Vincent's head, because he hadn't really seen it for fifty years, not since he was fourteen years old, attending his first big racket there. He had gotten laid that night for the first time. He still thought it had happened because his father had been the grand marshal. Getting laid to Vincent wasn't a big thing in itself. After that first time he could take it or leave it alone, but the first time had happened in the hat-check room with the forty-year-old hat-check girl who was only doing everything she could to get a renewal on the concession. Vincent thought of her as being ninety years old now, if she was alive, but a happy-minded person and a terrific piece of ass. In his mind, everything ran together into the splendor of Palermo Gardens itself.

Fifty years later Palermo Gardens was a dump that was still standing only because Corrado Prizzi wanted it that way. Palermo Gardens was his own memory, where he had brought all the people together to get his invisible hold on them, which had made the bank

possible, then the lottery, then everything else. It was
the social force of Palermo Gardens, the dances and
entertainments that he had organized for the people to
make them content, producing so many marriages and
children, establishing him as their leader the right
way, not with force. Palermo Gardens had made him
the center of their bounty and their confidence in him
had made possible the Prizzi family. The people still
saw Palermo Gardens as he saw it and as Vincent saw
it. The banquet for Vincent was a great triumph on
many levels, but none greater than on the level of
memory. The city had tried to condemn the building
four times in the last twenty years and each time Don
Corrado had told Ed to change their minds.

Angelo Partanna brought Maerose Prizzi and the
wives of two of the three *capiregime* to the banquet.
Special arrangements were made to get Don Corrado
there. Charley and Irene Partanna were busy making
plans for Filargi in Brentwood, and everybody wondered why Charley wasn't there. The three *capiregime*, Sal Prizzi, Rocco Sestero, and Tarquin Garrone,
formed a guard of honor to bring Vincent to the banquet in a black Lincoln limousine registered to the
Carolina Peach Congress, Inc., of Great Neck, Long
Island. Zingo Poppaloush was the driver. Everyone
wore a black tuxedo, with a white shirt and a black
bow tie; no faggy colors. A neighborhood crowd of
about forty people cheered as Vincent got out of the
car, because Rocco Sestero's people had organized it
as a little spontaneous tribute.

"Sit here and wait," Rocco told Poppaloush. "The
Boss wants the car right here when he comes out."

The three men surrounded Vincent, two in front
and one pushing behind him, and they propelled him
forward into the banquet hall. He was brought along
the aisles made by the crowded tables under the hanging streamers and the bunting and the garbage light

while everyone cheered hoarsely, men whistled deaf-
eningly through their fingers, women pushed up to
brush against him. Vincent tried to shake a few hands,
oozing forward through the excited crowd like a
heavyweight champion of the world after a popular
knockout. The force of the authority of the *capiregime*
got him to his place at the dais where Angelo Partanna had seated Maerose and the *capiregime's* wives.

A brigade of seventeen hired Bolognese and Vene-
tian cooks had been at work in the kitchens of the
Palermo Gardens since morning, preparing delectable
Sicilian dishes. Most of the banquet guests lived by
Sicilian food. The Prizzis certainly preferred it when it
was homemade, but when they ate out, and could control who cooked what, they had always used predictable cooks ever since Charley Partanna, nineteen
years before, had beat up an entire kitchen brigade for
what they had done to his mother's favorite dish,
focàccia di Fiori di Sambuco. For Vincent's banquet,
they were cooking for 735 heavy forks. There were
203 more people sitting down to eat than the Fire Department regulations of 1927 had allowed.

The guests were the elite of the Prizzi family: the
capiregime, their bravest soldiers, the outstanding ac-
countants, collectors, narcotics distributors and a few
dealers, bagmen, top labor-union leaders, pornography executives, stars, editors, the key suborners, the
top loan sharks, the senior fixers, the heavy muscle,
friends from the NYPD, and their wives. Although he
could not attend the banquet himself Ed Prizzi had
two tables down in front, which were honored by the
presence of six congressmen, five judges, and legal
counsel to the governor of the state. All the guests
lined both sides of strips of continuous tables on
sawhorses, which bore flowers, souvenirs, bottles of
wine, gleaming white linen and rented silver and
dishes. Everyone seemed to be manic with the idea
that they were going to see the legend, Don Corrado

Prizzi, the Caesar and Croesus of their time, walk into the spotlights on the dais in person. The noise was horrendous. Old friends greeted each other screaming across tables, rushing with outcries to embrace and kiss and laughing at everything because they were so happy.

The people at the dais sat, brilliantly lighted, under the eight-by-eight-foot sepia portraits of the men Corrado Prizzi admired most in the world: Arturo Toscanini, Pope Pius XII, Enrico Caruso, and Richard M. Nixon. They were his patron saints. At least one of them had been his long-time protector.

When everyone was seated, when each one was in his place on either side of the single empty chair on the dais, Cucumbers Cetrioli and Mango Passato brought Don Corrado into the building through the back door. When the old man appeared on the platform the applause and cheering were tremendous. Perhaps the applause would have been tremendous anyway, but Don Corrado, as always, had provided his entrance with insurance by having himself escorted by a man who neither he nor anyone else in the family had ever met before, who he had met for the first time twenty seconds before, who he knew his son regarded as the greatest *bel canto* singer in all history, although he, himself, preferred Enrico Caruso, the Italian master Giuliano Rizzo, whose manager had accepted a fee of twenty-five thousand dollars for the appearance, who had been flown directly from a benefit performance in New Orleans in an Air Force fighter-bomber in a special arrangement by Ed Prizzi with the Pentagon.

Before the 735 people, the don embraced one-eighth of the enormous tenor, then was lowered upon his seat while the crowd went wild with abandoned excitement.

The great singer stood facing them in a pool of pure emotion then, accompanied by an offstage piano, began Verdi's moving aria from *Les Vêpres Sicilienne*, which described the slaughter of the unarmed French by the Sicilian patriots.

People sobbed as he sang. Others were transformed to silence perhaps for the first time since their birth. When he finished the last magnificent note they all came to their feet, applauding maniacally, shouting hysterically, and weeping.

Rizzo kissed his hands and extended them in blessing to the family, bowed deeply, then disappeared from the building. The applause, whistling, and shouting ran on and on. Vincent stood up, raising his hands. For nine minutes he tried to quiet the exultation. Then Don Corrado stood, smiling. He did not raise his hands. He stood and smiled upon them and they understood that once again he had stopped at no expense or effort to bring them happiness. The shocking noise reduced itself to a clamor. The clamor became a few hundred voices; the voices fell into a murmur. Everyone sat down.

"We are here to honor my son," Don Corrado said simply. "He is going to leave us—" there was a shocked moan from the guests "—to live in a nine-hundred-and-twenty-five-thousand-dollar house overlooking his own golf course in Las Vegas, Nevada. I say to him, for you and from my heart—God speed you and God bless you, Vincent—and I present to him this small token of our combined esteem, the going-away present to which all of you have so lovingly contributed, a complete set of sterling silver golf clubs and five hundred of his favorite Mexican cigars." He smiled. The guests cheered. Sam Falcone and Willie Lessato came staggering across the platform under the weight of an elephant-hide golf bag that held more golf sticks than had been seen on the St. Andrews links throughout 1754. Phil Vitimizzare followed them, balancing twenty cigar boxes.

The banquet guests, stunned by Giuliano Rizzo,

pulverized by the unheard-of transfer of a Boss, all at once were brought to reality by the material manifestation and leaped to their feet, producing a response which almost—almost—matched what they had given to Signore Rizzo. A great surge of love and bodies carried several hundred of them toward the stage, reaching out to touch and congratulate, and Don Corrado was gently but swiftly moved out of the building by the three gift-bearers.

The three *capiregime* took charge. They formed a semicircle around Vincent and yelled at the people.

"Get the hell back to your seats!" Rocco Sestero bellowed.

"Whatta you think this is, a zoo?" Tarquin Garrone said.

"Get oudda here! Go ahead! Sit down, fahcrissake!" Sal Prizzi yelled.

The crowd moved back to their seats slowly. When the last banqueter was in his chair, Vincent stood up to address them.

A woman suddenly appeared at the back of the hall and screamed, "*Fire!*"

Instantly, the wall behind her burst into flame. Flames began to lick through the east wall at places and levels from the back of the large room to the stage. "Come on!" Vincent shouted. He grabbed his daughter's arm and pulled her behind him as he ran for the back door. Rocco Sestero followed him, pushing his wife. Angelo Partanna walked rapidly offstage toward the door. Sal Prizzi and his wife followed him and Tarquin Garrone closed in the rear. The phalanx gained momentum and crashed through, knocking down two waiters as they went. As they reached the alley and raced out to the street, Garrone stopped, cupped his hands over his mouth and shouted after them, "I'm going back for my sister." No one ever saw him again.

"Sal," Vincent said. "Get the women into a car. Rocco, stay with me and Angelo. The car's in front."

They sprinted to the black Lincoln. Vincent and Angelo piled into the back seat. Rocco got into the front beside the driver. "All right!" he yelled at Poppaloush, behind the wheel. "Get it going!"

Poppaloush sat there, disinterested. He didn't even watch the fire. Rocca stared into his face. "Holy shit, Boss," he said. "Somebody did the job on Zingo."

"What?"

"He's dead. They shot his fucking eye out."

"Then somebody lit that fire on us!" Vincent yelled. Hundreds of shocked, frightened people were pouring out of Palermo Gardens, embedded in black smoke that packed in around them like plague. "They did the job on Zingo so we would know they lit that fire on us. Am I right, Angelo?"

"Yeah. Right. Rocco, fahcrissake, dump Zingo and get us the hell out of here."

He leaned forward and opened the door next to the body. Rocco shoved it out into the street and got behind the wheel. The car moved slowly through the dazed crowd then roared away.

"Drive to my father's house then get to a phone and call my brother Ed to get ambulances over there and to handle the media so this don't come out like some gang massacre. Jesus, I can't get it through my head that somebody done this to us. Who would do it to us, Angelo?"

"Slow down, Vincent. You got blood pressure you gotta think about. We'll talk it out when we get to your father's."

"Listen, Rocco," Vincent said, "the first call you make is to get some soldiers over to the don's house. Whoever hit Poppaloush tonight—whoever set the fucking fire could try to get a shot at the don."

"We'll button up the whole house," Rocco said.

"Listen, Rocco," Vincent said. "The first thing you do is put six guys onna phone and they call all over town to find out who done this then we are gonna move my father outta town and blast the shit out of them."

Vincent and Angelo went slowly up the stone steps to the front door of the Sestero house. Vincent was breathing heavily and his face hung on his head like a gray mask. He pulled a large key chain out of his pocket and opened the door. A man with a sawed-off shotgun rushed forward as if to ram them but Angelo said, "Okay, okay, Freddo. It's the Boss."

"Jesus, sorry, Boss," the guard said. "There was no lights so I figure take no chances."

"You done right," Vincent said, brushing past him. The two men climbed the long flight of stairs to the first floor. Vincent leaned against the wall while Angelo knocked on the door to Don Corrado's room. "It's me, Corrado, Angelo," he said. "I'm with Vincent."

They heard the old man's voice calling out to tell them to come in. Angelo opened the door then stood aside for Vincent to go in first. Don Corrado was playing a complicated game of solitaire with three decks of cards. He looked up at them. "What happened?" he said.

Vincent fell into a chair. "You don't look good, Vincent," his father said. "Never mind what happened. Angelo will tell me. I want you to go across the hall to the bedroom. I want you to get undressed and get into bed. You have a night's sleep and we will talk tomorrow morning."

Angelo helped Vincent to his feet. "I feel lousy, Poppa," he said. He turned away and shuffled out of the room.

When the door closed, Don Corrado looked at Angelo.

"Somebody set Palermo Gardens on fire," Angelo said. "Just before that they shot Zingo Poppaloush. He was sitting in Vincent's car out front."

"Who did it?"

"The Boccas."

"Why?"

Angelo told him what Vincent had said at the meeting in the rented boardroom at the midtown bank. "He treated Bocca like a piece of shit in front of all the families. Bocca had to keep his honor. They are all going to back him up on this."

"How many were caught in the fire?"

"Vincent put Ed's people on the count with the cops and the fire department. We won't know until they put the fire out, like sometime tomorrow."

"How many do you think?"

"It was crowded, Corrado. They were all rushing for the front door when we left to go out the back door. It could be a hundred people. It could be a couple of hundred."

"That is the kind of revenge a pimp takes," Don Corrado said without inflection.

If anyone else had been listening they would have said that he felt nothing. But Angelo knew that Corrado felt the deep pain of a loss of honor and waited for what was to come.

"Vincent insulted him in front of the families so Bocca waited until all of our people were in one room and he had the torch put to it. Women were in there. Daughters were in there. What will the others say to that when they back Bocca up on what he did? There were big politicians in there—and five judges. There were at least three cripples at those tables tonight—what are the others going to say to that when they back Bocca up?"

"Corrado, no one is going to accuse Bocca of setting the fire. No one can prove who set the fire or maybe they can't even prove that the fire was actually started by anything but some accident."

"Then they are going to back Bocca for killing the young Greek, Poppaloush, for what Vincent, a Boss and my son, said to Bocca? Do you believe that, Angelo?"

"That is the formality of it, Corrado. That is what they will back Bocca on if we accuse him of the killing."

"What if we accuse him of setting that fire?"

"They will not back him on that. But they are fair. And they aren't all our friends. Some are Bocca's friends. They will ask for proof."

"Then we will wait a few months. When Charley gets back—because I am going to make a deal with Charley which he will accept—I want the people close to Bocca to die by natural accidents or bad illnesses. When only Bocca is left, surrounded by new people—and a few of the new people will be our people to get us the inside on his operation—we will have the police in eight or ten states move in on him and we will see that he is set up with consecutive sentences from a friendly judge to fifty years in the Federal prison on the Mann Act. We won't need the families to back us up on that because no one is going to be able to prove that we did it, any more than they can prove Bocca set the fire tonight."

Eighty-nine people burned to death in the fire at Palermo Gardens; 217 were severely burned; 4 were blinded. Miraculously, the congressmen and the judges came through the fire unharmed. Survivors were advised by Ed Prizzi's people to bring suit against the Palermo Gardens' owners but the building was owned, following a 1934 donation from its "anonymous" owners, by the blessed Decima Manovale Foundation Order, a nonprofit organization of religious ascetics who had taken vows of poverty.

Chapter Thirty-five

There were more cops at the Palermo Gardens fire than there were firemen: Mitgang, the commissioner, himself, chiefs in and out of uniform, captains, detectives, traffic cops, and plainclothes men. The PC, Vincent Mulqueen, in charge of the uniformed force, Joe Maguire, chief of detectives, and John Kullers, the chief inspector, stood apart from the mobs of police and firemen and, beyond these, a crowd of a few thousand pleasured citizens.

"How do you figure a thing like this?" Mitgang asked rhetorically.

"I can tell you where we start to figure it, Commissioner," Maguire said. "We can't figure the Prizzis set the fire themselves to get the insurance—although that's one of the few shots at grabbing money that they haven't taken—because every one of their top people were in there. No, sir. This fire is connected to the Calhane case."

"How?"

"Somebody—one of the families or all the families—is putting the pressure on the Prizzis to throw us the killer. It is absolutely one hunnert percent sure that the Prizzis snatched Filargi, and whoever snatched Filargi killed Vicky Calhane."

"The dirty prick," Chief Kullers said.

"Who makes the next move?" Mitgang asked.

"Corrado Prizzi is no dummy," Maguire said, "and that goes for Angelo Partanna. They have to be up there with the ten greatest schemers of all time. They have to be figuring out a way to give us the Calhane killer without any risk to them on the Filargi snatch."

"Yeah? How do they do that?"

"Believe me. They will figure a way. They have to move. After what happened tonight he knows that the families have declared war against him. They are leaning on him—and he knows this fire tonight is only the beginning—to force him to give us whoever it was who did the job on Vicky Calhane."

"So we wait?"

"We gotta wait, Commissioner," Chief Maguire said.

"What are you going to tell the press?"

"That's easy—and they'll eat it up. This is the whole nutshell. Gangland Orgy Results in Eighteen Deaths—or however many. Hoodlum Celebration Turns into Preview of Hell."

"Good," Mitgang said. "I think you got it figured."

The Palermo Gardens burned until 9:20 the next morning. During the night, while he was still with Corrado Prizzi, Angelo called the chief inspector's office and asked for Lieutenant Hanly. The cop who answered said Hanly wasn't there.

"Well, you better find him and tell him to call Angelo."

"Call *An*gelo? At one o'clock in the morning?"

"He lives in Brooklyn, doesn't he? All cops live in Brooklyn."

"What the hell is this?"

"Tell him to call Angelo, my friend."

Two hours later Hanly reached Angelo at Angelo's apartment. It was 3:10 A.M. They agreed to meet at Charley Partanna's apartment at the beach.

Angelo had hot coffee and some zucchini muffins ready when Hanly got there.

"Jesus," Hanly said, "I bet if you had known about the hours in your business, you woulda probably stood in Sicily."

"Who sleeps at my age?" Angelo said.

They sat down and Hanly got to work on the muffins. "What's this, fahcrissake! This is terrific!"

"That's one of my son's zucchini muffins," Angelo said. "He makes them up then freezes them."

"Charley can *cook*?"

"Charley is your typical all-around man," his father said. "Davey, listen—we know who tried to wipe us out last night."

"Who?"

"The Boccas."

"Yeah? How come?"

"Old Quarico Bocca is around the bend. He thinks Vincent insulted him."

"Well? Vincent did insult him. Right? At the Yariyaki Bank? Two days ago?"

"You guys are regular detectives," Angelo said. "Yeah. Vincent insulted him so Bocca set fire to a building which had the whole Prizzi family in it. Even Don Corrado himself was there last night."

"Still—you wouldn't have been wiped out exactly."

"No. There was a coupla dozen soldiers who wasn't there."

"Charley wasn't there."

Angelo didn't comment on that.

"Where was Charley, Angelo?"

"Charley went to Miami to meet a shipment that couldn't wait."

"When can I see Charley?"

"When he gets back."

"I can't resist it. I'm gonna have another muffin."

"I got a little surprise for you, Davey, I got another

haffa dozen muffins in a paper bag for you to take
with you.''

"I thought I was off the pad.''

"Never for zucchini muffins, Davey.''

Hanly buttered part of a muffin. "You have to admit that it is unusual for one of the New York families
to go to the cops about another family.''

Angelo shrugged.

"You guys have always been very strict about things
like that. Bocca tried to burn you down and that is
usually a thing about honor with you guys that you
pay them off yourself.''

"Nobody needs to tell Corrado Prizzi about honor,"
Angelo said. "We had a meeting. We decided that,
considering where the Department stands right now,
that this is no time to start a war with the Boccas,
that's all.''

"Yeah. It could also be that Prizzi didn't want to
start a war because he could be starting a war against
all the other New York families.''

"Why do you say that, Davey?''

"Look, Angelo. Why fuck around on this? At the
meeting at the Yariyaki Bank they all put it to Vincent
and you that they were tired of all the money going
out and none coming in. They told you they wanted
you to give us the Calhane killer so Vincent staged his
big insult scene and you walked out. Angelo, you
think only the families are pissed off about our clamp-
down? We are more pissed off than they are. We are
digging into our safe deposit boxes to stay alive and
comfortable the way it was meant to be. You guys
know and we know that the laws which keep the people from their pleasures, like gambling, shit, and
women, are not only impossible laws, but impossible
to enforce. You people don't have any pad for armed
robbery or arson or any other reasonable felony. We
nail you every time in your tracks when you pull any
shit like that. But gambling is a misdemeanor. Solicit-

ing is a misdemeanor. And we are not allowed to arrest the important half of any of those collars because the eager citizen who is out to put down a bet or get laid, the customer who causes the commission of the misdemeanors, isn't considered by the law to be any part of the offense. But the people have to have it so it throws off a lot of money. We both make money because, together, we supply the services the public wants. So this is costing us one huge pile of money, Angelo. Give us the piece man who hit Vicky Calhane and not only can we all get back to business, but I promise you we are going to look the other way when you go out to blow the Boccas off the street."

"You make one helluva case, Davey," Angelo told him, "but there's nothing else I can say."

Chapter Thirty-six

The Plumber was on duty outside the cellar door; Dom was sleeping upstairs. Charley went out of the kitchen, where the telephone was, to talk to the Plumber.

"That was my father. I got to go into town for a sit-down. I'll be back about eight in the morning."

"Bring me a couple of tit magazines."

"I'm embarrassed to buy them," Charley said.

"What?"

"I always think the guy will think that I think they are full of real girls instead of little pictures of girls. What good is a picture? How can anybody except a pervert get his jollies from a little picture?"

"I must be a pervert," Melvini said. "I like them."

"I cooked up a big beef stew. All you got to do is throw in a couple of cans of peas and carrots and cook the pasta to go under it."

"What kind of pasta?"

"*Farfalline*, the beef stew pasta."

"Make a big pot of coffee before you go, Charley. I am sick of Filargi complaining about Dom's coffee."

"Sure. See you in the morning."

Charley made the coffee then went out of the house and got into the Chevy van. It was five after one in the morning; no traffic. He would be at the beach by 4:30, catch a little sleep, then start back with Irene at 6:00 A.M. He'd have to work out with Pop the way they would keep in touch. He and Irene could go over their demands for giving Filargi back to the Prizzis on the way to Brentwood. He had to remember to bring a soft, heavy sap with him because he didn't want to hurt Dom or the Plumber, they were just workers and they were good guys. He and Irene would have to figure out a place to keep Filargi all during the negotiations. He would have to talk to Filargi and give him a feeling that he had something to hope for, the poor doomed son-of-a-bitch. They had to keep Filargi happy with the feeling that they were all screwing the Prizzis and that everything was going to work out great. A wave of bitterness hit him about losing Brooklyn, the sports book, Pop, and everything else he needed but, what the hell, he had got better than even money when he cashed in his bet on Irene. He had Irene. They could make it wherever they were going to have to go after the deal was made with the Prizzis so that the whole delayed ransom could finally get under way and so that Filargi could be sure to be arrested and tried when he was freed and reported to the police. What the hell. Filargi was an old guy. He had to be sixty-three years old and he had drunk heavy cream all his life.

Everything was going to depend on Pop. If they were going to get out of this with all their hair, he and Irene had to make a very hard deal, then Pop had to sell it to the Prizzis. Jesus, how he hated doing business with such devious people. Nobody in the whole deal had ever said what they meant the longest day of their life. Thank God Pop was the most devious of all of them, including even Don Corrado. Pop had a seven-tiered Sicilian brain so that when they said A to him, he knew right away that he should read it as Z but would always stand ready to switch it to the real meaning, inside the real meaning of the false meaning, which he would read as M.

He let himself into the apartment very quietly but Irene woke up just the same.

"Hey! Charley?" she said.

"Don't wake up. Go back. We got to leave here by six."

"To where?"

"Pop called and—"

"Turn the light on, I can't hear you."

He flipped the switch. Irene was sitting up in bed and her beautiful, blind boobs were staring at him just over the tops of the bed covers. "Jesus, Irene. You got a beautiful set."

"You already told me that. Tell me about Pop."

He sat on the edge of the bed and talked as he undressed. "Pop called. He said things were heating up and we should get Filargi out of Brentwood by noon at the latest."

"What happened?"

"That's all he could say. We're going to talk again as soon as we get Filargi stashed."

"Where are we going to stash him?"

"Well, we got a long drive tomorrow and a real short time tonight. We'll talk in the car. This is a bed." He threw back the sheet that covered her, gasped with pleasure, and fell upon her.

They left the apartment at the beach at five minutes to six and talked about what they were going to do with Filargi all the way out to Brentwood. Irene wanted to talk about what they would demand from the Prizzis and where they would go after they beat the Prizzis, but Charley said that they had to get Filargi first, then figure out where they were going to put him. "We got a logistics thing here," he said. "We can't take him like to your house in LA because we got to be near enough to deal with Pop, the middle-man. We can't take him where there are a lot of people around because by now, believe me, everybody knows his face."

"I know. Where we can put him, I mean."

"Where?"

"You put him to sleep in the back of the Chevy while I go out and rent a car and a big house trailer or maybe one of those trucks which are really like mobile homes and we'll keep moving. We'll drive out on the Island, way out, except when we have to meet Pop then we'll come a little further in and park the trailer in a trailer park."

"I was thinking more in the shape of a boat."

"A boat?"

"Like a cabin cruiser and we just cruise around the Great South Bay and Pop can get us on the ship-to-shore phone."

"That's great if you know how to operate a boat."

"I thought you just steer it."

"It's trickier than that. Besides, you ever been on a boat?"

"Once, at the boat show."

"The whole floor moves on the water. That's how people get seasick."

"The trailer is a better idea," Charley said. "A mobile home. Listen, maybe we'll like it. What's a better way to stay out of sight after we stick it to the Prizzis. We take it to Canada, then Alaska, and after a couple of years maybe the whole climate is changed."

"Sensational."

"How do we get one?"

"The Yellow Pages," Irene said. "There are even people who rent yo-yos in the Yellow Pages."

Two miles from the house, Charley pulled the van to the side of the road. It was a fine summer morning on the mariner's finger that pointed out to sea from New York. Charley said, "The Plumber will be up and Dom will be down. Dom is easy but the Plumber is an old campaigner."

"Why don't you go in the back, then I'll come in the front and get behind him," Irene said.

"Yeah. Good."

"When will the Prizzis find them?"

"Pop calls in at noon and at six. If nobody answers he'll send people out here. Okay? You all set?"

"Me? What do I have to do except keep the Plumber from shooting you?"

Charley drove into the driveway of the isolated house. He got out of the car and moved around the house to the back door. As soon as he was out of sight, Irene left the van and moved in the opposite direction to the front of the house. As Charley was letting himself in the back door, Irene was opening the front door, under a wide porch.

Charley moved into the kitchen. Halfway to the refrigerator he heard the Plumber's voice behind him.

"Hey, Cholly!" Melvini said.

Charley spun around. His back was to the front of the house. Melvini faced the direction of the front door with the door into the dining room at his left. Melvini had a .38 Police Special in his right hand. It was pointed at Charley's stomach.

"What's the piece for?" Charley asked.

"You were going to take the big banker out of here, hey, Charley? Jesus, that could make the Prizzis kind of sore."

"What are you talking about?"

"We all got a job here, Charley. I am the telephone man. I record all the calls on a tape machine and I got you and Angelo when he called you last night."

"Then I'm a dummy."

"Charley, I don't know a smarter cat than Angelo. If he has you taking the banker out of here, then we

are talking heavy money. If it's rich enough for you
and Angelo then I want in."

"*In?*"

"If we can make a deal, I'm your man."

"How much are the Prizzis paying you for your
stand?" Charley asked.

"Fifteen dollars."

"We'll pay fifty."

"When?"

"As soon as we settle with the Prizzis."

"How much do you figure they owe you?"

"Plumber, you were okay with fifteen dollars. Now
it's fifty. That's all you need to know."

Melvini grinned. "You're right, Charley. What do
we do now?"

"We put the piece away."

The Plumber tucked the revolver in his belt at the
small of his back. Irene moved into the kitchen at his
direct left, ten feet away, in the doorway to the dining
room, holding a gun on Melvini. "You made the best
deal you ever made, Plumber," she said, smiling that
gorgeous smile.

That broke the Plumber up. He laughed so hard it
rattled the dishes. "They doubled on you and I make
a big deal out of it," he managed to say, "and all the
time you are doubling on me."

"What the hell, Al," Charley said, grinning. "Doubling is just kid stuff."

Charley and the Plumber tied Dom to the bed,
making him as comfortable as possible. "Listen, I
could starve to death here," Dom said. "You take off
with the client while I could starve here."

"Come on," Charley said, "how can you starve?
They'll call in at noon and when nobody picks up,
they'll come out here."

"Listen, I'm the one who is in the shit," Dom said.
"At least I am entitled to a good breakfast."

"All right," Charley said. "Make him some breakfast."

"Not him!" Dom protested. "Did you ever try to eat it when this guy cooks it? You make it, Charley. Some fried pasta with a little tomatoes, a little garlic; some scrambled eggs with little peppers. What do you say?"

"Ah, shit," Charley said, and hit him with the sap.

When the two men went upstairs, Irene went to the classified phone directory. She found what she wanted, made the call and arranged to go into Bay-shore to get one mobile home. When the two men came downstairs to organize Filargi for the journey she told Charley that the trailer was all set. "It's one of those complete units on a big truck, Charley," she said, "just like you wanted. But I got to drive in to get it, then I need somebody to get the Chevy back here."

"What did I tell you?" Melvini said. "These jobs got to have three people."

"How long you going to be?" Charley asked.

"Maybe an hour, maybe more," Irene said.

"It's eight-twenty. Figure two hours. Be back here at half past ten and I'll have him ready to go."

"We going to miss the twelve o'clock call?"

"That's what my father wants," Charley said.

When Irene and the Plumber left, Charley went to the ice box and got out the stuff to make himself some fried pasta with some tomatoes and a little garlic and some scrambled eggs with peppers. At 9:20 he had eaten and cleaned up the kitchen and he went down the cellar stairs to the padlocked door. He unlocked, talking through the door as he did, then he went into the room.

"How are you?" he asked Filargi, who was fully dressed in a neat little blue suit, a white shirt, and a blue tie with small silver figures on it. The last time he had come out from New York, Charley had brought him three new shirts, three changes of underwear and, at Filargi's request, a tin of black shoe polish and a shoe brush.

"I'm all right," Filargi said.

"Food all right?" It was Charley's cooking.

"Excellent. Really delicious."

"You got enough books?"

"Well—"

"We'll get more books for you," Charley said. "Tell me something, you know who grabbed you?"

The banker made one short, emphatic nod. "The Prizzis," he answered. "And I know why. When I get out of here, if I get out, which doesn't seem likely, I am going to spend the rest of my life pinning this on them."

"You're a real feisty little guy," Charley said. "Now lissena me. We are taking you out of here. The Prizzis don't control this anymore."

"Why?"

"That is a private reason between me and the Prizzis. But it could be a better deal for you. At least there is nobody to tell us that we got to do the job on you. And, if it works out a certain way—" by that Charley meant if the Prizzis refused to meet his terms "—it could be a better deal for you all around because the Prizzis figured to take the bank away from you and I ain't got no use for your bank."

"Well, the way things are, what have I got to lose? What do you want from me?"

"Just cooperate. That's all. Just cooperate. You ready for some breakfast?"

"Yes, I am. I certainly am."

"Then come on. We'll go upstairs and you can eat in the kitchen for a change."

Chapter Thirty-seven

The two men of respect, Vincent Prizzi and Angelo Partanna, sat in the thirty-by-thirty, six-window office of Ed Prizzi on the sixty-seventh floor of the United Insurance Industries building, which Prizzi capital had built, and which the Prizzis owned.

Ed Prizzi sat behind a massive early Georgian table, which was his desk, holding in his hands the letter from Charley Partanna that threated the wreck Corrado Prizzi's monument, a seventy-million-dollar heist.

Vincent's eyes had curdled. He had not been able to speak once on the journey from Brooklyn to Ed Prizzi's office because his own man, the traitorous Charley Partanna, had deliberately emasculated him before the eyes of his father by directing the letter to his brother who was not even supposed to have anything to do with the part of the Prizzi business that this letter concerned.

Vincent had worked himself into an erratic anger but Angelo Partanna was objective, wary and cold. His single interest at the meeting was to use Ed Prizzi's sudden superiority over his older brother to secure the survival of his own son and the assurance that he, Angelo Partanna, was the only possible choice of go-between to repossess Filargi, so that he and Charley could proceed with their plans.

"'Dear Ed,'" Eduardo Prizzi read aloud from Charley's letter, "'You are probably hot right now because we took Filargi but when you hear the score at least you and your father are going to understand why there was no other way we could go.

"'Vincent put out a contract on me.'"

Vincent roared, "What the fuck is that? He's crazy. If I put out a contract on him he'd be blown away by now."

"Vincent, lissena me," Ed said. "You want to hear this letter then you sit there and keep your mouth shut. This is maybe sixty-seven million dollars here that's got to be renegotiated to get it back. So shut up and listen to this."

He picked up the message smoothly where he had been interrupted.

"'Naturally, he'll say it's a lot of bullshit but it so happens he hired my own wife and he gave her a down payment of fifty dollars, and my wife is sitting right here beside me while I write this down, laughing like hell. I personally think Don Corrado found Vincent on his door step because Vincent is like fifty times too dumb to be a Prizzi.'"

Ed looked up and grinned at his brother. "I never knew Charley was such a joker," he said, "lissena this.

"'So, the first thing I got to have before you get Filargi back is that you deliver Vincent to me where I tell you, when I tell you.

"'Don Corrado told my wife that he would forget the whole business about Louis Palo and the three hundred sixty dollars if she paid back the three sixty plus fifty percent. Now, from past experience with the Prizzi policy, it could be that Don Corrado was going to have my wife clipped after she paid back the money. Therefore, the second thing we got to have before you get Filargi back is that you pay to my wife the seven hundred twenty dollars she had to give up out of the Vegas scam, plus the fifty percent penalty on the three hundred sixty, plus the difference of fifty dollars which Vincent Prizzi would have had to pay her for giving her the contract on me. That is only the side money.'"

Vincent was the color of a bouquet of flowers. His blood pressure had taken off because of outrage and fear. His breathing was shallow. He made choked sounds while Angelo got out of his chair and patted him softly on the back, making comforting sounds.

"We are trying to do business here," Ed Prizzi said, his face as long as a horse's and as seriously disapproving. "You're going to have your chance at a stroke later, Vincent. Calm down, fahcrissakes."

"Charley is dead," Vincent said. He remembered Angelo and turned to him. "I'm sorry, Angelo," he said, "but Charley is strictly dead."

"Listen to Ed, Vincent," Angelo said softly. "For seventy million dollars."

"'For the main money, this is what I want,'" Ed continued reading from the letter. "'Twenty-three hundred and fourteen dollars and some change for expenses. That's what I figure it's going to cost me for the three weeks while you set it all up. Then I want fifty dollars for the fee for my helper and, of course, the fee that was promised to my wife as second man in the Filargi stand.'"

Ed looked up with surprise. "Charley's *wife* was the second man?" he asked Angelo incredulously.

Angelo nodded. "She was right," he said. "She was the only way we could take out the bodyguard."

Vincent passed a deadly look to Angelo. Angelo had held out on him.

Ed went back to reading from the letter. "'Then I want all of the full insurance coverage on Filargi's kidnap policy which is two million five hundred thousand. Altogether, that comes to eleven hundred to my wife, fifty for extra labor, the twenty-three fourteen for expenses, and two and a half million from the policy. That makes a total of $3,652,314—plus Vincent.

"'There is only one man I trust to deal with, my father. Talk it over. Make your mind up. If you want to do business, run the house flag of the New York Athletic Club on the pole on the thirty-third-floor terrace of the building at ten after twelve on Thursday. That gives you two days. When I see the flag I'll send you the letter about how we'll work this out. Charley.'"

The only sound was Vincent's breathing.

Ed Prizzi said briskly, "Look at it this way. On seventy million dollars that is only an eight percent sales cost if we were paying out the two and a half million. But we aren't. The insurance company pays and the premiums are deductible, so what we are looking at here is a sales cost of like two point two percent, plus overhead, to get the whole bank back. Listen, how can we not recommend a deal like that?"

"How? I'll tell you how," Vincent yelled. "Because I'm a part of the fucking sales cost, that's how."

"Come on, Vincent!" his brother said. "Charley is just making a point! That is negotiable. Right, Angelo? Am I right?"

Angelo put an arm across Vincent's shoulders. "You know Charley, fahcrissake, Vincent. You know he's got to make his point. It's a thing like honor with him. All right. He made his point. Now we dangle the three million six in front of him and we tell him take it or leave it and he takes it."

"Fahcrissake, Vincent. You don't think we would turn you over to Charley, fahcrissake?" Ed said. He didn't wait for an answer. "I am not saying the whole wad, Angelo. After all, what is negotiating? We make him an offer, then we settle."

"You never worked with Charley, Ed," Vincent said. "He don't settle. He is a very straight boy. If you want Filargi you are going to have to pay all the money." He left the rest of the payoff unmentioned.

"Then let's go over to Poppa's and get this thing settled," Ed said. He handed Angelo Charley's letter. Angelo folded it and put it into an inside pocket.

The three men rode down in the elevator just as silently as all the other passengers, no more, no less. Ed copped a feel from a nice-looking young head standing just ahead of him in the elevator car. She turned around and smiled at him. He got so hot that he would have gone out with her if Angelo hadn't grabbed his arm and held him back.

When they got to the entrance on Fifty-sixth Street, they were starting out to the curb when Ed said, "I got to pick up a Wall Street closing," and turned back toward the newsstand. A blue Oldsmobile 98, which had been parked fifty feet down the street, moved and sedately passed the three men, who were at different distances from the curb: Angelo was a few feet back of Vincent, turning to acknowledge Ed, who was ten feet farther back, turning toward the building, when Cheech Scaramanzia of the Bocca family opened rapid fire from the blue car as it went past. Vincent went down. The blue car moved out and turned with the stream of traffic at the avenue. Ed came running out of the building.

Chapter Thirty-eight

Vincent Prizzi was dead on arrival at the Roosevelt Hospital. Angelo Partanna and Ed Prizzi had faded into the crowd, watching the ambulance crew take Vincent away. Angelo told Ed to go back to his office, stopped a taxi and followed the ambulance to the hospital. Within ten minutes he had bribed two nurses and three orderlies so that he could sit in the visitors' room on the emergency floor and receive the medical bulletins. When it was confirmed that Vincent was dead, he telephoned Ed from a booth and told him he was on his way to Brooklyn to tell the don.

"Who did it?" Ed whispered in the phone.

"The Boccas."

"How's Vincent?"

"He's gone."

"That's terrible," Ed said into the telephone. Two large tears ran out of his dark eyes. "It's going to be very hard for Poppa."

"He's strong," Angelo said.

"Well, at least, now we won't have to give Vincent to Charley."

"No," Angelo said. "But the fact is something happened to Vincent. He lost it. He was a tremendous man, I never saw a tiger like him from the time he was just a kid, but something snapped and he lost it."

"It was the daughter," Ed said. "She wore him down. Well, you better go over and break the news to Poppa."

Angelo paid off the cab in front of the Sestero house at five minutes to six. He climbed the front steps and the door opened when he got to the top. Amalia was waiting for him in a front room, her face ravaged by grief. Angelo held her in his arms, patting her shoulder, murmuring softly. "Poppa can't understand why everybody is so late," she said.

Angelo climbed the stairs slowly and knocked on the double doors of the room that faced west. He could hear the voice telling him to come in. He entered, closed the doors behind him and walked toward Don Corrado.

"Who is dead?" the old man asked.

"Vincent."

"Who did it?"

"The Boccas."

"How?"

"Outside the building."

"You saw it?"

"Yes."

"He missed you?"

"I was about eight feet back. Ed was getting a paper. They were only looking for Vincent anyway."

The little old man looked out at Manhattan, caught in the dying heat of the summer light, the buildings standing like a crowd waiting to get into a bathhouse. "Vincent was a lovable man," he said. "He was shy, he couldn't show anything, but he felt everything. He loved his family. He lived for honor."

"We won't forget him," Angelo said.

"He was such a man. Then—I don't know—he got old. Something happened. He lost it. I told him he had enough and he agreed with me. Then I had Charley over here for lunch a couple of days ago and I told him he was going to take over Vincent's job. He will hold everything together."

Angelo felt a pain go through him that came up through his stomach and across through his left arm and it knocked him right straight down into a chair. "Angelo, *An*gelo," the old man said. "Jesus, you been under a terrific strain today. You ain't no kid. You got to take it easy."

Angelo got a vial of pills out of his right jacket pocket, took off the top very slowly, shook two pills out, and popped them into his mouth. Don Corrado handed him a half glass of red wine and he washed the pills down.

"I'm okay now," Angelo said.

"Can you talk or do you want to rest for a while?"

"I can talk," Angelo said. "Give me a full glass of that wine and I can sing."

The don poured out a glass of red wine carefully. He sat down in the Morris chair facing his *consigliere*. "What did the Filargi letter say?" he asked.

"Charley wants the earth," he said, drawing the letter out of his pocket. He opened it carefully on his lap, put on a pair of wire-framed eyeglasses and read the letter through, aloud, to Don Corrado.

"You know what?" the old man said. "I can see now that Charley thought I was setting him up when I told him he had Vincent's job."

"Well," Angelo said, "that's the way Sicilians think."

"Vincent's daughter wanted to make her suffer. Maybe they were two of those kind of people who are put here, side by side, to make each other suffer. That's why he put out a contract on Charley. He told himself that Charley made him suffer so she made Vincent suffer and he loved her and he wanted to have a life with her like a father and his daughter have a right to have a life, and then when Charley married the woman who ripped us off with Louis Palo in

Vegas, I suppose he just collapsed inside. He put out the contract on Charley, and because everything was against him by that time, he had the bad luck to pay Charley's wife to do the job on him.''

"I seen it go like that, too, Corrado. Vincent lost it. It all ran out of him.''

"Well, what did we expect from Charley—if we knew. He thinks I set him up so he wouldn't suspect anything while Vincent sends out a specialist to hit him, so he naturally figures that when I tell his wife that she can pay back the money and a penalty, because she is Charley's wife and we don't do numbers on wives, that I am only telling her to get the money and then set her up so our people can hit her. Charley is a man. He has to protect his wife. He has to fight back. And he does it with the fire that he gave to his family from the time he was a thirteen-year-old kid and he took Little Phil Terrone up in the Bronx. So we got to straighten this thing out. Sure, Ed wants to get the bank back and win the seventy million, and so do I, but just as much I want to get this all straight with Charley. Who is going to negotiate this?''

"Me."

"Good. All right, set the first meeting. Tell him that he's got to make the final deal with me. Tell him to come here. Lunchtime is good because he likes to eat but he's going to be tense so he can't enjoy it, so make it around five o'clock in the afternoon of a sunny day—if it rains we'll wait until a sunny day comes along—and tell him to come here. Tell him my daughter Amalia will go out and wait with his wife wherever he says—only you will know where—so that if I am lying to him, if I betray him, then the wife can take my favorite daughter. We've got to straighten this out with Charley.''

Chapter Thirty-nine

The mobile home that Irene rented had been built on a Macktruck chassis in 1961, and either it had been mothballed for fifteen years or they had built much better automobiles then. The housing was designed to provide two bedrooms, a combination living room and dining room, a galley, a toilet and a shower. Up front, behind the driver's seat, was a wide, comfortable bunk. Charley relieved the Plumber with the driving for two hours every five hours. The Plumber slept, when he wasn't driving, in the driver's bunk, which within two days he had decorated with nude beaver shots from the national magazines. The Plumber was the only student of the media on the team and didn't look at the news columns. The others never thought about reading a newspaper because they figured they knew what was happening, and that was what the newspapers would be conjecturing upon, and they had neither radio nor TV with them.

Not that they didn't know what was happening. Irene always looked at the headlines when she went shopping in towns along the way for food. But she didn't go shopping very often because Charley didn't think it was a good idea. "The vegetable department is always handled by a wop and they have brothers and cousins who could be looking for us," he said.

"Believe me, Don Corrado has a long arm." Still, Irene's eye caught a headline about the fire at Palermo Gardens and she brought the paper back to the truck. Charley and the Plumber were almost sick when they read the names on the list of people who had been burned in the fire. They had known every one of them for all of their lives. "This is the worst single thing I ever seen in my life," the Plumber said, "Jesus! Mary Gingarola! I almost married Mary Gingarola." He dropped the paper and turned away. They were took sick about it to read past the list and the front page. They never made the connection with the Boccas. They were away out on the Island after that, so they missed the news about Vincent getting hit.

Irene and Charley handled the shopping, the cooking, and the cleaning up. Filargi was settled in the forward bedroom. Charley had rigged a heavy shutter over its window for when they were parked, but the shutter was left open when they were running, which was most of the time.

The truck moved on a regular pattern between Riverhead and Montauk, going out to the end of Long Island along the South Shore roads, as far out as Montauk Point, coming back through Sag Harbor and taking the ferry from Shelter Island to Greenport to cruise the North Shore. As much as they could, they stayed off the main highways. At night, whenever they could they parked at trailer camps for water hookups. On the fourth day, the second day after Charley's letter had been delivered in New York, Irene took the morning train in from Riverhead, took a cab from Penn Station to Fifty-sixth Street and checked out that the house flag of the New York Athletic Club was flying from the thirty-third-floor pole. When that was confirmed she sent a messenger to Ed Prizzi with the second letter.

The second letter made simple demands. It said that Angelo Partanna was to take the Long Island Railroad to the Jamaica station, in the fourth car on the train, and was to wait on the platform to be contacted. Charley knew there was no chance of the Prizzi's notifying the police for a stakeout, and no chance that they would do anything but comply with the letter of the contract because of the amount of money involved for them, but the Jamaica station platform was a crowded place when three full trains came in to exchange passengers and the crowd would be the buffer until he could get Pop away.

Charley walked Pop through two trains, across three platforms, then down EXIT steps to the street, padlocking the gate after them to stop anyone who might have the idea of following them. The Chevy van was waiting at the foot of the EXIT stairs and they drove away just as clear as everyone, on both sides, had intended.

"How're you doing, Pop?"

"I got a couple of surprises, Charley. You want to talk about it now?"

"Now is when, Pop."

"The Boccas hit Vincent."

"What? *WHAT?*"

"They clipped him in front of the building."

"What is this? What are they starting up here?"

"The official reason is that Vincent dumped on the Boccas at the meeting about the police captain's wife in front of everybody so Bocca had no choice, but the real reason is what the meeting was about—the cops are outta their heads to get their hands on the second man who did the job on that woman, the cop's wife."

"I don't get it, Pop."

"Well, the Boccas hit Vincent to tell us that if we don't hand over the second man then they are going to hit somebody else in the family until we give them the second man to give to the cops because the cops are pouring the heat on the Boccas, which are the weakest family in New York because of the business they're in."

"Fuck them all," Charley said. He was driving slowly, making his way south. "Can't they see the standoff or don't they give a shit?" he asked.

"Charley—the answer is that anybody who knows can see the standoff. If we give them Irene, then Irene tells the cops everything about the Filargi snatch. Either that or she holds out and tells them nothing because they can't prove she was on the snatch, but unless Filargi is released so he can be arrested, the Prizzis can't get the seventy million bucks' profit when we buy back the bank, but when Filargi is arrested, he is going to identify Irene as the one who did the job on that cop's wife."

"Then you are telling me the Boccas want it this way? That no matter what the Prizzis do, if they turn the second man in, they get their backs broken?"

"If they turn Irene in, the Boccas take the credit with the cops. The heat comes off them. Then when Irene talks, and drags the Prizzis into the Filargi snatch and the two killings, the Boccas grab what they want. I'm not saying the Boccas know anything right now, but everybody is going to know it when the second man starts to talk."

"So with all those edges, they had to give it to Vincent."

Angelo shrugged. "They got their honor, too, Charley. Vincent's funeral is tomorrow from Santa Grazia's."

"I'm sorry I'm going to miss it." Funerals, births and weddings had great significance in the Prizzi family.

"You want to talk about the deal or do you want to wait till your people can listen?"

"I want to hear it now."

"The money you asked for is okay, et cetra, et cetra. Don Corrado personally okayed the entire package."

"You mean that's it? We don't negotiate? They are going to just give in—like that?"

"Well, not exactly, Charley, but let me tell you something first. I go to Don Corrado as soon as I see Vincent's death certificate at the hospital and he starts talking as soon as I give him the bad news. He talks about Vincent, then he tells me that he had fixed everything for Vincent to take over the sports book in Vegas and represent the Commission there. He tells me he had already told you that you was going to take Vincent's place as Boss. How about that?"

Charley was stunned. He stopped the car, pulling over. "You mean he wasn't setting me up? He was leveling? He was going to move Vincent out and move me up?"

"Yeah."

"Jesus, I don't know what to say."

"He only had one thing on his mind after I read your letter to him. He said twice that he had to straighten this thing out with Charley. That is all that is on his mind. He's got to get it all straight with you."

"Pop,—"

"You know how I see it, Charley? He wants that seventy million, sure. But Vincent is gone. Corrado and I are old men. He's gotta have you back to run the operation. Who else is going to do it? Nobody. They are all second men. That's why I told you that he is ready to give you everything, et cetra, et cetra. I'm a messenger boy here. I'm not the negotiator. Corrado wants you to go to him and talk to him so that he can straighten this whole thing. It's a tremendous deal."

Charley sat staring at a DRY CLEANING sign. He thought of becoming Boss of the Prizzi family. His entire life had pointed him toward that. He had trained for that since he was thirteen years old and now it could happen. He could feel the power as if it were the texture of fine, strong cloth between his fingers. He could taste it as if his mother had come back to

cook one more glorious meal for him. He thought of
the money. Vincent must have been good for eight
million dollars a year, every dime tax free, every dime
safe in Switzerland then reinvested in the thousand
ways that Ed Prizzi had set up. He thought about the
respect that everyone would have to pay. "It's good
but it's also dangerous," he said.

"It's a lot of things, Charley, but it's not
dangerous."

"You feel you can personally guarantee that, Pop?"

"I could always guarantee you. And I can guarantee
me. Even after fifty years with Corrado, I couldn't
usually make the same guarantee for him, but Vincent
is dead and Corrado needs you, Charley. He has to
have you as insurance for the family and he also has it
in his head that the seventy-million-dollar bank deal is
his monument. Looking at the whole thing, yeah—I
can guarantee to you that there is no danger for you to
meet with him at the Sestero house."

"When?"

"The day after the insurance company pays off for
Filargi."

"Don Corrado will have that money, I won't. I'm
not giving up Filargi until we are all straight."

"Look, Charley—it has to be the day after the
payoffs because the payoff is going to be happening all
around the world, the way he has it set up, but by the
time you meet with him, the money will all be confirmed and Filargi will have to be freed. It breaks the
whole logjam here. They pay off for Filargi. You meet
with Corrado and make your deal, then you release
Filargi, the cops grab him, and Corrado moves into
position to buy his bank back for ten cents on the
dollar."

Chapter Forty

The payoff for Filargi in Lagos, Hong Kong, Aruba, Panama, and São Paulo happened at the moment of Vincent's interment in the earth of Staten Island at the Santa Grazia di Traghetto cemetery amid the immense necro-architecture of high-rise marble tombs and monuments that recalled Prizzi, Sestero, and Garrone departed.

The funeral had been quietly spectacular. Vincent was one of the last of the old guard *mafiosi* who had been born across the ocean in Agrigento, and his last rites brought dignitaries, of organized crime and of secular life, from all over the United States and included a representative of the Spina family, who had been Don Corrado's sponsors and in-laws in Sicily. The newspaper estimate of the value of the flowers was put at "about" sixty-five thousand dollars. All national TV networks had their cameras at the church and at graveside. The attorney general, the secretary of the interior, the head of the FCC, six governors, and eleven senators personally telephoned their condolences to Don Corrado or to Ed Prizzi. The mourners assembled before the requiem mass in a sea of black garments; the black unshaven cheeks of Sicilian men were yet another sign of grief. A brass band, dressed solemnly, played outside the church as the casket was carried to the black hearse for transport across the Verrazano Narrows Bridge to its final rest.

Don Corrado stood at his son's graveside amid eight saddened bodyguards, engrossed in prayer, while the bishop intoned the collective farewell. Maerose Prizzi tried to throw herself into the grave upon the casket while sixty-four altar boys, dressed with the simulated wings of angels, sang a popularized version of Verdi's *Requiem*, transcribed by Scott Miller, which was simultaneously being recorded as a musical memory by a Prizzi-owned recording label.

Angelo Partanna worked his way through the crowd to Don Corrado's side and, putting a comforting arm around the frail shoulders, whispered softly through the sweet air of the perfect summer's day and said, "The money is in Zurich." Don Corrado blew his nose.

They returned to the house in the late afternoon to wait out the twenty-four hours until Charley would appear.

"How about we head out to Montauk and do a little surf fishing?" the Plumber said.

"Why not?" Charley said. The Plumber went out the back door to walk around the truck to the driver's seat. They were on their way in three minutes.

Irene said, "Does it still feel right, Charley?"

"No matter how I add it up it comes out that we got to win. No running. No face jobs or new paper. We pick up all the points, plus we run the whole thing from now on. Did you ever think you'd be married to the Boss of the biggest family in the whole country? It's fantastic."

"You are fantastic. If it wasn't for you we'd be up that creek."

"I don't know how it happened," Charley said, "but I'm not going to believe it until I hear it from Corrado Prizzi."

"Let's find a drugstore phone booth somewhere and I'll wait there tomorrow night so you can call and tell me how it went."

"Yeah! Anyway, we got to set up where we'll meet because the next step is that we have to spring Filargi, the poor bastard." He turned and stared compassionately at Filargi's door. "However that works out we're going to need the Chevy so why don't you and the Plumber figure to be in Brentwood where the van is at say six-thirty, seven tomorrow night and I'll call you there."

"Fantastic," Irene said.

Charley took the train from Smithtown to New York at two P.M. the next day.

Don Corrado wept as he spoke to Charley about Vincent. He went back to the family's earliest days in New York, when Vincent had been a small boy, and they had lived on Mulberry Street in Manhattan. "He was a serious boy, even then," Don Corrado said. "We had so much trouble keeping him in school because he wanted to help me to get the business started. The Spinas, my wife's people in Agrigento, were able to arrange good credit for me to be able to import cheese and olive oil. I began to expand out to Brooklyn. By the time we moved everything to Brooklyn Vincent was twelve years old and I had to beat him every day to make him go to the school, and he went until I was too busy to be able to think about it, just a few months more. I had the bank going by that time—a small, store-front bank for the Italian people of Brooklyn—and the idea came to me that with a bank behind me I could start an Italian lottery. It was a colossal success but I needed someone to run it so that I could go on expanding. I wrote to Pietro Spina in Agrigento, *the* friend of the friends, and he sent your father to me in 1926, when he was a young man of seventeen years, and he arrived just in time, right in the middle of Prohibition, so we prospered, we became successful. Your family has a great place within my family. The Prizzis and the Partannas have worked side by side for almost sixty years. Your father is my most important friend, my oldest and dearest friend, and now the great circle has come to rest and you are here to take up my work just as your father took it up for me so long ago. My son is taken from me and now you shall be the son of my family. I name you now, under your oath of obedience and silence, to be the Boss of the Prizzi family's most sacred operations. Do you accept, son of my friend and son of my family?"

"You have honored me, *Padrino*."

"We will seal that," the don said, taking a straight pin from the lapel of his jacket. He pricked the end of his forefinger with the pin and a droplet of scarlet blood appeared. He held the finger out to Charley, who licked the blood away. "You have gained," Don Corrado said. He took up Charley's hand and pricked his forefinger. When the blood appeared, he licked it away. "We are now of one mind and substance. My enemies are your enemies. My will becomes your will."

Charley felt dizzy with the power he had just received. "I will serve you well, *Padrino*," he said huskily.

"To the business," Don Corrado said briskly, blowing his nose. "The Plumber must go. His betrayal of the family on this Filargi matter must be faced. Also he now knows too much about you and your father. Soon he could be drinking and talking about how he worked both sides. Besides, he did what he did only for more money, I am sure. Isn't that right?"

"Yes."

"He wasn't defending his marriage, as you were. He wasn't even acting out of loyalty to you, his *sottocapo*. He betrayed his family only for money. If he had been loyal to me, he would have agreed to join you and your wife so that he could do the job on *you*. He dishonored me. Let him finish this job with Filargi. Let him believe I have forgiven him. In a week or two have your people handle it."

Charley was disgusted with himself. He had blown his first chance to show that he was a real leader. But he had learned a lesson.

"But that is incidental. We are talking about my monument, Charley. Listen to how you must release Filargi so that, step by step, it will lead to his arrest, his trial, his disgrace, his conviction, the shaming of the bank, and its return to my family for ten cents on the dollar." The old man shoved a box of Mexican cigars at Charley, talking enthusiastically. "The insurance company has paid over the money and it is now in the bank in Zurich. Beginning tomorrow, at any time you say, your share—the whole two and a half million—will be transferred to your own account."

Charley grunted, deep in his stomach, with emotion.

"Tomorrow morning at ten o'clock bring Filargi into New York and take him to Madison Avenue and Sixty-first Street and let him out. We must treat him courteously, it is a matter of honor. He will go to his hotel which is two blocks away. Angelo will tip off the FBI and they will be waiting for him when he comes into the lobby. They will take him downtown for questioning and he will be charged with criminal mismanagement of the bank's funds, and embezzlement. The right cops will be tipped off to look for the evidence, pushed by the insurance company, that Filargi rigged his own kidnaping and worked out the devious payoff so that he could steal his own ransom just as he has been embezzling the bank's money. They will get him for complicity to murder his bodyguard and that elevator woman, the cop's wife. The trail, with Filargi's scent all over it, will lead from Lagos, Aruba,

Panama, Hong Kong and São Paulo and end at a Filargi numbered account at the bank in Lichtenstein. The Justice Department will prove criminality so that the Swiss banks will be forced to impound the money in the Filargi account, but by the time that happens, all the money will have been moved on—nothing will be found except that the account was in Filargi's name. Gomsky has all the evidence planted against him at our bank. Filargi will go to jail for twenty-five years, the bank will be disgraced, the Italians will be happy to sell out for our price to our agents, and Filargi will know that he made the mistake of his life when he refused my offer to do business with him."

Don Corrado got to his feet. The audience was over. He walked Charley slowly toward the door. "Tonight, put the fear deeply inside him, Charley. He is a Neapolitan. He remembers things which his mind forgot. Tell him how our arm is everywhere and that if he mentions in any way anything to do with any of his suspicions of how all of these things suddenly happened to him, that no matter where he is—in prison, within a circle of police guards, behind the highest walls, that we will kill him. Make it strong, Charley. He is not Mr. Robert Finlay, the great banker. He is Rosario Filargi, a Neapolitan, and he will understand."

Charley rode away from Brooklyn Heights wearing a nimbus of exultation. One week ago he had thought that he and Irene would be on the run by now, running for the rest of their lives—homeless, faceless and friendless. Now he was the Boss of the Prizzi family. He had been paid two and half million dollars for defying the Prizzi family. They hadn't worked out Irene's end of their payoff demands and maybe Don Corrado would never talk about that but, what the hell, he would split the two and a half million with her as a consolation prize, and she would be as knocked out as he was when she knew he was the Boss and everything that went with that.

He was going to reorganize the whole Prizzi setup. All three of the *capiregime* were dragging their ass. He was going to ask Ed Prizzi to build them a whole new modern laundry from the ground up, a new building with the right kind of offices and good equipment—a place that was one hundred percent clean so that he could feel good about going in and working there, not like the dump they had to work out of now, a cockroach ranch. Let them build a big city-wide hotel laundry business and make the place pay for itself and put other laundries out of business.

He was dissatisfied with the loan-sharking operation. Vincent had built it up fifteen years ago so that he had reached the point where he figured he was getting the biggest dollar out of it, but Charley could see a half dozen wrinkles to add at least thirty percent more to the gross. The sports book handle was so tremendous, day in day out, that nobody seemed to stop and think about the losses they were taking on weak collections and no-pays. Vincent had always looked at the gross business instead of seeing that he could have added maybe eight percent more to that gross by putting a few more soldiers on the collection side, giving them their commission and letting them beat the shit out of a few sportsmen until the word got out and everybody paid their markers.

Charley wanted to talk to Don Corrado in a week or two about how their honor demanded that Vincent be avenged even if he had been taken out by an all-family-approved hit. The Boccas had to pay for clipping Vincent. Fuck the Grand Council.

He knew how to settle with Quarico Bocca. Their biggest business was running women. The Boccas controlled all the vice in New York and supplied women for Vegas, Miami, and other major U.S. cities, as well as the Caribbean and the Bahamas. Charley was going to talk to Ed Prizzi about getting new state vice commissions appointed and very heavy laws passed with big teeth written into them so that the Boccas would have to spend sixty percent of their time staying out of jail, or straightening out police raids, and losing buyers and johns because they were tired of being hassled. The Boccas had no political muscle. The Prizzis had *the* political muscle in the country on every level, so the Boccas would have to come to Charley, their hats in their hands, and ask him to straighten the law out, and Charley would explain it to them. He would tell them that if they gave him Quarico Bocca he would see what he could do. Nothing could happen—no reorganization, no improvements, no nothing—until Vincent Prizzi was avenged.

Also the price of uppers, downers, coke, and shit had to keep up with the percentage increases in inflation; just like every other business passed the increases along.

He realized they couldn't live at the beach anymore. It was too out-of-the-way and it couldn't be protected well enough. Maerose was probably going to move back to town so he would ask the don for Vincent's house, then steam-clean it from roof to basement. Thinking about Maerose gave him an erection. He parked the car near a drugstore and went in to a phone booth. He dialed her number.

"Mae? Charley."

"Charley?"

"I had to tell you how cut up I am about your father."

"Well—thanks, Charley."

"Family business made me miss the funeral."

"Yeah. I know."

"You all right, Mae?"

"I'm all right when I talk to you."

"What are you going to do?"

"I'm going back to New York."

"When?"

"Any minute now. Ah, shit, Charley. I lost all the games—the game with my father, the game with you, and the game I had going with myself."

"I think about you a lot, Mae."

"That's no big deal, Charley. Anyway, it's not enough. How can things go this wrong in one person's life? Since the time I began to have bumps on my chest all I ever wanted was you."

"What the hell, Mae. I mean, what's the use? What's done is done."

"Ah, in your hat, Charley, and right down over your ears." She hung up heavily.

It was all a blur to Charley. Being Boss, the way the Filargi war had turned out, and Maerose Prizzi were all parts of the same piece. It proved that it only seemed that the fixed things were meant to be. What was truer—that he become Boss or that Maerose got drunk and walked away from him with that guy, so that everything in his life, her life, and Vincent's life had to change? What was going to happen to her now? He felt it like his own pain. She was really gone now and there was nothing he could do about it. Irene was separate, but Irene was his life now, and it only went to prove that the past and the present not only weren't of the same piece, they weren't even compatible.

He drove out to Brentwood, remembered that he had agreed to telephone when he got halfway there and stopped at a gas station booth to call her. Irene picked up on the first ring.

"Charley?" she said breathlessly.

"Everything is great, I'll tell you when I get there. You won't be able to believe it."

"Oh, Charley!" she said, "it makes me so *horny*! Hurry, *hurry*!"

When he got to Brentwood, Charley gave the

Plumber a dummy American Express Gold Card that Ed Prizzi's office had made up for him in the name of Robert Filargi and sent him off to return the mobile home to Bayshore. "Everything is handled," Charley told him. "Everybody had agreed to make the payoff so I'm going to take Filargi into New York and let him go."

"He's a nice little guy," the Plumber said. "And very profitable."

"After you drop the truck off, take a train back to Brooklyn and I'll see you around next week about your end."

"Sensational," Melvini said, "but I'm going to miss your cooking. Listen—is it all right if I rent a car with this card instead of taking a train to New York?"

"Why not? Filargi would probably rent a car after he turned the truck in. I tell you what—rent the car then ditch it somewhere between Fifty-ninth and Sixty-second between Park and Fifth. Jesus, that is a nice little detail."

When the Plumber left them Charley and Irene hit the upstairs double bed and went at it for forty minutes, both of them putting their hearts and hips into it. After they had showered together, they went to the kitchen and Charley began to cook dinner while he told Irene what had happened with Don Corrado.

"Actually only two things were settled," he told her. "I get my end, the two and a half million plus, and this is going to knock you over—I am now absolutely the Boss of the Prizzi family. I'm the Boss. We got ourselves maybe three million a year plus so many extras that you're going to think every day is Christmas morning. I got twenty-one hundred men under me. I get the respect wherever I go. I sit on the Commission. I have to okay every piece of work everybody does. Not only that, but you are the Boss's wife. How about that?"

"That's terrific, Charley. Congratulations."

He felt let down. He expected more, but he had to remember that Irene was a Polish freelance so she probably didn't have any idea of the amount of respect that went with the new job. Compared to that, what he was now, Underboss, which was what he had been for eleven years, was like being one of the workers. Then, he had to personally run the *capiregimes* and he had to personally handle the heavy enforcing. But that was all over now. From now on he would have total insulation. No involvement in the work. He would have to close down on his social contacts with his people and eliminate all obvious links to the actual operations. The bosses have to be protected. Shit, he thought, the Plumber would have made a natural Underboss for him but now the Plumber was in the shit.

"What about my end for the second-man stand?" Irene asked.

"Well, it figures that if the first thing he tells me is that my end is ready, that it also means your end is ready—that goes without saying."

"What about my five hundred forty and the other three hundred sixty and like that we asked for? Did he talk about that? That extra was the biggest part my of end."

"Irene—fahcrissake—his mind was on the two big things of his life right now, his own son's funeral and the whole Filargi thing which is so big he calls it his monument. Things like he's going to talk about somebody's end doesn't even come to his mind at a time like that."

"He told you about your end. He guaranteed that."

"So all right!" We have to wrap up Filargi tomorrow morning then I am going to see the don right after that. You want me to get him to sign a fucking paper with guarantees for your end?"

"No. Just tell him to pay out my end. That's all. Fair is fair."

Charley went down to see Filargi in the room in the cellar.

"I'm going to let you go tomorrow morning," he said.

"It's all over?" the small, plump man asked.

"Yeah. You get out at Sixty-first and Madison at ten o'clock tomorrow morning."

"I can't believe it," the banker said dazedly. "Every day when I woke up I was sure that woman was going to come in and kill me."

"You were born in Naples, right?"

"Yes."

"You were a poor kid?"

"Yes."

"You remember the *Camòrra*?"

Filargi nodded.

"We are worse. They were small. We are big. We wiped them out in this country. There is no place we can't go in this country." Charley leaned over, closer to Filargi. "You could live in a steel room on a battleship in the middle of the ocean and we could get to you. Do you understand me? When you go in tomorrow, when you are free, the police are going to talk to you. If you say *anything* about who you think was the people who took you—*anything* then we are going to kill you. Wherever they hide you, we will find you. If you talk, we will kill you."

Chapter Forty-one

Charley set the alarm for 5:30 A.M., leaving them time to give the house a thorough cleaning and have a hot breakfast before leaving at eight o'clock, so that Filargi could surely be dropped off in New York at ten.

"What's to clean, fahcrissake, Charley?" Irene said as she struggled out of sleep against the noise of the alarm.

"Listen, we use this place. You might want to spend a couple of weeks here this summer."

"I just spent a couple of months here this week."

"Two total pigs have been living here. I made them clean up, but what do they know about cleaning?"

After the rooms had been vacuumed, the beds made tautly, the bathrooms and the kitchen floor scrubbed, Charley made Filargi a three-egg ham omelet, a stack of toast and some hot coffee and took it down to him. "We go into New York this morning," he said. "This is your big day."

"Thank God," Filargi said. "I can't believe it."

"We leave in forty minutes. See if you can tidy this place up after you eat. Okay? I'll appreciate it."

Irene had their dishes washed and put away when he came up from the cellar. "How are you going to take him in?" she asked.

"I'll blindfold him down there and plug up his ears then we'll lay him out on a mattress in the back of the van and we'll drive in to Long Island City. When we get there we'll unpack him and sit him up front in the passenger seat for the ride into New York. You call Pop from Long Island City and tell him I'll be letting Filargi loose in fifteen minutes so he can have the FBI at Filargi's hotel. Then you take a subway out to the beach, and I'll see you there at about twelve-fifteen."

"Okay."

"It's too bad about this little guy. He shoulda took the don's deal."

"Well—it's too late now," Irene said.

"Filargi is a witness," Charley said. "You got him scared so let's keep him scared. Give him the stone eyes when you go down there. Where he remembers your face from has to keep him quiet for the next twenty-five years."

Filargo flinched when Charley opened the door to the cellar room and Irene went in, grinning at him like a television actor's idea of a homicidal killer.

Charley sat Filargi in the only chair, put cotton pads over his eyes and plugs in his ears, and while Irene held them there he wound the blindfold around his head, across the cotton pads. He taped Filargi's hands behind his back, then picked him up like a sack and, carrying him over his shoulder, went up the stairs to the kitchen of the house then out the back door to the Chevy van. Irene opened the doors to the van and Charley lowered Filargi in, full-length across the floor, while Irene locked up the house.

They got into the front seat of the van and moved out the country lane driveway toward the city.

They drove in silence for ten or twelve minutes then Irene said, "Charley, what are you going to do about the money the Prizzis owe me?"

"Well—I'm going to bring it up. I'm going to tell them we want it."

"Suppose they say no dice?"

"Jesus, I don't know."

"Charley, we had Filargi. They needed to get Filargi back. Seventy million dollars is what Angelo said so what it probably is is a hundred million because they are going to get a whole bank back. A *bank*, Charley. Like maybe the eighteenth-biggest bank in the country. So you could do anything to them and they would have to say okay because we had Filargi. We still have Filargi. But they owe me five hundred forty plus they owe me one hundred fifty for doing this Filargi stand, plus the first three hundred sixty. There was also the understanding with Don Corrado and Angelo that they had to pay the fifty Vincent was going to pay me to do the job on you. That's a million one hundred, Charley. They owe me a million one hundred, more money than I ever got in one lump in my life. They tell you they are going to pay you two and a half million for your stand on this thing, but you never saw the money. You don't know that they ever paid that to Switzerland. So what are we giving them Filargi back for? For some money which they supposedly have in their bank in Switzerland, or wherever they hide it? What are you *getting* for Filargi? You are getting the job as Boss of the Prizzi family which, the minute Vincent was clipped, they had to give to you anyway just to keep their business running, because there was nobody else who could have taken over for them to keep their business running."

"Irene, fahcrissake, that Boss spot is worth maybe three million bucks a year to us."

"Charley, who else is going to do it except you? You do it for them and that's the going rates for the job. They aren't doing you a favor, you're doing them a favor. But we've got Filargi and they owe us two and a half million six hundred. They *owe* us that. They accepted your letter and said certainly, it is worth that to us to get back Filargi. So where's the money, Charley?"

"Lissena me, Irene," Charley said desperately. "The Prizzis didn't say they wouldn't pay us what they owe us. In fact, Don Corrado said he was absolutely going to pay us. I was there. He said it to me."

"That's a lot of Sicilian shit, Charley," she answered hotly. "Did you ever hear of a deal where the chump hands over his entire bargaining edge because some Sicilians said they were going to pay him what they owed him someday?"

"Irene—all my life I have been waiting to be the Boss of the biggest family there is. I'm talking about the biggest family in the country, the family that runs this country just the same as the Senate does or General Motors or Alexander Haig, junior. You think I'm going to throw that away for half of a three million six hundred score? Ten years in the Boss slot and we got thirty million dollars in Zurich. Twenty years and we got sixty million. We can't miss. We give up a little piece of money and we make fifteen times that much. We give them Filargi and they fall all over themselves to give us whatever we want. Fahcrissake, Irene!"

"Well, there is no way I can see them paying out any three million six to us. They would eat their kids first."

"It so happens I happen to agree with that first part," Charley said. "But eat kids—never."

"So okay. We forget the two million five from the insurance. All right. I'll even forget the rest of the contract from Vincent. Listen, I would even be willing to bypass the money they owe me for this stand just to have it on them. But there is one thing I will not give up on. I got to have my five hundred forty back. That is the one thing they absolutely have to pay—the five hundred forty."

They rode on through fifteen minutes of silence, then Irene spoke again. "It's hard for me to say this," she said, "because you are the only thing that counts with me, Charley. But, the Prizzis owe me five hundred and forty dollars and I have to take that very big. So I'll tell you what I'm going to do. I'll help you get Filargi all unpacked and into the front seat. I'll call Pop and tell him fifteen minutes, then I'm going back to the beach and I'm going to wait until five o'clock today and if I don't have my money from the Prizzis by five o'clock then I'm getting out of here and I'm going back to LA and that's the end of the world for you and me."

Her eyes were filled with tears. He reached out and took her hand. "Okay, Irene," he said, "you got a right. I'll dump Filargi and go and see Pop and we'll both go and tell Don Corrado what he's got to do. Like you said, fair is fair. But don't talk about getting out. I couldn't handle it if you got out. Everything's going to be okay, just like you want it."

Charley and Irene worked silently in the back of the van beside a vacant lot in Long Island City, getting the tapes, the earplugs, and the blindfold off Filargi then pulling him into the passenger seat at the front of the car. As the van moved away toward the bridge, Irene went into a phone booth at the corner and telephoned Angelo Partanna at the St. Gabbione Hotel Laundry.

"Pop? He'll be there in about fifteen minutes." She hung up and set out on the eight-block walk to the subway station for the beach.

At the laundry, Angelo took out a small black book and tapped a number from it into his telephone. "Davey?" he said into the phone. "Robert Finlay, the banker, will be walking into his hotel in fifteen minutes." He hung up. Hanly called the chief inspector, who told him to notify Chief of Detectives Maguire, *The New York Times*, and *The Daily News*, then the FBI. "They gotta make the collar," he said, "but we gotta make sure we get the credit for the detective work on this."

Charley drove the Chevy van, with Filargi sitting in

the front seat beside him, across the Queensboro bridge. "A few more minutes," he said, "and you'll be walking across Madison Avenue to your hotel. Do you remember what I told you?"

"Yes."

"Nobody can keep you safe. If they show you ten thousand pictures and you tell them that any one of them is any of us, then you are dead. Do you believe that?"

"Yes, yes."

"It's all over. You are alive. Breathe the air. Look at the people. Stay alive. You were blindfolded all the time, you understand?"

"Yes."

"You don't know nothing because you couldn't see nothing or hear nothing all the time we had you. *Avete capito?*"

"Yes, yes. I understand."

They rode in silence across Sixty-first Street. Charley stopped the car at the near corner of Sixty-first and Madison. "Get out," Charley said to Filargi. "Good luck."

Filargi stepped down to the pavement. He leaned into the window and stared at Charley. "I have forgotten you already," he said in Italian.

Chapter Forty-two

Filargi went into the hotel through a revolving door, crossed the lobby and went directly to the front desk. An assistant manager was on duty. "Mr. Finlay!" he said loudly. "You're alive! How wonderful to see you actually standing there."

Filargi said, "I need to rest and then I must telephone. But not in that same apartment, please. Give me another apartment."

"Certainly, of course, oh, yes, Mr. Finlay," the assistant manager said.

Filargi was aware of people standing on either side of him. "Mr. Finlay?" the man on his right side said. Filargi turned. A short man, built like a fire plug, was standing there with his hat on. "Agent-in-Charge McCarry," he said, flashing his ID. "You'll have to come with us."

Irene sat on the terrace at the beach and looked out across the bay. There was despair in her eyes. She could hear Marxie Heller's voice as it had drilled her over the years to beware of Sicilians. "The Jews in this business are bad enough, sweetheart, but the Jews, the Irish, the coloreds—they got a *little* heart. The Sicilians don't even spend their money. There are three thousand fucking button men out there who are mil-

295

lionaires. Just soldiers, button men, the dirty-work people, not even workers. Millionaires. But they can't spend it because it's all hot money and when they die what do they leave to their families? Five thousand dollars. That's it. The rest goes back to the bosses, like they were priests in a church. The bosses got ten, maybe a hundred times that money, so what do they do with it? There in only one thing they can buy with it and that's more power, so they always gotta have more money to get more power because that's all there is for them. But they can never corrupt enough people until there aren't any innocent people left, everybody is working for the Sicilians in the end. Stay independent, Irene. Stay a freelance specialist. They need what you got to get themselves more power but if you ever join up with them what good are you to them anymore?"

She had gotten too fat on Charley. She had pushed her luck right over a cliff. What is that love shit? Was washing the awnings in this Brooklyn dump better than making a nice steady five hundred dollars a year and living in the most perfect climate in the world? She thought pasta was like hot garbage, but that's what she had signed on for because of love—*love*! Pasta for every meal except breakfast. Marxie didn't hold her up for love. Marxie was a schlepper, but he was safe and he was good company and they could have been on a beach in Spain right now with the $720, plus what she already had in the boxes, and with new faces and with new paper, living the way people ought to live without this horseshit of love that was costing her over a million cash, the greatest distance she had ever put between herself and her father. She could have taken that and all the other money she had and been halfway around the world away from these fucking Sicilians *and* Charley Partanna, who might just as well have been sticking her up like she was some gas station and it was his first stand. Charley was very big with the love shit, but Charley had cost her more money than all the other people she had ever met in her life.

Chapter Forty-three

Corrado Prizzi and Angelo Partanna sat down to breakfast at 8:00 A.M. Don Corrado ate as he always did: one jigger of olive oil. Angelo had a bowl of *stracciatella alla Natale Rusconi*. Rusconi, the great Milanese cook of the thirteenth century, was a Partanna family idol. Don Corrado surprised him by talking business before breakfast was over.

"Filargi will be in jail before noon," he said, "everything will now proceed automatically until I own my bank again. We will have made a good profit with Filargi. Now we have to get back to our regular daily business by giving the police what they want."

"I don't see how you are going to do that, Corrado," Angelo said. "The police want us to give them the second man on the Filargi job. If we do that, the second man will sing, we will all be implicated and that would be the end of the family."

"I considered all those things, Angelo. I think I have found a way around it. I want you to tell the police that we have heard that someone is about to give them the person who killed the woman who pushed the wrong floor—within the next forty-eight hours, maybe less. Then call Charley and tell him we want to meet him here."

"What is your plan?"

"Listen to me, Angelo. This is what we have to do to put everybody back in business again."

Angelo called Lieutenant Hanly at 10:30 that morning.

"How is Mr. Finlay holding up?" Angelo asked.

"He's not holding up so much as he's holding out," Hanly said. "He says he was blindfolded and with ear plugs all the time they had him. He says he doesn't know where they held him or for how long or anything else and he sticks to the story."

"Well," Angelo said, "I got one break for your people. We got a blind tip early this morning that the Calhane killer is going to be turned over in forty-eight hours, maybe less."

"How reliable is the tipster?"

"I don't know. It was a blind tip, but I can tell you this much, the person who got the blind tip and passed it along to me is what the papers call an unimpeachable authority."

"How do we work it?"

"I am going to get my source to get his source to call me when the hitter is ready to be turned over, then I will call you, no matter what time, so that you can call the detective bureau to make the pick-up so that Robert Finlay can make the ID."

"Finlay insists he was blindfolded. How can he make the ID?"

"He wasn't blindfolded when they took him in his hotel room. The hitter must have burst in, shot the bodyguard and taken Finlay out just when Mrs. Calhane stepped out of the elevator. Finlay had to see the hitter."

"I'll be sitting right beside the phone."

"Davey? I have a little present for you."

"What present?"

"Bet the Young Turks against the Buccaneers. They

are gonna win by exactly eleven points. Bet the whole roll."

"Where can I put down a bet in this town?"

"I'm gonna give you a number in Jersey."

After watching Filargi cross Madison Avenue and start up the street toward his hotel, Charley turned the Chevy van into the traffic and went north to Sixty-second, then turned off again to go across town to the East River Drive, down to the Brooklyn Bridge, then to the St. Gabbione Hotel Laundry. Irene was right, in her way. She wasn't able to see the big picture, but if she wasn't right she had right on her side. The Prizzis had agreed to what it would cost them to get back Filargi. They had to live up to that. They were going to get a bank for practically nothing so they had to understand that they had committed for certain expenses to get the bank, and that they had to pay for their commitments.

He would lay it out to Pop, who had been in on the commitments every step of the way. Then he and Pop would call the don and go over to see him and get the whole thing straightened out. He was proud of Irene. It took a lot of moxie to stand up like that. He had himself a tremendous woman. He knew that. Pop knew that. It was time that it was laid out for Don Corrado.

Pop was looking out the window when Charley come into his office. He turned around in the swivel chair as he heard the door open.

"Hey, Charley!" he said. "You ready to take things over?"

"Yeah," Charley said. "I almost forgot."

"Who is going to be your Underboss?"

"You're the *consigliere*, what do you think?"

"You make your pick, Charley, then I'll tell you if I agree. You got to make the decisions now."

"We'll move up Sal Prizzi."

"Good."

"Pop, I got to talk to you."

"What's up?" Pop asked.

"Pop, it's simple. Irene wants her money like the don agreed when he got the letter from me when I had Filargi."

"She wants her money?"

"She wants what is coming to her. She even can see that there is no chance at the insurance money for Filargi, even though the family agreed to pay that. She is willing to forget the rest of the contract Vincent put out and, if absolutely necessary, her money for the Filargi stand. But she wants the five hundred and forty back. She has to have it by five o'clock today."

"Five hundred and forty?"

"The money she had to pay back to the don."

"But three hundred sixty of that is Prizzi money."

"It was, but we had Filargi. The don wanted Filargi and that was a part of the price."

"Charley—where have you been?"

"What do you mean?"

"The don made you the Boss. How could there be more than that? That is going to like pay off ten, fifteen times more than the Filargi thing and she is your wife."

"Pop, I know that. But Irene wants her cut. She sees Vincent's job as my end and, anyway, she has no way of figuring what Vincent's end can make. And if she did know it, she wouldn't believe it because the Prizzis and everybody else in her life have always shortchanged her."

"There is no way we can pay her, Charley."

"Pop, I am asking you to see this from Irene's point of view. I mean, it's like she's looking back on her whole life when she says we have to pay her. It was a crappy life, Pop, until she took over from all the people who told her what to do. And what did they tell her? They said she was nothing, but she knew better.

She knew she was as good as they were. She climbed
out of Chicago. They fixed her up with a great job in
Chicago peddling her ass so she could split what she
made on her back. She took on the slobs and the pimples and the stink so they could make fifty percent off
her. She quit. She got books on bookkeeping out of
the fucking library so she could understand numbers,
then she went back to Chicago and got a job pushing a
pencil for the main wire. They paid her nothing, but
she learned how to talk and what dresses to wear and
she talked numbers to them until they saw she was a
great-looking head and that she could be trusted and
they made her a courier for three families. But while
she sat in those airplanes, back and forth, back and
forth, she studied books on income taxes. Irene was
always ready, but nobody ever paid her her end. So
she went in where they lived. She opened up as a contract hitter and we know the rest, but they never let
her in. They still paid her nothing compared to what
they got out of what she did. And now—now—she has
delivered for the Prizzis on every count. It was her
moves that got Filargi out of that hotel, not mine. She
handled everything that happened out of nowhere
with fast decisions, so we were right every time. We
got Filargi and that is going to make the Prizzis seventy million dollars. She paid them back the money
out of the Vegas scam which meant they got paid
twice, once from her and once from the insurance
companies, but the don still whacked her with a fifty-
percent penalty for getting her to double his money.
What the fuck, Pop. We are always talking about
honor so we have to pay off Irene for every cent we
promised her we would pay her."

"There is no way we can pay her, Charley."

"Well, Pop, with all respect, I have to hear that
from the don."

Angelo picked up the telephone on his desk and
dialed a number. "Amalia?" he said into the phone.
"Angelo. Charley and me got to see the don today."

"The only way you can do that," she said, "is you come over for lunch."

Lunch at Don Corrado's, which didn't begin that day until 2:30, while Charley and his father waited for the call from Amalia because of the don's overlong nap, lasted until a quarter to five. Charley was almost distraught thinking about Irene's ultimatum—that she have the money by five o'clock or she would leave him—but the don would not speak of business that day while they ate. At last the two old men sat in the Morris chairs and Charley sat in a straight-backed chair facing them.

"You tell me what you have on your mind," Don Corrado said, "then I will tell you what I have on mine."

"*Padrino*," Charley said, "we delivered Filargi to you in the best of good faith. It was agreed at the time that if I agreed to give Filargi to you, that my wife would be paid her fee for doing her stand as second man, and that the five hundred forty dollars would be returned to her. With respect, on her behalf, I am asking for that money now."

Don Corrado and Angelo Partanna stared at him sadly.

"I am saying that we will forget the rest of the entire piece of money, a very big piece of money, but the return of the five hundred forty—that she's got to get back. It was all okayed by you and she's got to have it back."

"Charley," Don Corrado said gently, "there is a very good reason why she hasn't been paid. The Grand Council decided last night that we must give the second man on the stand to the cops."

Charley looked with horror from Don Corrado to Angelo Partanna. "Give her to the cops?" he said thickly. The words were like razor blades in his throat.

"Listen, Charley," Don Corrado said, offering him the comfort of his alligator eyes, "last night the Grand

Council, speaking for all the families in this country under a system which we have all accepted for fifty years, told me I had one week to give up whoever killed the woman who pushed the wrong floor or to find myself at war with every family in this country. The Grand Council sent Bavosi and Lingara here last night to tell me that. Do you know what a war would cost us? It could cost us our life as a family. It could cost us all of our people and everything we have. Nothing else can have any meaning to any of us except the family who made such a good life for us in America."

"What do you want me to do?" Charley said.

"You have to do the job on her, Charley. You are the only one who can get close enough to her to do it," his father said.

"Zotz her? Clip Irene?"

"You are thinking that Ed's fixers can get her off and that she could be given to the police alive," Don Corrado said. "But I have never seen them like this. The FBI is in it because it was a kidnaping. If they get her alive they will make her talk and if she talks she will drag all of us to prison. Maybe even to the chair. She would talk because she would have to talk. When she talks, then you, me, Angelo, and Ed will all be nailed. Filargi will go free. We will never get the bank back. There is no choice, Charley. The existence of the Prizzi family is in your hands."

"But how will clipping Irene ever satisfy the cops about the woman who pushed the wrong floor?"

"Filargi will identify her body as the one who shot that police captain's wife. There will be no one to question. They will have what they asked for and we can all go back to doing business."

"But she is my *wife, Padrino.*" Charley's voice broke.

"She is your wife, we are your life," his father said. "Tell us your answer, Charley."

"One woman who you have known for less than two months, or your family which is your life," Don Corrado said.

Charley felt that he must be drowning. He wouldn't have anything left if he did what they were asking him to. What else did he have except Irene? How could he do the job on the only person he loved? Everybody else—Pop, his job, the family—that was all only an automatic thing that had been massaged into him, beaten into him, fed and coaxed into him every day of his life. It was a Sicilian's instinct to feel that way about those things. But Irene was his need, she was the emotion on which his life rested. She was all the things that made him a man. She was the only important thing in his life.

Maybe he would get old. Pop and Don Corrado had made it somehow. What would he have when he got old if he did what they wanted? He would have a pile of money in a Swiss bank. He would have houses, and people, and cars, and power—not his but on loan to him. He would have more respect and still more respect. He would have quick-eyed men like the Plumber and Cucumbers Cetrioli around him wherever he went and he would shrivel up inside from the endless talk of sports and odds and fixes. He would go dead and dry because for every minute of every day until he was dying he would remember what he had done to the only meaning of his life. He would have killed more than Irene's body, he would be wasting both of their immortal souls. He would be passing a sentence upon himself to spend the rest of his life inside a 230-pound cake of ice. That was the bad part. If he blew Irene away he would be alone. No one could take her place. All his life he had never stopped looking, like everybody else, hoping to find that perfect match-up, edge to edge, of his body, mind, and spirit, and when he had found Irene he knew he had done it, that they were chemical complements, and could make each other safe forever.

What was the Prizzi family next to that? What was all of his life—apart from Irene—next to that? In his mind he stared blankly into her sweet, serene face as it smiled at him, completing him, saving him, and he knew that, no matter what she meant to him, because he had been formed by the history of the people he came from, by his father and Don Corrado, to become what he was, even though Irene was one being with him in his business—which was his life, too—even though she was the woman who was his mother and his lover and his partner all at the same time, he would be even more alone if he turned his back on his family than if he did what they were asking him to do. The family were what he had been since Sicily started breeding people. They were his food. They had been with him forever. There were hundreds of thousands of them, most of them ghosts, some of them bodies. They were all staring at him, waiting to know what he would do. He couldn't do it. They couldn't expect him to do it. How could he be the final one to cheat her out of her life the way her father had done it, the way the mob had done it? He would be the last of all of them to put her through the hoop. But the last one. She would never be able to start up again the way she always had done it. He would be finishing her courage. And in the few seconds before he could do it, he would see all of that in her eyes because, no matter what else, she trusted him and she knew he loved her. He wanted to drown.

"I will give her to you," Charley said to them.

"It's business, Charley," his father said. "You know it's only business."

"Well—we can't set her up without that money," Charley said. "She has everything going on that money."

"Then you'll bring her the money," Don Corrado

said. "It's in the same little case. It's under my bed. Bring it out, Charley."

Charley went across the room and got down on his hands and knees beside the big bed. He pulled a traveling case out and brought it to the don.

"Open it, son," Don Corrado said.

Charley unsnapped the clasps and opened the lid. Packages of thousand-dollar bills were stacked inside. "That's the five hundred forty dollars," Don Corrado said. "If that's what she wants, show it to her."

"Where you gonna take her?" Pop asked.

"She left for California." He couldn't look at them so he kept looking at the money. "She told me if I wasn't back at the beach with the money by five o'clock that she would leave for California."

"All right," Don Corrado said with finality. "After you take the stone out of my shoe, leave her in a rent-a-car at the airport, then call Angelo and tell him where. He'll tell the New York cops and they'll call the LA cops, then she can be photographed and they can show the pictures to Filargi in the slammer and he can tell them that she is the hitter who did the job on the woman who pushed the wrong floor and the wind will stop blowing. We can all get back to our business again."

Chapter Forty-four

By the time Charley got to the bottom of the stairs at the Sestero house, leaving the grimness of his father and Don Corrado two floors above, his body and mind felt as if they had been flash-frozen. He had spent his life with those two old men and he had carried out their devious and brutal orders as the ordinary course of his job, but although he spun around and around in his head what they had just told him to do, he could not make the jagged parts of it fit into any recognizable, coherent pattern. They had assigned him to do the job on his own wife, as if that were something that the *fratellanza* did every day. He was now the Boss of the Prizzi family and the first job they handed him was to kill his own wife. Charley had been brought up to believe that, no matter how vicious things got in business, the women were safe from it. That was the primary point of honor of the whole thing. No matter what you did for money, you never did the job on women—certainly never on your own women.

He could understand it, but he couldn't understand it, but as he thought about it, he thought about the seventy million dollars and how Don Corrado had not even made a move to avenge his own son's murder by a gang of pimps because, if a war started, it could get in the way of the seventy million dollars coming down the chute. That helped Charley as he walked away from the house toward the Chevy van. Don Corrado had had to put the considerations of honor to one side when the Boccas killed his son. Angelo had to see his own son in agony over what they had told him to do. The leaders had to sacrifice themselves first in order to make a better place for all those who followed them. He was a leader. No matter how he looked at it the family had been his life. What he felt for Irene was enormous, but it was separate. She had a different much paler, thinner meaning when he judged her beside the total meaning he got from his family. He was now Boss of the family. He had to set an example that would be remembered as long as the family stood. He saw dimly that it was right to sacrifice the woman he loved so that the family could go on and on fulfilling its honor, which was its meaning.

He suddenly saw clearly that Irene had stepped so far out of line that there was nothing left to do but to whack her. It wasn't her fault entirely that she had scammed the Prizzis for $720. She was a Polack, so what could she know about the real rules? But she had made her mistake when she had given back the $360 and made out like she was innocent so she could keep the other half of it, because what could she expect— that the Prizzis would hold still to be taken for that kind of money?

It could even be, he forced himself to tell himself, that in all this time she had only made out like she was crazy about him in case—like she, herself, said—he would have zotzed her. Marrying him and all that grabbing and kissing him and cooking and washing the awnings and scrubbing floors had probably been a lot of bullshit. She had certainly fooled him. She had convinced him that she was crazy about him—but how could she take the fifty dollars from Vincent to blow him away if that was how she felt about him?

She had screwed up on the Filargi stand and that

was what had finished her. He tried to go through the whole thing again in his mind. She threw the baby at the bodyguard just when the elevator door opened. The bodyguard went for his gun instead of the baby. What Irene should have done was to grab the woman who pushed the wrong floor and used her as a shield to make the bodyguard drop his gun or to give Charley a chance to get out there and sap him. Well, maybe she couldn't. She shot the bodyguard first so he must have been pressing her. Irene had nerve. She did everything right. But why did she have to clip the dumb broad on the wrong floor? She wasn't holding any gun on Irene. She was just standing there in inno-cent-bystander shock and Irene had done the job on her and put them all in the shit.

But what a woman. A clean woman in every way and a terrific housekeeper. Sometimes he had the feel-ing that she couldn't stand Sicilian food but she could cook it like she had studied under the whole Spina family in Agrigento. She was some woman. She never complained; she hated Brooklyn, hated Sicilians, hated the climate but she never complained.

No use thinking like that, he told himself. He had learned a long, long time before that a contract on anybody was just business. He had grown up with Gusto Bustarella. They had been made on the same day. They liked the same kind of broads. Gusto's fa-ther had spent maybe fifty hours showing them all the ways to use a knife when they had been fifteen-year-old kids, and, besides, Gusto was a very funny guy. He was a million laughs. He was the very best friend Charley ever had, except Pop, but when Vincent told him he had to do the number on Gusto, that was that. He did it. He even used a knife for old time's sake. What's the sense of thinking about things that had nothing to do with business whatsoever? Everybody had to die sometime.

And now he had to give it to Irene. When he had

gone into Don Corrado's house he had loved Irene but when he came out that was something that had happend to two other people a long time ago in a different country. Pop had said it. The family was his life.

He drove to the beach figuring out the best way to set her up. She wouldn't be easy, but if he didn't make a whole mountain out of that she wouldn't be too tough either. If she had left on the dot of five o'clock, and that was the kind of woman she was, it would take her maybe forty minutes to get to the airport if the traffic was right. She could have caught the six o'clock plane for LA and that would get her there at half past nine, maybe to her own house by half past ten, which would be half past seven her time. So he would call her at eleven o'clock New York time.

He got to the beach at half past five and took a shower. Then he went to the box he kept on the floor of his closet and took out the long, balanced knife he had taken from Marxie Heller. He chose a lightweight soft leather scabbard and strapped the knife and the scabbard around the inside of his left calf. Then he put on a pair of pajama bottoms and got up to look at himself in the long mirror in the closet door. He couldn't see anything under the floppy pajama trousers.

That was what he would use. He would wear a .38 Magnum in a shoulder holster, then when the time came for them to go to bed, he would take off the gun harness elaborately, so she could watch what he was doing, and hang it over the back of a chair away across the room from the bed, then he would get into bed with her and wait for the right chance to slide the knife into her. He wanted to do it the most painless way, the quickest way. He didn't want her even to know that he had done it to her.

He made himself a hamburger and had two glasses of red wine while he ate in front of the TV screen and the video machine. He played Irene's cassette over and over again. When its two minutes and forty-nine seconds were over, he pressed the button on his remote control and rewound it, to start it again while he chewed the hamburger and sipped the "Chianti-type" wine.

The cassette was as short as his life with Irene and many different pictures were crowded into it, but he was able to see what Paulie, and Pop, and that cameraman had meant when they hadn't gone out of their skulls, the way he had, about Irene's looks. She was a good-looking woman, sure. But no 12 on a scale of 10 the way he thought when these pictures were actually happening. He would rate her about a 7.

What tore him up as he analyzed it, watching the scenes again and again, was how he had been kidding himself when he thought that they had both gone crazy about each other the way he knew she had hit him. He had thought that she had been dropped by love at first sight, from the minute Mae had introduced them. Now he could see that it was Mae who had been standing there adoring him, not Irene. Irene just looked at him like a passenger on some sinking ship looks at a lifeboat. She had needed him all right, but she hadn't needed him for the reasons he had thought she needed him.

He didn't feel used, he felt sad. He was never going to be able to forget her. But Pop had been right. Pop was always right. He had been a part of the Prizzi family all his life and he had been a part of Irene's for less than three months. There was nothing to choose from there. She threatened the family—she stole from the family—and she had to go. But she was some woman. She was smart, she was brave, and she wouldn't take any shit from anyone, not even Corrado Prizzi. He wished he could stop his life anywhere right in the middle of that cassette.

After he ate he cleaned up in the kitchen, then got

out the vacuum to make sure there were no stray crumbs in the sofa or around the floor. The last thing he wanted was roaches.

When he was dressed he called the airline and booked a seat to LA, then sat down and filled in one of the hot tickets with the corresponding flight number. At 11:05 he tapped Irene's number into the phone. Irene picked up on the second ring.

"Hello?"

"It's Charley. Jesus, you really meant it."

"I always mean it, Charley," she said.

"He could only see Pop and me at lunch but lunch didn't start until after two and he wouldn't talk while he was eating so it was about a quarter to five when I told him what I wanted."

"Yeah?" She felt as tense as a junkie. No Sicilians were going to hand over $540 just because somebody asked for it. They had reneged on every other piece of money they owed her so there wasn't a chance, unless they were setting her up, that they would pay back the money she had scammed from them. She gripped the back of a chair and held the telephone tightly and waited for what Charley was going to say.

If Charley told her that the Prizzis refused to give him her money, she was safe. If he said he had the money, they were going to try to hit her.

"I got the money," Charley said. "It's in your same bag. He hadn't even unpacked it."

Irene felt like a camera that had been laid on tracks and was now photographing as it withdrew tens of miles, then thousands of miles, then backward into outer space, without ever losing sight of the vision it was recording, a vanishing memory of what she had felt for Charley. She took one last look, then blanked it out forever. She remembered that day when she had told him she loved him. She had told him that she didn't know how to say it, because she had never said it. She had never said it to anyone else. She had cherished the day she would say it only because it was true, then she had said it to Charley. She heard her own voice. "I never loved anybody. All my life I had to protect myself, and you can't protect yourself anymore when you love somebody."

She tore the past up as if it were a two-month-old telephone message. She had to protect herself. The Prizzis were sending a man to do the job on her and the man was Charley.

"No kidding?" she said. "Man, that's a real surprise."

"Yeah. You coulda knocked me over," Charley said.

"Well, I'm glad it's settled. You hang on to it. I got about three days' work to get this house sold and the office lease fixed up, then I'll be back in New York and we'll spend some of it."

London was where she was going, she told herself. They have the surgery and they have the right language and I'll be able to lay my hands on new paper. Nine hours' time difference. Over the Pole and I can be there tomorrow night if I get out of here tomorrow morning. Got to stay until the bank opens so I can get at the boxes.

"I got a better idea," Charley said. "I got a couple of days before I take over at the laundry. I just booked space on a morning flight to LA and we can have a ball for a couple of days."

She felt grief as if the new glacier had just moved in on her, embedding her forever as if she were a mastodon. How had she ever gone the fucking love route? She had worked for eleven years to build her business, the best business in the world, tax free and high fee with a front that was so legit it was absolutely foolproof. She had the kind of house her mother had never even looked at. If she wanted the occasional shot at grabbing cock, that was certainly no sweat to line up. She had the California climate, her car, her clothes, and her safe deposit boxes but built into that, the whole time, must have been some tilt toward destroying herself, to take everything she had away from herself plus her peace of mind by walking right into the trap of loving Charley with her eyes wide open.

What was Charley? An animal, a hoodlum, a Sicilian hoodlum who shot people in the kneecaps or choked them with a piece of rope. He was everything Marxie had warned her about Sicilians.

If Charley came to California, it would be his last trip to anyplace.

If Charley came to California before she could get away to London she would have to zotz him, and for the first time she felt loathing, not for Charley, but for the Prizzi money that had pulled her in and made her meet Charley. She had loved him but that was all over now. She had wiped out ever meeting him, ever knowing him, and everything else sappy like that.

"I know you, Charley," she said gaily. "You can't wait to get started in the new slot. Why waste time coming out here? I'll be right back in Brooklyn in three days."

"Listen—who knows when I'm ever going to get any time off again," Charley purred into the phone, sweat pouring off him. He knew she was trying to beat them. He knew she had gone to LA just to get into the boxes at the bank. "What the hell," he said, "I am practically on my way, I can't stop now."

"Okay," she said, "it's up to you. What's the flight number? I'll pick you up at the airport."

When she hung up she went to the wall safe in her closet and dialed it open. She took out a 9mm pistol and unscrewed the noise suppressor from its barrel. It was the right caliber for close work. She checked its mechanism carefully then loaded it. She locked the safe and took the pistol to her dressing room and put it in her makeup box with its lifted top facing the doorway to her bedroom. Jesus, he was a big mother.

Somehow she'd have to drag him out to the garage and get him in the trunk of the rental she had picked up at the airport. She would leave him in the rental at the airport just the way he had left Marxie to rot there. She didn't feel the grief anymore. Charley was a contract she had put out herself, and had given to herself; full fee.

Chapter Forty-five

Charley strapped the shoulder holster into place on the left side of his chest, felt the knife in its leg scabbard, picked up Irene's light case and his own bag and left the apartment. The telephone rang as he was closing the door. He went back in and answered it. It was Maerose Prizzi.

"Hey, Charley!"

"Hi, Mae. I was practically out the door."

"Where you going?"

"I gotta go to the Coast."

"I just heard the big news. Jesus! You really are a regular Horatio Alger."

"Who's he?"

"Your father told me you're going to take over our house."

"Well, yeah. This is too far from the laundry."

"I been thinking about it ever since he told me. You can't live in that dump. It's furnished like a Calabrian coal miner's hut. Lissena me. You got to let me redo the whole place. As a wedding present. Whatta you say?"

"That would be terrific, Mae."

"Will it be okay with Irene?"

"Yes," Charley said.

"I mean we have the access here. We can get the

best colors, the best stuff, the really right wallpapers. I mean, of *course* I'm going to do the whole job with her, the way she sees it, how she wants it to look. Believe me, Charley, she'll be crazy about it."

"You have great ideas, kid. Look, I gotta get to the airport."

"Call me when you get back, you hear?"

Charley drove the Chevy van to the airport and made his flight by an easy twelve minutes.

She was there when he came out of the chute into the airport building. Jesus, what a tremendous-looking woman, he thought. He was doing the right thing. A woman like this should never get old. She was ripe. She was at her peak, so what the hell.

They didn't speak. They moved into each other and hung on. Then they kissed and, for an exploded second, she almost changed her mind. For the first time in her life she wished she had been born a square and that Charley was the corner druggist. But he lived by the sword, she told herself, so it was against all the percentages that he could be expected to die in a bed. His time had come.

Together they carried despair on their backs like a mountain God had told them to carry three times around the world. This is the way it is with everybody, he told himself, they all do every day what I'm going to do tonight, they kill whatever they love. They take it in and let it warm them and expand them until they think there isn't any more room under the sky to hold their joy then, sooner or later, they drag it out into the snow and kill it before it can change them.

"Did you eat on the plane, Charley?"

"Whatta you think? We are a couple of miles from that spic place. Our place. That's where I'll eat if I can ever stop looking at you."

"Well," she said, "we *have* been separated for at least twenty-four hours."

"I love you, baby," he said, and his tongue turned to wood. He told himself that she knew he had been sent there to do the job on her, but she thought it was all because of the $540 so, in a business way, it made sense to her that Charley should try to set her up. He was the new Boss. He wanted to start out with a clean slate. But she hadn't looked at a newspaper in a week so she had no idea what a thing that woman who had pushed the wrong floor had become, he thought. She didn't know she was the only natural patsy anyone had to stop the wind blowing on all the family business in New York and hurting the business.

They walked out to the rented car, a big gas guzzler with a large trunk. Irene drove.

"Ah, what the hell, Charley," she said, "let's go to my house and lay down on each other."

"Not yet. We gotta go back to that spic place. I dream about that place and you are always there. It could be the last chance we'll ever have to sit out there and hear the ocean and drink that pineapple stuff."

"It'll still be there, Charley."

"Sure. But where will we be? I'm the new Boss. It's going to keep me pretty busy."

She drove the car along the Pacific Coast Highway and she thought, if I was a square and if Charley was out here for some other reason, like he had some other woman or something, and I knew he was getting set to zotz me, if this was a TV movie, I would drive this fucker with both of us in it right over a cliff and into that ocean.

Charley thought it would be a good place to clip her out here when it got dark. He could get her to drive up into the hills for a quickie and shove the knife into her, but that was only a tactical thought. It passed through his mind professionally, as a possibility only. He had to have time with her at the spic place where they had started. Then he had to go home with her, once more, for the last time.

Irene swung the car into the parking lot at the restaurant. "Ah, what do we want a lot of food for, Charley?" she said. "Let's get home and train for the Olympics on my bed."

"Just one whiff of the good old days," Charley said. "You know what I was thinking?"

"What?"

"We got that satchelful of ready money in the car. We could cut out of here right now and head for the San Diego airport, then we could fly into Dallas and change for anywhere. Where do you like?"

"I once saw a travel folder I never forgot. It was about the South Island of New Zealand. Very calm and very beautiful."

"Then, what the hell, let's go. Let's take the satchel and go right now."

She leaned over, lifted his hand and kissed it. "What's the use, Charley? You know they'd find us no matter where we went. I mean, the Prizzis' honor is involved, isn't it? You are Boss now. So let's count our blessings. We can go to the South Island next year."

He kissed her cheek softly. "Just one more of these crazy pineapple drinks then we'll get lost in the sheets."

She cut off the engine and opened the car door.

They sat at the same table as before and ordered from the same waiter. They were both cast backward into the first time. Each of them put away their separate deadly plans for a while. Charley held Irene's hand and stared into her eyes. He looked like a thousand other guys in love with being in love, but his mind kept telling him that he was a professional and that he had to keep the right balance on things so she wouldn't think she was being set up, and he wished bitterly that he could have poured everything out to her, to hear her say that she understood, that it was all right, until he could maybe even call the whole thing off, pack a couple of bags, and get the hell out of the country with the $540.

"Hey, maybe we ought to lock the car," he said. "All your money is in that satchel in the trunk."

"I never thought you'd get Prizzi to pay off like that," she said.

"He's grateful to you for Filargi. Five hundred forty is nothing. You are a big star around the Prizzi house."

"What a business!" Irene said.

What was the use of bullshitting around like this, she thought. It only makes it worse. Men really want to g⸱t the last drop of romance out of the Valentine card. Everything they did was always for the wrong reason. Charley used to be a wonderful guy, in her whole life she never met anyone like him for churning her up and making her want to pull everything together. Maybe they were those floating two halves of the same being that the poetry talked about, maybe all they needed was that one thing—to be true to each other right down the line on everything that happened and never fuck around with other people's reasons and the corny temptations. She wished they had talked all that over the day they had met. It was one of those things that both sides had to understand. It never worked when it was only clear to one of them. It was too late to even think like that. Thinking like that could slow her down and give her a bad case of the fatals. She reached out for his other hand and said, "It's time to go, Charley."

When they got out of the car in Irene's driveway Charley said, "Anyway, here's your five hundred forty."

She opened the side door of the house, smiling. "Bring it in," she said, "we'll put it back in the same closet where we found it." They walked into the pantry, then into the main hall. She opened the closet door. He put the satchel at her feet and, with her right foot, she slid the bag inside and shut the door.

"Aren't you going to count it?" he asked.

"What for? You counted it."

They went up the stairs with their arms around each other and Irene could feel the .38 Magnum under Charley's jacket.

"Hey, you're packing a lot of heat in there," she said.

"Why not? I was walking around with a half a million dollars."

"I hope you don't wear it to bed."

"I can't wait to get the whole harness off."

Irene's large bedroom had a wall-to-wall mirror on the ceiling over the enormous, turned-down bed. She sat demurely and watched Charley hang up his jacket, then unstrap the gun harness from around his chest and hang it up in a closet far across the room.

They sat back-to-back on either side of the wide bed while they undressed and put on night clothes. When Charley had his pajama bottoms on he got up, walked around the bed and crossed to the bathroom in front of Irene, naked to the waist, so she could see how unarmed he was.

"I am really ready," Charley said. "Twenty-four hours away from you and I come on like some sex fiend."

"Keep it warm for five more minutes, honey," Irene said, smiling, her eyes opaqued with phoney lust. When Charley came back and got into the low bed, Irene got up and went into the dressing room. He lay with Marxie's long, thin knife in his right hand, hanging down against the far side of the bed. He was propped up against the pillow watching her as she brushed her hair in the lighted dressing room beyond the darkened bedroom.

As Irene brushed her hair she made up her mind. Charley, being Charley, would be counting on a whole night of making love so he wouldn't be able to see it coming if she hit him now. She put the brush down and looked back into the bedroom. Charley was lying there with his eyes closed, working on himself so he could turn into a tiger in the sheets; waiting for her to come to bed.

She lifted the .22 pistol out of the makeup case and shielded it with her body as she let it hang down at her side at the end of her arm. She moved out slightly into the room and began to raise the pistol. Charley moved.

He lifted up the knife from the floor and threw it with tremendous force across the fifteen feet that separated them. Her pistol fired, missing him because the knife shattered her larynx and severed her spinal cord, nailing her to the frame of the door behind her. She had moved from glorious life into death in three short seconds.

Charley dressed himself methodically. He took his case down to the hall, removed Irene's traveling case from the hall closet and put them in the front seat of his car. He opened the trunk. He went back into the house and plodded slowly up the stairs. In the bedroom he had to use all of his strength to pull the knife out of her throat and, while her body slid grotesquely to the floor, he wiped its handle carefully with a handkerchief, put the knife into its scabbard and restrapped it to his left calf.

He went back to the body and picked up the pistol that lay beside it and, holding it close to the body, just under the bare left breast, fired once. As he picked up the warm corpse he discovered that he was sobbing.

Carrying Irene, wrapped in a blanket, over his shoulder, Charley made his way down the stairs to the side door. He opened the trunk of the car and dumped the body into it, thinking that at least he and Irene had never been married. Marriage was a sacrament performed in a Catholic church under the eyes of God, and no justice of the peace named Joseph Tierney Masters in a honkytonk town like Tijuana could perform a real marriage. Only a priest could do that and there had never been time to get that done. There had never been time for hardly anything.

Chapter Forty-six

Charley called his father from the LA airport at 4:30 P.M. "It's an El Dorado with California Plates," he said, "Three-one-eight-six-one-two. You got it?"

"Yeah."

"It's on the east side of the parking lot about half-way down."

"You did good, Charley."

"Yeah."

"What time is your plane?"

"Twenty minutes."

"I'll call the Man in a half an hour. We are off the hook."

Charley got back to the beach in Brooklyn at 7:30 in the evening. He unstrapped the scabbard from his leg and locked it up in the box in his closet. He undressed, took a shower, and went to bed. He fell asleep quickly.

He slept until three o'clock the next afternoon. He made himself a heavy breakfast then washed all the windows in the apartment. As he was cleaning out the closets he found two of Irene's blouses and one dress. He packed them into a large manila envelope, looked up the address of the Salvation Army in the Brooklyn telephone book and addressed the envelope. He sat out on the terrace until ten minutes to five, thinking about how he was going to run the family and realizing that Irene could never have fitted in among the Prizzis, Sesteros, and Garrones.

He telephoned Maerose Prizzi at her office.

"Mae? Charley."

"Hey, Charley! You know what? My sister Teresa just got back today from her honeymoon."

"Where did they go—outer space? How about we'll have dinner tonight?"

"Dinner? Whatta you mean?"

"What do I mean? I mean let's go someplace and eat."

"You and me and Irene?"

"No. You and me."

"What about Irene?"

"We separated. She went away. How about it?"

"How about it? Holy cow, Charley! Just tell me where you want to meet."